Enjoy the journey

Love & Light,

Kathe

A Return
to Innocence

A Return to Innocence

a tale of self-discovery

Kathleen Beales

Library of Congress Control Number:		2010908486
ISBN:	Hardcover	978-1-4535-1897-7
	Softcover	978-1-4535-1896-0
	Ebook	978-1-4535-1898-4

To order additional copies of this book, contact:
Xlibris Corporation
1-888-795-4274
www.Xlibris.com
Orders@Xlibris.com
81299

Daddy-O. I *know* you're with me, always.
Mom. Thanks for letting me be Me.

*

Sometimes the effect we have on others is never truly known.
Thanks Ms. Harrigan—for igniting the flame.

MEMORIES

Out of the corner of his eye, Bill watched curiously as his eight-year-old daughter Brooke tiptoed into his office and quietly meandered toward his desk. She knew the rules. Nobody was to disturb him while he was working.

"Daddy?" she whispered.

"Yes," he replied, staring down at the papers in front of him.

"What's in the box?"

He scribbled a few notes, then looked up and addressed his daughter, "What box, honey?"

"The box from the back of the closet upstairs."

He shook his head. "I don't know, sweetie." To him, the closet was simply a wasteland of old clothes, books, and pictures. He could not imagine what had so earnestly caught the attention of his inquisitive young daughter.

"Yes you do," Brooke said softly. She held her hand out, "Come on. I'll show you."

Intrigued, Bill placed his pencil upon his desk and stood.

The little girl eagerly escorted him out of the office and down the long stretch of hallway. As they approached the living room she pulled anxiously at his arm, attempting to rush past the door. She did not want to be seen by Mom or her little sister Breezi, who seemed engrossed in some movie.

Making it to the stairway undetected, Brooke tightened her grip around her father's index and middle fingers, her hand too small to wrap around his rugged paw. Grabbing the banister with her free hand, she silently ascended the steps with increasing anticipation.

On the second floor landing Brooke put a hand to her mouth. She extended her index finger over her lips and shushed her dad (although Bill had yet to make a sound). Then the little girl made a sharp left turn. She tugged at her dad's arm, hurrying him through the doorway of the walk-in closet. Sticking her head out one last time, she felt confident they had not been followed and tiptoed backward, closing the door behind her.

They were welcomed by an amber glow from the afternoon sun peeking through the closet's modest octagonal window. Ambient light filled the small room, illuminating several abandoned objects that inhabited the jam-packed shelves.

Bill was struck by an unexpected feeling of comfort. Solace perhaps. Dreamily, he spun around, brushing his hands along the shelves as he surveyed the clutter upon them; lingering at several items along the way.

For Brooke, the room was a treasure trove full of history, a place of discovery. She loved exploring its contents, rewriting the past with her imagination. She'd get lost in there for hours, rummaging through all the old forgotten trinkets. Sometimes, she would try on the array of abandoned hats and dresses she found. She'd strut about in her mom's deserted high heels, pretending she was a grown up. Not long ago she came across her mother's wedding gown, wrapped in tissue paper along with a handmade photo album from her parents' wedding. They had gotten married in Italy, which seemed so much different from what Brooke saw outside her bedroom window in New York. One day, she thought, I'll go to Italy to see where mom and dad met. She vowed to visit each place in the vast collection of photos.

Today, however, it had been a large sealed box that caught her eye. She had not noticed it previously. She managed to drag it out from behind a bunch of musty old clothes. The box in question now sat in the center of the closet. The peculiar markings on the tattered cardboard structure had piqued her interest. Heavily taped and re-taped along the sides in big thick black ink it read: **Private/ Do NOT open/Ask Bill First.**

Now alone and safe behind the closed door, Brooke asked more loudly, "What's in the box, Daddy?"

He spun around, startled. "What bo . . .," and stumbled over the brown, tattered parcel. Staring at it, for what seemed like an eternity to Brooke, he eventually knelt down in front of the object he'd hidden away so very long ago. Running his fingers along the tape he managed to answer, "Memories."

"Can we open it? Are they your memories, daddy? Why would you tape up your memories?" she reeled off.

His daughter's questions seemed to be floating in air, far off in the distance. Bill could barely hear them for he'd become consumed with the recollection of his life's journey.

"What memories are in the box daddy?" she asked again.

Taking a deep breath, Bill smiled as a tear fell down his face. He whispered, "The great kind my sweetie. The wondrous kind."

Over the years, he had dared to glance inside, only to re-seal the essence of his story. He never talked about what happened, what he knew to be true, what he chose to let go of and why. He had not shared these particular childhood experiences with anyone, not even his wife.

He was the same age as Brooke was now, when life became real for him. And, he was not much older than Brooke when the realities of life got in the way.

"What memories are in the box daddy? Are they your memories, daddy?" she asked once more.

Bill remained quiet a few moments. With a slight quiver to his voice he answered, "Yes, honey. They are *my* memories."

"Did you lose them daddy?" she questioned.

"Lose them?" He didn't understand.

"Your memories?"

"Oh," he paused, "Maybe, for a while." Bill let out a prolonged sigh. "It's more like I forgot them, on purpose. I put them in this box so I could remember them someday. And today, you found them for me." Patting the floor, he motioned for his daughter to join him. "Would you like to help me open it?" he asked.

"Yes!"

Plopping down on the carpet, Brooke was preoccupied by her own excitement over the discovery of her father's hidden treasures to notice his obvious emotional state.

Watching his little girl's earnest curiosity touched Bill greatly. "Okay then," he responded, "let's open this together."

He took a small knife from his pants' pocket and began cutting away at the thick bands of tape. His daughter proceeded to tug at the frayed layers, tearing away the barricade to her father's past.

"Will I lose my memories when I grow up, Daddy?"

Together they yanked off the last bit of tape then pulled back the folds of cardboard at the top of the box. "I hope not, sweetie," he replied tenderly.

"Wait, hold on a moment," he gently commanded.

By now the tiny room had grown quite dim as the sun gently slipped below the windowsill, making way for the illumination of a full moon. Bill stood up to flip on the light then returned to his seat, on the floor next to his daughter.

He looked at her and smiled. "It's time to remember . . ."

Calm Seas, Sad Thoughts

For miles blue skies were filled with clusters of pillow-like clouds. The water was a deep sapphire blue without the slightest ripple. A tiny breeze was evident but only once in a while; when a puff of wind would pass across the deck, never long enough to raise the sails. It was as if Mother Nature was chiding them, teasing them. They had been slowly motoring for almost five days now. The closest sign of land was at least three days away and the last time they stepped foot on dry soil was nearly two weeks ago.

Lying on his back, on the bow of his granddad's sailboat, Billy stared up at the sky, mesmerized by the antics of a small mass of nearby clouds. The young boy could not help but smile as he watched each one take shape, only to transform into something new within moments.

Dreamily he stroked the soft fur of his cat, Mishimo, who was curled up next to him. The silkiness of her coat soothed him. The silence of their friendship offered a sense of peace. Billy was grateful she had been allowed to join him along this journey.

As the clouds carried on with their performance, the eight-year-old continued to stroke his friend's belly while drifting off into daydreams, thinking of his mom. She would have loved this trip.

He envisioned her walking along the deck, toward the bow, the warm ocean breeze gently blowing long locks of blonde hair across her face. Billy imagined his mom laughing as she struggled to sweep the strands away with one hand while holding onto the stainless steel lifeline cable with the other. Closing his eyes, the small boy dreamed his mother was lying next to him. He could smell her perfume. He listened to her laugh as he envisioned sharing his explanation about the happenings in the sky, and smiled. He liked seeing his mom happy. Healthy. And he was grateful he could still find a place where the only thing separating him from her was the image of a gray and black striped tabby, snuggled between them.

When he heard Mishimo begin to purr, Billy's chest tightened. His daydream was slipping away. He squeezed his eyes shut more tightly, attempting to hold onto the peaceful images in his mind. But it was no use. His joyful musings were no match for reality. He could no longer forestall the impending floodtide and eventually gave in to the sting of tears. Grief had prevailed once more.

Toward the back of the boat, manning the helm from the cockpit, Papa Joe observed his grandson on the bow. His heart hurt as he recognized the expression of sorrow upon the youngster's face. He had seen it too often lately and longed to take Billy's pain away. He watched with concern while tears streamed gently down the little boy's cheeks.

Papa Joe's heart ached thinking of his daughter, Grace. It had been six months since she'd passed away. To him, it felt like a lifetime. She was so beautiful, so young. And he missed her. As if infectious, *he* became consumed by sadness, too.

Papa Joe shook his head in an attempt to break free from the spell grief had cast upon him. He clenched his jaw, fought back his tears and looked up to the sky. If only the weather would cooperate, he thought, they could reach their destination more quickly and begin.

They had set out on their journey almost eleven days ago, in the early morning of June 9, 1974. Having said goodbye to Nana, Billy and his grandfather left the dock at the dilapidated Chelsea Piers just before dawn. They raised the sails as they passed the Statue of Liberty, bound for the open ocean. Papa had looked back, only for an instant, to marvel at the beauty of the sunrise reflected in the overgrown buildings along Manhattan's lower east side. He was quite content in saying farewell for a while.

Originally a self-effacing, lowly field scientist, Papa Joe became a world-renowned marine biologist after conducting several famous, yet unconventional, exploratory expeditions. He was considered a pioneer in the study of marine mammal behavior and was an avid conservationist. Eager to share his passion with others, in January of 1966 (the year Billy was born) Papa became founder of the prestigious *P.J. McMillon Marine Mammal Research Academy*. Affectionately referred to as the "Mc4" by staff and students alike, it was an extension of the New York Aquarium.

Over the years, Papa had spearheaded some of the Mc4's most complex clinical research earning him both awards and accolades from around the world. Having been away from exploratory expeditions for the past several years following a tragic accident off the coast of Puerto Rico, Papa had become increasingly involved in the daily decision-making at the Mc4. But since his daughter Grace's death, he seemed consumed by it.

In order to subsidize his research, Papa had recently been pre-occupied by an unending number of fundraising activities. He did not like this part of his work. He was much more a hands-on scientist and country boy at heart. He'd rather be looking under a microscope in the lab or picking strawberries on his small farm out on Long Island. Instead he was hosting charity events in the city and asking for financial contributions for the academy. He preferred to leave these responsibilities to his beloved wife, Nana, a well-known socialite.

Papa was always impressed with what he called Nana's most dominant quality: the art of persuasion. She was constantly telling Papa how his presence was so important; that he symbolized the academy, that he consistently drew a generous crowd and that he was much more charismatic than he gave himself credit. It always worked. He attended every function she asked of him.

Nana loved fundraisers and enjoyed a busy calendar of events. She was incredibly poised in soliciting both investors and contributors alike. She also managed to stay unendingly patient with the many city officials required to keep the academy running. She found it all therapeutic. It kept her mind occupied.

It was not the same for Papa Joe. The death of their only daughter had, by comparison, caused him to become increasingly antsy at being in the city. The concrete walls surrounding him day by day and the constant chatter of the city at night had always worn on his nerves. But, the overwhelming sadness surrounding his daughter's death was too much for him to bear. Even weekends at the farm could not squelch his *need* to sail away for a while. So, one day he expressed a plan to Nana, who understandably agreed. They both felt that a new expedition would offer Papa a much-needed reprieve. However, it took much coaxing before Nana reluctantly acquiesced to her husband's argument that this was a wonderful opportunity for Billy. It seemed Papa also possessed the art of persuasion, or at least something like it.

Billy was thrilled at the chance to assist his grandfather in carrying out some of his essential research and loved the idea of (at least temporarily) foregoing his formal education. Wise beyond his years, with an innate need to be near nature, at only eight years old, Billy was a gifted child. He had been in an accelerated school for more than two years and found he was still not challenged very much. He yearned to explore and was excited at the possibilities of discovering new places and making new friends. But it had been a bittersweet goodbye for the inquisitive, curly-haired, blue-eyed boy, for he also longed to share this with his mom.

Papa Joe continued to stare at Billy and Mishimo lying on the foredeck. He thought back to the day he presented his grandson with his detailed plans. They had shared an open dialogue usually reserved for adult conversation. He always spoke to children with respect. Papa always said, "Knowledge is power, but only when balanced with heart." He believed an adult was a child's guide, a teacher, and a child was there to open the heart and mind of the adult—to keep them young. Their conversation had ended with Billy eagerly agreeing with his granddad's proposal.

That's how they came to be sailing the Atlantic Ocean, bound for a tiny group of islands in the eastern Caribbean aboard Papa Joe's 60-foot sailboat, *Amazing Grace*.

The intensity of his granddad's stare breached Billy's daydream. Billy opened his eyes and wiped his face with the back of his hand. Returning his gaze to the sky, he once again noticed the clouds playing their favorite game. He took a deep breath, filling his lungs with salty air and smiled.

"Papa Joe," he called out, "come here, I have something to show you."

With the boat on autopilot, in calm seas, Papa Joe felt safe to leave the helm. He approached Billy on the foredeck. "What is it my young man?" What is so urgent amongst this tranquil sea?" Papa lyrically questioned.

"Come here, Papa. I want you to meet my friends," the boy commanded.

"Friends?" his grandfather questioned, "Where?"

Billy motioned for Papa to lie down on the deck next to him. Then instructed him to close his eyes, relax and try to think of nothing.

"Now open your eyes. What do you see?" asked Billy.

Opening his eyes and looking up at the sky, Papa Joe began to speak—but was immediately interrupted by Billy. "Wait. Don't think Papa—just see! And describe it to me."

Taking a deep breath, Papa began, "I see three wolves. The center one bigger than the others. They are looking right at us. Friendly, not fierce. But definitely wolves," he finished.

Billy could not hold back his laughter. "Really?"

"Why, my child? What do you see?"

"I see three wise men with long bushy beards," Billy professed.

"Hmm. Okay, I can see that. Okay," Papa Joe repeated, amused by his grandson's imagination.

Squinting from the midday sun Billy exclaimed, "You see, right there!" as he pointed to the sky and outlined each image he saw in the clouds above them. "These are my friends." He continued, "Puff, Fluff and Snow."

As they lay there chatting and laughing the mood naturally shifted from sadness to joy. Papa breathed deeply, glad the dark moment had passed.

Billy's smile grew wide. He sat up and looked out over the bow, then scooped up Mishimo and cradled her in his arms. He wondered what their adventure would bring next.

Just then an unusual gust of wind kicked up. Papa Joe jumped up with delight over the unexpected change in weather. He returned to the cockpit to grab the binoculars. "I believe it's time to sail!" he bellowed with excitement, taking a closer look at the approaching weather. He could see the effects of the wind over the distant water. The once calm sea now contained choppy waves with breaking white caps. A large formation of clouds had developed and seemed determined to join the pillows that only moments earlier contained imaginative wolves and wise men. From what Papa could see, it seemed the clouds did *not* hold rain. They simply accompanied the wind.

Keeping the boat on autopilot, Papa Joe ran down below to his navigation station to look at his charts and do some calculations. There was no time for an updated weather report on the radio; this wind would be upon them quickly.

Billy, acting on instinct, gently placed Mishimo in her custom built basket inside the cockpit. He put on his life vest, took his place on deck at the base of the main mast and waited for his grandfather to return with instructions.

Up the stairwell and back to the helm flew Papa Joe. He looked at the approaching wind behind them with a huge grin. He loved to sail. He'd owned several boats throughout the years. *Amazing Grace* was his latest. A custom sloop, she was commissioned more than 15 years ago, as a fiftieth birthday present to himself. Originally recognized for her elegance and state of the art design, these days, *Amazing Grace* was admired for keeping passengers safe and comfortable in the calmest waters or during the most disturbing storms. Papa was grateful for her reliability as he took the boat off autopilot to raise the sails.

"Here we go, young Billy. Are you ready?"

"Yes, Papa!"

Amazing Grace had two huge sails, a mainsail and jib. They raised the main first, and then let out the jib. Papa Joe and Billy worked in unison and without chaos, each doing their respective jobs in order to make the task seem effortless. Within moments both sails were up. They were now on a broad reach in a following sea with the wind relatively behind them, off their starboard quarter. Strong twenty to twenty-five knot winds pushed them in a southwesterly direction. It was ideal. The boat quickly picked up speed, eight knots, then ten knots. Papa Joe looked out over the water, connecting with the wind, the water and his boat. Making a few acute adjustments to the sails, he received a momentous response from *Amazing Grace*. They were now sailing fast, on course and in relative comfort. At a speed of twelve knots he blurted, "That's my girl!"

Putting the boat on autopilot, Papa relaxed into his seat at the helm. He watched his grandson neaten-up the lines on deck, in awe of the young boy. At eight-years-old, his grandson was already a better sailor than many adult seamen. It simply came naturally to him and Papa knew Billy was destined to become a great sailor someday.

Papa watched as his grandson scooped up the hefty gray tabby from her basket and made his way to the cockpit. The young boy sat beside his grandfather behind the helm. "It's a wonderful wind my dear boy," Papa let out a grand sigh, "It's a wonderful wind."

With his best friend wrapped in his arms, Billy looked up at the stately silver-haired man and smiled. He was grateful for the wind as well.

For the next two-and-a-half days *Amazing Grace* glided along the water, surfing each wave like an adolescent on a board. The wind lingered, continuing to propel them in the right direction while the clouds came and went. It had been a record-breaking trip for Papa Joe's boat. At times they managed fourteen knots. Her usual cruising speed was around ten. Papa was quite proud of his *Amazing Grace*.

It was nearing dawn when Billy first spotted the tiny islands they had been yearning to reach for almost a fortnight. He called out to Papa who was down below making breakfast.

"Papa, we're here. We're here! I can see the islands," the boy bellowed with excitement.

With two pancake-laden plates in his hands, Papa Joe climbed the stairwell to join Billy in the cockpit. He placed the dishes down on the previously set table and took a look at what Billy was so excited about.

In the distance were several islands. The larger island to the right, off their starboard bow, was illuminated with streetlights that wrapped around the emerald mass, reminiscent of a Christmas tree. Many houses and buildings could be seen scattered along the hillside. This was St. Thomas. Directly in front of the boat was another large protrusion of lush green trees and rock. A few speckles of light could be seen on its northwest side, suggesting the existence of a small town. This was St. John. Both islands were part of the U.S. Virgin Islands.

"Which island are we going to Papa?"

"We're headed to the islands off our port bow, known as the British Virgin Islands."

Billy looked at the collection of islands toward the left. They seemed peaceful and uninhabited. The delicate sweet light from a new day offered a glimmer of sunshine on the otherwise darkened mounds jutting from the sea.

"Wow. Are there people on those islands, Papa?" Billy asked.

"Oh yes, my young lad. And, I am sure you will befriend many of them."

In that moment, their journey somehow became *real* for Billy. Until then it felt more like a prolonged trip on Long Island Sound, except for the fact that they had barely seen land in twelve days.

They continued their conversation over breakfast, not that Billy could eat. With the increased excitement surrounding their impending arrival, Billy's only concerns were the answers to his onslaught of questions.

Papa painstakingly answered them all, overjoyed by his grandson's amplified curiosity. He finished with one simple statement, "I have spent many a day exploring these waters, and now I am anxious to share them with you."

A few hours later, they reached the anchorage. The wind had tapered and the sun was shining brightly in the midmorning sky. Great Harbour was a picturesque bay on the southwest side of the island of Jost Van Dyke. There was a quaint village along the beach that consisted of several makeshift shacks, a tiny white church with a steeple, and an eclectic restaurant bar that was frequented by all the local and not so local sailors. At the center of the village was the Government House, a light blue, two-story building made of concrete block. It looked massive in comparison to the other structures along the beach, but consisted of only two rooms, one on each floor. In front of the Government House was a commercial dock, home to the local ferry that carried passengers and supplies to and from the surrounding islands. Attached to the larger dock was a small wooden structure with three tiny inflatable boats tied to it.

When the anchor was set, Billy remained on the bow. He looked toward shore, immediately impressed by the rudimentary construction and the charm of the unpaved road that paralleled the beach. He could see several cocoa-colored children walking toward the back of the church, apparently on their way to school. For an instant, he envisioned being back in New York. A jubilant smile appeared across his face. He was so happy he was no longer confined to a classroom.

The sounds emanating from shore amused him. Several roosters began to crow, as if carrying on idle conversation. He listened intently at what was obviously a baby cry, only to find it was actually a small lone goat along the hillside. He observed a nearby boat weigh anchor and sail away from the harbour. He wondered why anyone would ever want to leave this place.

While Billy was engrossed by the content of his new environment, Papa Joe had lowered the 12-foot inflatable dinghy from its cradle and tied it to the back of the big boat. "Come on, my young lad," he called out from the stern as he made his way into the smaller boat. "It's time to go ashore and check-in."

Billy's euphoric trance was halted, replaced by a mad dash down the port side in order to catch up with his granddad. He leaped from the stern platform into the smaller vessel. "Let's go!" he called out in mid air.

From the confines of the cockpit, Mishimo studied the blissful pair. She paced the deck as she watched Papa and Billy laugh all the way to shore.

Billy jumped from the boat almost as quickly as he leaped into it. He was on sensory overload as he took off running toward the light blue building. Back at the makeshift wooden dock, Papa Joe methodically tied up the dinghy. He too was fascinated by the magic of the village's simplicity. It was exactly as he remembered it.

He met up with his grandson on the steps of the Government House, where Billy was already making new friends.

"Papa, this is Charlie. He's from Cane Garden Bay on that *other* island over there," he exclaimed, pointing arbitrarily toward the water. "He can hold his breath and dive more than thirty feet! He likes to fish and says I can go with him next time. He has three kids: Keisha, Dante and Ritzel. Ritzel, he's the same age as me," the little boy spouted.

"Breathe, my dear boy. Breathe." Papa Joe gently patted his grandson on the back. "I can't imagine how you got *all* of that from my buddy Charlie in the short time it took to tie up the dinghy."

Extending his hand, Papa said, "Good morning, old friend. I see you've met my grandson."

"Oh, me goodness, Dr. P.J.," responded Charlie, "Good mornin'. You been gone too long, mon. It good you come back."

"Thanks, Charlie. It's great to be back. I see Great Harbour is as quaint as ever."

"Me favorite place next to Cane Garden Bay, ya know."

Looking back down at Billy, the local man concluded, "Dat mean dis must be Gracie's boy," pausing a moment. "Yep. You gots Gracie in ya. I see dat. I sees her in dose sparklin' blue eyes you got."

Charlie then asked, "Where Gracie be these days, Doc?"

Tears came swiftly at the sound of his mother's name. Papa gently placed an arm around his grandson's shoulders. He looked at Charlie with kindness. There was no way for him to have known. He swallowed hard, attempting to stifle his own rush of emotion.

"She passed six months ago, Charlie. Cancer returned to her, my friend." Papa looked from Charlie to his young grandson and back again. With an understanding nod, Charlie remained silent.

"Billy, let's go clear in," Papa said. "I bet Val is working this morning. If she is, I know a Johnnycake is not far away."

"Ooh, Johnnycake," Charlie commented, "You gonna love dem. I know Ritzel do and I do too. Ask for da one wit cheese, Billy."

Charlie paused. "It good to see ya, Dr. P.J."

Extending his hand, Papa stated, "You too, my friend." Then he guided his grandson toward the building in front of them. They'd see Charlie again for sure.

Opening the door to the Government House, Val's presence was obvious from the wafting smell of fried dough. Papa greeted the entire room with a jovial, "Good morning," as he walked through the entranceway; a custom that was mandatory if you wanted to be acknowledged (at all) by the inhabitants.

Standing behind the front counter were three women who all responded, "Good mornin'," looking up expressionless.

But Val recognized the distinguished older gentleman right away and smiled broadly. A rotund middle-aged black woman, she was friendly and polite with a huge smile, but only if she knew you. Otherwise, she took her job *very* seriously and said nothing except to ask the required questions to new visitors. She had been a customs and immigration officer for more than ten years.

"Mr. P.J., You gone to come back. It good to see ya," Val offered with sincerity. She had always enjoyed Papa's visits to the island. He seemed to brighten up the place, she thought.

They checked in with ease and were given a six-month visitor's entry. Val had been so preoccupied with Papa's return that she did not address the subject of Billy. Not wanting to press his luck, Papa chose to refrain from asking about her famous Johnnycake. He figured six months afforded plenty of chances for the young lad to try that specific dietary staple.

From the Government House, they turned right down the sand packed road. A mother hen with her six peeping chicks crossed in front of them. Under a nearby tree lay a group of heifers seeking shade. Billy stared in astonishment. Papa giggled, "Welcome to the BVI."

At the end of the road, in the far west corner of the village, stood an open-air restaurant bar. Flags, t-shirts and other paraphernalia hung from the ceiling, cross beams and walls. It was nothing less than eclectic.

Cheers from a modest crowd welcomed them into the establishment. Apparently, word had spread that Dr. P.J. had returned. Charlie smiled from the end of the bar, giving them a big wink as he took a swig from his beer.

After a brief greeting, Papa guided his grandson toward a quiet area overlooking the anchorage. They sat at a small wobbly table with bench seats.

Billy surveyed the room. "Does *everybody* know you, Papa?" he asked excitedly.

"Not everyone."

"It's like you're famous or something. I like it."

"Are you hungry, my dear boy?" Papa asked, ignoring his grandson's last statement.

"I can hear my stomach growling."

"Well, I'll take that as a yes then."

When the waitress finally arrived, Papa proceeded to order two hamburgers with fries and some sodas. It took quite a while before she came back with their food. But, neither noticed. They were both engrossed in their surroundings. However, when the burgers finally did arrive, hunger overshadowed excitement as they devoured their meals in relative silence.

They were just about finished when a tall, broad-shouldered man with a long, slightly graying ponytail strolled up to talk.

Danny was thirty-eight, originally from Massachusetts, with a very colorful background and robust Bostonian accent. He had earned a Master's Degree in Economics from Harvard. But, after college, he had decided to take off for Waikiki to pursue his dream of becoming a professional surfer. Not exactly a natural talent, he achieved only relative success and soon realized it was hard work with very little money. He returned to the states to 'grow up' and found he wasn't very fond of that either. So, when he came into a sizeable inheritance, he decided to migrate south, settling on the island of Jost Van Dyke. Within a month, he married Marta, a sweet local woman, and a year later they opened The Dive Bar & Grill. That was twelve years ago.

"Well, if it ain't P.J. McMillon!" Danny stated as he approached. "I thought I recognized that wicked beautiful sloop come in early this morning. How aw-yah my man? Welcome home!"

The juxtaposition of Danny's *strong* Bostonian accent next to the island patois made Billy laugh. He liked this man immediately. And, he could tell Danny must be one of his granddad's good friends because Papa immediately stood and rather than shake his hand—he hugged him. The two men then slapped each other on the back a few times. Billy had never seen his granddad this animated.

With tear-filled eyes, Papa began, "Harvard, it is so good to see you!" He then looked at his grandson, "Billy, I'd like you to meet one of my closest friends in the world, Mr. Danny Waters."

"Ah, call me *Hahved* like ya Papa," Danny boisterously exclaimed, extending a handshake to Billy—who was also on his feet now.

"Hello, Mr. Harvard," Billy answered with a bit more shyness than he anticipated. He wanted this man to like him.

Danny didn't notice. He was on a mission. The unexpected arrival of his old friend, Dr. P.J., offered him a chance to do something he'd been trying to do for over a year now. He felt no shame in impishly exploiting a young boy to do it. He proceeded with a rapid exchange of questions and answers with his best friend's grandson.

"Hey Billy, do you like sailing fast?"

"Yes." The question caught Billy off guard.

"Have you ever raced your Papa's pretty sailboat?"

"No."

"How about any other boat?"

"No."

"Want to?"

"YES!" Billy exclaimed.

"Did you know that your Papa is not only a world renowned scientist, but also a pretty famous racing tactician. He used to race on my boat. Nobody could beat us when your Papa was aboard."

At that point Papa Joe interrupted, "Harvard, what are you getting at?"

Billy was grateful for the break. He didn't know what a tactician was and felt too embarrassed to ask.

"Well, since you've been gone, Foxy has gone and bought himself a new race boat. He calls her *Hold the Mustard*. We've been unable to beat her and it ticks me off. Who names their boat that, anyway?"

Foxy owned another bar on the opposite end of the harbor. He was Danny's biggest competition, both in business and in racing. Papa listened as Harvard explained the multitude of circumstances (or excuses, Papa teased) that had thwarted each attempt at beating his most challenging opponent. He wasn't sure what Danny was more mad about—losing a race to his biggest rival or losing to a boat with such a silly name.

"So, what are you looking for, Harvard?" Papa asked.

"Well, you see, The Race Around the Dyke is tomorrow and I thought you might be interested in lending a hand aboard *Silver Bullet*. The boys and I could use you. Plus, Billy here would be our good luck charm. You did say he was a better sailor than most men who've been sailing their whole lives, didn'tcha?"

"Hey Billy," he added, "in case you're wondering, a tactician is the person who reads the conditions of the water, wind and surroundings. He anticipates what to do next and tells the helmsman, who then steers the boat and instructs the crew accordingly."

"Ooh, Papa is the *best* at that! He could be your tacman."

"Tactician," Papa corrected.

"What do you say, P.J., for old times' sake? Show the boy what speed is all about," Danny suggested.

Billy managed to pick up on Danny's eagerness for Papa's participation. So, as Papa mulled over Danny's proposal, Billy looked up and motioned for Danny's ear. He whispered a simple offer and waited for the captain's response.

Standing upright with a playful smirk, Danny looked at the small boy, impressed. Then offered a handshake in agreement to the boy's quiet stipulation for his assistance in persuading Papa to participate in the race.

Billy winked at Danny before gently taking his grandfather by the hand and prodding, "Please, Papa."

"You *really* want to race?" His grandfather asked.

Tugging gently at his Papa's arm, Billy pressed again. "Yes. *Pleeeeease!*"

Danny looked like he was about to burst. He wanted his friend to race so badly. It felt like forever before Papa spoke.

"Well," Papa paused, "I guess we better get moving then. We have our own boat to wash and we'll need a good night's sleep if we want to blow past the likes of Foxy's crew aboard . . . *Hold the Mustard*." He was unable to stifle a laugh.

"Yes!" Billy and Danny shouted together, high-fiving each other with big toothy grins.

Soon after, Billy and Papa Joe said their goodbyes to Danny and his wife, Marta, and made their way back to the sandy road. As they headed toward the dinghy, Billy remained quiet—lost in thought about all the events of the day.

He thought about what Captain Harvard had said, that he would bring good luck. He surely hoped so and silently asked his mom for help. He remained quiet on the short trip back to *Amazing Grace*, and kept relatively silent as they washed the boat. He was even quiet during and after dinner.

Papa assumed his grandson must simply be exhausted, the strain from their long trip must have finally caught up with him. When they were both finished eating, he suggested Billy get ready for bed.

The young boy showered, put his pajamas on and hopped into his bunk. His grandfather came in, soon after, to tuck him in for the night. He kissed Billy on the forehead and told him how much he loved him. When Papa went to leave the room, Billy stopped him with a few last minute questions.

"Papa, do you really think I am a great sailor?"

"You are well on your way to being the *best*, my young man," he responded proudly.

"Papa. Is Danny your best friend?"

"Next to you, yes he is."

"I love you, Papa."

The gentleman replied, "I love you too, Billy. Now, get some rest. It's been a very long day." He switched the light off and shut the door behind him.

The little boy would not sleep. Instead he talked to his mom in the darkness. He told her all about his day and all about what he anticipated for tomorrow. He told her that he loved her and that he knew she was there with him. He just knew it. Mishimo eventually jumped onto the bed to join him. She fell asleep under his arm. Billy followed soon after.

STRENGTH, LOVE & GRACE

Papa had been pacing the deck since putting his grandson to bed several hours ago. He could hear music in the distance, coming from shore. The Dive seemed pretty lively, he thought. But, then again, it was the night before a race. He was certain there were plenty of sailors already drinking their weight in beer. He walked down below and peeked inside Billy's cabin. Immersed in his dreams, Billy did not wake. However, the creak at the door had caused Mishimo's ears to perk up from beneath the warmth of the young boy's arm. He sensed the protective feline was annoyed by this intrusion as she glared at him with a profound intensity. Gently, Papa closed the door, confident Mishimo would keep a close eye. He left a note on the galley countertop, just in case Billy awoke before he returned. On deck, he took one last look to make sure the anchor was secure before heading to the stern platform, where he jumped into the dingy bound for The Dive.

On shore, standing behind the bar, Danny watched his old friend motor his way through the anchorage, tie up the dingy and embark on the brief trek along the beach, back to The Dive. Grabbing a cold six-pack of local beer, Danny walked over to Marta, who had also noticed Papa walking toward The Dive.

Kissing her on the forehead, Danny gave Marta a wink as he walked off. He knew she understood his obligation to his friend.

A moderate crowd filled the tiny dance floor. Danny strolled cordially through the group, greeting some of the patrons at the surrounding tables. He made his way to the entrance just in time to welcome his approaching friend. Their greeting was straightforward. "Saw me coming, didn't you, Harvard?"

"Yup."

Danny led the way. Walking toward the sandy beach, away from the bar, they retraced some of the footsteps his friend had just made. They walked in silence until Danny settled on a spot where the ruckus from the bar was less prominent. He took a seat along the trunk of an old palm tree that had grown askew.

"Come sit, P.J."

Papa remained silent for the first beer. It did not take him long to polish it off. Taking the last swig, he turned and held out his hand for another. It had been a long time since he'd reflected upon the events of the past several months much less shared them with anyone. He felt safe in the company of his trusted friend.

"You gonna to talk to me, old man?" Danny questioned impishly, but with sincerity. "Yup." It would take a little while before he offered more. Halfway through the second beer, P.J. let out, "She was so young, Danny." It was all he could muster. He felt depleted.

"Yes, She was," he paused. "Why didn't you tell me she was so ill?"

P.J. took a deep breath and began, "We didn't want to tell anyone. Grace knew she was sick again, long before she ever told me. I think I knew, but I ignored the signs. I didn't want her to leave and she knew that. I believe she feared telling me because if she were to let me know too soon, I would have tried to convince her to do any and all treatments to keep her here. And I would have. And she would have done them for me."

P.J. took a big swig of another beer before continuing, "It was a little over a year ago that she admitted she had been feeling poorly for a while. When she finally went to the doctor, it was too late. The cancer had spread throughout her body. She wanted to die on her own terms. She was given less than six months. She lived a bit over eight. Always on Gracie's time. Always." He took another big swig, finishing the bottle.

He reached for another, took a short sip, and proceeded with his story. "If she'd involved me too soon, she would not have been able to do that." Choking back tears he finished, "I think she believed her life's purpose had been fulfilled. She was finished here and willing to give into her illness."

"And how are you, my friend?"

Shrugging his shoulders, P.J. blurted, "Some days I am mad, some days sad. But, mostly—I am determined. I am determined to continue my daughter's work and my own along with it. I made that vow to her."

"And Billy?"

"He is an amazing young boy. I am so proud of him. He's also very, very sad. His mom was his best friend." P.J. remained quiet for a long stretch of time. Finally, with a quiver to his voice, he managed, "She was mine too," pushing an empty beer bottle into the sand. Tears fell swiftly now.

"Billy keeps me happy," P.J. continued. "I am doing this for him, you know? He is a boy with such promise. He is a boy with such *life* in him. I want him to be able to live *any* and *all* of his dreams. And, I want to protect him." P.J. stopped for a moment, lost in thought. "You see, Billy's not of 'concrete walls'. He's special. He deserves to be here at sea. I've always known that. I could tell, even from our short trips on The Sound or up to Nantucket and the Vineyard." P.J. turned to face his friend, looking him in the eyes. "And I've got to tell you Harvard," he paused, "when we left the confines of the city this time; Billy came alive. It was as if he could suddenly hear and see for the first time." Dreamily P.J. looked out over the water, then leaned back on the palm tree and turned his head toward the twinkling brilliance of the night sky. "Like I've always said—once the external noise of the city is gone, all things come to life in a grander way."

"Yup, *that* I understand, my friend."

They both sat quietly, consumed by the sorrow caused by their collective loss. Danny eventually offered another beer to P.J., who took a sip before turning his attention to another subject.

"He showed up for the funeral you know?"

Danny knew exactly of whom his friend was referring. "No way."

"Yup. I stopped him before he could see Billy. Told him it wasn't right for him to infringe on the poor boy's grieving. He told me he wanted to be a part of his life in some way. I told him he would have to earn that right."

"Being a little harsh?" Danny had always had a soft spot for Billy's father. He genuinely liked him and knew it took a lot for Peter to walk away from Grace and their infant child.

"Absolutely not!" P.J. rattled on, "I held no grudges when he left my daughter. I understood the pressure of being so young and having a sick wife and baby. But he chose to leave. He doesn't get to choose to come back. That was the agreement."

"But, that was *seven* years ago, PJ. And, now Gracie's gone."

"Yes. And she could have been *gone* back then. But she fought. She fought to stay alive and to raise her child! Peter didn't fight for anything."

"Except his own survival."

P.J. ignored the comment. "She always said—he was the love of her life."

"Until Billy was born," Danny whispered.

"He professed that *she* was the love of *his* life, too. And then, he left her with an eight-month-old baby and battling one the most aggressive forms of cancer." He paused. "I always told Grace he'd leave her one day."

Both Grace and Peter were passionate about their causes. Her passion was in the sea. His was in the sky. They met at the University of Hawaii when Grace was a freshman. Peter was a sophomore. P.J. knew his son-in-law was extremely smart and very driven. He also knew, from experience, the price of a calling.

Changing his tone P.J. continued, "He's remarried now, you know. Three years. Lives in Hawaii still. He told me they had been trying to have a baby ..." P.J. trailed off at the thought.

"Is he happy?" questioned Danny.

"He says he is." Sighing P.J. continued, "He happened to be in New York on business when he saw an article in the paper about her passing." P.J. squeezed his eyes shut. He took a deep, quivering breath and blurted, "He was in New York and ..." Pounding a fist in the sand, he couldn't finish the sentence. It hurt too much.

Eventually, he regained his composure, "I wasn't all that harsh, you know. I did give him the chance to redeem himself. I told him if he wanted to be a part of Billy's life, he would first have to meet with me, catch up, build my trust again, but not in the midst of my daughter's funeral. We made plans to meet later that same week. He told me he would call to confirm."

He paused, shaking his head.

"But he never did. He left for Hawaii without saying a word. Again, Peter did not choose to fight. In fact, he didn't even try." P.J. was exasperated. He let out another loud, deep sigh. "Then, about a month ago I received a letter. In it, Peter explained that he didn't call because he ..." (P.J. made a jester of quotation marks with his hands)—*just wasn't ready*. He wrote how he was confused and was still coming to terms with Grace's death. That he was sorry for being such a coward. He explained how he and his wife were expecting their first child, having left the funeral home that day to find out his wife was pregnant."

P.J. let out a sarcastic grunt. Finishing with, "He said he didn't want to come into Billy's life halfway and claimed that he did not know how to incorporate him into their lives just now."

"Did you tell Billy?"

"No."

"What did you do?"

P.J. looked to the sky. "It was the catalyst for me to get off my butt and onto my boat."

"So, are you running away then?

With a bit of irritation in his voice, P.J. replied, "No. I am not running; I am doing!"

Continuing the story in an almost defiant tone, P.J. proclaimed, "Peter's letter was the best thing that could have happened. Before receiving it, I was simply keeping my head above water, attempting to survive, when all I really wanted to do was drown. Peter's weaknesses reminded me of Grace's strength. His letter reminded me of the promise I made to her—to continue her research, to return to mine."

Suddenly he was quiet. He remained silent for a few minutes before humbly citing, "It always amazed me how she had the capacity to follow through with her commitments. She was gentle, yet tenacious. And she always did everything at one-hundred-percent!"

"Of course she did," Danny commented.

"What makes you say that?"

"Cause you're her father. It's what you taught her."

"Oh no," he professed, "Gracie was a much stronger individual than I could ever be. I have my own cowardly moments to overcome. My own demons."

Danny chose not to fuel the last statement; he knew the origin of his friend's unwarranted guilt. The demons his friend was referring to had to do with a tragic event several years ago, while he was searching for answers regarding the research he'd been working on. The incident had made him feel like a failure, a coward. But he was actually considered a hero by so many in the marine world. Danny wished his friend could see things the same way. Maybe one day, he thought. Some day. But, this was an entirely different subject, and it was not the focus of this evening's dialogue. There would be plenty of time to discuss P.J.'s demons.

He managed to maneuver the conversation back to the subject of Grace, letting his friend talk, let go and grieve.

P.J. continued to share his admiration for his daughter, which changed his mood considerably. He talked for hours, telling Danny the many stories of Gracie's work at the Mc4. He told him how Grace had given him the push he needed to pursue his own lofty projects and how it was Gracie's idea for him to return to the islands and further their research.

As P.J.'s final story came to a close, he was overcome with gratitude at the opportunity to let go of so many thoughts and feelings he had buried inside. He expressed how thankful he was for Danny's friendship and the safety he felt in feeling loved like a brother.

"Well, we have a big day tomorrow," Danny responded abruptly, ignoring the accolades. "Want one for the road?" he said, offering up the last of the six-pack.

"Sure. One last one." P.J. chose to keep the bottle unopened. Friendship, he thought; next to family, it is the most important thing.

The two men looked out over the harbor. The placid water glistened in the moonlight. The boats in the anchorage seemed desolate as their inhabitants slept.

A few scattered lights from the outer islands twinkled, seemingly in response to the amplified crowing from the nearby roosters. Both men noticed just how quiet The Dive had become.

It was now past three a.m. and a new day would be upon them soon. They decided to make their way back and call it a night. A few lights remained as Marta cleaned up behind the bar. Some stragglers lingered, having long surpassed their tolerance for alcohol. Danny took a look at the two men at the bar, and then back at his friend, letting out a sarcastic laugh. "Those boys better be ready tomorrow," he warned.

P.J. just smiled.

Walking behind the bar, Danny greeted his wife with a giant hug, swinging her in a circle as they kissed. "I love this gal." He commented, kissing her again.

"Put me down. You're like a big bull," Marta giggled, and punched him gently on the arm. She gazed into her husband's bright blue eyes. "You gonna break someting."

It was time to go. Raising the unopened bottle in the air, P.J. walked away, "I'll see you both in the morning. Thanks for the beer Danny."

"Ahhh . . . There is a price, my friend. Get us across that finish line—*First!*"

Halfway down the beach, Papa looked up at the bright, clear sky. He could not forestall his thoughts. His demons.

"I am going to make it better," he declared aloud. "I am going to fix things. I'll make it right. And, I am going to make my grandson proud." With each statement, the sparkling sky seemed to intensify. He noticed the full moon looking down upon him.

He swore he could see a smile.

What's in a Name?

"Dolila, Dolila, wait up!" screamed Phinny, out of breath and barely able to keep up. "Dolila!" he called out, exasperated, "Please stop and talk to me."

"NO!" she screamed without looking back.

She had always been a better swimmer than he, and when she was mad she was the best swimmer in the ocean. Eventually she stopped, just long enough for her brother to approach. Only then did she begin to dive. She dove as far as she could and for as long as she could. She dove until she could go no further and could no longer stay below. She had to come up for air. This was the routine when Dolila was mad at Phinny.

Out of breath and near exhaustion, Phinny was too fatigued to continue chasing his sister under the water. Instead, he rested, deciding it was best for him to regain his strength from the surface. Sooner or later, she was bound to come up and he wanted to be as supportive as he could when Dolila finally chose to vent her frustrations.

Looking around, he realized his sister's outburst had taken them far from the group. Phinny scanned the water until he found the others swimming near some rocks, way off in the distance. He'd keep an eye on them. But, he knew this incident was surely going to cause some trouble. Veering off from the rest of the swimmers was bound to infuriate their tour guide, Sir Thomas. That did not matter to Phinny. His main concern was Dolila.

When Dolila finally re-emerged, she had calmed down considerably. She was no longer angry, simply hurt. Hurt and overwhelmed by sadness. She began slowly, "Why don't you ever defend me when the others make fun of me. What kind of big brother are you?" she asked as her irritation with Phinny resurfaced. "You're supposed to defend me when the others make fun of me and *especially* when they make fun of my name!" By now, her anger had not only resurfaced but intensified. She continued in one breath, "You know I can't stand them teasing me about my name! "My name is Dolila! She screamed, "How hard can that be? What is wrong with Doh-Lie-Luh," saying the sound of each syllable distinctly, slowly and extremely loud. By the time she was done, her voice had reached an ear-piercing volume.

Phinny looked stunned. He had seen his twin sister mad before, but never to the point of hysteria. He was afraid this might be the day. He was not very good at these situations. He tried very hard to stay *in the moment* and respect his sister's feelings. Although, all he really wanted to do was crack a joke and get her to laugh.

These were the moments he missed his dad the most. Dad always knew what to do in these situations; when to be funny, how to be supportive without saying anything too stupid. He wondered if he would grow into being more like him or had he lost the chance to learn the secrets to his dad's success at being genuine and kind. He took a deep breath. Rather than say the wrong thing, he simply reached out and hugged his little sister. Dolila broke down and began to cry. She cried for a long, long time and for a lot of things. It wasn't just the teasing. It was everything.

Merely moments older than his sister, Phinny was a few inches longer and definitely broader. They joked about Phinny being the *big* brother. In actuality, it was Dolila who usually acted like the elder. After all, she was the rational one. She was constantly calming Phinny down, bailing him out of trouble and speaking on his behalf—mostly apologizing for his arrogant or unruly behavior.

Phinny was an adventurer, a free spirit. Dolila had somehow grown to be more reserved, even afraid of most things adventurous. She felt she needed to protect Phinny. If not from his antics, at least from himself. She felt responsible for keeping him safe and keeping him from being too wild. He had developed a *darkness* about him three years ago, and she had desperately been trying to keep it contained. She feared it would grow, eventually overtaking his lighter, gentler nature. He was all that she had, and she didn't want to lose him. And she was terrified of losing him. That fear fueled her current anger and frustration. She didn't want to be mad at her brother. She didn't want to have these resentments growing inside of her. But *here*, in this place, it seemed she could not stop them from pervading her mind and poisoning her heart with blame.

Dolila looked up and saw Phinny's stunned expression. He looked frozen with fear. Instantly, her floodtide of emotions passed. She laughed a bit uncomfortably, "I guess I got really, really mad that time, eh?" Adding, "You look terrified of me big brother!"

He wasn't terrified. He was concerned. "Dolila," he paused. "I am sorry," humbly offering, "I should have defended you." Softening his gaze he continued, "I know you don't like when they call you by anything but your given name."

"You would think I'd be okay with it by now. But, I am not. I'm just not," she said sadly.

"It's okay, sis. It's okay. But can I say something?

Dolila nodded.

"Promise you won't get upset."

"No," she pouted. "But I promise not to get mad."

"You see, I guess I don't defend your name so much because when they call you Dolly . . ." Choking back tears, Phinny turned away. When he spun back around, he looked into his sister's eyes, "I think about Mom. And I think about how much you remind me of her." He paused. "And it always makes me glad that I have you. That we have each other." It stung to think he'd contributed to his sister's anguish. "Are you going to be okay?" he asked.

It took a few minutes before she answered, "Yes. Thank you, Phinny."

"Okay then. We'd better get back to the group. Sir Thomas must be *furious* with us by now!"

Smiling playfully she offered, "That's okay . . . he'll just blame *you* for us swimming off."

Her brother laughed as he led them toward the others. She's right, he thought. Oh well, one more thing to get in trouble for. He didn't care. All he cared about was that his sister was okay. Safe. Happy. That's all that mattered.

Sir Thomas saw them coming. He was fuming! This was the last time he was going to stand for Phinny's antics. He understood his need to explore, but not at the expense of everyone else's experience, let alone their safety.

He had taken the twins' actions as a personal affront. What mattered most to Sir Thomas, next to his love of family, was education. He professed—knowledge was power, but a belief in oneself was also vital for sustaining life. And he believed that respect, hard work and dedication were required—no matter how big or small the individual.

He was making a stand, laying down the law. In his more than fifty-five years conducting reef tours around the globe, Sir Thomas had never had a student be so incredibly self-centered and reckless. There were no more excuses. Phinny's antics had to be dealt with immediately!

As Phinny and Dolila swam up to the group, they were both very well aware Sir Thomas was irate. The stern, yet (usually) composed director of the Reef Tour Program looked like he was about to burst.

"Phinny," Sir Thoms screamed, "That's it. You are out of the summer reef tour program!" Commanding him to head back to camp and meet up with Miss Tanya, Sir Thomas reported, "She will instruct you on tonight's dinner. You are to help her, and then you are confined to your quarters." Bellowing, "I am through dealing with your disruptions. You have absolutely no regard for anyone but yourself. And, I am tired of worrying about where you'll swim off to next. There is no room for it anymore." He finished, "I am done with you!"

"Fine, you got it sir," Phinny said in a smug, but unusually low, accepting tone. No lip, no backtalk. He simply turned around and headed off in the direction of camp.

Phinny's actions took Sir Thomas by surprise and before he could react, the young one had swum away, out of sight.

This ill-fated altercation terrified Dolila. She knew her brother *had* to be ticked off over being yelled at for something that was clearly not his fault. She tried to fix it.

"But, but, but, Sir Thomas . . ."

Sir Thomas wouldn't listen. "Dolila, I do not want to hear any excuses. I am tired of everyone defending him," he stated, shaking his head and rolling his eyes. "Heck, the whole class was trying to blame *you* for swimming off, unsupervised and without permission." He looked at her sternly. Stating with confidence, "Now, I know *that* would *never* happen."

"But, Sir Thomas, it was my fault," she begged. "I swam off because the others were teasing me." She tried to continue, but he wasn't listening.

Shouting over her voice, Sir Thomas looked at the rest of the group and commanded, "Alright troop, fall-in. I want to see each of you front and center. Right now!" The group gathered into a straight line as fast as they could swim, facing their belligerent guide in silence.

Once they settled down, Sir Thomas began, "It's time we head back to camp. With a demeaning tone he continued, "You can all thank Phinny for an early day." But, Sir Thomas wasn't quite done. He wasn't about to let them off the hook that easy. Looking each of his students in the eyes, with utter disappointment he launched into them: "Before you all go, I want you to think long and hard about the events of today. If I hear that *anyone* is teasing a member of this troop this summer, for *any* reason, you will be kicked out of this program—immediately." He explained further, "Out here, there is absolutely no room for picking on one another or ostracizing anyone. We are a team. Accidents happen when a team does not work together."

Sir Thomas thought back to that fateful day three years ago. At this point, his lecture became personal. With a pained heart he went on, "That is how someone can get hurt . . . or worse," he trailed off, temporarily pre-occupied with the memories that suddenly came flooding back. Regaining his composure, he shouted out a final command, "Now, head out two by two!"

The group followed orders, swimming off in the direction of camp. They returned to find Miss Tanya preparing dinner. Phinny was there, too. But, he wasn't himself. No jokes, no easy-going nature. He stayed to himself, uncharacteristically quiet.

When everyone finished eating, Dolila approached her brother, who was wading near the sandy shoreline—alone. "Big bro, are you okay?" she gently asked.

He did not answer her question. Instead, in a soft tone he said, "Meet me at my bunk when everyone is asleep."

A pang of nervousness pierced her belly. She looked at her brother with concern. Tentatively she asked, "Phinny, what are you planning?"

"It will be okay, Dolila. Just meet me."

"Okay," she whispered, reluctantly.

"It will be okay, Dolila," her brother repeated. "I promise."

The sound of Sir Thomas' voice, from behind a nearby sand dune, interrupted their brief exchange, "I thought I told you, you are confined to your quarters."

"Yes Sir," Phinny called back. "I am on my way."

"Good!"

"I'll see you soon, sis." Phinny whispered. Then he turned abruptly and headed toward his bunk.

As Dolila made her way to the opposite side of camp, she wondered what the heck her brother was up to.

It was after midnight when Dolila returned to find her brother very much awake.

In a low authoritative tone he stated, "It's time to go."

"What, where?" a stunned Dolila replied.

"Shush. You'll see." He whispered, "No questions. Just follow me."

Phinny had a plan. They left the confines of camp, bound for an undisclosed location. Eventually he led them far away from the reef and even further from the island it surrounded. It took some time before he got them out to open ocean. Along the way, Phinny created several elaborate diversions. He even backtracked a few times, only to loop around and head in the exact same direction. With each course change, he left conflicting signs to confuse anyone who might attempt to locate them. He wanted to ensure they were not found.

Phinny did not talk throughout their trek, except to bark orders for his sister to stay close and follow quietly. Meanwhile, Dolila's head spun with mounting questions that she dared not ask, like, what the heck were they doing? Where were they going? And why wasn't her brother telling her anything?

Instead, Dolila simply obeyed, remaining silent as she followed her brother's orders. Frightened and confused, she was exhausted by the time they reached her brother's secret destination. It felt as if they had gone in circles for hours.

Georgey Hole was a sheltered cove at the base of a steep hillside on the southeast corner of the island of Jost Van Dyke. With a palm tree-lined, pristine beach it was surrounded by boulders that projected from the azure waters and trailed up through the soft sand. It was relatively isolated, almost desolate, and offered protection from uncomfortable weather conditions. With a view of all the nearby islands in the area, it also offered a great vantage point to observe unwanted guests approaching. These were all the attributes Phinny had been looking for, when, earlier that summer, he secretly searched for a hiding place for him and his sister. He had been planning to run away for a long while. The only thing he had been waiting for was an opportunity. And, considering how mad Sir Thomas had been earlier that day, Phinny felt secure that this was the night to leave. He hoped his elaborate scheme was enough to avoid being caught by Sir Thomas—just in case the hard-nosed elder decided to search for them. Phinny did not want to be prevented from accomplishing his purpose for running away.

Declaring Georgey Hole their final destination, he looked at his sister, suggesting she get some rest. He said nothing else. Dolila was spent. Too tired to assault Phinny with a battery a questions, she remained quiet. There would be plenty of time tomorrow, she decided, drifting off to sleep shortly before sunrise.

She did not nap long. Sleeping with one eye open, once Dolila's initial exhaustion waned, fear crept into her slumber and haunted her dreams. She awoke, startled. For a fleeting moment she thought she was still within the confines of Sir Thomas' Reef Tour Camp—that their running away was simply one big nightmare after all. However, when she opened her eyes to spot Phinny fishing for breakfast near the water's edge, Dolila quickly realized the events of the previous night were *not* a dream. She felt uneasy as she recalled the hours leading up to their arrival at Georgey Hole, and she was troubled by thoughts of just how far they were from the safety and security of Sir Thomas' care.

They were more than fifteen miles and three islands away from their troop back on the east end of Anegada. Surrounded by one of the largest reefs in the Caribbean, Anegada was a flat, 11-mile stretch of land just a few feet above sea level. Phinny and Dolila had been spending their summers there since they were very young. And, until recently, it had been a place filled with happy memories.

Why did they have to leave? What were they going to do here, all alone? Dolila questioned as she stared at her brother.

Without looking up, Phinny addressed his sister as if reading her mind, "Isn't it beautiful here? So peaceful. So quiet." With a casual glance he continued, "Good morning, Sis. Would you like to join me for breakfast?"

"I don't think so," she answered nervously.

"Okay then. But you're going to want to keep your energy up, Dolila. So, please eat soon," he replied, while dining on his morning catch. He scooped several more small fish from the sea, offering them to her.

Once again, she declined. Her brother was acting as if nothing was unusual. It made Dolila very uncomfortable.

"Don't be nervous, Dolila. Think of this as an adventure," he offered in an amused tone.

An adventure, she thought, *more like a nightmare*. "Why are we here, Phinny?" she asked. "*What* is going on?"

"It's time we knew the truth," he asserted.

"The *truth*? The truth about what?"

"Come on Dolila," Phinny interjected, "if you won't eat, let me at least show you around this place. It's really cool. So much better than where Sir Thomas takes us to explore."

Overtired and scared, Dolila approached Phinny with a determined and demanding tone, "The truth about what?"

"I promise to explain everything to you, Dolila. But first let's go explore," he urged. Phinny breezed passed her, jumped into the air and crashed into the water with a huge splash.

Dolila remained motionless, drenched and not amused. She wanted answers, not foolish antics. And, yes, she could see they were in a beautiful place; it was impossible not to notice.

Swimming back to the surface, Phinny realized his brilliant idea had not worked. His sister looked more infuriated than before. He knew she wasn't going to allow him to keep her in the dark about why they had run away. But had hoped a little laughter would lighten the mood.

He took a moment to organize his thoughts. With a deep sigh, Phinny looked out past the confines and protection of Georgey Hole. A wafting breeze caused a slight ripple on the water. Several sailboats motored their way westward in the distance.

Taking a few deep breaths, he began slowly, deliberately. "I need to know the truth about what happened three years ago," he said choking back his emotions, "I have to. And I need you to trust me when I say—*that* will not happen while we remain under Sir Thomas' care."

Dolila was stunned. She had not expected that answer. And, she knew he was right. Under Sir Thomas' care they would *never* be able to probe into the deaths of their parents. Sir Thomas would not allow it. Phinny had tried. She'd seen it. She also knew her brother not only carried around immense guilt over their deaths, but had also suffered the loss of affection from the one individual he loved almost as much as them—Sir Thomas.

Until that day three years ago, Sir Thomas had always been Phinny's mentor, a friend. Summers at Anegada Reef were all he'd talk about during the rest of the year. Although very close with his dad, Phinny shared a special bond with Sir Thomas—the love of adventure. He'd listen to Sir Thomas' tales of the sea and his travels, demanding the most intricate details. And, in return, the elder had kept a watchful eye—remaining patient and understanding with Phinny's own need to explore.

Dolila realized her brother had not been reckless in his choice to run away. In fact, he had been surprisingly methodical in his plan, so far. "I trust you, Phinny," she said.

She meant it. They weren't running away. They were running *toward* something—toward him healing, toward the answers to some of his most burning questions. Dolila looked at her brother with immense pride. And, for the first time in many years, she truly felt he was her *big* brother. A sense of calm came over her. "I trust you, Phinny," she repeated. "You can count on me. I am not going anywhere."

They continued to talk, telling stories for hours—remembering nuances of both their parents. They reminded one another about what it felt like to be without worry or pain. And, for the first time, they actually discussed what happened that day and how each of them was specifically affected. Phinny even expressed his feelings about how much he missed his relationship with Sir Thomas.

Hour after hour, they continued—sometimes laughing, mostly crying. Listening to one another intently, as morning turned into afternoon. Their surroundings were ignored. Their concentration never wavered. They both had lots to say. The day had come and gone.

Looking out over the water, Phinny and Dolila watched as the sun's light grazed the vast blue stillness, creating a layer of amber reflections from the evening sky. The bright tawny semi-circle continued to disappear below the horizon.

Dolila chirped, "Well . . . I am definitely hungry now."

"Me too. Let's go catch some fish!" Phinny exclaimed.

They fished for more than an hour. Filling their bellies, they were exhausted. When they finally settled-in, Phinny wished his sister good night. "I love you, Dolila."

"Goodnight, big brother. I love you too. And Phinny, I am really looking forward to tomorrow. I have a *good* feeling about it."

Phinny was speechless.

Their journey had begun.

*   *   *

While Phinny and Dolila slept peacefully, fifteen miles away on the east end of Anegada—it was a different story. Attempting to wind down for the night, Sir Thomas could not relax. Rather, he remained tense and unnerved after a grueling first day of searching for the young twins. He had called upon his most trusted confidant, Wendy, to head up the search. He even had his students in the reef tour program take part. Breaking up into small groups, they had scoured the surrounding area for hours but to no avail. Each lead had ended in disappointment. Each possible clue was halted by another dead end. It had become apparent to Sir Thomas that the twins did not wish to be found and that they had gone to great lengths to confuse and mislead anyone who tried to locate them.

Sir Thomas approached his beloved Tanya, who was already nestled in for the night. She'd managed to finish her work early and decided to get some rest as her growing condition had begun to make her increasingly weary.

"Tommy, come to bed," she gently requested.

"I can't sleep, Tanya," Sir Thomas answered as he paced. "It's been almost twenty-four hours since they were last seen, Tanya. Twenty-four hours," he repeated with a quiver in his voice. "Being out on the water alone is dangerous. What am I going to do if we can't find them? What am I going to do when we do find them? What am I going to do if something happens to them out there? And, *anything* can happen," he trailed off, unable to shake the fear.

Tanya lay quietly. She patiently waited for his next outburst.

He attempted to quiet his mind. But, he couldn't. Sir Thomas knew the twins had not simply run off. He also knew, having queried the students for hours, that none of them had any involvement in helping the twins run away. In fact, they were all so surprised by the twins' disappearance that for a while it was Sir Thomas that was besieged by questions. Having no good answers for them, rampant rumors swiftly spread throughout the reef camp as increased speculation consumed his students. Sir Thomas felt depleted, frightened and incredibly guilty for his contribution in the twins' decision to leave.

Lamenting over his behavior toward Phinny, he began to rant, "Why did I have to be so darn hard on him? Why couldn't I have just been gentler? Why did I have to get so angry? How could I let Lamar and Dolly down like that?" He paused as his thoughts drifted, thinking of the young ones' parents. Swinging himself around, he looked at Tanya in desperation. "It is my fault the twins are orphaned. It is my fault they've now run off." He exclaimed, "I promised myself I would protect them. I promised Lamar and Dolly I would keep their twins safe!" He was at his wit's end. "I have to find them, Tanya. I have to keep them safe. I just have to . . ." Sir Thomas broke down, unable to finish his thoughts.

Pained by her husband's struggle, Tanya watched as he broke down for the first time in many years. She had worried, over the years, that he would not tolerate feeling so deeply again. That his masks and walls may never allow him to show his true emotions. For as hard and strong as Sir Thomas seemed on the outside, on the inside he was soft and warm. When it came to his loved ones, Sir Thomas was incredibly protective and extremely vulnerable. She watched as his sense of responsibility toward Phinny and Dolila overwhelmed him. His sense of guilt consumed him. She knew he felt responsible for their safety and survival.

Sir Thomas did not usually show this kind of vulnerability. Tanya had seen it only a few times in their long lives together. Usually, he remained so strong, calm and contained. He had the ability to command and keep control even in the most aggressive and horrific of situations. And, she knew—he had seen his share of horrific situations.

Looking up at him, Tanya waited a few moments before softly requesting that Sir Thomas lay down with her. Her voice was tender. Her request, a simple whisper, "Come here, darling. Lay with me a while."

Entranced by the sound of Tanya's voice and exhausted from his emotional outburst, Sir Thomas obeyed her gentle request. He sighed deeply as he made his way to the warm bed. He nestled in next to her, nuzzling her cheek.

"I love you," he stated.

"I know," she returned with a smile.

They lay together in silence looking up at the midnight sky. The moon peaked into view from behind a collection of cumulus clouds. Tanya turned and stared into her beloved's eyes. "Tommy," she stated in a soft voice—with undeniable strength and poise, "You are amazing. You are incredible. And this is not your fault. Phinny and Dolila are on their own path now. You have chosen the most worldly force possible to handle the efforts of finding them. Wendy is strong. She is also kind and comforting. She will find them. She'll look out for them. And she will bring them back to you, when it's time. You know this. It's why you hired her. Let her do her job. Trust that Phinny and Dolila are safe and protected. Know that Lamar and Dolly are proud of you and that they know you have done everything in your power to take care of their young twins."

Tanya waited for her words to sink in. She remained silent, waiting until Sir Thomas was calm enough for her to pursue their conversation. When Tanya sensed it was safe to continue she asked, "Can you share what Wendy said in her report today?"

A late afternoon meeting with Wendy seemed to magnify Sir Thomas' frustrations. Wendy was in charge of the investigative efforts surrounding the missing twins. She offered no concrete answers as to Phinny and Dolila's whereabouts, much to Sir Thomas' displeasure. He wanted answers! He usually had the utmost confidence in Wendy's abilities but this incident was too personal for him. He was having trouble maintaining a clear head about the circumstances and recovery efforts. As much as Wendy tried to persuade Sir Thomas to let her handle things, he could not help but feel the need to be actively involved with the search.

But, rather than get upset again, he chose to take several deep breaths before staring back into Tanya's adoring eyes, which soothed him. She was so gentle and wise, he thought. At that moment he loved her more than he ever had. He loved her for loving him. He loved her for balancing his gruffness. He loved her for accepting all that he embodied. There was no one else he could imagine spending his life with.

After a long, deep sigh he began, "She said she had things under control. She said she had a plan and that I must be patient." He rambled, "She said it may take a while before the twins could be brought back to me. She asked that I focus on what had happened in the past few months. She said it was evident that Phinny had planned their departure long before my outburst at Anegada Reef. She said she believed something else triggered the twins' motivation to leave." Sir Thomas stopped abruptly, lost in thought. He wondered what might have caused Phinny to go. He hoped Wendy was wrong and the young one had simply overreacted to being reprimanded. Taking another deep breath he finished, "She asked me to be patient. She said she had a plan. And she asked me to simply trust her," he finished.

Tanya waited a moment before responding. "Okay then. Well, it sounds like Wendy has things under control. Why not give her a while, my darling. What is it that you fear?" she asked.

Sir Thomas was resolute not only to find out why the twins' had run off but also why they seemed so determined *not* to be found? His words spat out, "I am worried about Phinny. I am scared for him." He continued, "I have noticed the *darkness* within him has grown recently. He has been asking a lot questions about his parents lately. It's as if something has refueled his obsession over what happened to them." Again, he looked deeply into his beloved's eyes, searching for comfort. "I have not shared that with Wendy." He looked away and continued, "I know I should have, but I was hoping to investigate a few things on my own first."

These last few comments were of great concern for Tanya but she knew not to push Sir Thomas for further clarification. She would revisit this conversation later. Instead, she chose to focus on another subject.

"Hey," she stated playfully, "Look here," addressing the bulge at her belly. "It is almost time."

An immediate shift came over him, the gruffness abating as he admired Tanya's belly. A small grin developed, as he stared. "Wow!"

They had a large family already, but Sir Thomas loved the idea of more children. "When?" he asked giddily.

"Soon," Tanya answered, "I have already made all the arrangements." She was getting older and delivery was not nearly as easy these days. She wanted to be safe, especially with multiples on the way.

"I'll be heading to Ft. Lauderdale soon."

"Who will be going with you?" Sir Thomas asked, knowing he would not be able to accompany her.

"All my sisters will be there and some of my cousins, too. Don't worry dear, I'll be fine." She gave him her most tender smile. "You have a camp to run with twenty-two young ones to keep safe and in high spirits. They are counting on you and I am too. Now, let's get some sleep. We both need some rest."

They nuzzled into one another again. Sleep came readily. Exhaustion had consumed them both.

A Race to the Starting Line

Billy awoke from his first night at anchor to the sun shining through a nearby porthole. Slowly emerging from an unencumbered sleep, his eyes half open, he rolled onto his side to give his cat her morning squeeze. "Good morning, Mishimo," he croaked groggily then gently placed his ear to her belly, awaiting her response. A bright smile filled his face as he listened to her hums of contentment.

Mishimo did not purr very often. It was simply not in her nature to purr. But, she always allowed this morning exchange of affection. Once she deemed it complete, she'd return to her stoic, seemingly unfriendly temperament. This morning was no exception. It took only moments before she became impatient with the weight of Billy's head on her belly. Consistent with her fickle nature, the persnickety gray tabby quieted her internal motor and pushed up with her back, a clear indication she was through being demonstrative. Managing to wiggle her way free from Billy's grasp, Mishimo tensed up her back to let him know she was serious; her tiger-like stripes standing on end.

With a smile still spread across his sun-kissed face, Billy ignored her signs of defiance. Grabbing his friend around her chubby belly, he pulled her close, landing one last peck between the ears before she broke free from his embrace and jumped to the floor. He loved her. And he knew she loved him.

Still sleepy, the young boy whirled onto his back for a prolonged yawn and a lengthy, involuntary stretch. He took a deep breath. He recognized the smell of chicory and cinnamon seeping through the crack at the base of the door. His smile grew. *Papa's up*, he thought. Acting as a catalyst, the familiar aroma transformed the boy's content dreamy state into overwhelming excitement as he realized it was the morning of the big race. His eyes opened wide and he jumped from his bunk. Sprinting out the door, through the empty salon and up the stairwell he found Papa sitting in the cockpit looking out over the bow, a fresh cup of coffee in his hand.

"Good morning, my young man," welcomed Papa. "It looks like a great day for a race," he commented while admiring the slight chop on the water. A warm breeze filled the air.

"Hi Papa. Is it time to go yet?" spouted the eager boy.

"Not yet. We're about one cup of coffee away. Why don't you go wash up?"

"Okey Dokey!" Billy called out as he dashed back down the stairwell.

Meanwhile, Papa went back to what he was doing. He looked out over the bow, admiring the beauty created by the morning glow. He could not imagine a more perfect place than here on the water, surrounded by the mystical nature of the islands. He thought of Nana. He should call her after the race and let her know they had arrived safely. He took a sip from his cup. Good ol' Danny, he thought. Racing was surely a cure-all. It made you forget everything else.

They arrived back at The Dive shortly before 8:00 a.m. Papa Joe followed by Billy, who slowly trailed behind him—holding a special basket.

—

The small boy's face beamed with excitement as he followed his granddad through the restaurant, dawdling to read some of the notes scribbled on the plethora of t-shirts, dollar bills, and business cards that lined the walls, crossbeams and ceiling. Billy could not help but stare at the artwork of intimate apparel that was strewn throughout the place. Eventually he made way, greeting a smattering of patrons as he meandered past them. When he saw Marta, bustling around refilling coffee, Billy got excited. He liked her. Smiling brightly, he quickened his pace to chase her down, say hello and give her a morning hug. In so doing, he had lost sight of his granddad. Marta was happy to help. She pointed the boy in the direction of the bar and off Billy soared, dashing around the corner to catch up with his Papa.

Once around the corner, however, Billy stopped abruptly. His eyes widened like saucers as he became fixated on his grandfather ambling over to four men sitting at a table in the back of the establishment. Billy's heart began to pound hard within his chest. His hands became clammy. He had never seen a group of men quite like this. The whole scene made him extraordinarily nervous.

Two of the men had their heads down on the table, eyes closed. Neither of them moved, but every once in a while, they let out some despondent groans. They both had dark tans and long blonde hair, bleached from the sun. Big guys, their muscles protruded from their ripped up t-shirts and threadbare shorts. One of them had a huge tattoo of a long-legged girl on his left shoulder. The other, a nasty scar down the back of his leg. Adjacent to them were two other men, both much smaller in stature. One was ebony with long strands of matted black hair pulled back with what looked to be a rubber band. He sang continuously as he tapped the table with his weathered hands and kept rhythm with his bare feet in the sand. Every once in a while he'd stop just long enough to take a sip of coffee.

Listening attentively to the black man's melodious musings was another bleached-blonde light-skinned bloke. Obviously amused by the lyrics of his buddy's tune, the attentive listener chuckled heartily, throwing his head back and displaying a tooth-filled grin.

Involuntarily wiping his sweaty palms on his shorts, Billy inched his way toward the table, anxiously staring while his granddad interrupted the singer and his one fan.

He could hear his grandfather address the men, "Scat and Spidy, how are you fine men?"

"Dr. P.J.!" They both proclaimed, standing.

The dark man welcomed Papa back to the islands with a handshake and slap on the back. He spoke with the same local accent Billy had been introduced to the day before. The other man shook Papa's hand and let out a boisterous laugh, "How are you, mate? It's been too long." He spoke with a lilt in his voice that Billy had never heard before.

"Billy," his granddad called out as he turned around to find him, "Come over here. I would like you to meet some of the guys we'll be racing with today."

The young boy slowly made his way to the table where he clung to his granddad's side as he was introduced to the two men.

"This is Scat and Spidy, two members of the crew aboard *Silver Bullet*," Papa continued proudly, "Guys, this is my grandson, Billy."

Scat extended his hand and smiled widely. His teeth were almost luminescent in contrast to his dark skin. "It great to meet you, Billy," he said.

Still clutching the basket, Billy freed his right hand and wiped his palm on his khaki shorts. He was unusually aware of his own presence. As butterflies danced in his belly, he sheepishly replied, "Hi Mr. Scat. It's nice to meet you too."

Scat was amused by the young boy's formality. He leaned over and patted Billy on the back, "No need for the 'Mistah', he stated, "Me name just Scat, ya know."

"Hey Billy," Spidy chimed in, holding out his hand, "It's awesome to meet you, mate!"

Cautiously the young boy shook the man's hand and replied, "Hello Mr. Spidy." He was still feeling unusually nervous.

"So you're joining us out there today?" Spidy inquired.

"Yes," Billy answered, astounded by his sheepish one word reply.

As if on cue, Marta walked up. "Hey guys," she offered, before kneeling beside Billy and handing him a small pie-shaped disc of fried dough. "Compliments of the man at the corner of the bar," she said.

Billy looked up, surprised. It was his first Johnnycake with cheese. He smiled and looked over at Charlie who was watching the exchange from behind his local paper. He waved over at Billy before burying his head back into an article about the ongoing difficulties of bringing electricity to Jost Van Dyke.

Taking a big bite of his Johnnycake, Billy savored the fried dough, which was still warm. The cheese, although not melted, reminded him of home. Soon, the mutterings in his belly began to fly away. "Yes, Mr. Spidy, I am going to race today." This time he answered with increased confidence. Fearlessly he continued, "Mr. Harvard said I could." He decided there must be magic in the fried sweet dough as he took another sizeable bite before questioning his new acquaintance. "Is that your real name?" he asked Spidy.

"No mate," the native New Zealander laughed. He was amused by Billy's quick transformation from a scared little boy to a curiously bold young man. "Spidy is my nickname," he continued, "My real name is Troy, but nobody calls me that."

From the table came a groan, interrupting the conversation. One of the sleepy men lifted his head to take a quick gulp of caffeine. Marta walked over to fill his cup. In response, he groaned again. The other man grunted. Billy stared at the lethargic men. He found their sounds amusing. He was no longer afraid of them. They no longer seemed that scary. In fact, they reminded him of hibernating bears, nothing was going to wake them.

Papa found the men with their heads down quite amusing as well. They were the two stragglers that Papa had seen hanging out at the bar the night before. Wearing the same clothes, it seemed they had not made it home. With just a hint of a smile he decided to tease them. "Must have been a late night there boys. How you and your brother feeling this morning, Big John?" he chided.

Lifting his tattooed arm, Big John indicated his feelings by making a fist and pointing his middle finger in the air. Bubba just grunted.

"Ooh, that good I see," Papa commented.

Up walked Danny. Excited and eager to begin the pre-race meeting, he ignored the teasing exchange. He was focused and determined to win!

"Let's get this meeting started, boys!" he exclaimed.

At the sound of Danny's voice, Big John and Bubba raised their heads and sat upright.

Papa and Billy took a seat as the entire group gathered around the table. Focused and determined, Danny was all business when it came to racing. He began the meeting with a tactical discussion. Billy sat quietly, listening intently.

For the next twenty to thirty minutes, the crew mapped out a cohesive plan, building their strategy to beat *Hold the Mustard*. When they'd finished, Danny changed the subject. He wanted to formally introduce Billy to the team by offering a brief background on each of his crew.

First there was Spidy, who was from New Zealand and had grown up in a boat yard, climbing masts before he could walk. He was famous for his acrobatics and agility.

Then there was Scat, a musician who played reggae for his fellow locals but also had a not-so-secret love of jazz and blues. He would create new lyrics and sing all day long. His real name was Damon. Scat was the Bowman aboard *Silver Bullet*. He managed the jib and spinnaker sails and was responsible for getting them up and down—*fast!*

Next there were the Carolina Boys, Big John and Bubba. Way over six feet tall, with a full beard, Big John looked more like a lumberjack than a racer. He and his brother lived on St. Thomas. Nobody ever called Bubba by his real name. He didn't like it and everybody was too afraid to ask what it was. Bubba looked exactly like his brother, only clean shaven and tattoo free. They were both originally from North Carolina on the Outer Banks near Cape Haterras. When they weren't racing, they could be found either on their surfboards or at the bar.

Then there was Captain Danny Waters, otherwise known as Harvard, and his Tactician, who the crew affectionately referred to as Dr. P.J.

Billy liked all their cool nicknames. He wanted one.

"You, my boy, will be referred to as Rail Meat," Danny explained, "It's a generic nickname for those hanging off the rail in a race with no other duties except to offer ballast." He continued, "You'll have to *earn* a real racing name."

"He looks more like a Rail Feather to me," Bubba quipped.

Billy was okay with the generic nickname but didn't like the meaning behind it. "I can do more than just hang off the rail," Billy suggested, ignoring Bubba's comment. He looked to Papa for help.

"Billy, racing is different. It can get very hectic and even dangerous at times. Serving as ballast will allow you to watch and see what racing is all about." He added, "You must move quickly from side to side when we tack. Always remember to duck under the boom. Can you do that?"

"Yes." Billy answered with a bit of an attitude. He wondered why he was being asked such a silly question; he had been sailing his whole life and had just completed an 1800-mile trip from New York. He wasn't about to forget to duck from the boom!

P.J. ignored his grandson's disgruntled response, "Racing can be a lot of fun, but you must listen to Danny when he gives a command, okay?"

Billy responded with a blank, "Yes." He was starting to wonder about Papa. Why was he treating him like a little boy? He wasn't used to it.

"Okay, listen up," Danny called out to his crew. He stood behind the young boy. Towering over him, he placed his thick leathery hands on Billy's shoulders, "Billy here, is our VIP passenger. You are to treat him as such," he commanded.

As a gentle reminder, Billy lifted his special basket over his head. The contents did not stir. Danny grinned as he took it by the handle. He could not help but admire the young lad's power of persuasion—remembering the bargain he'd struck with the boy the day before. This was the price for Billy's help in convincing his grandfather to take part in the race. Raising the basket in the air, Danny addressed his crew once more, "And we are going to have another guest aboard today, boys. Her name is Mishimo. She will be our mascot for the race," adding, "Be nice to them both. And, no playin' with the pussy!"

Raucous laughter ensued. Billy did not know what to make of it.

Rustling the youngster's hair and patting him on the back, Danny handed the basket back to the boy. He raised a fist in the air, and roared, "Now let's go catch some wind and leave *Hold the Mustard* in our wake!"

The meeting adjourned. They all let out a *huge* cheer, jumping up from the table (some more quickly than others), bound for the commercial dock.

There were many other boats in the harbor now. Twenty-three would be competing in the race. Piling into a large dinghy with Marta at the helm, six men, one VIP passenger and a feline mascot, hiding in her specially constructed basket, made their way through the busy anchorage toward *Silver Bullet*.

Marta pulled alongside the boat. Her husband gave her a huge kiss before jumping up onto his boat. One-by-one Danny's crew climbed over the lifelines and onto the deck. Handing up the basket, Billy was the last to board. They all screamed and whistled as Marta made her way back to shore. She looked back at them, waving as she walked down the beach toward The Dive. She had a lot to do before the post-race party.

A classic 32' Alden wooden sailboat, *Silver Bullet* was Danny's pride and joy. She was built in 1947 of mahogany and had a full deep keel. Danny had purchased her on a Tuesday in 1962. Three weeks later he arrived in Great Harbour. He'd lived there ever since. *Silver Bullet* was kept in immaculate condition and had all the state-of-the-art sails and equipment. Her primary function these days was racing, although Danny would occasionally take her on short trips to the other islands nearby.

Onboard *Silver Bullet*, organized chaos ensued as the three-minute whistle sounded. Mishimo was safely secured down below, under the stairwell. Scat manoeuvered sails while Spidy flung himself up the main mast to untangle some lines. Big John and Bubba brought up the anchor while Harvard kept the boat into the wind. P.J. squatted down on the stern looking out past the committee boat, watching the chop on the water and assessing the wind direction. Their sails went up. Billy's eyes became wide as saucers, studying each of the men. Meanwhile, he did what he was told. He sat on deck with

---

his legs dangling over the starboard side, listening for further instruction. He was fascinated.

Within minutes Great Harbour had transformed from a quiet little anchorage into a multi-lane highway where boats crisscrossed as they raised sails, some heeling dramatically. Members of other racing teams could be seen scurrying around the decks of their respective boats. When the one-minute whistle sounded, the harbor became a bustling artery for twenty-three racing hulls—all vying for the best position between the starting markers.

"Okay boys, are we ready?"

"Ready!" they all bellowed.

They grabbed the wind on a starboard tack and headed for the committee boat. They would have to time it perfectly. Another boat came up behind *Silver Bullet*, attempting to overtake them. To Billy, it looked as if they were going to collide. He could see dangling legs along the other boat's starboard side; the boat was completely out of the water on a hard tack. Bubba took two turns on the winch, tightening up the jib. Big John took care of the mainsail. The start whistle sounded. Inching away from the competition, *Silver Bullet* sailed between the starting markers first, setting the pace for the race.

Billy loved it!

Papa stayed glued to Danny's ear, sharing his thoughts on wind and weather. Danny instructed the crew. Outside the mouth of the harbor, they let out a bit more sail as Danny steered to port, turning left with the wind nearly behind them. Their strategy was to take the most direct route—staying close to shore, hugging the coast, and hopefully not losing too much speed. It was a risky move because the wind direction might shift, causing them to slow considerably and even have to change course, which would slow them even more. Several of the other boats decided to use another strategy; they would sail higher on the wind, sailing away from the shoreline, with the hopes of gaining speed. *Hold the Mustard* could be seen in the distance, having taken the latter route.

P.J. pointed out the competition to Danny, who took a long glaring look at *Hold the Mustard*. Then, P.J. whispered something to him. Billy could see the smile on Papa's face. He knew his granddad was happy with the decision to stay close to shore.

The race required them to circle the island completely, including the tiny island cluster at Jost's most eastern point. It was a thirteen-mile trek and was expected to take less than three hours to complete.

The wind was relatively light, consistently around ten to twelve knots. However, at times, it would get gusty. From the bow, Scat continued to make adjustments to the sails. He looked back at Harvard, who made a few hand signals. Scat then called the other boys over to him.

Big John and Bubba had been straightening up the deck. Billy watched as the two men dropped everything and walked over to pull out some additional gear before making their way to the bow. Billy guessed the plan—the spinnaker was going up! Brought out in only very specific conditions, this *huge* lightweight sail could give them the edge they needed. But, it would take some manpower to get it prepared and was cumbersome, sometimes even challenging, to get up.

Billy stood up and headed into the cockpit to get out of the way. He watched closely as the three men prepared the huge, tubular cover that contained the spinnaker sail. When they were finished getting things ready, Bubba walked back into the cockpit to man the jib's lines. These lines controlled how much sail was let out or, in this case, brought back in. Bubba would have to bring in the jib completely in order to make room for the massive spinnaker to fly.

Billy offered to help.

"Nope. I got it kid," the burly man responded as he leaned over to grab the line.

Suddenly a scream came from the foredeck. Scat had tripped, fallen and was now lying on the deck—hurt. Bubba hastily placed the line from his hands into its safety block and ran toward the bow, not realizing the rope had not been properly locked-in.

Billy could see it was not secure, but there was no time to yell. Without being locked into its safety block, the line would continue to pay out and the sail would surely unfurl. Losing control of the jib could be disastrous, especially with three men in its path on the bow—one already lying on the deck, apparently hurt. A jib line flailing around was like a whip at high speed and could cause major injury, or worse, if someone was slapped with it. And, the sail whirling about, uncontrollably, would only add to an already dangerous situation. The little boy had to act—before the wind filled the sail and caused more line to pay out. He jumped up, ran over and yanked as hard as he could on the line, wrapping it around the winch several times before locking it securely into the safety block. He then grabbed a handle and inserted into the winch, cranking as hard as he could. A puff of wind filled the sail as Bubba looked up and saw what Billy (who was now returning to his position on deck) had done. The whole maneuver took a matter of minutes, but at the end of the day, would be considered the most vital of the race.

Things settled down almost as quickly as they'd gotten out of hand. Scat was okay, having only suffered the wind being knocked out of him. Without saying a word, all three boys got back to getting that darn spinnaker out of its chute and into the air. Up it went—an enormous deep-blue sail that seemed to fill the sky. A massive decorative scene was embroidered on it—a *gigantic* six-pack of beer. On each can—the Rocky Mountains graced the background while Danny's face (with a big toothy grin) was embedded in the foreground. A small jagged hole, with liquid pouring out, pierced each container. In the top-left corner of the image was the culprit—a distinct silver bullet casing.

Billy had seen several spinnakers before, but never one quite like this. Usually they were decorated with numbers or an emblem of some sort. He thought it was funny, watching Danny's exaggerated expression flapping around on the cans.

"Nice spinnaker, Harvard," P.J. quipped, "Looks like you're running for office."

Danny snapped, "Thanks a lot," before launching into a spirited explanation. "Just a little sarcastic nudge to the old coot," he said, referring to his uncle, whom he didn't like very much and enjoyed doing things to annoy. Looking up, admiring the artwork that draped the sky, he continued, "Thought this would adequately piss him off."

"Now, before you say anything there Doctah," he went on, "*I* realize *every* time I serve the stuff, I add to my inheritance. But boy—does that man tick me off. This is the only way I can stand it!"

Danny and his uncle had never seen eye to eye. His uncle thought Danny was wasting his life (not to mention education and talent) by *running away* to the islands. Danny preferred to think of it as *living his life*, as opposed to simply existing.

Well aware of Danny's disdain for that particular member of his family, P.J. decided not to tease him any further. He didn't like watching his friend's otherwise mellow, liaise-faire persona mutate into venomous rage. But, it was too late. Danny was on a roll. He continued with his rampage for a few more minutes, explaining that his uncle had most recently infuriated him by making several derogatory comments toward Marta. Since he didn't believe his uncle had any real feelings, he was going to get him where it really hurt—the family fortune. Spending his inheritance on the latest, greatest, most expensive, sometimes unnecessary, equipment for his boat was the only way Danny knew how to inflict some type of pain on his uncle—while still enjoying himself. It was that thought that changed his mood. Chuckling, he commented, "I thought you'd get a kick out of it. It's state of the art, ya know?" Proudly bragging, "It's a brand new type of fabric. Supposed to be the best."

P.J. was glad to see his buddy's little tirade was finished. He did, however, appreciate his friend's protective nature for the ones he loved. "Okay, if you say so." he responded. "But it hasn't helped ya win yet," he teased. "How 'bout we work on giving you a real reason to gloat, *six times*, on that spinnaker of yours."

Danny ignored the comment. Instead he turned his attention to his crew. "Okay boys, pay attention," shouted Danny, "No more mishaps."

Everything worked like clockwork after that. *Silver Bullet* rallied nicely, making up for lost time, resulting from the jib sheet fiasco. They were now enjoying the effects of having raised the unwieldy sail, picking up enough speed to remain competitive with the other boats. If things went well, they'd hug the coast, peacefully, for the next forty minutes and arrive at the most eastern tip of Little Jost in a good position to take the lead as they rounded the north side of the island.

It took a little while, but after the boys finished jabbering about the semantics that caused them to get tangled-up, things finally got back to being quiet on deck. Billy couldn't help but think—it was he who had gotten them out of trouble, although he didn't hear anything being mentioned. No reason to linger on the thought, he was just happy to have been able to help.

Grateful for the quiet, the little boy took a seat along the port side railing, dangling his feet over the boat and casually folding his arms along the lifeline. He laid his head upon his forearms and took a deep breath, soaking in the sea air and closing his eyes for a moment. When he opened them back up, he noticed how much lighter the water had become, having transitioned from a deep sapphire to a pale turquoise as it became shallow beneath them. Looking back toward the stern, staring at the ripples the boat created along the near placid water, the small boy admired the coral heads and sea grass below. He could see schools of fry and a few larger fish. A broad smile spread across his face as a large sea turtle emerged to catch some air in front of him. How cool, he thought.

A sudden puff of wind caused the spinnaker to flap. Billy lifted his head and sat erect—on high alert, in case any action needed to be taken. But, all was calm. The crew remained seated together on the bow as the captain made a slight turn of the wheel. The huge sail became taut once more and the captain's artwork could be seen in all its glory again, filling the sky with multiple mischievous grins.

Realizing the wind had also managed to blow his hat off, Billy looked around, in search of it. The red cap with 'The Mc4' stitched along the front, was lying on the deck behind him. Placing it back on his head and tightening the strap, Billy was reminded of the purpose for this trip—Papa's research. He became excited about the thought of exploring things not only above the water, but also below it—in order to help find the answers Papa was searching for.

He tilted his head back, imagining what it would be like to get a closer look at the coral heads on a reef or gliding alongside a sea turtle, perhaps swimming into a school of tiny fry.

He became distracted as a gathering of white puffs of cotton filled the sky. He loved clouds. They always seemed to want to tell a story. Today, though, the story wasn't *in* the clouds but more about what they were *doing*. To Billy, they appeared to be heading in the exact same direction as *Silver Bullet* and, oddly, at the same rate of speed. With a furrowed brow, he stared at them, trying to decide whether they were actually following the boat or somehow attempting to lead the boat along its way. It was weird.

"Hey Rail Feather, mind if we take a seat?"

Billy's body jumped, startled by the sound of Big John's voice.

"Didn't mean to scare ya. Just thought you might like some company."

The little boy looked at the two huge men standing over him. "Yeah, okay," he squeaked out.

Each of the men took a seat, Bubba to the left, Big John to the right of the small boy. Their sheer mass engulfed Billy in shadow.

Billy stared at them. They didn't look as ominous as they had earlier that morning. In fact, he thought they looked kind of cool, friendly in fact.

After sitting silently for a moment or two Big John uttered, "Thanks for the help earlier, kiddo."

"You're welcome," Billy gleamed, glancing up at the man thinking, *I guess he did notice.*

Feeling confident, he asked, "Big John, may I ask you a question?"

"Sure. What is it?"

"Who is that on your arm?"

"Ah . . . it's just a girl I used to know," he said.

"Why did you put her on your arm?" Billy asked.

"Good question."

That was it, short and sweet. Billy decided he'd asked Big John enough personal questions for the moment. But, he had thousands.

He sat in silence, eventually lulled by the gentle downwind sail. He marveled at the wall of lush green trees and rock that was Jost Van Dyke. Shaking his head in amazement as he looked down at the azure water and asked, "Hey Bubba, how deep is the water here?"

It took a moment for the guy to answer, "'Bout twenty feet."

"Wow! It's so clear," the youngster announced.

"Yup."

That was it—end of dialogue.

Billy contemplated whether or not to ask Bubba about the scar on his leg. But, decided not to disturb him. He'd ask some other time.

Curious to his surroundings though, Billy decided one more question couldn't hurt. "What's that over there?" he asked, pointing to a small, secluded cove, "It looks nice."

"Hey boys," the captain interrupted, "it's time to take this spinnaker down. We need Sandy Cay to port if we are going to make it round Little Jost."

Both men stood immediately, "Time to go," Big John declared. Before taking his place on deck, he turned back and asked, "Billy, why don't you get into the cockpit in case I need a hand." And gave the boy a wink.

Billy jumped up proudly. "You got it."

Things got busy, but this time they were ready. Even with the threat of two boats approaching, things went perfectly. The crew got the colossal sail down and the jib was back out within moments. The boat was in a great position, clearing Sandy Cay and ready to round Little Jost with the least amount of maneuvering. And, hopefully, leaving the competition in their wake.

They all stood, at the ready, awaiting instructions from their Captain. They could see the committee boat in front of them. The tricky part was keeping *Silver Bullet* between the markers as they rounded the turn. One misstep could mean having to make an additional maneuver, which would surely take them out of the running to win, not to mention create absolute chaos for the other boats. Danny looked to his tactician before making the call.

Suddenly Danny screamed, "Ready about?"

The boys each responded, "Ready," before Danny turned the wheel sharply.

The boys worked smoothly, Billy ducked from the boom and everything came together perfectly as they made their first turn of the race. It would not be long before the next one.

"Good work, boys," Danny called out. "Stay alert."

Papa Joe studied the weather as well as the actions of the other boats nearby. He closed his eyes a moment, listening. Opening them, he scanned the scene again and calmly instructed Danny. In turn the captain called out, "We'll clear the northern edge of little Jost, squeak past the port marker and jibe on three. Keep focused and work fast boys," adding, "Billy, we jibe, you move. Got it?" Danny didn't require answers, just action.

Billy was nervous. Movement needed to be orchestrated and precise. His adrenalin was pumping as he watched the collection of boats surrounding them. Where did they all come from. He'd been so lost in thought a while back that he'd almost forgotten they were in a race. Pay attention, he told himself. He did *not* want to make any mistakes. He wanted to make a good impression on Danny. He liked Danny.

"One, two, three. Jibe Ho!" Danny called out.

They all did their part. Billy ducked under the boom and moved quickly to the port side of the boat where he grabbed the lifeline and took a seat, hanging his legs over the port side. He was glad to be safely nestled on the rail again.

They cleared the marker, and safely turned the corner. Some of the other boats weren't so lucky. One of them hadn't judged the turn well and almost crashed into some rocks along the edge of the island. Another misjudged their point of sail and had to tack before reaching the marker. Both lost momentum and were no longer major contenders to place in the race.

Looking back, Billy could see *Hold the Mustard* round the corner just moments after them. She was gaining speed off the starboard stern quarter of *Silver Bullet*. Everyone onboard was alert and on the ready. Papa watched his friend's nemesis approaching. He looked up at the sky, then at the water, then back at *Hold the Mustard*. Billy heard Papa say, "Listen, Danny," before his grandfather leaned in to tell him his plan.

As the captain looked around, it was obvious, by the expression on his face, he did not agree with the tactician's proposal. But, he trusted his friend.

"We are going to play a bit of chicken, boys," Danny called out. "I am gonna need ya to work fast," and provided them with precise instructions.

They were in very deep water now. The north side of Jost Van Dyke faced the open ocean. Sailing almost directly into the wind, they remained on a port tack, beating to weather. Boats were scattered along the water, spread out now, with *Hold the Mustard* not far away. It was choppy and not nearly as comfortable as their sail along the island's south side. Billy looked out, above the mountainous, rocky terrain to see a large formation of black clouds approaching. He looked at Papa, who continued to carry a contented smile. Billy had never seen the man so happy.

"Hey kid," Harvard called out, "did ya bring any foul weather gear?"

"Nope."

"Well, you're about to get wet, my boy."

"That's okay. I can take it."

"Good answer."

They proceeded to beat to weather with *Hold the Mustard* hot on their trail. The wind came upon them in a flash. The pelting rain stung Billy's face as he stared at the competition, who were not only being pummeled by rain, but were suffering from the effects of being unprepared for the dark cloud's hidden wrath. In a rush to catch up to them, *Hold the Mustard* had not anticipated the additional wind in the rain. The bright yellow boat heeled sharply and its crew grabbed onto anything they could find. As they were thrust hard over, the top of their main mast slapped the water and each of their crew disappeared under the surface. Suddenly, the boat popped back up again.

There was a huge tear in *Hold the Mustard's* jib sheet and it was flapping around madly. Billy stared, wide-eyed, with mouth agape. Broaching a boat was not an uncommon occurrence in racing, but it was the first time he had ever witnessed such a thing. He was mesmerized, watching the other crew act swiftly, getting the torn sail down and putting up another in its place. It took them a while to recuperate, losing precious time and slowing considerably. By the time their new sail was up, *Silver Bullet* was *way* ahead of them.

Unless *Silver Bullet* was to make a large tactical error (which was not likely with P.J. McMillon aboard), there was no way *Hold the Mustard* could ever catch up to them.

Without wishing any ill-will on his competition, Danny could not help but feel elated. He turned and slapped P.J. on the back in gratitude.

Danny wasn't the only one who knew what it all meant. Foxy knew it too. And, even from afar, Billy could see that the guy was not a very happy man.

Silver Bullet had no competition after that. They had judged the wind in the rain better than any of the other boats in the race, turning the final corner, at the west end of the island, with no visible opponent.

Back in shallow water with a strong following sea, they surfed the waves all the way back to the opening of Great Harbour, where they crossed the finish line more than ten minutes before the second and third place boats (*Noah's Arc* and *Barefoot Contessa*).

Overall, it was considered an easy day. It wasn't too hot. A nice breeze pushed them at a good pace (mid-June was always questionable where wind was concerned) and except for some minor issues—all the boats made it safely to the finish.

Although not part of the official racing circuit, The Race Around the Dyke was a regular favorite, mostly because of the after-party that Danny put together—and the fact that the winning crew all won their weight in beer. As the owner of The Dive, Danny figured it was his way of giving back (and, of course, another way to spend his inheritance).

"Yes!" Danny howled, with both fists in the air. "We did it boys!" He grabbed P.J. in a bear hug, lifting him off the ground. The boys were scattered around the deck; all jumping around wildly, screaming, "We won!"

As the adults all cheered, Billy remained seated on the port side deck. *Rail Meat*, he thought, *Well, I don't care what my nickname is as long as I get to do this again.* He quietly proclaimed that he would someday be known as 'The Best Racer in the World'. Closing his eyes, he imagined a large crowd roaring in his honor as he was awarded a huge trophy for his racing mastery.

"Hello."

The little boy opened his eyes. He looked around. The crew was still on the bow, rejoicing. He shook his head, closed his eyes once again, and turned his attention back to the imaginary crowd in his mind.

"Hello."

He could not tell where it had come from, but he distinctly heard someone offer a greeting.

"Hello."

There it was again, a little louder this time, almost in song. It sounded as if it was coming from mid-air. Spinning around, Billy looked at Danny and his granddad, deep in conversation on the stern while the boys on the bow packed the sails away. *Where is that coming from*, he thought.

Again he heard, "Hello."

Billy leaned over and looked out past the lifelines, down at the water. Surprised, but not alarmed, he gazed at the greeter and said, "Hello."

They stared at one another for quite some time before a very angry feline pounced into Billy's lap, manning her position. She had overheard the exchange from the stairwell and was not happy about it. She hissed in the direction of the water.

"Mishimo, don't be mean," Billy scolded.

"What's going on Billy? What's wrong with Mishimo?" Papa called out as he walked toward the boy.

"Nothing, Papa. I think she's just jealous."

"Jealous of what?"

"The dolphin."

Looking down over the lifelines, the older gentleman asked, "What dolphin?" There is nothing there, Billy." His grandfather shook his head.

"There was a minute ago. He said *'hello'* to me. Twice."

Suddenly Billy was scooped up off the deck.

Placing the boy upon his broad shoulders, Big John called out, "We must celebrate, Lucky Charm!" as he swung Billy around in circles.

Laughing uncontrollably, Billy almost missed his new nickname.

"What about our mascot?" Bubba wailed as he chased Mishimo around the deck. She ran below, hiding in her basket—wanting nothing to do with this human celebration.

Putting the boy back down, Big John escorted him to the bow where they were joined by the rest of the crew. One by one, Scat, Spidy, Bubba and Big John rustled the boy's hair before Bubba grabbed him from behind, tossing him in the air like a beach ball. They all let out a huge cheer in recognition of the boy, "Let's hear it for our Lucky Charm!"

Watching the festivities on the bow, Papa decided to keep a close eye. He knew the boys could get out of hand quite easily. It was funny though, he mused, that a fifty-seven pound, eight-year-old boy would be so revered for his contribution to such a great race. Rail Feather was pretty accurate. But, Lucky Charm suited his grandson equally well. He laughed, glad to see his grandson so happy.

Turning his attention to the water, the older gentlemen looked out passed the harbour, along the horizon. Squinting from the mid-day sun, he thought he caught a glimpse of something.

I wonder what that was all about? he asked himself.

He put a hand over his eyes to block the sun's glare and squinted a bit more. *Maybe.*

Screams of laughter drew the man's attention back to the onboard activities. He turned around to find his giggling grandson being tossed in mid-air again. Papa called out for them to be careful. In so doing, he missed the festivities from the water, way off in the distance.

The owner of the discolored dorsal fin leapt into the air, jumping in delight over the excitement of his own day. He shot into the air a second time, this time doing a double flip, causing his blackened dorsal fin to become even more apparent.

Splashing back into the water, Phinny dashed off in the direction of his new home. He could not wait to tell his sister what just happened.

Angelica's Influence

The Race Around the Dyke post-race party had continued into the wee hours. However, while Bubba and Big John danced and drank the night away to Scat's musical talents, P.J. and his exhausted grandson had departed early. Both slept deeply, engrossed by amusing dreams of the day's events, undisturbed by the ongoing boisterous sounds that emanated from the beach bar.

Anxious to begin the next phase of their journey, P.J. awoke just before daybreak. He grabbed some coffee and made his way on deck. As he studied the shoreline and the lush green mountainside, he listened for any signs of life. But, even the goats and roosters seemed to be sleeping in after the late night festivities.

Churning the engine of his *Amazing Grace*, in the otherwise muted anchorage, P.J. slowly exited Great Harbour. He turned left, motoring southeast, as the blue-gray sky of twilight welcomed the morning sun. "Good Morning, Gracie," he whispered, wondering if his daughter could somehow hear him, "Here we go, my darling."

This brief moment of quiet contemplation abruptly ended, as P.J. noticed a small mop of curly hair coming from the stairwell, followed by a furry companion.

Groggily ascending the steps, Billy took a seat on the starboard settee, next to his granddad. He rubbed his sleepy eyes and watched as Mishimo jumped into his lap and proceeded to knead at his tanned flesh. Shaking his head, he looked down with a smile as his cat curled into a ball, inside his crossed-legs, and covered her eyes with a white-mitten paw.

"Why didn't you wake me to help bring up the anchor, Papa?" Billy croaked as he stroked Mishimo's soft tiger-like stripes.

"You looked so peaceful in your sleep, I didn't want to disturb you."

"I was dreaming," the little boy responded. "Talking to mom."

Swallowing hard, P.J. closed his eyes, and craned his neck toward the sky. He took a deep breath and filled his lungs with salty air as thin streams of saline crept down both cheeks.

"Are we really going to that place I asked about, Papa?"

Clearing his throat and wiping his face with his palms, P.J. returned his gaze to the horizon. He leaned back on the settee, rested his right foot at the base of the oversized wheel and rotated it slightly to the right. "I promised, didn't I?"

"Yeah. But I thought you only said that to get me back to the boat last night."

P.J. chuckled, "You're right."

The sun continued to climb as P.J. steered toward Georgey Hole with his grandson quietly by his side. It was a beautiful morning filled with a majestic blue sky, scattered with streaks of white. He hadn't bothered to raise the sails. There was no wind. No rush. No worries. He also felt physically depleted. The race, compounded with their lengthy journey from New York, had taken a toll on his aging body. However, his mind remained sharp, focused, and filled with questions for his grandson.

Meanwhile, Billy had his head buried deep within his books, feverishly doing some homework. He'd spoken with Nana the evening before, after getting back from the big race. He excitedly explained all the details, but she was preoccupied with reminding him of their non-negotiable stipulation. Billy had to keep up with his studies in order to stay with his grandfather.

The little boy knew his Nana was serious. And, there was no way he was going to jeopardize this trip. So, although he was finding it incredibly difficult to concentrate, he was trying his best.

About 30-minutes into their trip, they both spotted a small paint-chipped blue vessel crossing the channel in front of them. They could see a lone charcoal-colored fisherman.

Papa grabbed his binoculars. He took a long look, before placing the binoculars on the settee. He lifted his hand to his mouth, rubbed his chin and tapped his left cheek with his index finger. "Hmm," he mumbled then picked up the binoculars again.

"Who is it, Papa?" his grandson questioned.

P.J. thought he remembered the boat from his last trip to the BVI several years ago. The more he thought about it, he was sure it was the one he'd seen beached under a tree in Cane Garden Bay, near his friend Charlie's home. He vaguely remembered Charlie telling him a story about the guy who owned it. They had some kind of falling out or something. He'd have to ask Charlie the next time he saw him.

"Looks like a local fisherman," he answered.

As he watched the boat round The Point and slowly motor into the tiny cove ahead, P.J. responded in a mildly aggravated tone, "I guess we're meant to have a bit of company today." He'd been looking forward to having Georgey Hole for themselves.

He put the binoculars down and looked over at his grandson who already had his head buried back into his book. "Hey, Billy," he called out, "I have a question for you."

Billy remained engrossed in his studies.

Undeterred, P.J. continued, "Yesterday, when you were looking over the side of the boat. What was that all about?" He asked.

When he didn't get an answer, P.J. decided to elaborate. "After the race. When the guys were celebrating our win. You said you saw something. Heard something."

"What?" Billy responded, head still down, looking over his work.

"Can you tell me a bit more about what happened yesterday?" His grandfather pressed.

"When?" Billy was only partially listening. He was determined to finish his work *before* they reached the anchorage. He wanted to explore.

"Yesterday, after the race. What did you see in the water?"

Mishimo's ears perked up. She squirmed in Billy's lap.

The little boy soothed his friend, petting her gently with one hand while holding the open textbook with the other. He let out a long sigh. "I already told you, Papa," he answered.

"Can you tell me again?"

He didn't understand why his granddad was so curious about all of this. But, it was about to be his excuse for not getting his homework done. He put the book down.

Billy lifted his head and turned toward his granddad. "I was sitting down, looking out at the water and I heard somebody say hello. At first I couldn't figure out where it was coming from. Then, I looked down and saw a dolphin." He paused. "So, I said hello back. Then, Mishimo jumped into my lap and started hissing at him. That's when you came over and, ah . . . well, I guess the dolphin got scared cause he swam away."

Listening intently, dissecting every syllable, Papa asked, "And, the dolphin said *hi* to you?" He leaned in toward his grandson. "What did this greeting *sound* like?"

The little boy pulled back with a grimace. His grandfather was acting very strange.

"The dolphin didn't say *hi*, Papa. He said . . . *hello*." Billy let out a little giggle. He leaned in to meet his grandfather's gaze and continued very slowly, "And, it sounded like . . ." Billy moved his mouth in an exaggerated expression, "h-eeel-l-oooo."

"Waahaha!" They both cracked up laughing.

"Really, Papa, that's it. The dolphin said *hello*. So, I said hello back." Giving his granddad a sideways glance, lifting an eyebrow and tilting his head, the little boy smiled impishly. "After all Papa, *you're* the one that taught me to *always be polite*."

Mishimo tensed up and lifted her hindquarters, making her fur stand on end. It caught Billy off guard. He tried to comfort her. But it was no use. She hissed at Papa and jumped from Billy's lap.

"I don't know what's wrong with her these days. Maybe I should take her ashore later, so she can chase some iguanas and lizards for a while?" Billy suggested.

"She's probably just feeling a bit jealous or left out," P.J. offered. He leaned over and rumpled his grandson's sun-kissed brown curls. Suddenly filled with memories of his daughter, he muttered, "Hmmm," as he envisioned Grace, healthy and vibrant, diving off the bow with her long, golden hair trailing behind her. He patted Billy on the shoulders, "Soon *you'll* be as blonde as you're mom," he said with a melancholy smile.

Billy stopped laughing. "I don't think so, Papa."

They both fell silent.

"Well, maybe not, but you're still one heck of a good looking young man," P.J. winked. "Guess what?" he paused, "We're here!"

Billy turned around. The small cove was even more amazing than the day before. The lush green mountainside was devoid of any man-made structures. The natural barrier of rocks jutting from the sea protected the pristine white sandy beach from erosion and weather.

On his way up to the bow to help Papa navigate through the reef, Billy noticed the local fisherman he'd seen enter the cove earlier. The man was now leaving Georgey Hole and was about to pass *Amazing Grace* on her port side. Billy leaned over the lifeline, offered a huge smile and flailed his arm in a vigorous wave. The man's boat was empty, except for a few makeshift fishing poles. Billy called to him, "Better luck next time, Mister!"

Once safely inside the reef, Billy struggled with the anchor. Papa eventually had to come up and take care of it himself. The boy was mesmerized. He studied the details of the cove and silently declared Georgey Hole his secret home.

"Hurry up and finish that homework while I make us a nice breakfast," P.J. announced as he headed down below. "We're going to explore today!"

Billy sat on the settee and opened his book. "Ick," he said aloud. A few minutes later, he called out, "Papa, is it ready yet?"

"I just got started." P.J. rolled his eyes. He knew his grandson wasn't going to get any more schoolwork done. Nana would just have to wait. "Why don't you get the table ready?" he called out.

Billy slammed the book shut, jumped up, and immediately got to work. He wiped the morning dew from the cockpit table. As he put the placemats down, he could smell freshly cooked bacon wafting up from the galley. It made his stomach growl. He placed the utensils on the table then poured himself a cup of orange juice and took a big gulp, attempting to quiet his grumbling belly. He could hear his grandfather singing below. "Would you like to swing on a star, carry moonbeams home in a jar . . ." P.J. sang as he flipped the last pancake. "Hmmm, hmmm, hmmm, hmmm, hmmm, hmmm, mmm . . ." he continued, as he tossed it onto a plate.

"What are you singing down there, Papa?" Billy asked, poking his head down the stairwell. He could see his granddad at the stove, swaying to this strange melody.

The old man smiled, remembering how he used to bounce Gracie on his knee while Bing Crosby played the piano and sang to the schoolboys in the movie 'Going My Way'. They must have watched the film a hundred times while she was growing up.

"An old classic, my dear boy. An old classic," P.J chuckled. He looked up at his grandson. "Now we'd better make sure you get that homework done for your Nana. We don't want you turning into a mule."

Billy wrinkled his brow, shook his head and rolled his eyes, "What?"

He picked his head up and turned back toward the table.

Putting the final touches on the two huge plates of food, P.J. made his way to the stairwell. As he began to climb the narrow steps, his mind wandered to what needed to be done in order to get started exploring; *It shouldn't take more than twenty minutes to show Billy how to assemble all the dive and snorkel gear. The tender is already in the . . .*

"Papa! Papa! Hurry! Quick!" Billy screamed.

CRASH. The food splattered across the steps and floor, as P.J. flew up the stairwell. He swirled in circles. When he heard the outboard engine turn over, he ran to the back of the boat. Billy was in the dinghy, screaming.

"Get in. We have to help!"

P.J.'s feet barely touched the ground before Billy revved the engine and took off.

Within minutes, they'd arrived at a small patch of reef on the western corner of the beach. The older gentleman stared as a bottle-nosed dolphin jumped in the air, squealing hysterically. Shaking his head, he tried to compute what was going on. He could see a second dolphin, under the water, frantically shaking her snout back and forth.

Billy cut the engine. "Papa, Papa, where is your knife? Give me your knife!"

"What?"

"Give me your knife!" Billy screamed.

He handed the knife to his grandson who then dove into the water. The dolphin squealed and dove in after him.

Leaning over the side of the dinghy, P.J. could see Billy, wielding the knife back and forth, as one of the dolphins paced in front of a large school of fish. The other dolphin was at the little boy's side. The old man leaned in closer. Then he saw it.

About six feet below the surface hundreds of fish struggled to break free from the ultra-thin green netting that trapped them along the reef-line. Hundreds.

Caught in the taught, barely visible trap, many of the fish's gills were stuck between the small squares. Some struggled, breathing laboriously. Others kept relatively still. Many were already limp. Lifeless.

The salt water stung his eyes as the small boy swam toward the net. He gasped, almost choking, briefly paralyzed by the sight. He shook his head, exhaled slightly, and began swimming along the net, cutting away. One by one, he worked to free them.

In front of Billy, pacing back and forth, was a beautiful bottle-nosed dolphin screaming, "Angelica, Angelica. Where's Angelica? You have to save Angelica!"

Trailing behind the boy was a male dolphin, with a blackened dorsal fin, shrieking arbitrary commands, demanding Billy *save them all*.

The boy attempted to follow the dolphin's panick-driven instructions, but they seemed contradictory and began to slow Billy down. He was becoming fatigued and needed to get some air.

"Over here. Please! She's over here!" Screamed the female dolphin, from about 40 feet away.

Billy swam toward her, kicking his legs as fast as he could. But without a mask or fins, he was becoming sluggish. He needed to breathe.

"Hurry, Hurry!" She squealed.

Suddenly, the boy was being propelled toward the shrieking dolphin. Once upon her, the pushing stopped and so did Billy.

Trapped in front of them, was an incredibly beautiful Queen Angel Fish. Her brilliant blue body was trimmed with a majestic gold glow and a luminous, regal looking spot sat upon her head.

She remained poised as she gasped for air. "My . . . my left gill . . . it's caught," she managed between breaths.

Billy nodded. Carefully, he began to cut through the threads from the opposite side. With three strokes of the knife, the netting opened up. He gently placed his hand under the fish's body and pulled her forward slightly, releasing the netting from between her gills.

The female dolphin nudged Billy's arm.

He could see many scrapes and marks along her snout and wondered if they'd all come from her attempts to free her friend. He placed the fish upon the dolphin's back and watched as she carried the small, limp, blue mass to safety and hoped he'd been able to free the fish in time.

Suddenly, someone else was pushing at Billy's left shoulder, screeching, "Come on, come on, we have to save the rest of them."

The little boy turned around as the dolphin with the blackened dorsal fin swooped up the netting and began tugging to make it taut. It had become loose, and began to sag, collapsing around the many entangled fish.

"We have to save them!" the dolphin squealed.

But Billy couldn't help anymore. His chest hurt. His lungs felt like they were about to burst. He had to get to the surface, fast.

SPLASH!

His grandfather entered the water about 50 yards away. But the little boy could not wait for him.

Kicking and pumping his arms, Billy swam to the surface, gasping for air as his head popped out of the water. He swirled around in search of the dinghy, which was bobbing back and forth on the outside of the reef. *Too far,* he thought.

Lying on his back, floating, he attempted to catch his breath. But there was no time to rest. He inhaled deeply, turned over onto his belly and dove under the water.

It had only been a few minutes, but he could see the difference in the reef fish. They all seemed to be dying.

He swam over to help his grandfather, who was cutting away at the net as the dolphin pulled at it with his mouth. By now, many of the fish were lifeless. Most had already been freed, but they were too weak to swim away and lay limp upon the coral or in the sand.

Together, the little boy, his grandfather, and the male dolphin worked until every fish was free. Papa had to swim up for air twice. Billy, four more times. The dolphin never let go of the net.

When they were finished, Papa and Billy gathered what was left of the webbed trap. It wasn't heavy, but it was bulky and made it difficult to swim.

Slowly, they made their way to the surface. Billy could see the dinghy at the opposite end of the reef. He was exhausted.

"I can carry it from here, young man," Papa suggested in a calm, soothing tone. He took the net from his grandson. "Not much longer now. Why don't you lie on your back a minute and float. Catch your breath."

Billy did as he was told. He didn't think he could swim anymore.

"You did great, young man. Just rest a bit."

The frayed netting was beginning to weigh P.J. down, making it difficult to remain idle in the water. He was going to have to keep swimming, but didn't want to leave Billy on his own.

Suddenly, his grandson was gliding through the water on his back.

P.J. watched as the boy turned onto his belly and grabbed the blackened dorsal fin that protruded from the water. The male dolphin was back and was now carrying the young boy toward the dinghy.

By the time P.J. caught up with Billy, the dolphin was gone and the little boy was holding onto the side handles of the boat, crying.

"Are you okay, young man?" Papa asked, concerned.

"I am good, Papa. I am okay."

The old man threw the netting over his left shoulder and hauled it on to the boat. He then swam to the rear and climbed inside. He pushed the netting to the corner and leaned over to pull his grandson aboard. But, just as he was about to pull, Billy was hoisted in the air.

Papa put his arms around Billy and lifted him gently off the dolphin's back. With his grandson wrapped in his arms, he looked down at the dolphin.

Nodding his head, the dolphin made a few high-pitched remarks and swam away.

P.J. watched the blackened dorsal fin slip below the surface.

Tears poured down the boy's face as he stared at the green netting in the corner of the boat. Remnants of gills, fins and flesh remained attached to the ragged green mesh. "Who would do such a thing, Papa? Who would want to kill all those pretty fish?" the little boy said as he lay down across the seat behind the steering column.

P.J. knelt down next to his grandson, "I don't know, my dear boy. I don't know." But, he was pretty sure he *did* know, and he had every intention of doing something about it. He patted the boy's head, turned around and started the engine.

Back at *Amazing Grace*, P.J. tied up the dinghy, lifted Billy over his left shoulder and carried him up the aft-deck stairwell, toward the cockpit. He could feel heat radiating from the boy's body.

Making his way down the salon stairs, P.J. carefully navigated past the broken porcelain and scattered breakfast-covered steps. Inside the little boy's cabin, he wrapped a towel around his grandson and placed him under the covers. Grabbing some extra blankets from the closet, he tucked them tightly around the boy.

Billy laid very still, eyes closed, crying.

Mishimo jumped onto the bed, gently climbed onto the boy's body and laid upon his chest. She licked his tear-stained cheeks with her jagged tongue.

The boy slowly turned to his side.

She followed his movements and found her place. She curled up under his chin, against his chest, and purred.

Papa leaned in, fiddled with the blankets, tightened them around the boy's feet, then stood erect and paced back and forth in the tiny room.

He stepped back, staring.

The boy's tears stopped as he drifted off to sleep. Mishimo purred all the while.

—

P.J. backed out of the room, closing the door behind him.

He worked tirelessly, cleaning the mess from the plates he'd dropped earlier that morning. His mind raced, vacillating from concerned grandparent to inquisitive scientist. He was worried about his grandson, had a million questions for him, and wondered how these two dolphins ended up at Georgey Hole.

He put on a pot of coffee and went to sit down at his desk to scribble some notes. But first, he walked over and placed his ear to the closed door. All was quiet in his grandson's cabin.

"I don't know if I can do this, Gracie. I just don't know." He said shaking his head and turning away. With eyes to the floor, he walked over and slumped into the half-moon shaped settee in the saloon. The coffee pot buzzed. P.J. remained seated. Quiet.

Bang. Bang. Bang. There was a thumping on the hull.

Bang. Bang. Bang. It was louder this time.

P.J. stood up and made his way up the stairwell to see where the noise was coming from. He poked his head out and looked around. Stepping into the cockpit, he watched while the two dolphins, jumped in unison, off the port side. He walked alongside the lifelines, following as the dolphins circled the boat.

The dolphin with the spotted dorsal fin swam closer. He sat upright and stared at P.J., who was now standing along the port side. He squealed and screeched then propelled himself backward. Then turned and dove into the water. The female remained still, a few feet away. Once her brother was finished, she approached the boat. Turning on her side, she swam back and forth. She stared up at P.J., without making a sound. Suddenly, she dove below the surface and disappeared.

P.J. looked out along the water, awaiting their return. But, they did not come back. He made his way inside the cockpit to sit, never taking his eyes from the water.

Eventually, he walked back down the stairs and into the saloon. At his desk, he feverishly wrote notes in his diary.

Every once in a while, he'd get up, lean his ear to the closed door, and check for sounds of movement from his grandson. He was afraid to peer in, not wanting to awaken the exhausted child.

The hours passed and he kept writing.

He'd written tens of pages when Billy's door slowly opened. P.J. watched as the young boy walked out, rubbing his eyes with both fists.

It was late afternoon and the saloon had grown dark. But, there was still enough light to cause Billy to squint as he looked at his grandfather.

"Papa, is it night time?" he asked.

P.J. smiled. "No, young man. But, it will be soon enough. Are you hungry?"

"I don't think so," the little boy answered, still half asleep.

P.J. watched as his grandson walked over and sat on the settee. The little boy groggily attempted to focus.

"What are you working on, Papa?" asked Billy.

Bang. Bang. Bang. The sound startled them both.

"I believe that's for you," P.J. commented.

Billy looked at him, raised one eyebrow and pulled his head back.

Papa leaned over and rubbed Billy on the shoulder. "Go ahead. Go on up top. They're waiting for you."

The little boy stared at his grandfather for a few moments, before standing up and walking toward the stairwell. He looked back at Papa and smiled. Then briskly climbed the steps. As he ascended, Mishimo walked out of the cabin.

She watched her friend make his way outside. She did not follow him.

But P.J. did.

Outside, Billy sat in the cockpit and watched closely as the dolphins put on a similar display to the one they'd given his grandfather earlier in the day. This time, however, the dolphins did not swim away. Rather, they swam to the back of the boat and waited near the stern platform.

Once again, Billy turned to his grandfather.

P.J. could hear the dolphins calling. "Go on. They've been waiting for you," he said gently.

As the little boy made his way to the back of the boat, P.J. slowly trailed behind him. He watched as his grandson descended the stern steps, took a seat on the edge of the swim platform and dangled his feet over the side.

Immediately, the dolphins swam up to the boy, stood upright and began clicking and squealing. The male dolphin, with blackened dorsal fin, was incredibly animated in his display. He thrashed and whirled around while screeching and clicking.

At the top of the steps, P.J. sat on the teak bench along the edge of the back deck. He leaned over the stainless steel railing, as far as he could, to hear what was going on. Fascinated by the exchange, he didn't want to miss a moment and wished he'd remembered to grab his notebook from his desk. But he was not about to thwart this amazing interaction by making unnecessary movements or gestures.

He studied his grandson chatting with his new friends. It was too difficult to hear through the wind, but there was a definite dialogue. At times Billy was silent, listening intently to the dolphins' squeals. At other times, the little boy talked a great deal. Every once in a while P.J. picked out a few words from Billy, but he never understood the other half of the conversation.

P.J. studied the character and mannerisms of each dolphin. He was happy to see they both seemed healthy. Although concerned with the blackened markings on the male dolphin's dorsal fin, he was pleased at the dolphin's energy and excitement. The female dolphin seemed a bit less comfortable, but joyful none the less.

Nearly an hour later, Billy waved goodbye and the dolphins swam away. He climbed back up the stern steps and sat next to his grandfather on the teak bench, excited!

"They asked us to hang around here for a while. They want to come back tomorrow and show me some things they found here on the reef. They also want to introduce me to Angelica. That's the name of the fish I saved today. She's *Doh-lie-luh*'s (Billy made sure to pronounce it like he'd been told) friend."

"Hold on young man, back up, back up. Let's start from the beginning," P.J. said.

"Sorry."

Billy talked to P.J. till late into the night, explaining how the dolphin had arrived in Georgey Hole a few days before. They were twins, very rare for dolphins. Their names were Phinny and Dolila. He explained how sensitive she was about her name.

"They've run away and made Georgey Hole their new home. Just like us, Papa."

"What do you mean they ran away?" Papa asked.

"They lost their parents three years ago. They are searching for answers to what happened to them. Or, at least Phinny is. I think Dolila is keeping him company. She's shy.

P.J. listened. He had dozens of questions, but only asked a few. "Did they explain how their parents died?"

"No."

"Did you ask anything about the male; about his dorsal fin?"

Billy shook his head, no.

"How do you know what they're saying?"

The little boy didn't know how to respond.

"What does it sound like to you?" P.J. clarified.

"Like they're talking."

"But, what does it *sound* like?"

Billy looked at his grandfather, confused. Once again, Papa was acting weird. "I just listen, Papa. I don't try to figure out what the words *sound* like. I just listen."

"You just . . . listen?"

"Yup."

They sat beside each other looking up at the sky. It had grown dark outside. The stars were out and the moon shined brightly. All was quiet in the cove.

"I am sorry about today, Papa. I know you wanted to go exploring."

Patting Billy on the head, he motioned for his grandson to make his way back down below. "Nonsense, my dear boy. Today, like all others, was a perfect day. I am very proud of you. Don't worry about me, simply enjoy your new friends."

Once the little boy was safely tucked in for the night, P.J. closed his grandson's door, returned to his desk and began to write. It was almost daybreak when he closed his journal. Rubbing the worn leather-bound cover, a gift from Gracie, he breathed deeply and smiled. His research had begun.

BACK IN THE OFFICE

Bill sat at his desk clutching a tarnished picture frame, staring.

His grandfather looked older than he remembered. The crew from *Silver Bullet* was not nearly as imposing as he'd once thought. Even the tree they were standing under seemed stunted. But the backdrop of blue sky, sandy beach and azure water, sparkling with reflections of the multitude of sailboats in the harbor, appeared just as magical as the day the photo was taken more than 25 years ago.

Charlie, who'd prided himself on his photographic prowess, had taken the picture just moments after the *Silver Bullet* crew had stepped onshore, following their big win in The Race Around the Dyke. He'd made them all stand under that tree until everything was perfect.

Rubbing his index finger across the image of his grandfather, Bill swallowed hard and took a few deep breaths as he recalled the silent declaration he made that day: to be 'The Best Racer in the World'.

Shattered dreams, he thought as he lowered his head and slowly shook it back and forth. He bent over, opened his desk drawer, placed the picture frame inside, then leaned back against the plush, tanned leather chair.

What the heck am I doing opening this can of worms, he thought. *The past is just that—past.*

He sighed deeply, swiveled his chair in a full circle and looked around his office. Behind his desk were two beautifully crafted, floor-to-ceiling mahogany bookshelves that spanned the width of the room. They were lined with volumes of architectural design and engineering books, leather-bound originals of all the great literary classics and scads of marine manuals. In the center of the vast library, encased in security glass, sat a replica of *Vigilant*, the Herreshoff-designed sloop and winner of the 1893 America's Cup trophy.

Adorning the remainder of the windowless walls was an ample supply of plaques, trophies, awards and commendations which spanned Bill's expansive nautical career.

He walked over to the collage of recognition. With an arm outstretched, he glided his hand along the metal plates and browsed the inscriptions—In Honor of *This* and In Honor of *That* or Outstanding *Blah, blah blah.*

When he reached the framed letter from Richard Branson, extolling his gratitude for Bill's part in the success of *Virgin Challenger II*'s attempt to break the world speed record for crossing the Atlantic, a tear fell down his cheek.

What a joke, he thought.

His entire career was based on building the most efficient, fastest racing boats in the world, but he'd never even stepped foot on any of them. How could the accolades be real if he didn't actually man, or even see, the boats he'd designed?

He bit his lip and shook his head again.

"I don't know," he said aloud. "I don't know."

Walking back to his desk, Bill repeated, "I just don't know."

He slumped into his chair, swiveled around to face the front of his desk and slowly shook his head again, teary-eyed.

The room was devoid of photographs except for a lone photo in the corner of Bill's desk. He picked up the image; his wife and daughters were laying in the snow, nestled inside three bright, new snow angels—smiling. It had been taken in Central Park the previous winter.

He knew he hadn't been the most demonstrative or *present* of fathers, but wasn't it more important to take care of them, provide for them? He never wanted to disappoint or hurt them and wondered if sharing his childhood memories had been a good idea after all.

He'd been sharing his stories with his eldest daughter, Brooke, for a while now. Each night she'd surround herself with the contents of the box they'd opened several months before. When he checked on her that evening, he'd found the picture frame, with the photo taken after the big race, sticking out from underneath her pillow.

She was enthralled, and he loved watching her excitement as she listened to the adventures he'd taken with his granddad when he was a young boy. He loved re-living them with her. But what if it wasn't the way he remembered?

Like him, Brooke was curious. Like him, she required concrete answers.

She'd gone to bed, once again, without answers from him. And he simply couldn't provide them for her.

She'd asked if he would take her to the islands some day. He didn't want to lie. He wasn't sure he could ever go back.

Manhattan. Such a loud, busy city, he thought.

She wanted to know if she could talk to the dolphins too.

If only I could be sure.

He bent over, opened his desk drawer, took the picture back out, and placed it next to the one of his angels.

A desk full of smiles, he thought. For the first time he noticed how much his daughter's smile resembled his own. She was so proud of her perfect snow angel. He was so proud to have participated in the race aboard *Silver Bullet*.

There was a knock at the door. Startled, Bill placed the older picture face down, on the edge of the desk.

Nodding, Bill silently watched as his wife, Ella, a petite, slender woman, with long brown hair, strolled over.

Chin tucked, with an impish grin, Ella sat in her husband's lap, facing him. She offered a gentle hug.

Feeling the tension in Bill's body, she began to caress his back. *"Amore mio,"* she said, nuzzling her head in the nape of his neck. "You are such an amazing Papa. Your daughters and I love you so."

She sat up and looked into his eyes and put her palms on both his cheeks. "It's so beautiful how you talk with Brooke each night. It means so much to her."

Bill loved to listen to his wife speak. Her soft voice combined with a strong Italian accent, always seemed to soothe him. He wrapped his arms around her and leaned his face against hers. His rough stubble scratched against her smooth cheek as he sighed, deeply.

They hugged in silence.

She'd always believed he could be such an open and loving father. She was so happy his stoicism had waned.

He'd been a loving husband and great provider, and although she knew Bill loved their daughters tremendously, until a few months ago, he'd always kept his guard up with his girls.

She understood why. She never compared her loss with his. She was simply grateful her husband finally let Brooke 'in' a little.

A curious child, Brooke had longed for her father's affection and yearned to hear all of his childhood stories.

Ella was not privy to the content of their private conversations, but it didn't matter. She was thrilled her husband and daughter had somehow found a bond that had been missing in their relationship. They had each longed for it. Now they had it. So, it worried her that her husband was troubled and seemed to be growing distant once again.

"*Mi Amore.* Come to bed, *my love*," she offered.

"I will. In a little while."

She looked over on his desk. She noticed the overturned photo, but it was the manila envelope in the center that was of particular interest. She could see it had been opened, and she knew its contents were the source of Bill's trepidation.

"Are you sure?"

He pulled away slightly. "I promised I would never go away again." He paused, "I promised. And, I won't. But, you know how I like to think. I may have to do that tonight."

She could see him struggling. There was no way to take the pain from him. She didn't even understand it.

"Trust me. Please," he whispered.

He loved her. He credited her for all that he'd managed to become. He knew, when he got like this, it made her nervous. He understood why. He'd left before, many years ago and he promised he'd never do it again. He promised he'd always come back, even when he needed to disappear for a little while.

He stared at the envelope. He needed to do this. He needed to understand. And, he hoped she'd be okay.

"*Tesarina, my treasure*," he picked up the envelope, "Why don't you go up to bed?"

A feeling of dread welled up inside Ella as she asked, "Are you coming up?"

"I promise to be back. I have to go do something."

She looked at her husband with apprehension. *"Promessa?"* She asked in earnest.

He lifted her face in his hands and spoke softly, "*Prometto,*" then kissed her gently. "I promise," he repeated in English.

It somehow felt more real when he said it in Italian. Ella wrapped her arms around her husband, not wanting to let go. She listened to his heart pound within his chest. It had been a long time since she'd been frightened by her husband's behavior.

They were married only a few months after they met. She always knew he was the man for her, so she was willing to be patient with him. After all these years, she knew her husband well and could feel him growing distant. He'd come such a long way these past few months. It pained her to think he was slipping away.

Bill placed Ella's hands in his, stared into her eyes and declared, "I promise, I'll be back. I just have to do this." He then embraced her tightly, before guiding her to the door.

He watched as she walked down the hall and climbed the stairs.

He stared at the package on his desk. It arrived from the lawyer's office several days before and had been laying on Bill's desk ever since. The final portion of settling his grandmother's estate, it had been in her safe-deposit box for 25 years, a safe-deposit box that only she and her attorney had access to or even knew existed.

Bill had opened the envelope earlier in the evening, just before he checked on his daughters and found the picture underneath Brooke's pillow.

He turned the envelope over and dumped the contents onto his desk. There was a lengthy set of legal documents, a set of keys, and a framed photo he hadn't seen since he was a boy. The sight of the picture immediately brought tears to his eyes.

He studied it briefly then shook his head. "I am sorry," he said and pulled the photo to his chest, "I am so sorry."

Placing the picture in his lap, Bill picked up the legal documents. He noticed the original date: February 2, 1974, three weeks after his mother's death. Shaking his head, Bill flipped through the pages, faster and faster. He grimaced, seeing his grandfather's repetitive signature, at the bottom of each page. *Why didn't he tell me? How could Nana keep this from me all these years?* He thought to himself.

Bill bit his top lip, shook his head and closed his eyes a second. Sniffling, he put the papers and picture back in the envelope, slipped the keys into his pants' pocket and headed for the door.

In the darkened hallway, Bill studied the walls, ceiling, and flooring that lead to the staircase at the other end of the hall. Ornate sconces, dimly lit, acted as a guide as he walked along the impeccably waxed hardwood floor. Although he'd lived at his grandparents' east side penthouse for much of his life (both as a child and for the past six years) the stark white walls, intricate crown molding and strategically placed artwork suddenly seemed foreign.

When he arrived at the base of the staircase, Bill placed his left hand on the banister and took the first step, then abruptly stopped. His mind became filled with the recent memory of Brooke excitedly sneaking him up the stairs to show him the box she'd found. He looked up and listened for any sounds, closed his eyes and imagined his daughters tucked safely under their covers, breathing rhythmically, dreaming. He hoped Ella was dreaming, too.

"*Devo andare,*" *I have to go* he whispered in Italian and stepped back down, away from the steps. "*Sogni d'oro,*" *sweet dreams* he said softly.

———

He turned around, stepped into the elevator across from the staircase and stared at the floor. His stomach churned with butterflies as the doors closed. Tears streamed down his face.

Upstairs, Ella opened her eyes. She listened to the elevator whine as it made its descent. *He'll be back*, she told herself. *He promised. He'll be back.*

Looking up at the full moon through the window, she watched the snowfall, unable to shake the uneasy feeling welling up inside. They'd married very young. He was 21. She was barely 20. And after 18 years of marriage, much about her husband remained a mystery to Ella, especially when it came to the complexities of the McMillon Family. She wished she understood or could at least relate to her husband's angst over his past, his family, his life.

Ella had her share of losses. But she didn't carry them with her the way her husband did. He seemed plagued by them.

They'd moved to the States to live in this big city, this big apartment six years ago, when his Nana had become gravely ill. Brooke was barely two at the time and Ella was not yet pregnant with Breezi. Ella knew she would miss Italy, but had been happy to relocate for her husband. She thought it would be good for Bill and for their family.

But being back in the States, back in New York, didn't make things better for her husband. In fact, it had been an emotional rollercoaster for him.

It hurt to see him in such turmoil. She'd always remained patient with Bill. She adored him, having fallen in love with him the very moment they were introduced. But she found these moments, when he would disappear *to think*, excruciating. It was what he used to do . . . before they were married.

In fact, she wouldn't agree to marry him until they came up with a compromise for his need for extended bouts of solitude. The agreement was: he had to stay close enough to hear her sing. He loved to listen to her sing.

In Italy, he always chose the barn. In New York, it was his office and on Long Island, he'd go to the guesthouse. There was always somewhere close by to get far away. And in return, she promised he'd never be disturbed.

And, Ella was diligent and respectful about giving him the space he needed. She had taught her girls to do the same. She didn't know about Brooke coming into his office, without permission, a few months ago. Bill never mentioned it.

Recently Bill had made great strides. He'd become more receptive toward the girls and would sometimes even leave his office door ajar for them to come and go as they pleased. Each night he'd tuck Breezi in and then sit with Brooke, sharing bedtime stories. Ella loved that they were growing so close.

When Nana finally passed a few weeks ago, after a long agonizing battle with cancer, Bill had become increasingly distant. She realized there was a lot to contend with regarding the complexities of the estate and wanted to believe it was the culprit for his irregular behavior. But, deep down, she knew there was more to it.

Tonight, she clung to the hope that whatever was in that envelope and wherever her husband was going on this late night might provide the answers for which his heart was longing.

"I pray for you my love," she said aloud, "Buena fortuna. Good luck."

But, it would be hours before she finally quieted her mind and was able to drift off to sleep.

Meanwhile, on the lobby floor, Bill stepped out of the elevator. Tightening his grip on the manila envelope, he walked toward an impeccably groomed, uniformed man. They exchanged pleasantries before Bill asked him to hail a cab. There was no need for a town car, Bill protested. A simple yellow cab would suffice.

"Very well sir," the doorman responded, although he disapproved. "Is there somewhere specific you are looking to go?"

Fidgeting with the envelope Bill said, "Home."

The doorman raised an eyebrow and looked at Bill with a puzzled expression. He went outside, flagged down a cab, opened the yellow door, then waved for Bill to approach.

The cold air slapped Bill's face as he walked out onto the street. "Thank you, Gregory."

"My pleasure, sir," the doorman offered in an obligatory cheerful tone, "I am sure this guy can get you wherever you wish to go. Goodnight, Mr. McMillon."

After giving careful instructions to the driver, Bill twisted around and looked out the back window. "Prometto," he whispered, "*I promise*," before turning back in his seat. He closed his eyes and let out a heavy sigh.

It was nearly midnight. The streets were relatively quiet, but the city was not completely devoid of activity on this blustery winter night. They drove through Central Park and over to the Upper West Side. The driver made a left on 85th Street and stopped halfway down the block.

Snow began to fall, covering the sidewalks with a fresh film of white powder. Gray, slushy mounds lined the curb and pressed against the tires of some of the cars along the street.

With his face against the glass, Bill stared out the window at a chestnut-colored brownstone wedged between two lighter buildings. He counted the steps up to the doorway. Nine. Just as he remembered.

Turning his attention to the tree at the edge of the curb, he tried to imagine his six-foot-two frame was ever small enough to climb the fragile limbs.

"Hey, buddy. You gettin' out or what?" the cabbie questioned.

Bill jumped. His heart thumped so loudly, he was convinced the cabbie could hear it. He removed twenty dollars from his wallet, almost twice the cab fare, leaned over the seat and handed it to the man. Clenching the door handle, Bill hesitated before exiting the cab. Standing on the pothole-riddled pavement, he studied the intricacies of the pre-war architecture and the ornate design above the double-doors of the entrance to the four-story brownstone he once called home.

He walked toward the building, stopping in front of the tree. A select few branches were still covered in powdery snow from the first storm of the new year. The others seemed gray and lifeless without their leaves. He reached up and grabbed some of the icy snow from a top branch, shaking the remainder of packed white powder, causing it to fall to the ground. He looked at the snow in his palms. It seemed a bit grayer than the nice white flakes found on the farm on Long Island. *Too much dirt in the city, even the snow is dingy.*

Suddenly he was mad. He dumped the handful of snow out of his hand, wiped his palm on his pants and walked toward the steps leading up to the mahogany double-doors he'd entered every day as a child, when his mom was alive. *Why didn't Papa tell me he'd kept this place? And, why the hell didn't Nana tell me about it while she was alive?*

He had dragged his family away from a beautiful, serene life in the hills of Tuscany to come back to New York—for her! *And she leaves out massive chunks of information regarding my life. How dare she!* No. He didn't know if he would have chosen to come back here before, but he at least deserved to be given the option. "Humph," he grumbled.

Gritting his teeth, Bill sat at the base of the steps shaking his head. He knew better. There were never options when dealing with Nana. There was only her way or no way.

The last time he'd been at this address was the day of his mother's funeral. He was seven-and-a-half years old. Papa and he sat on the steps, looking at the tree, sharing stories about Grace, until Nana pulled up in the limo to take them to the service.

Gracie had been cremated because she didn't believe in taking up any unnecessary space in an already overcrowded city. She'd made all the arrangements herself before filling Papa in on the details. She'd also openly discussed her wishes with Billy. She didn't want him having any questions regarding her death.

Nana had been upset. She didn't believe in cremation and she'd felt it was important to have a full service so people (contributors and associates of the Mc4) could attend. Papa wouldn't allow it. Gracie didn't want it. It was the first time Papa ever put his foot down with Nana. It may have been the only time.

Although very young, Billy unfortunately knew the severity of it all. He'd helped take care of his mom when she was ill, this final time as well as once before when he was only five.

Gracie had been very open with her son. She'd ask him to sit with her as she told him stories and talked, sometimes for hours. She'd tell him, "The more you know of my thoughts and feelings, the more you'll be able to carry them with you when I am gone."

But, I forgot, he thought, shaking his head.

He still missed her, after all these years, but the memories had faded. Imagination had taken over to fill in the gaps. She was beautiful. He knew that. And, although he had never acknowledged it openly, he saw her every day in his girls. Each had different characteristics of Grace. Breezi in demeanor, Brooke in looks.But he never mentioned these things to his children or his wife. He couldn't.

"Up the stairs. Third floor. Apartment 3B," he said aloud. His hands trembled as he stood up. Gingerly, he walked the steps, counting them like he did when he was young. At the top, he read the names on the six buzzers to the right of the door: Ramirez, Spencer, Feinberg, Annesley, Winchester, McMillon.

Seeing his last name in print made him gulp. Hard. Placing the key in the lock, he pressed down on the door handle and pushed. It opened easily.

Everything looked darker and much smaller than he remembered. Even the staircase seemed shrunken. It was not nearly as grand as the one at Nana's.

The smell of fresh paint permeated the foyer.

He walked up to the third floor and stared at the door. Suddenly, he was transported in time. Above the peephole there was a shiny brass nameplate—MCMILLON.

How could it remain so well polished after all this time?

His hand trembled as he struggled to fit the key into the door. Gripping his right hand with his left, he was able to control the shaking enough to get the door unlocked and opened it.

Welcomed by the scent of fresh flowers, for a moment, he thought he was going crazy. Then he saw the vase of roses atop the living room table, in front of the fireplace.

He scanned the room. Well-kept and tidy, it looked like someone was living in it. But the only thing living in Apartment 3B was a memory.

The fireplace was spotless. There wasn't a speck of dust on any surface and all the furnishings remained the same. The simple, cream-colored curtains were drawn and the room was dimly lit from a standing lamp behind the green cushy chair in the corner, next to the fireplace.

Bill pulled back a curtain and peeked outside the bay window to the street below. It was still snowing and the sidewalks and parked cars were completely white. He watched as a man, in a blue ball cap, stepped out of the building to shovel the snow from the steps and wondered if he might be the owner of one the five names on the buzzer.

The man looked up and met Bill's gaze. Bill jumped back and shut the curtain. Should he have notified someone he was coming by? Looking down at the papers in his hand, he thought, *Who would I notify? I own the damn place.*

Turning around, Bill walked out of the living room, down the slender hallway, past the tiny kitchen, toward a door at the end of the apartment. He hesitated and wondered if Papa would really have had someone maintain the garden in his dead daughter's home.

The large garden terrace was the reason Gracie had chosen the apartment. There was nearly as much room outside as there was inside. That's the way she liked it. She may have lived in the city, but she didn't have to give in to the city. It was a place to surround herself with nature. Every spring she would plant vegetables, especially tomatoes. And every year, she and Billy would add something new to the garden.

As Bill pushed open the heavy metal door, the spell was broken. His mother's beautiful clay pots, collected over years of traveling as a youngster were all there. Perfectly aligned, empty. Except for the snowfall.

He made it to the wrought iron bench before breaking down, crying. He didn't actually know why. His connection with this place had long past. But somehow, for that brief moment, he thought it was real. All his happy memories of living here with his mom, of his childhood growing up at the Mc4, laughing and being silly, being free, came flooding back. *Why do things happen the way they do? If she'd only gotten treatment and let us take care of her, maybe she'd be here. Maybe Papa would be here. We could have had more time. Things could have been different.*

He shook his head, inhaled deeply and wiped his face. No. This is NOT what his mother taught him. In fact, this thinking was exactly what she taught him not to do.

He wondered if she'd be disappointed in him as a man, a parent. He felt the failure so often lately.

Looking over his right shoulder, he admired the beauty of the French doors that led to the apartment's lone bedroom. A petite room, it measured 12 feet by nine-and-a-half feet. But Grace had managed to make it work for both their needs. The room was split in two. Half was in the motif of an active boy. The other half filled with the beauty of an elegant young woman.

It had been his room alone, until his mom became ill. Before then, she had slept on the pull-out in the small living room, moving the table each night and putting it all back together again before Billy awoke each morning.

When she got so sick, he let her have his room and he would sleep on the couch. Eventually she became so ill, he didn't want to leave her anymore and would camp out on the floor next to her bed.

He'd hold her hand, get her ice, and wet her forehead when she needed it each night. When she would finally drift off to sleep, her dreams overcoming the pain, he would make sure it was all neat and tidy before she woke up in the morning. He'd kiss her good morning after the nurse arrived and then walk down the stairs to head off to school.

There would be a driver waiting for him, opening the door as he approached. It was a formality Bill was born with so it never seemed out of place, until he was older, and found freedom in opening his own car door.

Tears streamed down his face as he recalled his mom sometimes whimpering in pain, vomiting blood, and wasting away, unable to eat.

Staring down at the bed, he could still see her pleading with him not to call Papa on that last day. She simply wanted to let go on her own. She loved her father, but he had controlled so much of her life. She didn't want him controlling how she chose to die.

Billy lay next to her. They hugged until she stopped breathing. He knew she was gone, but he still believed she was with him—as she said she always would be. It was more than an hour before he got up from the bed.

He remembered walking into the kitchen, grabbing the ice pick and heading out to the garden. Leaning over the bench, he carved the words *Grace's Garden* on one of the horizontal wooden slats. When he was done, Billy picked up the phone and called his grandfather.

Rushing to the apartment, Papa found the little boy sitting at the side of the bed, in the dark, staring at the ground. It was the last time Billy had been in the apartment.

He never minded taking care of her, and he never resented her for it. Her illness was his illness too, in some strange way. But as Bill's thoughts focused on his own daughters, he could not imagine either of them ever having to see him that sick, or worse, having them take part in his care. He could not fathom ever asking them to.

In spite of all the sickness and sadness in the apartment, there were also incredible memories of joy, fun, happiness. That's what Bill clung to as he sat on the bench in the garden again. He hadn't realized he'd walked back out there.

He sat, looking around at the empty pots. He cried deeply. Sobbed deeply. The snow continued to fall, filling the pots and covering the ground that once contained life.

It was late and he was exhausted. Even the lights in the city seemed to dim a little. But he couldn't bring himself to leave. He did, however, need to get out of the cold. He'd been sitting there so long even he was covered in snow.

He walked back through the French doors and over to the bed. Loosening his grip on the envelope, he pulled out the contents. Placing the deed to the apartment building on the nightstand, he stared at the picture. A sepia-toned tightly cropped photograph of his mom with a huge, toothy grin. Her long hair pulled back in a ponytail.

Slumping down on the bed, he looked over at the pillow and rubbed his hand across the sapphire blue coverlet. He lay down on the bed. He could smell the same fresh scent he remembered as a young boy.

He pressed the picture frame tightly to his chest and wept. Eventually he was met by dreams.

Walking the halls of the Mc4, Bill was searching for something. Someone. He slowly approached the stark gray door with the words RESEARCH LAB *on the front, and peaked through the slim vertical piece of glass below the nameplate.*

She was there, working.

Without knocking, he turned the knob. When he entered, a blonde woman looked up from behind the microscope and swiveled in her chair. She smiled at Bill, but did not address him. Instead, she leaned over and excused the young child that was playing next to her. "Go ahead now, go on over to the other lab," she suggested tenderly, "I'll be by soon to check in on you."

The young boy jumped off the seat and left through a doorway at the other end of the room, never turning back. Bill could not make out his face, but thought he recognized him.

"I am so glad you're here," Grace said to her adult son. "I missed you," she stated simply, with a peaceful grin.

Bill was dumbfounded. He hadn't seen his mom in his dreams in many years and realized just how much he missed her. Suddenly, he wasn't mad anymore. He had so many questions for her.

She requested Bill sit where the young boy had been moments earlier. Then, she bent over the microscope and peered through the lens.

"What are you working on?" Bill croaked.

"My life's work," she said without looking up. "Do you remember?" she asked.

"The dolphin?"

With a soft lilt to her voice, she answered, "Yes," and continued to gaze into the lens. "That's part of it."

She motioned for Bill to look into the microscope the young boy had been fiddling with when Bill had come into the room.

He looked down and attempted to adjust the focus.

"I can't see anything," he said.

"It's important to let go of the darkness, my darling," Grace offered.

Bill continued to struggle with the knobs, but he couldn't see anything. "I don't understand!" His voice cracked with frustration.

"You will."

When Bill picked his head up, his mother was no longer there and he was no longer in the RESEARCH ROOM at the Mc4.

He was now standing at the base of a huge, lush green mountain. The wind was howling and the trees rustled with each gust. He recognized this place.

He looked around at the familiar path. Instinctively, he began to climb.

He was alone on his ascension.

Within moments, he was at the top, having made his way more than nine thousand feet almost instantly.

At the top, there was a lookout point and a large building with a walkway surrounding it. In the center were several telescopes. He recognized the place immediately.

He spun around, looking for confirmation that he was, in fact, in the same place. Then he saw it. A huge, old, indigenous Ohi'a tree with yellow tentacle-like blooms. Toward the bottom of the mangled trunk there was an engraving. Bill approached and extended his hand, tracing the letters with his index finger: PA ♥ GM.

He spun around again. Looking at the huge valley below, he could make out the palm trees, beach and water. He recognized the view, but it was not the place he'd been describing to his daughter all these months. No, this was a different place. A place he'd come a long time ago, the last time he ran away to think—searching for answers.

"Remember." He heard from behind him. The wind seemed to be carrying the words. "Remember."

Bill turned around sharply, trying to catch a glimpse of the voice's owner. But he was alone.

"Mom?" Bill called out in his sleep. His eyes remained closed. His body curled up, still clutching the picture frame. "Mom?"

From behind the tree, with her long blonde hair blowing in the breeze, Grace walked up to her son. She was wearing a fluffy white blouse and blue jeans.

"It's good to see you, sweetie. It's been a while."

He looked at her. Stared at her. She looked so healthy, young.

He had so many questions for her. But didn't know how to begin.

Tenderly, Grace offered, "Why don't we sit? Tell me what's on your mind."

For the first time in years, Bill slept deeply. He pressed the picture tightly to his chest as he lay on his side, with his legs curled into a fetal position. In his dream, he shared the details of his life, his triumphs, his fears, and his disappointments.

His mom sat lovingly beside him and listened. When her son was finished, Grace responded, "It's all there for you, waiting for you. There's plenty of time," she paused. "You'll find your way. When you're ready." Then, she was gone.

Slowly, Bill opened his eyes. Rays of sunlight were poking in from the French doors. He rubbed his eyes and stretched his legs and arms with a few big groans and a huge morning yawn. Looking around the room, he suddenly stood up, made his way to the hallway and headed for the kitchen. The cupboards were bare, but all the utensils, glassware and dishes were in place. Opening a drawer, Bill grabbed something and headed for the back door. Outside, about a foot of snow had fallen. The garden looked beautiful, even without a plant or tree. He stomped over to the bench and wiped away the fluffy white powder. It looked brighter this morning. *Maybe I was wrong about the dinginess.*

Beneath the weathered carving he'd made the day of his mother's death, Bill carved something new. *Her Garden is Your Garden.* Then made his way to the front door.

He could smell the fresh pancake batter the moment he stepped out of the elevator. Walking down the hallway, Bill stood in the kitchen doorway, smiling.

The girls squealed, "Daddy, you're back!"

Ella swung around and looked up at the clock. It was a few minutes past seven. Managing to hold back the tears, she looked at her husband and smiled. Then quickly turned back around flipping the pancakes on the stove and exhaling deeply.

"Mama, are you okay?" Brooke asked, standing at her mother's side. Breezi was in her daddy's arms, hugging him tightly and whispering in his ear.

"I am fine, sweetie. I am fine." She hesitated, "I am just happy daddy's home in time for breakfast." Leaning down, she handed her daughter a plate of pancakes. "We made his favorite, remember?" and gently touched Brooke's cheek.

The young girl walked the plate over to the table but did not take her eyes from her mom.

Strolling over to the doorway, Ella placed one arm on Breezi's back and the other upon her husband's upper arm, meeting his gaze.

"*Tesarina*, go wash up for breakfast," Bill said, kissing his daughter's nose before setting the five-year-old back on the ground. He then hugged his wife and rubbed her back softly, "I said I'd be back. I promised," he whispered.

Ella placed her head in his chest. She closed her eyes. Tears gently glided down her smooth skin. "I know," she replied softly.

"Mommy, Daddy, come eat already!" Brooke spouted.

Both parents giggled. Bill grabbed his wife around the waist. "We're coming," he said. Placing his hand upon Ella's lower back, he guided her toward a chair.

As they sat at the table, eating pancakes, Brooke leaned over toward her dad and whispered in his ear, "Can you tell more about Phinny and Dolila, Daddy?"

Playfully, he pinched the edge of his daughter's chin. "Of course I can. Right after you finish your breakfast."

Brooke took three big bites. With her mouth still full she announced, "Done!"

The Importance of
Good Weather

They'd been in Georgey Hole for six weeks with no plans of leaving anytime soon.

Each morning there had been a knock on the hull. Billy would open his eyes, give Mishimo a quick peck then bolt out of bed, excited to share another day with his new friend, Phinny.

P.J., who was usually in the cockpit drinking coffee and writing in his notebook, would help Billy put on his life vest (and snorkel gear when needed) and watch the little boy dive into the water to meet up with his friend. He'd then sit, observe, and take copious notes of each day's activities.

This morning, however, Papa was not taking notes. Instead, he was determined to finish going over Billy's schoolwork. Weeks behind getting it done, he knew the mail from the BVI to the States was extremely slow and Nana would be very upset with him. He'd been avoiding calling her because of it.

The sun shone brightly, and the air was already sweltering as P.J. sat on the back deck. From to time to time, he glanced over at Billy and Phinny playing

---

near the reef and curiously noticed how Dolila seemed to peek her head out of the water whenever the breeze picked up.

Looking back down at Billy's worksheets, Papa erased some of his grandson's writing and replaced it with his own. Why bother the boy? P.J. surmised. They were only minor mistakes and Billy was enjoying himself. They were simple errors, really. No need to interrupt him.

Some of the answers were missing altogether. "Ah, he's smart. It'll be fine," he said as he penciled in the blank spaces. With the corrections all made, Papa stood up. He looked out over the water, "There's his *real* education," he said aloud.

His grandson was now holding onto Phinny's blackened dorsal fin while the dolphin swam around in tight circles. Billy was laughing. His feet dangled behind him.

"Watch this, Papa," the boy called out as he jumped onto Phinny's back. Riding the dolphin like a bronco, Bill squealed, "Look Papa, no hands!" as they passed by the boat's swim platform.

P.J.'s head bent back as he let out a huge laugh. "Good for you, young man. Good for you!"

He placed the schoolwork neatly in an envelope, wrote out the address and sealed it. Now he could call Nana.

From the saloon, Mishimo poked her head out of her basket. Her eyes were fixed on P.J.'s every move as he descended the stairs and sat at his desk. When he picked up the radio receiver, she jumped from her wicker haven and stood at his feet. Glancing toward the stairwell then back at P.J., Mishimo hissed at him before she leaped up the stairs. At the top, she looked back and hissed at him again, before making her way toward the bow.

P.J. shook his head, "Crazy Cat."

Hailing the ship-to-shore operator on channel 16 Papa said, "Virgin Islands Radio, Virgin Islands Radio, Virgin Islands Radio" he paused, "*Amazing Grace. Amazing Grace.*"

The operator was based out of St. Thomas. Always gracious, P.J. enjoyed dealing with her. It only took a moment before she replied, "*Amazing Grace,* this is Virgin Islands Radio. Please respond and switch six-eight."

"*Amazing Grace* switching six-eight," Papa said and switched channels.

He conversed with the operator a moment then gave her the number for his home in New York. Nana picked up on the second ring. P.J. could hear a polite female voice explain, "Good morning, Ma'am. I have P.J. McMillon on the line for you."

"*Doctor* McMillon, dear. Thank you," Nana responded.

"Yes, ma'am," she answered. She then addressed Papa, "Go ahead, *Doctor* P.J." The young woman giggled. Papa did too. But Nana remained silent.

"How are you dear?" P.J. asked.

Nana detested ship-to-shore conversations. It made her feel like she was talking on a two-way radio and found it impossible to have a proper conversation. But she remained pleasant, "Very well, thank you." She knew the female operator could overhear them.

They talked briefly. She caught P.J. up on things at the Mc4 and he promised to send Billy's schoolwork to her the next day.

When she asked to speak with Billy, P.J. told her Billy was still sleeping. He knew his wife wouldn't approve nor understand what the little boy was doing swimming around with dolphins all day.

P.J. expressed enthusiasm over the progress he was making with his research and he hoped to have something to share very soon. But, he also warned it might take a while before this delicate research was complete.

Nana didn't try to hide her emotions. She didn't want her husband keeping Billy from school for more than one semester, expressing how important it was for Billy to do well in order to qualify for the new school she'd chosen for him.

It was still summer, P.J. told her. He understood her concerns and suggested they chat about it a bit more next call. "Why don't you come down for a visit," he urged.

Gracie was the one who'd shared his love for the sea. Nana, on the other hand, had never been to the islands nor joined him on any of his oceanic research expeditions.

"You know I prefer the city, dear."

They ended with mutual *I love yous* and she with an *I miss you both*.

He put the receiver back in its cradle and made his way on deck to check on Billy. Mishimo was sitting upright, on the bow, watching the boy intently. She did not turn around as Papa approached.

"Oh, Mish. He's okay. You don't have to stand guard *all* the time."

The cat turned her head sharply and glared at P.J. a moment, then turned back to watch Billy snorkel around the reef with his new pal trailing close behind him.

"Okay. Fine. Be that way," P.J. grumbled as he walked away and sat under the awning on the back deck. As he opened his notebook, he called out to the cat, "I should write something about how strangely you've been acting since we got here, Mish."

Mishimo did not respond.

From opposite ends of the boat, they both watched as Phinny pushed Billy with his snout.

The dolphin gathered speed, raised Billy in the air then propelled him forward. Billy threw out his arms and turned his body at the last minute. He splashed into the water on his back then popped back up, giggling. Phinny leaped into the air, did a full twist and crashed back into the water, creating a huge splash. They repeated this over and over again. Each time Billy attempted a new entry into the water, mimicking his new friend.

After several hours of this, Phinny approached the stern of *Amazing Grace* with Billy on his back. The little boy climbed off and sat on the swim platform with his legs dangling in the water.

A few feet away, on the back deck, P.J. leaned-in, attempting to hear their conversation. He didn't want to disturb his grandson but was curious to what was being said. Moving closer to the railing, he desperately tried to understand.

As they spoke, Phinny stood erect with almost half his body out of the water, responding with rigorous nods and several clicking sounds.

They'd been chatting for a while, when a strong breeze blew past. Phinny stopped abruptly. His smile dropped as he lowered his body back into the water and looked around. Suddenly, Dolila appeared behind him. They spoke privately for a moment before Phinny turned back toward Billy. The young dolphin apologized for having to leave so abruptly, but it was time for his sister and him to go.

"Okay, but will I see you tomorrow?" the young boy asked with a newly formed frown upon his face.

"Absolutely. I promise."

Billy waved goodbye and watched his friends hastily swim away.

Up on deck, P.J. was feverishly writing in his notebook. He was fascinated by his grandson's ability to communicate with these mammals and longed to understand how it was possible. In fact, he'd been working diligently on an elaborate code to decipher the meaning of each sound the dolphins made.

Meticulously detailing the dolphins' movements, body language and personalities, each day P.J. recorded their interactions with his grandson. In the evenings, he'd listen closely as Billy recounted his experiences. Often, P.J. had compiled a list of questions pertaining to a specific incident or activity he'd overseen.

But, anytime P.J. asked questions about the dolphins' general health or appearance, Billy would become uncomfortable.

"Why do you ask so many questions about Phinny's dorsal fin, Papa?"

"I don't know. Maybe because it's different and I am curious."

"Phinny says you stare at him a lot. It makes him nervous." The boy paused. "I always tell him it's because you're a scientist and you study *everything*."

Before the Mc4 opened, P.J. was in charge of an expedition team studying marine mammals' sensory, cognitive and communicative abilities. Focused on dolphins and whales, the team's mission was to better understand the social interactions of different species and enhance conservation by educating the general public. P.J. was considered a pioneer in the field and his expeditions were filmed. From 1960-1965 his work titled: *Sounds of the Sea* was showcased on National Education Television and continued to air in syndication when PBS was established.

Since the Mc4's inception, P.J. had become consumed with his efforts to combat the mysterious illness plaguing bottlenose dolphins and had recently taken a more active role in the political arena regarding the safety and security of marine mammals in the wild.

One of the earliest projects at the Mc4 was the recovery and research on groups of blackened dolphin carcasses found beached in several areas of North and South America. The ailment was an infection of unknown origin, degenerative in nature and ultimately fatal.

P.J. was worried about the blackened discoloration on Phinny's body, which completely covered his dorsal fin and had seeped onto the right side of his back. Through conversations with his grandson, P.J. ruled out the possibility of it being a simple birthmark. He was glad to see Phinny's overall health seemed unaffected and although unable to measure it specifically, he believed the general structure of the abnormality had remained unchanged in the six weeks since they'd been at Georgey Hole.

P.J. wanted to examine Phinny. He needed substantive facts rather than observational hypothesis in order to rule out this disease.

His sister, Dolila, showed no signs of the abnormality.

"So, what did you learn from your friends today young man?" Papa asked. They were sitting down in the dining area, having dinner.

Scrunching his brow, with his eyes looking toward the sky Billy answered, "We just played." He paused. "Oh, and Dolila likes you, now."

"Huh, huh, huh," P.J. chuckled.

"She didn't before because you stare at Phinny all the time and don't ever say hi or try to play with them. But Angelica explained to Dolila that you're just being protective of me like she is with her brother." He continued, "Angelica's really smart, Papa."

"Hmmm. Yes, she is," Papa remarked as he removed the plates from the table. "Well, maybe I can come play with you guys tomorrow."

When they finished cleaning up, Billy put on his pajamas and crawled into bed. His eyes were heavy and his small body ached from the day's activities. But, when his grandfather went to shut off the light, Billy felt compelled to ask the question that had been gnawing at him. "Papa, is Phinny okay?"

"What do you mean?"

"You keep asking me about his dorsal fin. Is it bad that it's black?" he paused. "Is he gonna . . ." The young boy squeezed his eyes shut tightly before taking a labored breath. "Is he going to die like mom did?" he blurted as tears poured down his face.

Papa rushed over to the side of the bed. He wiped Billy's face with his palm. "Phinny is going to be just fine." He wished he could do or say something more to ease his grandson's worry. "I promise." He bent over and kissed Billy on the forehead then stepped out of the way so Mishimo could work her magic.

The gray tabby curled up closer and comforted the little boy. Billy put his arms around her and turned onto his side. Slowly, the sobs subsided and eventually he fell asleep.

Papa hoped his grandson's dreams would be peaceful. He gently closed the door behind him and headed for his desk. Tears fell fast. He wiped them away just as quickly. He could hear Gracie telling him there was no time to cry. It was time to get things done!

He grabbed some pens and highlighters from his desk drawer, pulled out a new notebook and wrote on the outside cover: Comparisons, Conclusions & Solutions.

Opening the double doors of a small cabinet to the right of his desk, he stared at the volumes of hand-written notebooks from Grace's research on blackened dolphins. There were fifty-seven, spanning Grace's short tenure at the Mc4. Running his hand across their spines, P.J. decided to start with her earliest work titled: *The San Francisco Recovery Effort.*

Sixteen notebooks pertained to this project. It was Grace's first field assignment and was one of the Mc4's most notable recovery efforts to date. He pulled out the first volume in the series and methodically read each line, highlighting some of Grace's notes and findings.

He'd managed to get through eight of the notebooks when he finally stopped sometime after daybreak. He'd found comfort in Grace's writing. It felt as if she were talking with him.

Switching the percolator on, he walked up top. He'd missed the sunrise. The morning sky was filled with clouds and P.J. noticed the gusty breeze right away. "Hmmm. Not much of a day," he proclaimed aloud and returned to the galley to get some coffee.

When he came back up, the weather looked marginally better. *Perhaps the rain will stay away*, he thought as he leaned his head back on the settee, contemplating the notes he'd just read.

The *San Francisco Recovery Effort* referred to 36 dolphin carcasses found on the East Beach of Crissy Field on the morning of April 11, 1966. Part of the Presidio of San Francisco, a military airfield, East Beach was on the bay side of the San Francisco Peninsula near the Golden Gate Bridge.

The dolphins were strewn across the sand along the shallow water's edge. Originally thought to be a new species, when they later conducted autopsies, they found the carcasses all had the biological structure of the common bottlenose but suffered from a mysterious black discoloration. Additionally, their organs had drastically aged. Even the juveniles showed signs of premature aging. Further testing showed no new genetic strain or mutation.

Researchers from the Mc4 were sent to investigate and arrange transport for several carcasses to the labs in New York. Grace was one of the first scientists on the scene. She was also who discovered—one of the carcasses was actually alive.

According to the passages in the notebook, back at the Mc4 Grace spent several long days and nights with the female who'd managed to survive the beaching. In the weeks to follow, it became apparent she did not suffer the same affliction as the others. She had actually been injured and her body badly bruised. As the bruising healed, the darkened areas of her body lightened. Her dorsal fin was in tact, and she looked otherwise healthy, but she was lethargic and weak.

The incident deeply affected Gracie. Her entries about it were much more personal than the entries in the other notebooks.

P.J. remembered the *San Francisco Recovery Effort* well. The story had received national attention. Bottlenose dolphins were rarely seen in the colder waters of the North Pacific. Rumors flew regarding the mysterious beaching, the discoloration of the dolphins and the reasons the young female survived.

Anti-war protestors, hippie gurus and spiritual healers sensationalized the incident. East Beach became a campsite for vigils, group chants and conspiracy theorists for weeks following the beaching.

Nana loved the publicity. The Mc4 had only opened in January and the phone was ringing off the hook. She used the incident to the Mc4's advantage, exceeding all donation goals for the year in only one month.

The thought of Nana reminded P.J. of the promise he'd made. Shaking his head, he rolled his eyes and sighed deeply. He *had* to get that package in the mail.

Making his way down below, P.J. quietly walked over to his desk and scribbled a note to Billy. He explained how he was headed to Great Harbour to run some quick errands and would be back shortly. He left a list of chores and instructed Billy to radio The Dive if he had any problems. Plus, he was not to play with Phinny until Papa returned.

Leaving the note in front of Billy's door, P.J. headed to the back of the boat and pulled the tender around from the side. He climbed in and started the engine. As he pulled away from *Amazing Grace*, he noticed a fairly decent chop had developed in the channel. It was the first day he'd seen any sign of weather since the race.

As he entered the channel, he noticed Phinny and Dolila near The Point.

They were facing west, looking up at the sky. Their body language was serious and it looked like they were in deep discussion.

P.J. got the feeling something was bothering them. But, he shook it off, determined to get to Great Harbour and back again before his grandson awoke.

Around eight a.m. P.J. stepped onto the dock with two big garbage bags and a thick envelope for Nana. They only collected garbage once a week. It was burned at the other end of the island every Wednesday. He placed the two big black bags alongside the massive pile of trash at the base of the dock and walked over to the Government House. Placing the envelope in the mail slot, he decided to stroll up one of the sandy side streets toward a tiny makeshift general store. "Good morning," he announced as he walked through the door.

The woman at the counter muttered, "Good morning." She looked like she'd just gotten out of bed.

The room was quite dark and smelled of overripe fruit and fertilizer. There were only two aisles and a very limited selection of items. P.J. poked around at the fruit and canned goods. He grabbed some boxed milk, a few mangoes and a carton of fresh local eggs. At the check-out counter, there was a sign for some local foods. P.J. asked for some Johnnycake and some Goat Water (local stew).

He was looking down at his pocket, getting some money, when Danny walked through the door.

"Good Mornin'!" Danny bellowed.

Startled, P.J. jumped back. He hadn't seen Danny since the day after the incident with the fishing net. He'd come into town with Billy to report it to Danny and let Charlie know about his neighbor in Cane Garden Bay. Charlie was peeved. Said he'd talk to the guy. Danny was glad to see nobody got hurt.

"Didn't mean to scare ya," Danny said, patting P.J. on the back. "How you doin' this morning, Doc? It's good to see ya. Where's that handsome Lucky Charm?"

Danny was surprised to hear P.J. had left Billy alone in Georgey Hole. "You think it's a good idea to be leaving Billy on his own like that, my friend? Especially in weather like this. He's only eight, P.J."

How dare Danny question his judgment! He knew what he was doing. Billy was fine back on the boat. He was probably still sleeping. If Danny knew what that little boy had been through these past few months, he wouldn't worry about Billy taking care of himself.

Tat-tat-tat. Tat-tat-tat-tat. P.J. looked up at the roof. Tat-tat-tat-tat-tat.

Outside the doorway, the wind howled while huge raindrops pelted the sandy road. P.J.'s eyes widened as he watched bags of garbage, corrugated metal and other loose articles being flung down the road.

The sky was black. The rain was coming down in sheets. He looked down the street toward the harbour. Boats were rocking and rolling. "I've got to get back to Billy!" he screamed and ran out the door, leaving the groceries and supplies behind.

Danny ran after him. "You can't do that, P.J.!"

The storm raged. The wind wailed. Jagged raindrops stung P.J. as he ran down the road toward the dinghy dock.

His heart ached at the idea that Billy might be in danger. *What the hell was I thinking, leaving the boy on his own?*

Danny was right behind him. "You're not gonna be able to get back there now. Get inside, P.J. We'll radio him from The Dive."

P.J. was distraught. He followed his friend to his restaurant and radioed *Amazing Grace*. No response. He paced the floor and tried again. No answer. *What the hell was I thinking? How could I have not noticed the dark clouds coming?* Again he called *Amazing Grace* on the radio. Nothing.

Danny saw P.J.'s coloring change and ran over to help him sit down. P.J. was pale and looked unsteady. His body was clammy and cold.

Danny had never seen his friend this way. "Let me get you some water, P.J. Don't move. I'll be right back."

* * *

Back in Georgey Hole, Billy awoke on his own. He came out of his room and lay down on the settee in the saloon, still sleepy.

Mishimo stood outside his door. The note was under her right paw.

"Good morning, Mishimo." Billy said and waved for her to come over to him.

She didn't move.

"You're silly," he said and rolled over. But he couldn't fall back asleep.

He got up to look for Papa.

Mishimo meowed.

"What's wrong with you this morning?" Billy asked. Mishimo never meowed. He walked over to the stairwell. Mishimo meowed louder.

"Mish, I'll be right back," the little boy called out as he made his way up the stairs.

Papa wasn't in his usual morning spot drinking coffee. "Hmmm, maybe he's asleep," Billy said aloud.

He turned around to head back down below when he saw Phinny swimming toward the boat. He smiled and ran to the stern. Taking a seat on the swim platform, Billy waited for his friend.

Phinny was jittery and pacing as he spoke. "Come with me," he commanded.

"Phinny, what's wrong?" asked Billy.

The palm fronds ruffled and the sand kicked up on the beach.

Phinny looked out past Billy's shoulder. "Hop on. Hurry!"

The young boy turned around to see what his friend was looking at. The black sky was approaching quickly. He hadn't noticed it when he came up top. It seemed to appear out of nowhere.

"Jump on. We have to go. Now!"

Startled, Billy jumped on the dolphin's back and grabbed onto his dorsal fin. They took off fast, away from the blackened sky. Billy's head bent back sharply. He held on tight as Phinny darted around the eastern point of the cove.

Suddenly, Phinny stopped. He instructed Billy to take a deep breath and get ready to dive. The dolphin pointed his snout to the water and dove straight down.

Billy opened his eyes under the water. There were a group of giant boulders beneath the surface, all stacked together. As they weaved between the rocks and continued to descend, Billy's ears began to ache. He held tight to Phinny with one hand while he pinched his nose with the other. Keeping his lips pursed securely, he pushed his tongue against the roof of his mouth and attempted to equalize like his grandfather taught him. There was a crackling sound in his ears as the pressure was released and the pain subsided.

He leaned forward, flat against Phinny's back as they approached the base of a boulder and swam underneath. Billy's lungs hurt. He didn't think he could hold his breath much longer.

Phinny swam up the other side of the boulder, through a slim passageway and turned left before finally popping back out of the water on the other side of the massive rock. Dolila was there waiting.

Billy gasped for breath and looked around.

They were inside the hollow space between several massive boulders leaning in on one another. About twenty feet above the water line, there was a large crevice, which allowed air and light to illuminate the otherwise darkened cave. A small fissure at the base of another boulder allowed water to enter from the crashing waves outside.

Phinny had chosen to live at Georgey Hole because of the cave. It was the perfect hiding space. The only way in was to choose the right set of twists and turns under the water, on either side of the boulders. Any other combination led to dead ends beneath the surface.

Across from the cave's entranceway was a tiny ledge. Phinny swam over to it, lifted Billy high enough for him to reach a groove in the rock and instructed him to climb up and rest on the sandy shelf.

Billy thought it was a pretty cool place. He could hear the waves crash against the boulders outside then watch as water spewed through the fissure beneath the ledge he was perched upon.

"Why did you bring me here?" Billy asked.

"I wanted you to know how to find me."

Billy shook his head and raised his shoulders, "I don't understand."

Phinny continued, "I have to leave for a while. I have to go take care of a few things."

The weather outside was building. Blustery gusts sounded like howling dogs as they resonated through the small area, followed by claps of thunder.

BOOM!

Billy jumped and looked around the cave.

Phinny looked agitated.

"But, where are you going?" the little boy questioned.

"Back to Anegada," Phinny explained, "but only for a little while. My plan is to be back in less than three days. I'd like for you to come look for us here in the cave. This is where Dolila and I will be."

Dolila chimed in. "Phinny, you're scaring him. Don't scare him." She looked at Billy. "Don't worry. It will be okay."

Dolila had somehow found her courage since living in Georgey Hole. She had grown to understand her brother's reasons for leaving Sir Thomas' care and she didn't want to go back. But she knew they had to.

—

The cave grew darker. The squall outside was raging. Billy shivered. He didn't like this place anymore.

*   *   *

P.J. was hunched over a bench with his head in his hands. The howling sounds sent shivers down his spine. He looked up and stared at the ominous sky, wondering if it would ever let up. Squinting, he thought he saw a small break in the weather outside Great Harbour. He stood up, ran out of The Dive and sprinted toward the dinghy dock. Jumping into the tender, he started the engines and sped off, exiting the harbour.

Pelted by raindrops, P.J. struggled to see. It didn't matter. He had to get back to his grandson. He screamed, "What the hell was I thinking? He's just a little boy." He wiped his eyes with his arm, struggling to see, "Protect him, Gracie. Please!" he called out.

*   *   *

Phinny silently swam in circles inside the cave. He paced. And he dove.

Eventually the violent sounds subsided. The slapping of the waves stopped and the sun began to peek through the cracks of the cave-like structure.

Addressing his sister, Phinny said, "Okay, I think it's safe now."

"Safe from what?" Billy asked. "What *was* that?" He'd never heard a squall sound like that.

"Storm. I think Sir Thomas sent him."

Billy looked confused. "What?"

A short, brisk breeze snuck through the crack between the boulders. The sun shone brighter now.

Phinny popped up out of the water. "Come on Billy. It's time to go. I want to get you back before your grandfather returns and begins to worry about you." His tone was abrupt, almost harsh.

Billy barely noticed. "Papa. Oh my goodness I forgot about Papa!" He jumped on the dolphin's back and hung on tight. His mind raced with thoughts of his grandfather.

They dove fast and deep, coming up on the other side of the boulders with sunbeams shining upon them. The breeze was warm, light.

Billy could feel the tension in Phinny's body as they rounded the corner of Georgey Hole.

Returning Billy to the stern platform of *Amazing Grace*, Phinny asked, "You *will* remember how to get to the cave, right?"

Billy hesitated, "Yes. I'll remember. But ..."

"I'll be back, I promise." And the dolphin was gone.

Butterflies dashed around Billy's belly. He didn't understand what just happened. But, he was very worried about Phinny and the dinghy was still gone.

He stood up and made his way down below.

Mishimo was standing in the center of the saloon.

"Oh, Mish." He'd forgotten about her. "Are you okay?" He picked her up and gave her a hug. "I am so sorry, Mish. You must have been so frightened. I am so sorry."

Mishimo squirmed and jumped from Billy's arms. She shook her body then and each leg, ridding herself of the salt water.

Billy looked down. There was a puddle underneath him, his shorts were drenched and his body was dripping.

"Oops. Sorry Mish." He grabbed a hand towel from the galley counter. "Where's Papa?" he asked, wiping the floor.

Mishimo walked over and stood on the piece of paper. Billy picked it up.

Realizing his grandfather didn't know he'd left the boat, Billy scurried into his cabin. "Mish, Let me go clean up and then I'll sit with you." He didn't think he wanted Papa to know where he'd been. Not yet.

Papa called out, "Billy! Billy!" before he'd even tied up the dinghy. He ran up the stern ladder and looked around the deck. "Billy! Where are you?" he called out as he made his way down the stairwell and into the saloon.

Billy rushed out of his room and met his grandfather at the base of the stairs.

"Are you okay, my young lad?" Papa asked, out of breath. He grabbed the boy and hugged him. "Oh my God, are you okay?" The old man was shaking. Tears streamed down his face. He pulled back and looked his grandson up and down.

All of a sudden Billy looked so young, so fragile, so inexperienced. All of a sudden he was no longer *mature beyond his years*. Rather, he was simply a 55-pound, eight-year-old boy who had lost his mom recently and had spent the past eighteen months taking care of the grown-ups in his family. A boy who had to grow up much faster than he should have and who was now being asked to fend for himself again while an old scientist ran off to do errands on land. *What the hell was I thinking?* P.J. asked himself.

He stared into his grandson's eyes, attempting to figure out how Billy was feeling. *He must be so traumatized, so frightened,* P.J. thought.

"I am okay, Papa." Billy reassured his grandfather. "I am okay, really"

The older gentlemen put his hand to his chest and tried to catch his breath.

"Come on over here," Papa motioned toward the settee. "Come sit with me."

"But, Papa, you're all wet."

P.J. looked down at his drenched body. "I don't care. I don't care." There was a quiver to his voice. "I just want to sit with you."

Billy skipped off to the bathroom and grabbed a dry towel. "Here Papa. Sit on this." The little boy placed the towel on the cushion and helped his grandfather sit.

"I am so sorry I left you, young man. I am so sorry. I won't do it again. I promise."

More promises, Billy thought, *Phinny* promised *he'd be back in three days. Three days.* Billy wasn't sure he liked promises anymore.

Billy grabbed a blanket. They snuggled together, quietly, both wondering what the other must be thinking—each afraid to find out.

About twenty minutes after Papa returned, there was a knock on the hull. Danny called out, "Hey! You guys okay in there?"

P.J. and Billy walked out on deck and welcomed Danny aboard.

He walked up the back steps with a six-pack in his hand and offered it to P.J. "I figured you probably needed a few of these after that scare."

They all sat in the cockpit. Billy was very quiet. P.J. was too. Danny did most of the talking, attempting to keep things light. He managed to get them both laughing, telling stories about his time in Hawaii, braving some killer waves; how it took three weeks to win-over Marta's six brothers, before they'd let him date her. He also told them what it was like to live on an island of less than 100 people, with no electricity or fresh water reserves.

In between stories, Papa showered while Danny made lunch for everyone. When they were done eating, P.J. and Billy were ready for a nap.

"Mind if I stick around a while?" Danny asked.

"No. Not at all," P.J. said. "Make yourself comfortable. You're welcome to stay as long as you'd like."

"Great."

It was several hours before P.J. emerged from his cabin to find the table set. Danny, newly sunkissed and smelling like coconut tanning oil, was drinking a beer and tossing some onions in a pan.

"You just can't help yourself, can you?" P.J. asked.

"Whaaaat? Ya gotta eat."

P.J. laughed. It was good to have Danny around.

It didn't take long before Billy came out of his room. Cradled in his arms, Billy rubbed Mishimo's belly. He walked over to the table and looked at the immense amount of food. "Are we having company?" he asked.

"Hey, ya gotta eat like a man if ya gonna grow to race like a man, Lucky Charm!" Danny proclaimed.

They ate dinner, talked, laughed and told more stories. This time Billy and P.J. shared some too. It was getting late by the time they were cleaning up.

"Hey, is Marta okay on her own at The Dive while you're out here?" P.J. asked.

"I told you. She's got six brothers. She can take care of herself. Besides, it's not busy at The Dive these days." He smiled. "But I am gonna radio her in a bit. Gotta tuck my baby in."

Billy liked how Danny treated Marta. He thought she was one of the nicest ladies he'd ever met, next to his mom.

When it was time for Billy to go to bed, Papa kissed him goodnight, followed by a final visit from Danny.

"Hey, you wanna go play in Cane Garden Bay tomorrow?" Danny asked. "You can meet Charlie's son, Ritzel, and hang out on the beach all day. He might even take you to the Sugar Mill."

Billy's belly fluttered as he thought about Phinny's familiar knock on the hull. He knew he wouldn't hear it in the morning. He hoped Phinny and Dolila were safe, wherever they were. And wished they'd be back soon.

"We don't have to, if you don't want. I just thought it would be fun to explore other places and maybe make some new friends while you're here."

"No," Billy protested. "I want to. If it's okay with Papa?"

"Don't you worry. I'll make it okay." Danny winked. He patted the boy on the shoulder and went to leave the room.

Danny was about to shut off the light, when he commented, "Wow. That was some wacky weather today, huh. That storm was aaaangry! And I haven't seen it windy like that since our last hurricane scare."

Billy sat up. With a furrowed brow he stared at Danny. "What did you say?"

"Ah, nothing. Just commenting about how crazy the weather is acting. I am sure it will be peaceful tomorrow. Get some sleep, Lucky Charm." Danny switched the light off and shut the door.

—

Cane Garden Bay

The air was steamy when Billy climbed into the cockpit, dressed in swim trunks and ready to go. P.J. and Danny were sitting across from one another at the table drinking coffee and casually chatting.

It was nearing 7:30 a.m. Billy looked around at the tranquil cove. The palm trees along the beach remained still. The sky was clear blue and there wasn't a ripple on the water as it gently brushed against the shore. Beating down upon the deck, the sun's scorching rays were unencumbered by clouds or wind.

Billy found it troubling. Georgey Hole felt desolate, isolated. Abandoned. He wondered where his friends were and if they were safe?

"You okay young man?" Papa questioned, noticing the uneasy look upon his grandsons face.

Billy nodded. "Mmhmm."

"Why don't you get some breakfast and we'll head out." P.J. offered, "It'll be fun. I promise."

Bigger and faster, they took Danny's 26-ft. Boston Whaler across the channel thinking it would be more comfortable. Although it wasn't necessary, the water was like glass.

Sitting on the bow, Billy remained unusually quiet. He did not ask questions or even look around. Instead, he kept to himself, staring out upon the water. He took no notice of the spectacular view as they approached the large mouth of Cane Garden Bay.

Cane Garden Bay was much larger than Georgey Hole or Great Harbour. It stretched for almost two miles. There was a colorful reef along its western shore, and it was surrounded by lush green mountains. Palm trees were scattered along the sand, and the water was a glistening turquoise. Along the eastern shore there was a banana tree farm, and when the northerly winds kicked up, there was usually great surf along its eastern point.

It wasn't until a familiar voice called out that the little boy looked up.

"Hey Billy, trow me dah bow line!" Charlie was standing at the water's edge, along with his sons and daughter, to welcome them ashore.

It took a moment for the boy to compute what was asked of him. He stood on the bow cushion, grabbed the line that was tied to the front of the boat and threw it toward the tall dark man standing ankle deep in the barely visible surf.

Charlie tugged and found the bitter end. He walked up the white, sandy beach and wrapped the line around one of the many palm trees.

Meanwhile, Danny lifted the outboard so it wouldn't hit the sandy bottom. "Okay, Billy, jump on out!"

Beaming proudly, Charlie introduced his family. Keisha was the eldest. She was almost thirteen, very tall and slim with braids in her hair. Her skin was a deep, rich bronze. As she smiled at Billy, her hazel eyes sparkled in the sunlight.

He thought she was the prettiest girl he'd ever seen.

Only six and very small for his age, Dante didn't need an introduction. Jumping in the water and flailing his arms, he stomped his way toward Billy. "Hi.

I am Dante, wanna play?" he asked before he threw himself backward, making a huge splash. When his head popped up, out of the water, he was cackling.

Billy shook his head and giggled.

Charlie pushed his eldest son's right shoulder. Unlike his little brother, Ritzel was reserved and mellow. Tall and stocky, he was also the darkest of the three. His skin was black as night, but his eyes were brilliant like his sister.

Almost twice Billy's size, Ritzel towered over him as he held out his hand. "Nice to meet you," he said flatly.

Billy looked up, shook the boy's hand and said, "Hi."

Silence.

"Well, okay then. Everybody's met everyone else!" Danny shouted, "Now go play!" He walked up the beach toward a pink building. "You ready for a Bloody Mary, P.J.?"

The kids remained in and around the water. After a few minutes with Dante, Ritzel asked Billy if he wanted to take a walk down the beach. Keisha let them alone. She stayed with her baby brother.

"You been here before?" Ritzel asked.

"No. I'm from New York. It's a big city. I like it better here."

"I never been to a big city. But, I like it better here too," Ritzel agreed. "You ever see a sea urchin?" he asked Billy. "Look." Ritzel pointed to the water in front of them. There was a cluster of black, thorny round mounds embedded in the sand. "You don't wanna step on dem," he cautioned, "They hurtcha and the only way to make it stop is to pee where it sting."

"What?" Billy' raised an eyebrow. "If it stings you, you have to pee on it?" He asked, fascinated by this idea. "Does it hurt like a bee sting?"

"I don't know. I never been stung by a bee. But, I been stung by a sea urchin."

"Hmmm," Billy muttered. He leaned over to look at the objects in the water.

Ritzel bent over and carefully picked one out of the sand. "We eat dem, though. Can you eat your bees?"

They both cracked up, laughing.

They spent the rest of the day exploring, talking and giggling. Ritzel took Billy over to the sugar mill where they met back up with his sister and brother. They played hide and seek through the sugar cane field, and when they got hungry, Ritzel broke off a stem and showed Billy how to chew on the stalk and suck the sweet sap from it.

Back at the pink building, they found Papa and Danny laughing at the bar. Charlie was behind the counter mixing cocktails. In the back of the room, there was a man making food at a barbeque pit. Frying oil permeated the air.

A band was setting up, getting ready to play their first set for the afternoon, although there wasn't much of an audience. The long stretch of beach was pretty empty and Papa and Danny were the only patrons at the bar.

"Go find a table kids. Tiko will bring you over some food in a minute."

Dante ran over and plopped himself in a seat at a table along the restaurant's railing. The other kids followed. Soon, four big plates of burgers and fries were brought over. The kids devoured them.

Halfway through the meal, a voice called out to Billy, "How you doing, Lucky Charm?" It was Scat, one of the *Silver Bullet* crew. "You bringing us some good luck today, keeping dah storm far, far away?" He asked as he walked over.

Billy didn't know what he was talking about, but the word storm made his belly ache.

"You see it out dere? Scat asked, pointing toward the open water. "It been sittin' dere all day, not movin'. Just sittin', beyond the mountain of Jost Van Dyke."

Billy swung his body around to see where Scat was pointing. The sky was completely black behind the eastern edge of Jost Van Dyke. It looked like a looming monster in the sky. He felt sick to his stomach and turned around. Again, his thoughts returned to Phinny and Dolila. He hoped they were okay.

"Me glad you come to listen to us play. You were sleepin' dah last time. Me gots a friend from the States coming down to jam later. Maybe you and Keisha can dance together while I sing."

Billy's face turned bright red. He put his head down and looked away.

"Ah, you blushin'. Oooh, you got a crush on me cousin, do ya?" Scat patted Billy on the shoulder and walked back to the band equipment.

Noticing how uncomfortable Billy seemed while talking with Scat, Papa kept an eye on the little boy until his smile returned.

They listened to the band for an hour or so before P.J. decided it was time to go. The sun was setting and P.J. wanted to be able to get back while the sky was bright enough to monitor the weather. He didn't like the looks of the dark clouds.

Danny was in no shape to drive his boat back across the channel, and he protested leaving so early.

Charlie offered to watch Danny for the night, suggesting Papa and Billy come back for him in the morning.

P.J. thanked Charlie then packed up their things and jumped aboard the Whaler. Billy waved incessantly until he could no longer see his new friends on the beach.

Back on *Amazing Grace* Papa asked, "Did you have fun today?" as they climbed down the stairwell into the saloon.

Shaking his head, yes, the little boy answered, "I ate sugar cane." He hugged his grandfather good night. "I like Ritzel. We had fun. Thanks for taking me to Cane Garden Bay, Papa."

P.J. was glad he'd listened to Danny. It was good for his grandson to be with children his own age and simply be a kid for a while. He decided not to bring up the subject of Phinny and Dolila, although he did wonder how they were.

Shutting off the light and closing his grandson's door, P.J. lay on the settee to read. He fell asleep before finishing the first page.

In the morning they headed back to Cane Garden Bay. They found Danny at the bar drinking coffee. His hair was tousled, and he looked a bit weak-in-the-knees as he climbed onboard his boat.

It was a steamy morning. The air was hot, without a stitch of a wind. They scooted across the flat channel in silence, each lost in his own dreamy contemplation on the way to Great Harbour.

Marta was standing at the dinghy dock, waiting for them. Papa stepped off the boat, greeted Marta and strolled up to the grocery store to pick up the items he'd left during the storm.

Billy and Danny remained on the dock listening to Marta as she explained how the entire village was preoccupied with theories behind the menacing clouds that continued to blanket the sky several miles northeast of Georgey Hole. "Everybody is talking about it," she told them, "Sailors are taking great care to avoid it, and several boats have left the harbour because they are afraid of it."

"I guess nobody's heading to Anegada for a while then," Danny commented as he kissed his wife and jumped back into the boat. He could see P.J. approaching with a big brown bag in his arms.

Billy, who was already on the boat, walked up behind Danny, "How come?"

Danny put his hand on Billy's shoulder with a questioning grin. It took a moment before he understood what the boy was asking about. "'Cause the only way to Anegada is through those clouds." He pointed northeast. "There's a wicked storm in those clouds. Nobody wants to sail into a storm like that, especially near Anegada. There are lots of unmarked shallows," he paused,

"You've got to know where you're going or you *will* run aground. Gotta watch you don't hit the reef."

Walking up with a handful of Johnnycake, Papa interrupted them. Danny devoured the fried dough, attempting to remedy his pounding headache. When he was finished with his own, he helped with Billy's.

Danny called out to Marta, "I'll be back soon my love."

P.J. threw the boat in reverse and headed toward Georgey Hole. When they arrived, Danny took the helm from P.J. He said his goodbyes and told them he'd check on them from time to time. Then he sped away.

Billy remained on deck for the afternoon, doing schoolwork and staring at the water as well as up at the distant sky. The ominous clouds worried him. He studied even the slightest movement out at The Point, hoping he'd see the tip of a dorsal fin. *Anything* to let him know—his friends were safe.

When the sun went down, he came inside. He and his grandfather dined quietly and the remainder of the evening was uneventful.

Papa lay on the settee reading a novel when Billy offered a hug and announced he was going to bed.

"Are you okay, young man?"

The young boy's stomach churned as he lied. "Yes, Papa. I'm just tired."

Mishimo was fast asleep while Billy lay in the dark for hours, unable to quiet his mind. He wondered what was happening with his friends and tried to convince himself they were safely in the cave, waiting for him. After all, Phinny had promised he'd be there.

But Billy could not help thinking about Phinny's actions in the cave. He wasn't afraid of the storm. He seemed *mad* at the storm.

Eventually, Bill slept. But his mind remained filled with dreams of the menacing sky.

—

In the early morning, the little boy came out of his room to find Papa's door still shut. He walked out on deck and watched the sun make its way into the sky. The water was still and the cove was silent. Pacing the deck, when his grandfather hadn't come up after an hour, Billy decided he couldn't wait anymore. He changed into his swim trunks, grabbed his snorkel gear and jumped into the water.

Making his way over to the reef, he noticed how quiet it was beneath the surface. By the time he'd arrived at the reef, he was aware he hadn't seen a single fish. He dove seven or eight feet to the base of the coral heads. Swimming around each formation, he searched for Angelica. The sea fans barely moved as he passed. The blades of sea grass remained still. Angelica was nowhere to be found. Neither were the others. The entire reef was deserted.

Billy swam back to *Amazing Grace*. He dried off with a towel and ran down to his grandfather's cabin. Opening the door, he walked up and shook P.J.'s shoulder. "Wake up, Papa. Wake up!"

"What? What is it?" Papa asked groggily, shaking his head. "What's wrong?" He blinked and squinted, attempting to focus.

"Papa we have to go find them. I have to take you somewhere. Papa we have to find them." The little boy trembled.

"Who, Billy? Who?"

"Phinny and Dolila. We have to find them. You have to come with me." The little boy was crying now. He ran out of the room and up the stairs.

P.J. jumped up and ran after his grandson. He found him sitting on the swim platform. "Give me a minute," P.J. called down to him. "I'll be right there."

Moments later P.J. returned with his swim trunks on.

"You'll need your dive gear, Papa." Billy had already pulled out his grandfather's equipment. "I don't think you can swim this far."

"I am sure I'll be fine, young man," his grandfather argued, "Go ahead, I'll follow you."

Billy grabbed the snorkel gear and jumped into the dinghy. "It will be faster this way."

His grandfather did not protest. He got in and let the little boy drive. They dropped an anchor just outside the east side of the cove. Holding his mask, Billy put on his fins and fell back into the water. He waited for his grandfather, gave him some general instructions and dove.

Twisting and turning beneath the surface Billy kicked his feet hard and equalized more readily this time. He got to the base of the giant boulder turned to make sure Papa was behind him and slid underneath. He swam as fast as he could to get to the surface quickly.

Papa popped out of the water right behind him. The older gentleman gasped for air and twisted around, searching for his grandson. The light in the cove was soft and made the stone boulders shimmer. Papa was amazed at how perfectly the boulders had collapsed to form such a spectacular place.

Billy pulled his snorkel out of his mouth and lifted his mask. "They're not here, Papa. They're not here." The little boy was shaking his head. "Something is wrong. Something bad."

P.J. had never seen his grandson this upset. He watched as the little boy frantically spun around in the water. He wasn't quite sure what to do.

"The fish are all gone from the reef and Phinny and Dolila are missing."

"Okay. It's okay," P.J. said as he swam over to the ledge. He stayed in the water and held onto the rocks. "I am sure they're fine." He thought a moment. "Tell me why you think they'd be in here. How did you know about this place? How did you know how to find it?"

Billy turned away. "Phinny took me here the day of the storm." He paused. "I was afraid to tell you. I am sorry, Papa." He lifted his head and gazed at his grandfather. "I didn't see your note until I got back. I didn't want you to be mad at me."

P.J. swam closer to his grandson. He could not imagine what it must've been like to wait out that horrendous storm in this place. "I am not mad," he said softly and shook his head.

"Papa," Billy frantic called out, "They're not here!" He spun around again. "Phinny promised he'd be here. He *promised*."

Attempting to ease his grandson's worry, P.J. offered calmly, "It's okay. It's going to be okay. They probably got held up with that storm out there.

"No! You don't understand." Billy explained how strangely Phinny was acting the day of the storm.

Papa brushed it off, explaining that the dolphins would be back. He promised to come back tomorrow with Billy and every day after if he wanted.

"No! We have to find them."

"What's wrong Billy," his grandfather asked. "What is it?"

"I think Phinny is sick." The little boy swam over to his grandfather and explained how agitated the dolphin seemed as he told Billy of his plans. "When he brought me back to the boat, I watched him. I watched him swim away." The little boy paused. "The black stuff. The black stuff on his body, it's bigger. Papa, what does that mean?"

P.J.'s eyes grew wide. He bit his lip and looked away, deep in thought.

Turning back around, he called out, "Come on, Billy," and placed his mask back on his face. But, before he stuck his snorkel in his mouth he emphatically declared, "We're going to Anegada."

The Baby is Okay

The phone rang at 3:30 a.m. Grace was already awake. She'd been up half the night with a persistent cough. She grabbed the phone quickly as not to wake Peter.

"Gracie, we need you in San Francisco as soon as possible." Her father sounded harried. He'd been working such long hours these days.

Although incredibly passionate, her father was a very clinical scientist. Grace was much more sensitive and became more emotionally involved in her work. He always told her it was both her greatest asset and sometimes her biggest flaw.

"Well, good morning to you too, Daddy," she teased, "or is it still considered night?" Sometimes he forgot the niceties most people used. He was always the scientist, always focused.

He ignored her playfulness. "There's been a mass beaching of dolphins on East Beach in San Francisco, and they're asking us to handle the case." *They* referred to the New York Zoological Society, the major benefactor for the new P.J. McMillon Marine Mammal Research Academy.

He was putting her on as lead scientist. There was a plane waiting at LaGuardia airport for her and a team of six. They would be working alongside the scientists from both Scripps Institute of Oceanography Research and the California Academy of Sciences.

Grace had interned at the California Academy of Sciences, and P.J. thought it would give her an advantage when it came to collaboration on the project.

She hung up the phone and began to pack. Her flight was in an hour. This would be her first assignment as lead scientist in a field operation. She was excited, although troubled by the situation. Any time animals acted out of character, especially to their demise, it bothered Grace. A beaching of thirty-six dolphins was significant.

"What's going on, Gracie?" Peter asked groggily. He reached out for her hand, eyes still shut.

"There's been an incident. I have to fly to California. A mass beaching of dolphins near the Presidio of San Francisco. It doesn't sound good."

He tugged at her arm, pulling her gently to the bed. Caressing her back, he said, "You feeling up for this? That cough is still hanging around, and the baby is getting pretty big in there." Peter reached around and rubbed his wife's tummy.

Grace leaned back against his chest. "He's doing just fine in there."

She was nearing her third trimester. They wanted to keep the sex of the baby a surprise, but Grace always referred to the baby as He. Peter would ask how she could be so sure they weren't having a little girl. She'd always say she just knew. The baby was part of her. She just knew.

Grace was a very slight woman. With long flowing blond hair and sweet smile, she could come across very gentle and demure, but was actually quite tough and resilient. There was no way she was going to lose out on this opportunity because she was six-and-a-half months pregnant.

"Hey," she pushed herself up and turned to face her husband, "P.J. is sending me out as lead. Isn't that great?" Grace beamed.

Peter looked at his wife in wonder. She was one of those incredible people able to juggle a vast number of things at once. She was only 22 years old, but was managing to climb to the top of her field. Granted, she had her father's help, but Peter knew his wife would be successful even if her father weren't P.J. McMillon. He was happy for her, but couldn't help but think how a massive project like this would affect Grace's already intense schedule. He immediately felt he was about to head down the priority list another notch.

"What does that mean?" He asked. "With the baby coming, do you think this might be too much?"

"The baby isn't due for another three months. We'll be fine. Don't worry, honey." She stood up to resume packing.

Peter watched for a bit then eventually fell back to sleep. When she was done, Grace came over, kissed him gently and said good-bye.

With his eyes still closed, he put his hand to her cheek. "I love you, babe."

"I love you, too," she offered in return.

Before leaving the bedroom, Grace walked over to the French doors and looked out upon her garden. In the twilight she could see the bright pink, yellow and purple snapdragon and pansy blossoms. She expected they'd be in full bloom soon. She rubbed her belly as the baby kicked. "New Life," she said aloud then headed toward the hallway. She turned back for one last peek at her sleeping husband.

It was raining when Grace and her team arrived in San Francisco a little after 7 a.m. They rented two cargo vans, packed them with their equipment and headed toward the East Beach at the Presidio.

Twenty minutes later, Grace pulled into a makeshift parking space and assessed her surroundings. There was already a small gathering of onlookers, and several vans were parked near a grassy knoll across from the beach.

Representatives from the two other marine agencies were on the scene and working. Police officers, T.V. and media crews were also present.

She sent her team across the sandy field to check out the beach while she headed over to a tall, gray-haired man wearing an emerald green jacket with the California Academy of Sciences logo. She recognized him from her time as an intern there.

"Good morning, Dr. Stevens." Grace extended her hand, "It's good to see you. I am Gracie McMillon from the Mc4 in New York. I believe you were expecting us."

He didn't look as stern as she remembered. But, he did look a bit worn out. Without addressing her, he started talking. "They were all dead when we arrived. It's the third mass beaching in a month. My team is stretched pretty thin between here, Isla Mujeres and the Florida Keys." He was staring toward the beach. "We can use all the help we can get," he said. "Here are the instructions for your team." He looked down at Grace. "You sure you should be doing this in your condition?"

"You'd be surprised at what I can accomplish in my condition," she said and briskly walked away.

She weaved in and out of the parked cars and headed toward the beach. A dense fog permeated the air, obstructing the view of the Golden Gate Bridge and the rich green landscape across the bay. When Grace got to the sand dunes she took a deep breath and closed her eyes a moment, preparing herself for what she was about to see. This was her first major assignment. She wanted to appear confident and professional.

But as she made her way through the thick haze that encompassed the thirty-six beautiful creatures strewn across the far corner of the half-mile stretch of beach, tears streamed down Grace's face.

Most of the dolphins had managed to propel themselves high above the water line, embedding their bodies into the sand. She watched the volunteers and staff from all three organizations working together to discreetly gather information and prepare the dolphins for transport to the labs.

Two canopy tents had been set up as stations for the workers. Several of the Mc4 staff hustled to set up a third while others gathered their supplies from the van. A bulldozer sat in the corner of the beach, awaiting instruction to pick up the carcasses and transport them to three flatbed cargo trucks that were on their way. A forklift and a dozen marine mammal transport cases were also en route.

The workers and volunteer staff were assigned sections of the beach. The Mc4 team was given the farthest corner, where six dolphins lay. Each team was to appropriately tag the dolphins, take an initial blood sample and record the outward appearance and any unusual markings.

Grace walked along the shoreline and up to a cluster of the dead. She'd never seen this species of dolphin before. They had similar characteristics to the bottlenose but were completely black in color and seemed a bit stunted. Three of the dolphins were tightly bunched together, partially submerged, lying near the rocky northern shoreline. The center dolphin seemed perched slightly to its side. It had different coloring than the others and its belly was distended.

Moving in closer to the clustered threesome, Grace thought she saw the center dolphin's right pectoral fin flutter.

She stepped up, leaned in and touched the center dolphin.

"Guys, guys!" she called out to her crew, "come over here. Bring a bucket, sponge and some towels."

Grace grabbed a bucket from one of the men, filled it with water and began to gently pat the dolphin down. She could see the dolphin was injured and believed it to be a pregnant female. They had to act fast if they were going to save her.

"Jason, take Shay and go get the stretcher canvas and poles," she commanded. "We need to get this girl into the water as soon as possible. She won't be able to handle the strain of carrying a calf outside the water for much longer. Go!"

Jason and Shay ran for the stretcher material and the medical kit. People from the other agencies noticed the commotion and followed them.

Arriving back at the scene, they awaited Grace's instructions. Grace remained calm and concise in her management of the rescue. Once the stretcher poles were in their sleeves, she had four people on either side of the dolphin and the stretcher was placed in the sand, in front of the dolphin's belly. "This is going to take precision and coordination, guys. We get one shot to save this dolphin and her baby." Grace paused. "I don't want to hear a peep. Everyone is listening to me. On three, lean her toward the stretcher, you two pull it under her as the others lay her back down." Grace took a deep breath. The entire team was silent. "One, two, three!"

In two quick movements they had the dolphin on the stretcher and were now moving her to the water. There were four people on each side of the stretcher now. The water at East Beach was relatively calm, allowing them to hold the partially submerged 400-plus pound dolphin with some ease. She thrashed her tail a bit, but was too exhausted and dehydrated to put up much of a fight.

The trucks and other equipment arrived on the scene as Grace's team was placing the dolphin in the water. The next step was coordinating the transport of the live female.

The police were able to keep most of the cameras and onlookers off the beach. The heads of the California Academy and Scripps descended upon

Grace, asking a bunch of questions. She knew what they wanted and they weren't getting it. Grace was taking this girl back to New York.

There were lengthy phone calls and much arguing back and forth, but in the end, The Mc4 had been assigned six bodies and Grace had been the one to find the female dolphin alive. Grace would take all five carcasses to the Mc4 lab along with the live pregnant female, whom she would treat in the quarantine pool until the dolphin was ready to be set free.

Grace wasn't wasting any time. She had them on the cargo plane within four hours from the time she arrived on the beach.

They transported the female in a container that resembled the bed of a truck. The 12-foot steel box stood four feet high and six feet wide. The back unhinged to allow them to place the animal inside, seal it and pump salt water into it.

The tank was filled slowly with roughly three-feet of ocean water, to take pressure off the animals body. Grace was careful not to sedate the dolphin fully for fear of damaging the fetus.

Emotions ran high and spirits remained cautiously optimistic. It was a five-hour flight back to New York, and although the plane was outfitted with a seated section, the Mc4 team spent most of the trip standing over the container, patting the dolphin down with wet towels and praying.

P.J. was waiting for them at LaGuardia.

It would be touch and go for a while. The next three weeks were a blur. P.J. and the Mc4 staff were inundated as they conducted diagnostic evaluations on all five carcasses from San Francisco plus the remains sent from the beachings in Isla Mujeres and the Florida Keys. Collectively, a total of 73 bottlenose dolphins beached themselves amongst the three locations. All of them displayed varying signs of the affliction P.J. referred to as *Blackened Dolphin Syndrome*.

The young female and lone survivor of the San Francisco beaching incident, was responding well to treatment. Her minor wounds, mostly cuts and abrasions from being dragged through the sand, were healing. But her dorsal fin had curled over to the right and she wasn't eating enough. She'd consume about thirteen to fifteen pounds of fish per day, not nearly enough to sustain a 400-pound animal that would soon give birth.

Grace was her primary care provider and remained close by, almost around the clock. She spent hours walking around the quarantine pool each day talking to the dolphin she named Dee. She was concerned about how despondent and depressed the dolphin seemed. She'd try to play games with Dee to get her to exercise, knowing the dolphin needed to move if she was going to carry her baby to term.

Administering tests on the animal was difficult. Dee would not let anyone touch her or even get close to her. P.J. gave Grace a lot of leeway. He continued to report visual findings to the board and managed to forestall their demands for substantive test results.

P.J. would come by once in a while to check on the dolphin's progress as well as his own daughter's health.

"You have to go home sometime, Gracie." He'd tell her each night. "You have to rest. That cough is not going to get better if you don't get some sleep."

Grace had trouble leaving the traumatized, lonely dolphin for any length of time. A bond had formed on the beach, and Grace fought hard to have Dee placed under the Mc4's care. She felt personally responsible for every part of her progress.

"I am fine," she'd answer. "Peter's taking good care of me."

Peter would come by each evening with dinner for his wife. He'd let Grace talk for hours about the day's experiences: how much the dolphin ate, exercised, played. She'd also tell him full details about the testing and results regarding the blackened carcasses.

Her work consumed her. Peter understood because he was also passionate about his work. But his work had nothing to do with marine mammals. Peter was an astronomer. He'd always been fascinated with the happenings in the sky. And although he had more aspiring career goals, he was currently enjoying the opportunity to work with the famous Zeiss Projector at the Hayden Planetarium.

As new discoveries were made in space, Peter was responsible for making sure that what was projected at the planetarium was accurate and current. He hoped to someday be the one making the discoveries. But for now, with the baby coming, he was willing to take some time away from his own research to ensure his family was happy and healthy.

"Where is Peter now?" Papa asked. "It's 7:30 and you haven't eaten since lunch." P.J.'s relationship with his son-in-law was somewhat strained. When Peter asked for Grace's hand in marriage, P.J. had said no. He wanted them to wait until Grace was finished with her studies and preferred if she also had some extensive field research completed. She'd always said she wanted to travel the world and teach others about the sea.

But then Gracie called to tell her dad she was pregnant. There was no way Nana would allow her daughter to have a child out of wedlock and began making plans for an elaborate wedding. Two weeks before heading to New York for the huge cathedral ceremony, Peter, Grace and five of their closest friends hiked two-and-a-half hours up to the first summit of the Olomana Trail in Oahu. Dirty and sweaty, Grace and Peter exchanged their vows in an intimate ceremony overlooking Kaneoha Bay.

P.J. managed to convince them to stay in New York at least until the baby was born. The Mc4 was about to open and P.J. needed her help. She could treat it like an extended internship, he proposed, and return to her studies in Hawaii

—

157

once the baby was old enough. P.J. also managed to pull some strings for Peter to get a job at the planetarium, for which he never seemed grateful.

A brilliant scientist with a promising future, Peter hadn't planned on being a father at 24, and he was aggravated by P.J.'s intrusion into their lives. He definitely didn't appreciate P.J.'s self-imposed role in finding Peter work. He would have preferred a position at a prestigious university doing research. In fact, he'd been offered several interviews. But the McMillons were well known and well respected in the city, and Peter didn't feel he could turn down the planetarium because of his father-in-law's involvement in securing the position.

After talking with Grace, he gave in. He wanted them to enjoy lots of time together before the baby was born, and the planetarium was an easy gig. It meant he had more time to devote to Gracie.

It was almost 8:00 p.m. when Peter arrived at the Mc4 with two brown bags of Chinese take-out. He looked through the large glass window of the quarantine pool lab. Grace was leaning over the edge of the pool. Both arms were on the ledge and her chin was resting on her hands. She looked like she was talking as the dolphin waded back and forth on the opposite end of the pool.

He peered his head in the door. "Hey babe," he said softly. The echo in the room was loud enough to carry his words across the pool.

Grace looked up at him and smiled. She extended her hand and tapped the water. "I'll be back soon, beautiful," she said to the dolphin.

They ate in her office. Stacks of papers lined her desk. They held their containers in their hands. "Do you want to go to the lounge?" she asked her husband.

"No, I'd rather sit quietly alone with you. I don't get to see you much these days." He leaned in and gave her a peck on the cheek. "I don't want to share you."

Grace appreciated her husband's patience. They were opposites when it came to organization. Peter would never let his desk get like hers.

The food went down fast. When Grace was finished, she looked at her husband with a childlike grin.

He knew what she was looking for, but he'd make her wait a little bit.

"Is that *all* that's in the bags?" she asked playfully. She knew he hadn't opened the second one yet.

"Maybe."

"Ahem—ah huh ah huh, ahem."

Peter dropped the bag on the floor and raced to his wife's side.

Grace leaned over, holding her belly. She'd grown quite large in the past few weeks and sometimes it hurt when she coughed.

"Honey, are you okay?" he asked. "Oh honey, you shouldn't be working so much. I don't think it's good for you or the baby."

Grace sat back up, slowly. A bead of sweat rolled down her forehead. She rubbed her belly and took her husband's hand. "I am fine, honey. I just need some of my favorite chocolate cake." She smiled broadly. "This little man is hungry and he's tickling my throat."

Peter shook his head, bent down and picked up the brown bag. Inside was a small box. Opening it, he grabbed a fork and broke off a piece of the luscious multi-layered dark chocolate extravaganza hidden inside and fed it to his wife.

Grace leaned her head back and closed her eyes. "Mmmmm. It's a little slice of heaven."

As much as Grace argued over not being tired, Peter managed to convince her to come home for the night. He waited for her in the lobby while she checked on Dee one last time.

—

Inside the quarantine pool area, Grace called out, "I am back, beautiful." She walked up to the pool and saw Dee lying on the bottom. Leaning in, she gently splashed the water and repeated, "Hey, I am back, beautiful."

The dolphin picked her head up slightly, but did not move.

Grace waved her hand along the water. "Hey, it's okay if you don't want to come up. I am sure you're tired. I know I am." Grace leaned both arms on the pool's edge with her head in her hands like she did earlier. "But I need to know you're okay. Can you come up and let me see you're okay?"

The dolphin didn't move. She simply stared through the water at Grace.

"Hey, what's happened since I've been gone?" Grace said. She didn't like what she was seeing. She didn't know how long Dee had been under the water and knew she had to come up soon. Dolphins could only stay submerged for about 20 minutes before needing to take a breath, and Dee was quite far along in her pregnancy. She'd need to come up sooner.

But as Grace kept attempting to coax the dolphin out of the water, the dolphin didn't move. She simply looked up at Grace.

Grace had never seen Dee act like this before. She removed her shoes and leggings. Anytime she was working near the pool, she'd wear her swimsuit. There was always the possibility of getting wet during a feeding or playtime.

Walking over to the ladder, she carefully maneuvered up the vertical steps. It wasn't easy with her pregnant belly. She sat down and dangled her feet in the water. "Please come up, beautiful. I am worried about you."

The dolphin stayed under the water, but began to move her head up and down.

Slowly, Grace lowered herself into the pool. She held onto the ladder's railing. "Wow, the water feels good," she said as she gingerly waved her right hand underneath the surface.

The dolphin began to stir. She lifted herself off the bottom of the pool and swam back and forth. She then ascended straight up and rolled her head back, gently slipping under the surface again. She repeated this two more times, then waited with her snout peering out of the water. Her eyes were glued to Grace.

Trying to figure out what the dolphin's actions meant, after watching the third time, Grace asked, "Is that what you want me to do? Do you want me to do that too?" And she pulled herself away from the ladder. She kept one hand on the rail, tilted her head back, closed her eyes and slipped beneath the surface. When she popped back up, she opened her eyes and saw the dolphin had swum up to her.

Grace didn't panic, but she held on tight to the rail. This was the first time she'd been in the water with Dee. And it was the first time the dolphin had ever been this close to her, except when feeding. Grace took a deep breath and sunk back underneath the surface. She watched carefully as the dolphin turned to her side and swam back and forth within a few feet of touching her.

On the next go around, the dolphin gently pressed her body across Grace's belly then swam to the other side of the pool. Grace came up for air. She grabbed a life ring and let go of the railing. Kicking her feet slightly, she managed to propel herself to the center of the pool, watching the dolphin as she did. Holding the life ring with one hand, she gently let her body sink into the water. When her head was under, she opened her eyes and watched the dolphin approach.

Once more the dolphin turned to her side and gently pressed her body across Grace's belly. When the dolphin came around again, she spoke, "Your baby is okay. Your baby is okay, but you're not. You are very sick. You have to do something. Please let me go. I made a mistake. I am not supposed to be here. Please let me go." Then the dolphin swam away.

——

Grace jumped back and pulled herself to the surface. She began hacking and coughing, choking on the water she'd just swallowed.

Peter came running through the door. He ran up the steps and jumped into the pool, fully clothed. "Oh my God, Gracie!" He pulled her to the ladder and placed her hands on the rails. "Turn around, let me pull you up." He climbed the ladder and pulled his wife onto the swim platform.

All the while Grace called out, "Take me to the hospital. Take me now. I've got to get to the hospital." Panic-stricken, she shrieked, "I need my dad. I've got to tell my dad."

At the hospital, they sedated Grace. She was sleeping comfortably when P.J. arrived. "What the hell happened?" he screamed at Peter. "One minute I see her in her office with you and the next you're calling me from the hospital. What the hell happened and why was she in that pool?"

"I don't know," Peter returned with a stern voice. "This is not my fault."

The doctor came over to the two of them. "Excuse me, Mr. McMillon."

P.J. swung around. The doctor was not Grace's Obstetrician. P.J. immediately turned back toward his son-in-law, "You have some stranger looking after Gracie? What the hell!"

The doctor responded, "I am the physician on call. There was no need to call Grace's doctor. Miss McMillon is not in labor and her baby is doing just fine."

"It's Mrs. Annesley," Peter chimed in.

P.J. shook his head and glared at his son-in-law. "What?" He then addressed the doctor. "Then why is she here? What's wrong with my daughter?" P.J. looked back and forth at both men. "Somebody tell me what's wrong with my daughter!"

Both the physician and Peter backed away from P.J. It took a moment, but the doctor regained his composure and stood tall. "I am not sure, but we're running a few tests. We're going to find out. She's awake and asking for you."

"She's awake," Peter interjected. "I want to see my wife." He charged forward toward the hallway.

"Wait. Wait, please," the doctor commanded mildly. "She specifically asked to see her father. Alone."

Peter clenched his jaw and inhaled deeply. His eyes narrowed as he glared at his father-in-law. He shook his head, mumbled, "Fine," and walked back into the waiting room.

They kept Grace in the hospital for three days while they ran a battery of tests. At first they thought Grace might simply have a touch of pneumonia. When the results came back, she asked the entire family to be there when the doctors presented their findings.

Grace was suffering from Stage II Bronchioalveolar Carcinoma (BAC), a very rare form of lung cancer that develops along the lungs' air sacs. They believed it to be operable, but were afraid to do so during pregnancy. Grace would have to undergo chemotherapy post surgery. The baby was just fine. Healthy, strong. And it was a boy.

Grace lay in the hospital bed, softly relaying her wishes to the family. She wanted to name the baby William, after her two favorite writers: the Irish poet W.B. Yeats and the American playwright Tennessee Williams. But she wanted to call him Billy because William was too adult for a little boy. She wanted to make sure he had his own room and asked Peter to start looking for a new apartment for them. And she didn't want anyone to worry. She was going to be okay, and it didn't matter what the survival rate was for patients with BAC. She assured them she was a fighter and she was going to see her baby live.

—

Peter was shocked. He grabbed hold of his wife and held her tight. They cried in each other's arms. P.J. reached for Nana's hand. They both looked at each other, faces flushed, eyes fiery red. Nana was shaking.

"Why don't you keep your place, and just come to the penthouse for a while? You can have the upstairs wing. You won't be disturbed and we have staff to help when Peter is at work," her father offered.

"Dad, I am not going to sit at home. I have work to do. And you know what needs to be done. I want to be there. I *have to* be there," Grace insisted.

Nana and Peter didn't understand what Grace was talking about. It was another one of those secret moments between Grace and her father. Peter stood up and stepped away from the bed. Nana walked toward the window.

"I am working on it, sweetheart. I am working on it," P.J. replied firmly. He walked over to his daughter's bedside, opposite his son-in-law. He held out his hand and carefully placed it atop the tips of his daughter's fingers, not wanting to disturb the I.V. protruding from the back of her hand. "Of course you'll be there." He leaned over and kissed Grace's forehead. "I'll make sure of it."

Two weeks later, P.J., Grace and her research team flew down to the Florida Keys. Her father had to pull a lot of strings, use every bit of his clout and many hours of Nana's persuasive talents to convince the board at the Mc4 this was a good idea.

It was a bright, warm Sunday morning when they dropped the stainless steel cargo case into the water and set the pregnant dolphin free.

Forever Young

The girls had been asleep for more than an hour. Bill and Ella sat on the couch in his office. Ella was leaning on Bill, with her back against his chest. He massaged her shoulders gently, leaned over and kissed her neck. "I am sorry for getting so upset today, he whispered."

Earlier in the day, they'd met with Brooke's school advisor, Ms. Klein, who was concerned Brooke was beginning to daydream, doodle, and seemed otherwise pre-occupied in class. Brooke's grades remained high, but Ms. Klein was afraid if Brooke wasn't careful her overall academic performance would suffer. Ms. Klein wanted to "nip this in the bud."

Brooke was an exemplary student at the prestigious Arelbery School, a private all girls' school on the Upper East Side. She'd been there since Pre-K and was halfway through the third grade academic year. She loved to learn and until recently her advisor had only the utmost praise for Brooke's academic performance and interpersonal skills.

Ella remembered how difficult it had been to get Brooke into Arelbery. There had been a waitlist for enrollment. Nana had managed to pull some strings and secure Brooke's placement at the school.

The meeting with Ms. Klein had not gone well. It had ended with Bill abruptly walking out. He'd sat in the hallway, waiting for Ella while she politely thanked the woman and excused herself.

Bill and Ella were discussing the possibility of removing Brooke from the school, but at this point, Ella thwarted the idea.

She argued, "It's one of the top-rated schools in the country and all of Brooke's friends are there." She'd been pleased with the varied curriculum at Arelbery. Brooke was adequately challenged, had many friends and seemed happy. However, she realized as the bond between Bill and Brooke grew, her daughter's needs were changing, and she did have concerns about whether Arelbery's intense structure would allow her daughter to continue to flourish.

Education was very important to Ella. Her parents had encouraged a rich and diverse body of learning. Early on, her parents knew Ella's talents lie in art and music, and they were very supportive of her interests. She'd attended school in Italy and England and had fond memories of her formal educational experience.

Ella did not come from a lot of money. Her father's family had lived in the tiny village of Montisi, Italy, for generations. Her father, Brizio, was the local butcher. Her mom, Eloise, was British and a primary school teacher in Siena. Their home was on a meager farm where they raised pigs, goats, and chickens. They also had a small family vineyard and olive orchard. It was a modest household, and Ella's father prided himself on working hard to provide for his family. Ella was the elder of two girls. Her sister, Mary, was six years her junior.

Ella's artistic talents were paramount from a very young age. She loved to draw, sculpt, paint and sing and she was incredibly proud of her accomplishments in school and the opportunities her father worked so hard to provide. It made her want to excel, which she did. School was difficult for her. Learning did not come easy, unless there was a brush in her hand or she was singing.

She was outgoing and warm. Her sister, Mary, was the same. And anything Ella did, her sister wanted to do, too. They were a very close family.

Her father was a very progressive thinker. He liked the idea of raising strong, independent women and encouraged Ella to hold on to what made her better than any man: her femininity.

Ella's bond with her dad was very special and she loved him very much. She always wished that if she was blessed with a daughter (or daughters), the relationship with *their* father would be as special.

On the other hand, Bill did not speak highly of his educational experiences. The subject of formal education always seemed to agitate him. Ella figured her husband was unaware, possibly ungrateful, for the opportunities afforded him simply because of his family's wealth and status. She knew school had been a breeze for her brilliant husband. Everything came naturally to him. It didn't matter what the subject, he seemed to excel.

Bill was perplexed by his wife's insistence on keeping their daughter in a school that professed individual creativity and thinking, but was judging Brooke for her imagination and story-telling. As they lay there, he explained, "My formal education was not a happy memory for me. I did not enjoy school. It didn't matter whether I was at the top of my class. Nothing seemed good enough for Nana. She just kept pushing and pushing for me to do more and do it better. I was never allowed to talk about what might be on my mind at any given time. And forget talking about my feelings." He paused, lost in thought a moment. "I don't want that to happen to Brooke." He took a deep breath, leaned his head forward and kissed his wife's temple. "I am afraid there might come a time when Brooke no longer wishes to hear my stories, share my past, listen so intently." He took another, deep, deep breath. "These past few months, Ella, have been so special. I feel like I have a part of me back again."

Nuzzling her head into Bill's right shoulder, Ella placed her left hand on his arm and rubbed it gently. "Honey, I understand. And I am grateful that you and Brooke have been building this wonderful relationship. It is beautiful to see. I wouldn't want to jeopardize that."

Bill sat up. With both hands on Ella's shoulders, he gently turned her around. Looking into her eyes, he started slowly. "Really? Because I've been thinking. This contract I am working on, they've asked me to oversee the completion of the project and possibly take part in her maiden voyage. She is a huge carbon-fiber hull, and I believe it will end up being my fastest design," he said excitedly. He then paused a moment. "It would mean leaving here for a while. Move to Holland for several months."

Ella's body tensed up immediately. She pulled away from her husband. Stood. Gritting her teeth, she walked over to the door. She grabbed the handle, turned around and stared at him. She spoke very slowly. "I am glad to hear you are thinking about actually sailing one of your own builds," she responded. "That's wonderful. But it is not about to be the excuse for running away." She attempted to stifle her anger. "Whether Brooke remains at Arelbery is one thing, but I refuse to uproot our family because *you* don't feel like dealing with some school official's concerns over your daughter's interpretation of your private conversations. There is a better way!" The door slammed as Ella walked out.

Upstairs, Ella climbed into bed and sobbed. She couldn't do it. She wouldn't do it. The children were happy in New York. And if there was any place she was going to go, it was home to Italy. There was no way she was uprooting her children. No way.

Downstairs, Bill waited several hours before heading to bed. It was after 1:00 a.m. when he finally left his office. Slowly he walked up the stairs, gliding his hand along the smoothly polished banister. He paused at the top, staring at the door to the walk-in closet. It had been 10 months since his daughter led him into the jam-packed room.

Tiptoeing down the hallway, Bill could hear his daughter's gentle rhythmic breaths. He peeked through the half-opened door of Brooke's bedroom. Soft light from the grand window at the foot of the bed gently framed her face as the glow of the streetlight shone through the sheer white curtains, replacing any need for a nightlight. The sounds of the bustling city outside, muffled from the thick glass, were no match for his daughter's imagination. He could see her smiling and wondered what she might be dreaming.

Tucked-in under a pink floral duvet, Brooke clutched a brightly striped, makeshift stuffed toy under her arm. Sticking out beneath her pink satin pillowcase was a bent metallic frame.

Bill looked up at the bare shelves on the far wall of the room. He had them built to house the majority of contents from the box they'd opened together.

It had become a nightly ritual. After dinner and homework, Brooke would race upstairs and get ready for bed. Once she was settled in under her duvet, Bill would come in and slowly remove items from the shelves. He'd surround Brooke with them before sitting at the edge of her bed and beginning a story.

Each night he came back to check on her and each night he found her sleeping, surrounded by the many stuffed toys he made back in college. He never let them be seen by anyone before. Until they opened that box, he'd forgotten he made them at all.

By the time Bill was in college, he never spoke about his time in the islands. He gave up trying to talk to Nana about anything except schoolwork, and he became fairly quiet and reclusive around others.

—

Not wanting to return to the city in the summer of his sophomore year at MIT (Massachusetts Institute of Technology), Bill took an internship, working as a sail-maker with a luxury sailboat builder in New England. After work, he'd hang around the yard. Sometimes he'd walk down the dock, studying the sailboats, but most of the time he'd walk around, asking questions regarding boats under construction or the ones being repaired. On the weekends, he'd hang out in Newport, watching the regattas, daydreaming.

But he didn't socialize with people in the yard and never addressed any of the sailors from the races.

At the yard, the sail loft was adjacent to the interior design department, and one day Bill found a pile of old remnants of fabric, bright greens, tawny ambers and deep rich blues, Bill began collecting the remnants until he could make something. By the time he was finished with his internship, he'd filled an entire box with rudimentary replicas of his past.

Sixteen months later, he graduated with honors at MIT. Packing up his dorm room, he added a few pictures and personal effects to the box, taped it up and carried it with him along his travels, but he rarely looked inside.

He let Brooke keep the entire contents of the box on her shelves, less a stack of letters and some legal documents. Each night she'd sleep surrounded by them, and each morning, as Bill asked his daughter about the happenings in her dreams, they'd neatly place the items back on the shelves, dash down to breakfast and eventually out the door for work and school.

Three weeks after their meeting with Ms. Klein, Bill and Ella were summoned to the head of the school's office. They arrived a little past 9:00 a.m. on a Monday morning.

Brooke had a writing assignment in class titled: *What Interests Me?*

She'd chosen to write about dolphins, swimming in the open ocean and studying marine life. It was beautifully written but when questioned about some of the content, Brooke's teacher, Ms. Henry, became concerned with a few of the young girl's answers. Afraid Brooke may be having trouble discerning the difference between things that were possible and fantasy, Ms. Henry decided to seek the advice of Ms. Klein who in turn set up this meeting between Bill, Ella, the head of the school, the school nurse and Ms. Henry, who innocently mentioned to Ms. Klein that Brooke's source was the stories Bill had been sharing with her.

After a quick exchange of introductions, Ms. Klein was the first to speak. She looked directly at Ella.

"It is this school's commitment to prepare our students for the demands of the future based on a strong foundation and discipline for academic excellence, without distractions. We pride ourselves on being a progressive school that allows students to express their individuality. However, we also have rules. When we see a student with such potential possibly endangering her academic opportunities, we prefer to address the issues head-on rather than let them fester." She continued without taking a breath, "Re-telling whimsical bedtime stories to classmates, on the basis that they are real, making claims we all know cannot be true, is worrisome to me and the other staff."

Ella explained how Brooke's essay was simply a child conveying enthusiasm over the stories her father had shared with her.

"Mrs. McMillon, I assure you we understand and appreciate your daughter's enthusiasm for the time spent with her father. It's wonderful to see a parent so involved in his child's daily life. Believe me, we have many parents who do not share your dedication. However, introducing Brooke's personal stories from home into the classroom has recently become disruptive." Ms. Klein reached into her desk drawer and pulled out a patch-work designed stuffed turtle made from scraps of fabric. "I recommend Brooke leave her personal effects at home," she said, placing the article on the desk in front of Bill.

Bill was not listening anymore. He wanted to slap Ms. Klein. He stood up and paced the room, glaring at the insidious woman.

Ella explained how she realized bringing in articles from home was against school policy, but had a hard time believing carrying around a stuffed toy was harmful to Brooke or anyone in class. "As adults, we display pictures of loved ones on our desk. For Brooke it's a makeshift plush queen angelfish or dolphin that her father made when he was young. I do not see the harm in it."

Bill chimed in, "To quote the man I was named after, "Education is not the filling of a bucket, but the lighting of a fire." He walked over and met each woman's gaze. "My daughter's flame is burning bright now. And you guys want to put it out. *No!*" he barked, "For many years I was a father who went idly by, letting my inquisitive, loving child's heart smolder. She awakened me. She ignited the flame in me when I thought it had been extinguished forever. I will not let you people throw water on hers." He took a breath. "I was constantly pushed to be the best and to go to the best schools, to lose who I was so I could be who someone else wanted me to be. My daughter is only eight years old. If it were up to me, she'd be forever young. But she won't. She'll grow up and have to face challenges, stress, loss, heartbreak. Where will her fire be then? If you squelch her dreams, what's in her heart, who she is today, what will be left? A Harvard graduate who knows nothing except to be *the best* without being true to herself? I won't stand for it. I am taking her away from here today!"

The Dean leaned over her desk, hands clasped in front of her. She spoke in a mild tone. "Mr. McMillon. Mr. McMillon," she gently repeated. "I assure you, we are not attempting to discredit your daughter's dreams."

Ms. Klein interrupted, "No. I simply wish to place them in reality. This little girl is talking about befriending wild dolphins and communicating with fish." She swung around and walked up to Bill.

Ms. Klein stood inches from Bill's chest. At barely five feet tall, she had to wrench her neck and look up to meet his gaze. "I am sorry, but we cannot have your daughter sharing such tales with the other girls here at Arelbery."

He stepped back, bent his knees slightly and stuck his face in front of hers. Seething he responded, "Do you know who my grandfather was?" He didn't refer to P.J. McMillon very often. "The man was a damn pioneer!" Bellowing, "A dedicated scientist, who was committed to furthering human understanding of marine mammal instinct and intelligence." He stood tall, pointing at his chest. "And I was blessed to be part of just a tiny bit of what he did. Don't you *dare* tell me what *is* or *is not* real and what *is* acceptable for my daughter to discuss!" He stormed out of the office. He was halfway down the hall before Ella could get up from her chair.

Ella had never heard her husband speak so boldly, so passionately. She picked up her purse and headed toward the door. Turning around to face the women in the room, she wiped a tear from her eye and stood poised and erect, "Ms. Klein, my daughter has become a more . . ." she paused a moment searching for the words, "a more well-adjusted and well-rounded child because of her father's involvement in her life. I suggest that unless this becomes an issue that directly affects her schoolwork in a negative way, that you embrace the enthusiasm and newly imaginative spirit within my daughter."

She shook her head and exhaled deeply then addressed the Dean, "For my husband and me to even consider keeping Brooke at Arelbery, I expect both a written and verbal apology, not only to my husband but also to my daughter! Good day, ladies."

Slam!

—

Dean Williams huddled with Ms. Henry and the school nurse for a few moments before she addressed Ms. Klein, who was huffing and puffing as she looked out the conference room window. "You'd better get writing, Ms. Klein. I expect to see those apology letters on my desk by the end of the day. And for the record, if you pull another stunt like that I'll send you straight to the board for disciplinary action."

Dean Williams had incentive to rectify this situation immediately. A hefty endowment was promised upon Brooke's graduation from Arelbery. There was no messing with Nana McMillon's wishes, even posthumously.

That evening, back at the penthouse, at Brooke's request, Bill retold the tale of how he and Papa Joe helped save Angelica and the other reef fish from the fisherman's net.

Wrapped in her fluffy pink duvet, surrounded by all her favorite things, Brooke hung on her father's every word.

As the story came to a close, he leaned in and removed some strands of hair from Brooke's eyes and gently kissed her forehead.

Fiddling with the duvet and rearranging some items on the bed, Bill asked, "Honey, may I ask you some questions regarding school?"

Brooke felt her tummy jump. Slowly she nodded her head yes.

"Do you like going to Arelbery?"

The little girl nodded her head rapidly and smiled. It wasn't the question she'd expected.

"What do you like about school?"

"Ms. Henry asked if I wanted to be the lead in our class play this year. She said I am smart. We're doing *Jungle Book*."

"Do you have many friends there? Tell me about your friends."

Brooke suddenly got nervous. She was *sure* she knew where her father was going with these questions and wondered how much trouble she was in.

"Well, yeah. But I think Sara's the nicest." Brooke paused. She looked toward the floor. Her forehead wrinkled and she rolled her eyes. "I don't like Penelope very much. She's mean sometimes."

"Who's Penelope?"

"She sits in front of me when our desks aren't in a circle. She's a year older than me, but in my class. And . . . she took something from me the other day."

Brooke hadn't told her father about Penelope swiping Sir Thomas from her desk. She'd had a geography test that day and was worried about it. She thought Sir Thomas could bring her luck.She hadn't asked her father if she could take his stuffed toys to school.

"Daddy?" The little girl pursed her lips. "I took Sir Thomas to school. Ms. Klein has him in her office. She said she was going to call you to pick him up." The little girl's eyes welled up. "I am sorry daddy."

Bill pulled out the stuffed turtle from his jacket and placed it under his daughter's arm.

"It's okay, baby doll. It's okay," he reassured her. "Have you been sharing my stories with your friends at school?"

Brooke clutched the plush toy tightly, kissed it and shook her head, yes.

"I bet you get excited telling them, don't you?"

"Yup! I tell the kids all the time that I am going to grow up to be just like my grandmom, Gracie. I am going to be a scientist like Papa Joe, and I am going to swim and talk with dolphins like you!" She sat upright and leaned-in toward her dad, disrupting the collection of toys surrounding her. "Do you think I'll *really* be able to talk to them like you do?"

"Did, honey. I *did* understand them, a long, long time ago." He changed the subject. "Promise me you'll let me know if you have any problems at school, okay?"

She nodded her head in agreement and brushed passed the last question. "What about now, daddy? Could you understand them now?"

"I don't know, honey," he lied. He had stopped being able to understand things in nature a very long time ago. If he remembered correctly, he was about eleven the last time he even tried.

"Am I like you were Daddy, when you were little? Do you think I would be able to understand Phinny and Dolila?" She hesitated a moment, "Or, am I like Papa Joe?"

Suddenly a memory came to him. In it, he was on his knees at his mom's bedside. She was holding his hand, telling him something. Bill looked at his daughter and smiled. "My mother used to tell me—*when you listen from your heart, there is no message you cannot comprehend.*"

Brooke fell back into her pillow, closed her eyes with a peaceful grin and re-opened them slowly. Squeezing Sir Thomas, she whispered, "I wish I could meet them."

Bill picked up some of the objects that had fallen to the floor. Once again, he tucked his daughter snuggly under the covers and placed the items all around her. As he fluffed his daughter's pillow, he felt the metallic frame and smiled.

"Baby doll, if ever you have any problems at school or anywhere else, you know you can come to me, right?"

Brooke nodded.

He rubbed her cheek and said, "Tennessee Williams used to say, *"Oh, you weak, beautiful people who give up with such grace. What you need is someone to take hold of you—gently, with love and hand your life back to you."* This might not make sense to you right now, but someday you'll understand. The day we opened the box filled with this stuff," he pointed to the cluster surrounding her, "you handed my life back to me." He leaned over and kissed Brooke lightly on the forehead. "Now, get some sleep."

He glided over to the door, turned around and met his daughter's gaze. Staring up at him with a peaceful grin, she looked like an angel in her butterfly bed.

"I love you very much," he said then turned out the light and walked out the door.

She's *listening*, he thought and hoped some day his daughter would get the chance to experience life the way he had so many years ago. Maybe. Someday.

Early the next morning Bill made a phone call.

"No. I am sorry, but I am unable to take the position you are offering. Thank you for your time and consideration." Bill placed the phone in its cradle. He could never leave his daughters, and he could not imagine life without Ella. The Netherlands would have to wait.

—

THE DROWNED LAND

P.J. hastily raised the tender the moment they got back from the hidden cave. "Billy, go get things stowed below and meet me back up here," he commanded. "You're going to need your life vest. And bring up our foul weather gear, too, please."

The palm trees stood motionless and surf remained still as they picked up anchor and headed out of Georgey Hole. Rounding the small scrap of land known as Sandy Spit, P.J. pointed *Amazing Grace* northeast, toward the black clouds that hovered over the open ocean. It would take them several hours to get to Anegada.

Neither of them spoke.

Billy stared up at his grandfather, then out at the storm and back again. His left leg dangled over the settee, twitching.

P.J.'s eyes remained fixed on the enormous storm ahead. He removed his right hand from the wheel and placed it firmly on his grandson's knee.

Billy lifted his leg and crossed it over the other one, then leaned his elbows on both knees to stop the motion.

"Keep a sharp eye, young man. I'll be right back." Papa quickly ran down below. He rifled through some charts and placed the Anegada and Anegada Passage charts on top. He studied them a moment and hurried back upstairs.

They'd be in deep water for a while, but there were some tricky shoals and pockets of reef to avoid along the way.

Named *The Drowned Land* centuries ago by the Spanish, Anegada was an 11-mile piece of flat sandy coral with patches of sea grape trees and hearty brush that peeked out from turquoise waters.

Anegada was surrounded by the third largest coral reef in the Caribbean. Horseshoe Reef stretched 39 square-miles, curved outward along the northwest corner of Anegada and swung southeast, past the lush green mountains of Virgin Gorda (another landmass in the more than 60 tiny islands in the British Virgin Islands).

There were only a few breaks in this lengthy treacherous reef, and unless you were familiar with them, navigating near the area was incredibly dangerous. Shipwrecks along Anegada's northern coast were common, as the wide expanse of the Atlantic Ocean met the shelf at the edge of the shallows.

There was also no route around the island via water. Parts of the reef were so dense, sharp and shallow not even a small tender or kayak was safe from the rugged terrain beneath the surface.

Back up on deck, P.J. assessed the sea conditions. He instructed his grandson to let out a bit of the main sail. "We'll keep her reefed. But, if I see any wind in that storm, we're taking her down, *fast*. Got it?"

The little boy looked out at the blackness lining the sky like a fortress. "Yes, Papa." He stood up and climbed over to the main mast. His hands trembled as he pulled on the line to raise the sail. He let out only a small percentage of the large fabric and tightly secured the remainder with ties that wrapped around the boom, before returning to the cockpit.

—

He'd never felt nervous sailing with Papa Joe before, but the menacing sky worried him. Billy stared at the older gentleman behind the helm. His voice quivered, "Are we really going to sail into that, Papa?" He searched for any signs that his grandfather might be nervous, too.

P.J.'s face was somber, strong. "You're *sure* Phinny and Dolila returned to Anegada?"

With a pained expression the little boy raised and lowered his head slowly.

P.J. pictured the blackness on the young dolphin's back and wondered just how far it had spread. "Well then," Papa Joe declared, "there is no way this storm is going to stop us from getting there!"

Ominous clouds swirled and lightning flashed as the angry weather blanketed the horizon.

*   *   *

On the other side of the blackened sky, a conversation was taking place inside a patch of sea grass along the northern edge of Anegada.

"You can't make them stay, Tommy. If they want to go, let them go. It may be time for them to venture out on their own."

The twin dolphins had been back in Anegada for almost four days. Tanya didn't like the way Sir Thomas was handling the situation. The aged guardian of the orphaned dolphins had threatened to send Storm out over Jost Van Dyke if Phinny and Dolila left the reef again.

"Using Storm to keep Phinny and Dolila from leaving is wrong. Eventually they will find a way to leave. And you can't really sic Storm on those unsuspecting people because you're mad Phinny disobeyed you. It's not right, Tommy. It's not natural."

She turned away from him, propelling her petite 515-pound soft-shelled body up through the thick blades of sea grass. Swimming along the jagged edges of coral, she glided through a crowd of tiny, shimmering silverfish and headed away from the shallows. A purple sea fan slowly fluttered from the turtle's movements. Several schools of parrotfish abandoned their feast on algae to let the rare leatherback pass.

Sir Thomas followed close behind.

When Tanya arrived at the deep drop off at the reef's northern edge, she tucked her front flippers and dove. Now swimming in the rich cobalt-colored abyss, along the gray limestone wall, her body was more adequately camouflaged and her movements were no longer restricted from the obstacles that lived amongst the shallows. She could now twist, turn and swim more freely.

About a half-mile west she stopped abruptly. Using her flippers as breaks, she turned around to study some markings along the limestone shelf.

It took a few minutes for Sir Thomas to catch up. His enormous 1300-pound, 97-year-old body moved slightly slower than Tanya, who was thirty years his junior.

"The boy and his grandfather have done nothing wrong," Tanya explained as Sir Thomas approached. "And the others don't deserve to have their lives turned upside down because of this. Don't pit Storm against Wendy. You know he'll win. He loves the challenge of getting her all riled up, and she doesn't handle losing her temper well, especially near people."

Sir Thomas moved closer to the limestone wall and traced the markings with his right front flipper. "Why would Phinny want to befriend any of them? *They* are the reason he lost his parents in the first place."

Tanya chose a gentle, yet sobering tone, "Who are you to decide. Look at what our offspring must do in the first few precious days of life, in order to survive. They must brave enormous obstacles, relentless predators and sometimes-treacherous sea conditions. And *they* do it alone. Even now, as we await their arrival—they are alone and only a few will survive. Why are you so stuck on keeping these two dolphins from doing what they feel they must do?"

Unbending, Sir Thomas shot back, "I promised to keep the twins safe. And I am going to do whatever it takes in order to do so." He hesitated a moment. "I've been against the involvement in humans' lives for years. It only creates problems. They've given up using their instincts," his frustrations escalated, "Choosing to rely solely on intellect, they've forgotten—One must hone both skills in order to achieve wisdom. They don't care about us, Tanya. They don't respect the oceans, Wendy, even Storm."

"Wow. You're getting pretty crotchety, Tommy."

He glanced over at her. "I just want Phinny and Dolila to be safe and happy." He looked up at the markings on the limestone. "The way it used to be."

"Then tell Storm to go. Leave them all alone. And meet with Phinny. Answer his questions. Be honest, then let him go."

"It's too late. What's done is done. I cannot help Phinny. And, if by some chance, the old man and the boy can make it past Storm, I can assure you—he'll blow out of here and won't come back."

*   *   *

P.J. and Billy had been motoring for about an hour. Billy held tight to Mishimo as his grandfather steered in silence. The storm, which had stalled a few miles off the flattened shore of Anegada, had grown darker and more threatening as they approached. The water remained extraordinarily smooth.

P.J. left the helm and walked toward the bow. He glanced over the port side and peered through his binoculars. Slowly, he turned his head. When he looked to the right, he stopped.

Billy squeezed his cat more tightly. Only a few miles behind them were the islands of Jost Van Dyke, Guana Island, Tortola and Virgin Gorda. But they seemed so much further away. He wondered if they shouldn't go back and wait for the storm to pass.

P.J. peered through the big, bulky lenses for a while. He then hurriedly made his way back to the cockpit. "Billy, go grab my harness from the nav-station below. Secure Mishimo and come on back up here," he instructed.

Billy froze from the uneasy tone of his grandfather's voice.

"Quickly now, Go!"

The young boy grabbed Mishimo under his right arm and fumbled down the stairwell.

When he came back up, Papa was standing behind the helm.

He took the harness from the boy. After wrapping it around himself and tightening the buckles, he strapped one end to the side of the wheel stand. His head darted back and forth and he moved the wheel slightly.

"Billy, I'd rather you wait this storm out down below. I am not sure how much power it's got."

"But . . ."

"Go. Shut the companionway door and make sure everything is secure. Wait in the saloon for me. I'll call you, if I need you."

Billy's heart pounded. He took a last look. A huge sheet of pelting rain was headed their way, fast. Beneath the advancing black sky, the water changed from a deep blue to morbid gray. He closed the companionway's top hatch and backed down the steps, trembling.

Inside the saloon he sat on the edge of the settee and leaned over the back cushion with his head on top of some pillows. He kept one hand on the wooden railing that hugged the outside rim of the settee frame. He listened, blindly, to the horrid sounds of the approaching storm. His imagination toyed with him as he envisioned what was happening outside.

Papa will get us through this, he thought. *He can sail through anything.* But Billy's mind could not escape visions of the boat being torn apart from the angry storm. He tightened his life jacket and took a seat on the floor. The gray tabby poked her head out of her basket and licked Billy's arm.

Up top, fierce bolts of lightning flashed in the nearby sky. With a mast that stood 85-feet in the air, *Amazing Grace* would be an easy target for the blazing strikes. If the boat suffered a direct hit, she'd surely lose all her electronics, and the wooden hull could possibly catch on fire.

P.J. glanced at the depth sounder. They were in 52 feet of water. He pulled back the throttle to slow the boat down, preferring this unavoidable altercation occur in deeper water rather than in the Anegada shallows.

He picked up the binoculars again. The rain was streaming straight down as the clouds churned eerily.

Craaaack, Boom!

P.J. jumped and the binoculars fell as a bolt of lightning shot through the black mass and struck the water a few miles from *Amazing Grace.*

Poking his head out of the hood of his foul weather gear, he quickly leaned down and grabbed the binoculars. Steadying himself, he stood upright and widened his stance as the torrential downpour encroached upon the lone sloop. "Come on Gracie, do your thing!" he bellowed as a wave flew over the bow, soaking the foredeck.

From the starboard beam, a sudden gust of wind filled the reefed mainsail, followed by thunderous claps and a blaze of lightning. P.J. gripped the wheel tightly as the boat heeled to port. A bright tentacle-like blaze smacked the water about 40 yards from the boat's starboard bow.

He lost his footing and let go of the helm. He fell hard, banging his cheek on something as his body hit the deck. Disoriented, he shook his head and blinked repeatedly then grabbed the base of the wheel to stop it from spinning. He wedged his right foot against the side of the settee and stood back up. Eyes agape, P.J. pulled the wheel sharply to the right to avoid the spectacle in front of him.

The rush of wind pressed against the hostile clouds. A huge lengthy brawl ensued. The battle lasted more than 40 minutes, but the thunderous black mass, filled with violent rain and threatening flashes, was no match for the wind's fury. The lightning eventually fizzled and the rain double-backed, almost horizontally as the storm finally surrendered.

Behind the wind was a clear blue sky with a few puffy clouds and bright sunshine.

As the rain retreated further and further to the northwest, P.J. called out, "Billy! It's safe to come up now."

The companionway door remained shut.

"Billy, are you okay down there?"

No answer.

The deep blue water had transformed to a silken turquoise. The wind had churned up the sand from the bottom, making it more difficult to see the darkened patches of coral amidst the shallow water.

P.J. looked at the depth sounder. Nine feet. Not a lot of leeway for a boat with a seven-foot draft. He pulled the throttle back all the way to idle, ran over to the companionway, pushed the top hatch open, and quickly poked his head inside.

Billy was on the floor. His eyes were squeezed shut with both hands wrapped around the thick mast step. Mishimo was wedged between the boy and the mast, as Billy held on tight. His knuckles were white and his face, even more ghostly.

"It's okay, Billy. It's all over," his grandfather gently called out. "Come on up. It's all over."

P.J. ran back to the helm and looked at the depth sounder again. 15 feet. It flashed. Eight feet. It flashed again. 12 feet. He needed to pay attention. The patches of reef were not his only worry. Running aground in the sand wouldn't be much fun either.

"Billy," he called out from the helm, "Are you hurt?"

From deep inside the companionway door, P.J. heard a muffled voice, "I am okay Papa."

A few minutes later, Mishimo stepped out into the cockpit.

Eventually Billy crept up the stairs. Caked with dirt and tears, he kept his head down as he slowly stepped outside. "I am okay, Papa," he croaked.

He picked his head up and looked around. The cockpit was a mess. When his grandfather turned his head Billy, eyes widened. "Papa, you're bleeding!"

"Oh, it's okay my boy. It's just a little cut. I took a small spill."

P.J. had a gash under his right eye. The front of his shirt was smeared with blood where he'd continually wiped it as he steered. He took off his foul weather jacket and asked Billy to get him a clean shirt and the first aid kit. "But first, look out there. We made it young man."

Billy turned around to find the sun shining brightly in every direction. The black clouds had completely vanished. They were surrounded by spectacular milky-blue water with patches of dark areas. A long sandy stretch of land with a smattering of green brush lay a few miles ahead.

"It's cool, Papa. It's so flat."

"We'll have to *really* pay attention now. The entry into the anchorage is unmarked and pretty narrow. Those patches of coral heads and rock are only a few feet below the surface." Papa looked down. "We're in 11 feet of water now." P.J. smiled. "Go ahead and wash your face and come on back up. Don't forget that clean shirt and the first aid kit for me, okay?"

Billy zipped down the stairs. He was back, all cleaned up, in minutes. He helped his grandfather with his bandage, threw everything down the stairwell and ran up to the bow.

Not many sailors came to Anegada because of the treacherous reef and the unmarked channel at Setting Point, which was the only place for a boat to safely anchor. With a seven-foot draft, P.J. would not be able to get *Amazing Grace* very close to shore, but he knew he could maneuver close enough to be in the lee of the island and protected by the reef.

"Papa," Billy called out, "all the trees are bent! Hey, I think I see a turtle!"

P.J. shook his head and giggled.

On shore, P.J. could see a small fishing boat beached near a cluster of vine-ridden, abandoned buildings. He picked up his binoculars. The name, *Fish Tales* was hand-painted on the boat's stern.

"Come on Billy. Let's get the anchor set. I believe there is someone here who can help us."

Lowell was a native BV Islander. Originally from Virgin Gorda, for years he'd make a daily 12 mile trek to Anegada to fish, before he decided to call the island home, in 1969. He had his mind set on buying the land at Setting Point where an unfinished dilapidated development stood. He dreamed he'd someday turn it into a thriving hotel with outdoor dining with the best lobster in all of the Caribbean. He looked forward to the day when the anchorage was full and his restaurant was packed. Lowell would always say, "They'll be dancing in the sand to live music with their bellies full of lobstah and their minds fuzzy with rum!"

P.J. had crossed paths with Lowell on one of his many first exploratory exhibitions along Horseshoe Reef. They shared a common love for the simplicity of the island and mutual respect for inhabitants in the waters that surrounded it. They'd shared many a beer after helping free an unsuspecting sailor who'd run aground while attempting to reach this majestic place. If there were anyone who'd know the whereabouts of the twin dolphins in the waters surrounding the island, it would be Lowell Wheatley.

How tall are we now?

Phinny and Dolila were playing in the deep water off Anegada's northern coast on the morning of their fourth day back at the reef. Above them, the black clouds grumbled, and every once in a while the water lit up from an arbitrary lightning strike.

Phinny became engrossed in watching Sir Thomas chase after Tanya, about a half-mile away, along the limestone shelf. He'd hoped to speak to Sir Thomas this morning. The old sea turtle had been ignoring him since they'd arrived back and Phinny was getting frustrated. He was angry at Sir Thomas' lame attempt at using Storm to keep them from leaving.

Dolila spun her tail in a wide circle and called out to her brother, "Come on Phinny. Remember how we used to play this all the time?"

Dolila lay on her back, spinning her tail faster and faster until the friction created a ring underneath the surface. "Jump through, Phinny. Bet you can't do it without touching!" she challenged him.

When her brother finally turned around, he chuckled, "I remember."

He propelled himself toward the circle. At the very last minute, Dolila backed away to let him through. Phinny leaped through the ring of bubbles and did a flip under the surface, then turned back around to see how he'd done.

The circle had already begun to dissipate, but it was clear he had not touched its edges. "Huh! I knew I could still do it!"

"Ah, it's only cause you're so skinny now. Why don't we go fishing for a while?"

Phinny hadn't eaten since he'd arrived back in Anegada. His skin had become slightly ashen which made the blackness more pronounced.

"Hey, Dolila follow me." Phinny darted through water toward the edge of the drop off, where he'd seen Sir Thomas and Tanya a few minutes earlier. "Remember *this*."

Carved in the limestone were two sets of horizontal lines with names and dates etched next to them.

Dolila stared at her name. "I always wanted to be taller than you," she commented, "but I never was. You're still bigger than me," she said looking over at her brother. "But, I am faster!"

"Do you remember the last time we were here?" His voice was somber.

Dolila's head slumped forward. She would not meet her brother's gaze. Of course she remembered. How could she ever forget *that* day?

> *It was a little more than three years ago during their family's fifth visit to Anegada. Every year their mother, Dolly, made them stretch out vertically in the same spot along the drop-off while she recorded their information in the limestone. Dolila had been upset when she looked at the scratch and saw she still wasn't as tall as Phinny.*
>
> *Upset, she challenged him to a race to see who could dive further and faster. That's when Phinny asked her if she would distract Sir Thomas and their parents long enough for him to swim off to the Forbidden Trench. He'd heard rumors about the trench, and every year he'd ask Sir Thomas to explain why nobody was allowed to go there.*

"It wasn't your fault, Phinny," his sister offered.

"Of course it was. That's why Sir Thomas hates me. That's why he won't tell me how to fix it." Phinny was referring to the blackness that had developed on his dorsal fin. "I have to know, Dolila. I have to know what happened to them!"

Phinny stared at the limestone growth chart; his mind raced with the details of that day.

The twins had never been allowed past the boundaries of Horseshoe Reef's northwestern edge. He promised his sister he'd be back shortly and swam off.

Navigating through the jagged coral of the western shallows, Phinny was soon in deeper water and able to swim much faster and freer. Twenty minutes later, he was in a patch of shallow water again. Directly in front of him was a huge mound that extended both below and above the surface. It was the marker he'd been looking for. "Stay to the left of round rock," Char (a dolphin he'd met the year before) had instructed him. "But approach slowly and be very careful not to be seen."

Phinny came up for air about 100 yards south of Round Rock. He saw a big white boat on the other side of the mound jutting from the sea and assumed he must be in the right place. He figured Sir Thomas didn't want him coming into contact with people.

But, Phinny wasn't afraid of people. Several years before, his family had come across a lone sailboat on the ocean. His dad, Lamar, had shown Phinny how to surf along the boat's wake. Phinny enjoyed watching the people aboard, smiling and gawking while he played in the surf.

He became excited. He took off under the water at full speed. He circled the mound and unexpectedly dove into the trench.

Screeching to a halt, he gazed upon the sight below.

A group of dolphins were behind a massive cage. They all had the same strange black discoloration that Char (and his brother Ash) displayed. Most lay limp. Three of them were pacing back and forth and another was pressed up against the cage, staring up at the surface. None of them looked happy.

Three people were in the water. They did not look like the ones Phinny remembered from the boat. These people had blackened bodies. Their faces were covered, and they had big metal things on their backs. Quickly, Phinny tried to hide, but there was nowhere to go.

Tanya startled the twins, interrupting their solemn recollections. She'd come over to tell Phinny that Sir Thomas was waiting to talk with him over in the southwest shallows, near Setting Point.

"I know he can get pretty grumpy. But if you can manage to look past his hard exterior, he's actually a real softy," she told Phinny. "He cares about you very much. " Phinny stared at Tanya in stoical silence.

"He's worried about you, Phinny. He doesn't want this obsession to consume you, possibly hurt you further."

"Huhh. If Sir Thomas truly cared, why is he threatening to hurt me or others if my sister and I leave here?" The young dolphin wanted to scream. "Where is he?" Phinny asked.

Whenever Sir Thomas needed to think, he nestled in his favorite patch of sea grass. "Make a left when you come to Shipwreck Rock. He's waiting for you a few yards from there."

Phinny took off, without another word. He chose the longer route around the outside of the reef, so he could swim faster. When he approached Shipwreck Rock, he surfaced and was surprised to find Storm had completely disappeared. As he swam up to the massive, 97-year-old leatherback camouflaged amongst the long grayish strands beneath the surface, he thought—*maybe the old turtle has finally come to his senses.*

They sat together silently for quite a while before Sir Thomas began speaking. There was no gruffness in his tone. "I've been on this earth a very long time, young one. And I have seen and taken part in a lot of things. I want you to know, none of my actions have been out of true anger. They've been out of love, protection and an overwhelming feeling of responsibility for your safety."

Sir Thomas also felt extreme guilt for cultivating Phinny's curious nature. He worried that in sharing his own audacious tales with Phinny, he'd painted a false picture, filled with heroism and excitement without warning him of the, sometimes, unavoidable dangers and devastation. Sir Thomas had filled Phinny's mind with glorified images of him helping capsized boats and saving others' lives. But he left out the unsuccessful attempts that had occurred in his life like the death of more than sixty sailors from a submarine that was destroyed or most notably, the horrible incident with Phinny's parents.

Sir Thomas talked as they swam along the hidden path inside the western portion of the reef. Phinny did not interrupt him. Instead, he listened with undivided attention.

"When I look back on these accounts," Sir Thomas said, "so much of the trauma was caused by human interference or interaction." His voice softened, "I have grown impatient with people, and I disapprove of you wanting to befriend them."

When they approached the reef wall, Sir Thomas swam over to the carved piece of limestone and abruptly stopped. He stared at the etchings. "Do you remember this?"

"Of course I do."

"I've come back to this spot a lot over the years. When I close my eyes, I can almost hear your mom insisting you and your sister stop squirming and stand tall."

Phinny gulped. "I don't understand how you could send Storm to find us."

"I was afraid you wouldn't come back otherwise, and I was very concerned."

"I got *so* angry with you," Phinny said before swimming to the surface to breathe.

Sir Thomas contracted his head slightly. He looked up at the young dolphin's body above him. "I can see that."

Phinny swam back down beside the old turtle. "Do you know why I ran away?" He didn't wait for a response. "It wasn't only to find out what happened to my parents but also to find out what's happening to me."

Sir Thomas looked away.

"Why wouldn't you help me before this blackness began to grow."

"I thought I was." Sir Thomas lowered his head, "I thought I was," he whispered. He had declared himself responsible for keeping Phinny safe and stopping this black disease from spreading inside of him. For three years it had worked. Ironically, it was Sir Thomas' actions to protect Phinny that caused the young dolphin's illness to spread.

"I saw what happened to Char and Ash. I saw you talking to them. How did their blackness go away? How did they get rid of that aggression, anger and poison inside of them." Phinny's voice became louder and more labored. "You helped them, but you wouldn't help me."

*   *   *

A year before Phinny's incident at the trench, Sir Thomas found two young dolphins, Char and Ash, wandering around the reef's edge. They were ripping out sea fans and breaking off brain coral just to watch it crumble into pieces as it tumbled down the limestone wall.

Their dorsal fins, backs, lower underbellies and chests had discolored. When Sir Thomas asked them what happened, Char explained how they'd spent several months behind the cages at the trench. One day Char and Ash teamed up against their captors, injuring one quite badly. They were immediately released back into the wild, but by then the blackness had spread.

Sir Thomas took them in, and Tanya and he cared for them. Eventually their anger subsided, but the physical effects of their time in the cages remained. They constantly struggled to stifle their emotions and resentments.

Phinny met Char on the first day his family arrived at the reef. They became friends and would fish together daily. The other dolphins were afraid of Char and would talk about him when he wasn't around. Phinny was used to his sister being sensitive about her name, so he understood his new friend's indifference toward the others.

There were many rumors about the trench, and Sir Thomas made it *off limits* for discussion. But, Phinny kept asking.

Char had never meant for things to end the way they did. He tried to explain to Sir Thomas that he thought Phinny would look around Round Rock, see what was going on and race back to the reef. He'd only wanted to scare Phinny and stop him from asking so many questions.

But, Sir Thomas wouldn't listen. He banished Char and Ash from ever returning to Anegada or anywhere near The Reef Camp. Sir Thomas didn't see Char or Ash again, until three weeks before Phinny ran away when he and Ash came back to tell Sir Thomas how they'd changed.

Sir Thomas explained, "I wasn't the one who helped them, Phinny. *They* were the ones. They had to do it themselves."

Phinny screamed, "I just want to be better. I don't want to be mad anymore. I don't want to be mad at *them* anymore."

"Who? Humans?"

Phinny lowered his head and remained still. He could not meet Sir Thomas' gaze. He struggled to get the barely audible words out, "Mom and Dad."

Sir Thomas clenched his jaw. He dove deep along the limestone shelf, pacing back and forth. When he came back up again, he stared into Phinny's eyes.

Sir Thomas suddenly looked fragile—old.

"I see now that it was wrong of me to keep you here all these years, not letting you be free." Sir Thomas confessed. "I am sorry." He paused a moment. "My time here will be coming to an end soon. I must make sure things are in order before then. At least," he paused, "that is how I wish it."

Phinny didn't understand.

"Storm has passed. He will not return. And your friends are fine. They are safely anchored at Setting Point."

"What?" Phinny exclaimed. "Billy is here?" He did three flips and a twist. "He must have come to find me, to help me. See, there *are* good people!"

The aged turtle looked away. *I hope he can always remember that.*

Blackened Dolphin Syndrome

Perched in his office at the Mc4, P.J. remained engrossed in the latest lab report. A stale, half-eaten bologna-on-rye and cold black coffee sat on his desk. A huge stack of papers obstructed the view of a newly framed photo of his five-year-old grandson; a recent present from his daughter, Grace.

Nothing new, he thought, leaning back in his chair, head still buried in his most recent documentation. P.J. had been collecting data regarding the disease-riddled carcasses of bottlenose dolphins since the initial beaching in San Francisco. Eight more beachings had occurred since then, in varying parts of the world.

From time to time, P.J. received reports of blackened dolphin sightings, mostly off the coast of South America. They were usually spotted in groups of two or four. But, when a larger group was reported lingering off Chile's northern shore two months ago, P.J. assembled a team and headed down to South America.

By the time the team arrived, the dolphins were gone. Several days later there was a new beaching, in Baja. All dead. P.J. spent the next several weeks exploring the South American coast, searching for any signs of remaining blackened dolphins.

He was frustrated. They'd reached a dead end. There was not much more he could do except continue to collect and study data. The origins of this deadly ailment were a complete mystery, and there was no way to find a cure or even slow the disease without a live specimen.

The Mc4 specialized in the study of marine mammal communication. But, it had become famous for its research on blackened dolphin. A recent PBS special had given the academy some national publicity, which had been great, but also caused many false sightings from people anxious to help with the academy's quest to stop the spread of this mysterious disease.

Tap, tap, tap.

P.J. flung forward in his chair and twisted his head toward the sound.

Grace was standing in the window, smiling. She held one hand up to her ear, in a fist with thumb and pinky sticking out, and with her other hand she pointed at her dad.

Looking down at his phone, P.J. motioned for his daughter to sit beside him in the chair on the other side of his desk.

She poked her head in. "It's about your research," she whispered.

"O.K." He leaned back in his chair. "Whatcha got?"

Grace continued, "The man says you may be able to help each other. He knows where there are some blackened dolphins but said he needed to speak with you directly."

P.J. nodded and scrunched his chin before placing his hand on the phone. He'd had these types of phone calls before. He was done getting excited about them. He picked up the phone and pressed the blinking button. "This is P.J."

Grace watched her father grip the phone tightly, lean over his desk and begin taking notes with an intense expression on his face.

"Mmm hmm. Mmm hmm. I see. And how long have you been working with these dolphins?" her father questioned.

More scribbling.

Grace leaned left, then right attempting to see past the piles of papers. Finally, she saw what he'd written. *Hans Vitters. 10-24 months.* Next to it he wrote—*under the radar.*

"I see. And, when did . . . Well, I have a few more questions before I can . . . Yes, it's very possible, but . . . I see." He scribbled some more—*SCT.*

"Tomorrow?" He hesitated. "Let me clear my calendar, and I'll call you when I make the arrangements." Another long pause, "You're welcome. Goodbye."

P.J. hung up. With a furrowed brow, he stared at the phone. His hand still grasped the receiver.

Grace was on the edge of her chair. "Well? What did he say?" Her right leg was twitching, and she was tapping her hand on the desk. "Well?" she repeated.

Her father looked up. "Hmmm."

Grace threw her arms in the air, "P.J., what did the man say?"

"I am flying to Puerto Rico tomorrow morning to meet him at their remote office. I have to get clearance before I can help them. *If* I want to help them."

"What do you mean, *if* you *want* to help?" Grace asked. "What is SCT, anyway?"

"It stands for Sonar Capability Testing."

BMD Engineering & Technologies International had been developing some high-tech equipment that worked in conjunction with the sonar capabilities of

—

bottlenose dolphins. They were about to launch their newest product but had been having trouble with the dolphins in their study.

The company had invested a lot of money in their research and wanted P.J. to find a treatment for the ailment plaguing the dolphins.

The man on the other end of the phone seemed incredibly knowledgeable about the species and was fixated on the bottlenose dolphin's innate speed and sonar/echolocation capabilities.

P.J. explained, "I have to get clearance in order to have access to the dolphins." P.J. looked at his daughter a moment. "The man asked me to recall my own advice, quoting an interview I gave many years ago—*Do not judge what you see but may not understand. Instead, strive for a grander perspective.* He said he hoped I'd be willing to take on the project."

Grace looked at her father with a bit of a grimace. "I don't like the sounds of this, P.J."

"They have a dozen dolphins—all showing some signs of what might be Blackened Dolphin Syndrome. Whether I like it or not; It's my best shot at possibly treating this thing."

She knew he was right. "Okay, Dad. What can I do to help?"

"First, I've got to clear my calendar, which means telling your mother I can't make the benefit dinner tomorrow night. Want to handle that one for me? Hahaha." He gave Grace a wink. "I'll need you to fill in here for me again. It won't be too long. Just a few days."

"Of course." But deep inside, Grace wondered how long her body could keep up this rigorous pace. "I'd better get busy then." She stood up and walked out of her dad's office.

That evening, after tucking Billy into bed, Grace strolled through the French doors with a cool glass of fresh lemonade (she and Billy had made earlier) and headed toward the new bench she'd had installed amidst the flora. Grace sipped from her glass, her mind drifted far away from any concerns building within her as she admired her horticultural handy work.

It was late August and the vegetable garden was thriving. There were long stalks filled with huge beefsteak tomatoes. Beneath hearty leaves dangled immense zucchini. A long rectangular pot housed fragrant stems of lush green basil leaves, covered in black netting to filter the hot summer sunlight. Along the wall of the building, near the fire escape, other fresh herbs thrived.

Adjacent to the vegetables was a flourishing mélange of summer colors. Green brush intermingled with the globe-shaped red and pink flowers, in full-bloom. White petals protruded from their yellow center and gently swayed with the night breeze. A sturdy row of amber sunflowers lined the long wall at the back of the garden.

Concerns about her son began to disrupt her quieted mind. There had been a battle over his education from the moment he was born. Nana, who was determined to have more guidance in her grandson's life than she'd had with her own daughter, secretly placed Billy on a waiting list at one of the top pre-schools in New York the moment she'd gotten hold of his birth certificate.

But Grace had been putting off enrolling her son in kindergarten. She desperately wanted to keep Billy with her another year. She'd been so ill after his birth, she felt she'd missed out on so much already. He made her busy days more enjoyable. He never seemed to mind the long hours she put in, and he had plenty of interaction with the students. Plus, the playroom at the Mc4 was always filled with staff members' children or several of Billy's neighborhood friends.

She could hear her mother's persuasive arguments, "Your son needs a more structured environment. He's smart and needs to be challenged academically.

—

You'll regret it later if you selfishly keep him from developing his talents. He'll always wonder why he was held back."

She didn't necessarily agree with any of her mother's arguments; however, raising a rambunctious five-year-old on her own and relentlessly working at the Mc4 had recently taken a toll on Grace's worn out body. She'd become fatigued over the past few months and now had an added concern. If things went well in Puerto Rico, a new phase of her father's research would begin. Things at the Mc4 would only get busier, and she knew her father would rely on her to assist with it all. She wanted to do what was best for Billy and had begun to rethink the idea of keeping him from attending school for another year. She felt the sting from her mother's words. *Selfish.* Nana always managed to strike a nerve.

Grace took a sip of lemonade. The ice had melted. She leaned back against the bench and lifted her eyes to the moonlit sky. She imagined the vivid formations camouflaged from the dazzling lights of the city below. Her thoughts drifted to a time and place when she could lay on her back, look up at the heavens filled with an endless abundance of twinkling stars, and listen to the enchanted tales of how they were named.

She asked aloud, "What should I do my love? How will I know what is right for our son?"

Grace smiled as a brilliant light flashed across the sky, passing the moon before fading away. Nodding her head, she blew a kiss into the air, stood up and walked back through the French doors.

*   *   *

P.J. left for Kennedy airport before dawn. Seated in first class, he boarded TWA flight 372 to San Juan, Puerto Rico and fidgeted, unable to get comfortable. His stomach grumbled, but he had no appetite. His heart raced as he ordered a third cup of coffee. Pulling out his journal, he began feverishly writing notes along with a list of questions that had been rolling around his head all night long.

He'd given Grace his flight information, the company name and Hans' contact numbers. But as the plane flew further away from the city, P.J. became increasingly uncomfortable. Staring down at the page, he began tracing and retracing the words—*Why am I here?*

He placed the book next to the mug of black coffee on the small table beside his plush leather seat, leaned his head back and closed his eyes. He envisioned the collective results of the 11 beachings on the shores of more than seven countries of North and South America in the past five years. A total of 328 bottlenose dolphins had been found, all having suffered from the mysterious ailment—Blackened Dolphin Syndrome.

Opening his tear-filled eyes, P.J. shook his head back and forth. He didn't care how odd this whole scenario felt. This had to be the answer. The opportunity to study a dolphin with the ailment, in the wild, would surely offer some insight and a better understanding of this deadly disease. He wiped his eyes with the back of his hand, pulled out some papers from his bag, grabbed a highlighter and picked up his journal again.

He didn't look up until he heard the captain over the loud speaker, informing the passengers of their impending arrival into San Juan's international airport.

An escort, holding a black-inked sign with the name MCMILLON, was waiting for P.J. outside his gate. The man silently led him to a remote section of the airport on the lower level. A small, six-seater, dual-prop aircraft sat on the tarmac. P.J.'s eyes widened and the hair on the back of his neck stood on end as an armed officer, standing beside the plane, held out his free hand to assist P.J. climb on the wing and into the aircraft.

The back two seats were filled with supplies. The pilot told P.J. to sit in the middle row and drop his backpack behind him.

Buckling himself in, P.J. forced a smile as the unnamed man sat beside him. His body stiffened as the tip of a semiautomatic weapon poked through the doorway. *What the heck have I gotten myself into*, he thought as he watched the armed guard take a seat in front of him. Hans had mentioned BMD Enterprises' work was highly classified and the company prided itself on discretion and safety. But the armed guard and creepy escort were incredibly disconcerting.

The nameless man leaned back and instructed P.J. to relax and enjoy the flight. "What is your name?" P.J. asked

"It's a short flight," the man answered. "Mr. Hans and Dr. Silver will answer your questions when we arrive."

P.J. leaned his head against the window. It was loud and stiflingly hot as the plane taxied down the runway. *Just relax and enjoy the flight* he told himself, but his stomach continued to flutter.

At an altitude of around 6,000 feet, they left behind the concrete buildings and busy roads of San Juan. They flew past the green mountains of the remote hillsides and were soon over brilliant sapphire-colored water, with a slight chop and breaking whitecaps.

An agonizing ten minutes later, they made their descent toward a tiny airstrip on the small neighboring island of Culebra. P.J. noticed a smattering of anchored sailboats and thought of his last trip aboard *Amazing Grace. Too long ago*, he thought, and promised himself he'd take little Billy and Gracie out on Long Island Sound when he got home.

The plane taxied toward a couple of dark blue sedans sitting on the gravel at edge of the tarmac. P.J. watched two men get out of the second vehicle and stand a few feet from the parked aircraft. One of them was tall, fit, and well dressed with dusty-blonde hair, and the other was short and stocky with big black-rimmed glasses and wearing a white lab coat.

When P.J. climbed down from the wing of the plane, the tall blonde man extended his arm and said "Glad you could make it Dr.McMillon. Welcome to Culebra."

Befuddled, P.J. held his hand out and stared at Hans Vitters, who sounded more like a neighbor welcoming him to a barbeque weekend in the Cape, rather than the forceful bully from the phone who demanded P.J. drop everything and get on a plane to Puerto Rico, only to be transported via armed guard to another island.

Unrelenting, Hans patted P.J. on the back, "I hope your flight was comfortable," he offered and guided P.J. toward the car. "The lab is just down the road."

Inside, Hans explained how the facility on Culebra was BMD's main headquarters but most of their studies were conducted at a remote area, "A bit northeast of here," was all Hans would offer for a location. He also introduced P.J. to the man in the lab coat, who smiled broadly as they shook hands.

Dr. Silver was BMD's Security Clearance Advisor as well as Head of Recruiting. Hans explained that Dr. Silver would be overseeing P.J.'s physical examination for clearance to continue to their next destination.

"Don't be nervous, Dr. McMillon, your physical is simply routine to make sure you can endure the extended dives," explained Dr. Silver, "I am sure *you* will pass with flying colors."

The car came to an abrupt halt. P.J. had been so engrossed in Hans' explanation that he hadn't noticed the car was moving at all.

"You're in good hands, Dr. McMillon." Hans offered, "I'll be back to pick you up in an hour or so." The car pulled away and sped off down the paved road lined with caramel colored, A-framed buildings that lead up to a massive concrete structure.

"Humph." P.J. shook his head with his hands in the air.

"It's okay. He gets like that sometimes," Dr. Silver offered. "Please follow me, Dr. McMillon."

They walked through a set of large double doors marked MEDICAL WING and entered a small cardio examination room. P.J. burned off some steam on the treadmill, but his questions kept mounting as he did jumping jacks, push-ups, pull-ups, and eventually held out his arm so Dr. Silver could take some blood.

Meanwhile, Dr. Silver was almost giddy. "I didn't want to say this in front of Mr. Vitters, but I am a *huge* fan of your show, *Sounds of the Sea*. I *love* the narratives," he said and proceeded to give five years' worth of excerpts from his favorite storylines. "I used to watch it every week."

P.J. wasn't listening. He wanted to know what activities BMD was engaged in that required armed guards and mysterious escorts. He decided to take full advantage of his star-status.

"Do you mind if I address you by your first name?" P.J. asked.

The young doctor stood up tall with a toothy grin. "Of course not." He panted, "Wow." Holding out his hand, "It's James."

P.J. shook hands with him, again. "Tell me about yourself, James. Where did you go to school?"

"Well, I did my undergraduate studies at North Western."

"Good school. I lectured there a few times after my first circumnavigation."

James pushed his chest out and grinned. "Really? I majored in Psychology with minors in Biology and Social Sciences."

"So, how did you come about working for BMD?"

"Well, after growing up in the frigid cold and having never been any place warm, I applied to the medical school at The University of Puerto Rico. My mom is from here. I always wanted to be a surgeon." He paused, lowering his head, "But I dropped out after I failed my third Practical." He picked his head back up and looked over at P.J. "It turns out I have one of the rarest cases of Monochromacy (an extreme form of color-blindness) ever reported. It was affecting my depth perception amongst other things. I didn't want to go back to Illinois. A few weeks later I saw BMD's ad and applied. I've always been fascinated with dolphins, or at least since I began watching your show, and I wanted a job that made me feel like I was making a difference."

"Aha. So, what is BMD *doing* with the dolphins?"

"We conduct studies on their ability to deliver and retrieve information as well as their sonar capabilities. I am in charge of recruitment of the animals. We look for certain traits and put them through a series of tests to help decide which ones are best suited for our program."

"How do you find them?"

"We have several methods. Mostly, we take teams into the wild, work with pods and see which are adventurous enough to choose to follow us. We work with them in the wild for several weeks before bringing them to our facilities here. That's when we begin to give them increasingly challenging tasks to perform and formally study their progress. Once they've worked with my team for a while, they are sent to our remote location where they work with Hans' team."

"What do *they* do with the dolphins?"

"I am not quite sure what occurs once they leave my care. But, when we're done here, I'll take you over to The Toy Box, where we conduct our studies.

P.J. was happy to finally be getting some information. He decided to keep probing.

"How many dolphin are in the study?" he asked.

"It depends. We like to have twenty or so actively in the program but we've had a lot of turnover these past few years."

"Turnover?" The phrase piqued P.J.'s curiousity.

"Yeah. When a dolphin displays negative characteristics toward the program, he is released back into the wild and replaced by a new dolphin."

"What is the longest amount of time one particular dolphin has remained in the program?"

"Hans would like to see it be several years. But, I've found 18 months is all the animals can handle. I think they get too fatigued after that."

Dr. Silver finally plunged the needle into P.J.'s arm. The vile rapidly filled with blood and a moment later, he pulled it out and covered the tiny pinprick with a Band Aid. "Okay, you're all done!"

P.J. remained seated while Dr. Silver ran into the next room to process the blood work. He returned a moment later bursting at the seams. "Okay. Here comes the fun part. Follow me." Outside the main entrance of the medical ward, James scurried down a dirt walkway lined with limestone rocks. "Hurry up, P.J., the dolphins should be entering the pool any minute now."

It was a sweltering sunny day. P.J. strolled along, unhurried behind his anxious fan. He was parched and his stomach growled which caused him to look at his watch. It was already past 1 p.m. He hadn't eaten since the evening before, but suddenly, as they approached the huge concrete structure along the beach, P.J. forgot about his empty belly.

The bright blue building had a mural along one side of an underwater scene filled with dolphins, turtles, coral heads and plenty of reef fish. On the front of the building a painted sign hung over the doorway: The Toy Box.

Inside there was a set of bleachers along the right wall, which overlooked a massive partially submerged dive pool in the middle of the room. There was a conference area and offices along the left side of the building. At the far end of the room was a multiple glass-paned window that looked out upon a spectacular view of the azure water outside.

Inside the pool were a bunch of hoops, several metal objects that looked like goal posts and a gray barge that resembled a ship's hull. Otherwise, the pool was empty.

P.J. looked over at James and asked what the bleachers were for.

"Every Sunday, BMD opens The Toy Box to the public. They put on a 30-minute show and offer a tour of the facility. BMD is very sensitive to the islanders, and Mr. Vitters likes the positive press it offers. He's *very* involved in the local community."

"Where are the dolphins right now?"

"They start their afternoon exercises at 13:30. Tony will open the pool gate in just a few minutes. This group has been really great. They are scheduled to head over to the trench later this week."

"What is the trench?" P.J. asked.

"It's where Hans' team gets the dolphins ready for their missions. I think you're heading there this afternoon, if all goes well with your lab results. By the way, you're in great shape for 63."

P.J. was stuck on a phrase James had just used—*get them ready for their missions.* He was about to ask what kind of missions they could possibly be sending dolphins on, when a large gate at the back of the pool opened and five bottlenose dolphins swam inside. Moments later a man in a black wetsuit walked over and sat at the edge of the pool. The man put his fins on and waved to Dr. Silver, before strapping on his tank and leaning back into the water.

"That's Tony. He'll get them all warmed up for a while, and you can see what they've been working on," James informed P.J.

Two other men wearing swim trunks walked up to either side of the pool. They didn't wave.

James ignored them. He gave P.J. an impish grin. "Come on, let's get a closer look."

They stood at the pool's edge. James leaned on the pool with his head in his hands. "I am not supposed to name them, but I always do."

"Huh." P.J. was amused by the young man's excitement. But scowled at the men on either side of the pool. He fidgeted, looked around and shook his head at the oddity of his surroundings.

The dolphins seemed healthy with no signs of discoloration or fatigue.

Tony sat at the bottom of the pool with his right hand out. He waited for each dolphin to dive, touch his hand and then bolt upward, out of the water, spin around twice then dive back down and form a line next to Tony. He rewarded each one with a handful of fish.

The maneuvers became increasingly complex. In one instance, a dolphin picked up a small canister from a shelf, passed it off to another dolphin, who, in turn, swam over to the large barge. After attaching the canister to the bottom of the metal surface, the dolphin swam to a stockpile of round tubes that lay under the water at the opposite corner of the pool. The dolphin pushed at them with his snout, put one in his mouth, swam back to Tony and placed the tube in the man's hand. Tony opened the top of the cylinder, nodded his head and rewarded the dolphin with some fish.

P.J. rubbed his eyes and frowned.

James looked over. "It's a lot more involved than it looks," he professed. "These procedures help us decide which dolphins are ready for full training with Hans' crew over at the trench."

"What happens to the dolphins that don't advance to Hans' team?"

"Most of them eventually do. Some simply take a bit longer to train than others. The few that do not are typically sold to zoos or aquariums."

P.J.'s whole body quivered.

"The ten cent tour turned into a full show, I see," Hans remarked walking up between the men. "Dr. Silver, hasn't it been an hour yet?" he asked.

The young man looked at his watch. "Oh my goodness. I am sorry sir. I guess I lost track of time. I'll head back now and compile my results for you."

"No need. I looked at the reports. He's fine." He turned away from the young man.

"You must be starving by now, Dr. McMillon. Why don't we dine in my office so we can talk, privately?"

James suddenly remembered a phone call he was expecting. He said a hasty goodbye to P.J. and made a quick exit out the double doors.

Hans Vitters' office was on the top floor of The Toy Box. It was filled with plaques and framed commendation letters, in both English and Spanish, regarding BMD's outstanding community service in the past seven years since Hans had been in charge of operations in Culebra.

They sat at a small meeting table in the corner of the room. Hans' personal chef had prepared a beautiful local lobster salad, beans and rice and some fried plantains.

In between bites, Hans explained why he wanted to wait until the next day to take P.J. to the trench. "I'd like you to have adequate time to evaluate all twelve dolphins at once."

"How many of them are displaying signs of the disease?"

"All of them."

P.J. was stunned. "Is this the first outbreak or has this happened before?"

Hans patted him on the shoulder. "P.J., finish your salad."

He pulled back. "Has this happened before?"

"Yes."

"Have you quarantined the infected mammals?"

"We have the situation contained, yes."

P.J. squinted, took a deep breath and pushed his chair away from the table.

Hans repeated, "Yes." He took another bite of lobster. "That is why I had you rush down here. The five healthy dolphins you saw today are scheduled to go to the trench by the end of the week. I am hoping, with your help, we can quickly integrate them without any complications. I'd like to find a way to combat this thing so I don't have to keep training new recruits."

Standing, P.J. asked, "What the heck does that mean, new recruits? They're dolphins, not soldiers? And why was I brought here with an armed guard? What exactly are you up to, Hans?"

Hans' tone was eerily calm, firm, and matter-of-fact. "I don't know if I properly thanked you for dropping everything and coming down here. I know your work is important to you, as is mine." He pushed his food away, leaned on the table and gave P.J. a brief company history.

Specializing in sonar and GPS technologies, The Brewster Group had spent years studying dolphins' natural sonar capabilities. In 1963, The Brewster Group was acquired by MD Corporation, a think-tank focused on *Government Conflict Resolutions*. BMD Enterprises was formed and the company saw an opportunity. Rather than expend their energies on creating new technologies that matched that of a dolphin's, they decided to focus on harnessing the animals' abilities. They began training them to find specified targets and deliver top-secret messages and supplies to covert, and sometimes clandestine, locations. The program began in the summer of 1964 and was initially very successful.

But by the middle of the second year, BMD began battling outbreaks of (what Hans believed to be) Blackened Dolphin Syndrome.

Hans stood and walked over to his desk. "Tomorrow I'll show you the facility known as the trench. It is used to further the dolphins' skills in delivering our products efficiently and accurately. Meanwhile, tonight you may simply relax and enjoy." He walked over to the door and opened it. "I want you to know the facilities are at your disposal. You are welcome to use the lab or science library if you need. And please let me know if I can do anything to help." He paused a moment. "I hope you can keep an open mind." He motioned for P.J. to follow him. "Please let me know, if you cannot."

P.J. stood, speechless. Like a zombie, he followed Hans out the door.

The sun hid behind some clouds as they walked toward the dark blue sedan. Hans opened the back door. "My driver will drop you off at your bungalow. It's packed with cold beer, wine and some light snacks for later. It also has a spectacular view." He looked at P.J. squarely in the eye, "There are some sensitive operations going on here, Dr. McMillon, and our clients like things on a need-to-know basis. If you don't think you can take part in this, please let me know by tomorrow morning. Have a good rest."

Hans walked away before P.J. got in the car. He did not look back.

P.J.'s eyes were like saucers and his heart raced. He stared out the window, wondering what the hell he'd gotten himself into. He almost hit the roof, when the driver opened the door.

"Yours is unit twelve. Your bags are already inside."

He looked around at the series of uncluttered canary yellow concrete block structures perched along the mountain. Impeccably manicured, each was separated by beautiful pink and white bougainvillea bushes.

This is crazy, P.J. thought, shaking his head.

He walked inside, ignored his bags, and walked out onto the terrace. It was a beautiful, blustery late afternoon. The sun sat low in the sky but remained warm upon P.J.'s face. He closed his eyes, breathed in the salty air, stretched his arms wide and let the air out.

He continued this for several minutes before his shoulders finally dropped and his muscles relaxed. He sighed deeply, shaking his head once again.

Cock-a-doodle-do!

P.J. almost fell off his chair. He looked over the railing at the rooster perched in the tree beneath him. "Huh." Regaining his composure, he walked inside to the modest kitchen, opened the fridge and grabbed an ice-cold beer. It went down easy. He grabbed another and headed back to the veranda.

Along the way, he bent down in front of his two bags. "Hmmm," he muttered as he opened his knapsack. One of his notebooks was upside down and his tape recorder was gone.

He recalled the waiver the nameless man had given him to sign before he was permitted to board the tiny aircraft. In it, he'd agreed—*not take pictures or any recordings of any and all events or exercises while on the properties of BMD Enterprises.*

Bing. Bong.

P.J. jumped. His knapsack went spewing across the foyer. He stood up, leaving the contents on the floor, and walked over to open the door.

The same nameless man who'd met him at the airport stood in the doorway. "Hans asked me to give this to you," he said extending his arm out. "Enjoy your dinner, Doctor." Stepping aside, the man made way for two waiters who carried several silver covered trays into the bungalow. They carefully stepped over the scattered contents of P.J.'s knapsack and placed the trays on the white Formica counter separating the living room from the small kitchen, before marching back out the doorway and closing the door behind them.

Eyes glued to the note, P.J. stumbled over his eyeglass case. Tearing open the envelope, he read the handwritten message:

Dr. McMillon,

I hope you enjoy the meal. A car will be by at 07:00.
The boat leaves the dock promptly at 07:15 for the trench.

I'll brief you then.

Hans

"Sure," he bellowed, "Feed me gourmet food while you have someone rifle through all my things." He grabbed his beer off the floor and marched back onto the veranda.

He downed the cool liquid while feverishly writing in his notebook, never touching the covered dishes in the kitchen.

P.J. tried to capture every *minute* detail of the past 24 hours. It all seemed wrong. *I'll have to be sharp tomorrow,* he thought. His memory would have to suffice. *Details Patrick. Pay attention to the details,* he told himself.

He wrote for hours. When he was done, he rushed over to the knapsack, emptied the few remaining things onto the floor and slid his hand along the bottom of the bag. He ran his finger along the edge until he felt the first of several small snaps. Unhinging the false bottom, he rubbed his finger along the edge again, looking for the zipper. Opening the second false bottom, he felt around for the contents; two stacks of U.S. currency, a certified copy of both his passport and birth certificate, and an unopened letter addressed to Nana and Grace.

He'd learned this trick after he was robbed while on an expedition in Mexico many years ago. With no money or ID, it had taken almost two weeks before he could leave the country. Since then, he no longer carried his personal effects in one place and always carried his secret emergency stash.

He never thought he'd be using it like this. He ripped the pages from his notebook, folded them neatly, placed them inside the hidden compartment and shoved all his things back in the bag.

It was after 1:00 a.m. by the time he laid his head down on the arm of the couch. His body quickly gave in to sleep, but dreams consumed his restless mind.

Beep, beep, beep, beep. Beep, beep, beep, beep.

P.J. shook himself awake and smacked his watch alarm. It was 5:30 a.m. He got up, made a pot of coffee, took a shower and anxiously waited for his driver.

They headed down the mountain and rounded the corner. P.J. could see Hans standing at the end of the dock alongside a white-hulled 31-foot Chris-Craft sport fishing boat. The boat had a small swim platform at the back, and there were two men on the wide-open white deck, fiddling with dive gear. The cuddy-cabin door was closed and the captain was already sitting inside behind the helm. P.J. heard the engine fire up as he stepped from the car.

"I am glad you made it, P.J. I wasn't sure after our conversation yesterday. You looked . . . you looked distressed."

"A bit overwhelmed by it all. That's all," he said with a forced smile. "I am ready if you are."

"I've instructed the trainers to take the dolphins through a series of exercises and have you observe their behavior. Afterward, Rodolfo will accompany you while you examine the dolphins more closely, if you wish." He paused. "They (the dolphins) shouldn't give you any trouble."

"Trouble?" P.J. winced. "Why would the dolphins give *anyone* any trouble?"

"They can get a bit riled up sometimes. But, they are familiar with Rodolfo and Eduardo. I am sure you'll have a fine day." Hans waited for P.J. to jump onboard the boat. "I'll be waiting for you when you get back. I look forward to a full report of the day's events." He then turned around and walked up the dock.

P.J. shook his head and raised his eyebrows as the boat pulled away. *Focus, P.J., focus.*

It was a smooth ride. The water was like glass and the sky was clear. They were about twenty miles off the northeast coast of Culebra in some of the deepest portions of the Atlantic Ocean when P.J. noticed a giant boulder, peeking out from the otherwise empty expanse. A few yards to the east, he could see a lengthy sandbar protruding from the azure water.

P.J. had traveled these waters for more than thirty years. He couldn't recall ever seeing an area like this marked on a chart. He stood up, walked into the cuddy cabin, greeted the captain with a quick hello and walked over to the tiny dining table where there were some folded charts.

None of the charts were open. "How'd you guys ever find this place?" he asked, unfolding the huge sheets of paper and scanning the pages. The depths on the chart were in the thousands of feet. How could they suddenly be in shallow water?

P.J. looked up and pointed to the large sheets of paper on the table, "Captain, I don't see that rock or this shallow area on the chart. How'd you guys ever find this place?"

The Captain lowered his binoculars, smiled at P.J., nodded his head and turned back to what he'd been doing.

"Oh, come on. This is crazy." P.J. shouted, "Answer me!"

The man jumped. He turned and faced P.J. with a frightened expression. He put his hands up and in a mild tone he said, "Lo siento. Lo siento. No hablo Ingles."

P.J.'s face turned bright red. "Oh my gosh. What the hell is wrong with me? No, no, no" he protested, patting his own chest, "Lo siento." Repeating, "Lo siento. I am so sorry," He shook his head and darted out the door. He sat at on one of the bench seats and put his head in his hands.

"You okay Dr. McMillon?" Eduardo asked.

P.J.'s face was still flushed when he picked his head up, "I am okay, son. Thanks."

Eduardo was preparing the dive equipment. P.J. noticed three dive tanks rigged up and ready to go. Next to them were several small stainless steel cylinders, about twelve inches tall and a few inches in diameter. They each had a black strap and a clasp around them.

Rodolfo walked up. "Anchors all set."

P.J. looked around. He felt like he was in a fog. He hadn't noticed the boat slowed down or that they had anchored only a few feet from the huge boulder.

"I am told you are a seasoned diver," Rodolfo said from the swim platform. "Do you use a lot of air Doctor?" He asked as he grabbed a boat hook and reached for a mooring floating in the water. "We can set up a second tank if you think you might need it."

He then secured a line from the boat to the mooring.

"I am usually good for 40-45 minutes on a tank," P.J. answered, watching.

"Okay then. Your gear is ready. I'll go first. Eduardo will take up the rear. Don't forget to grab onto the line attached to the mooring to help guide you under the water. There's a pretty decent current running through here, and we don't want to lose you." Rodolfo leaped off the swim platform. Splash. He popped up. "See you down there," he said and dove.

P.J. walked over to his equipment. His vest was perfectly adjusted for his weight, and his fins matched his shoe size. He walked onto the swim platform, put on his gear and plunged into the water. His hands were shaking as he grabbed hold of the line and dove. Sucking in air faster and harder than usual, P.J. stopped a moment to regain his composure. There was no way this dive was going to be cut short because he'd blown through air like an amateur. He continued. His head darted back and forth as he studied every detail along his descent.

The trench was actually a long, jagged fissure in the ocean floor. The split was about 50-feet wide. The deep valley seemed to stretch for miles in either direction. The cliffs on either side of the fissure were uneven. The northern cliff sat only a few feet below the surface. The sandbar was perched atop a small portion of the cliff and poked out of the water for about 100 yards. On the opposite end of the fissure was the southern cliff. It sat about twelve feet below sea level. The giant boulder sat atop the southern cliff with almost as much of it out of the water as there was under the water.

As P.J. descended beyond the cliffs' edges, he looked westward. About fifty-five feet below, there was a submerged object that looked like a stationary submarine or some type of simulator. P.J. wondered if it was manned.

When he looked to the east, P.J. almost choked on his breathing apparatus. Inside a huge, reinforced-steel cage that began at the surface and continued to the depth of the fissure, were twelve bottlenose dolphins.

Horrified, he listened for sounds. There were no clicks or chirps, only a sense of foreboding. Some of the dolphins looked completely undernourished, and their faces were ashen. Others were a charcoal-gray, including their typically white underbellies. All of their natural smiles were broken, and their dorsal fins were jet-black. Each dolphin had a black strap, with a metal clasp, wrapped around its left pectoral fin.

P.J. noticed three metal cylinders attached to Rodolfo's weight belt. They looked exactly like the one's he'd seen next to the dive gear earlier. The black clips on the side of each cylinder looked like they'd fit the clasps attached to the dolphins' fins. On top of each cylinder was a red flashing button he hadn't noticed before.

When Rodolfo approached the cage, a few of the dolphins became agitated and charged the cage. Rodolfo took out a large black stick with a metal comb on the end and swam back and forth in front of the cage. Eventually, the group of mammals became still.

Suddenly a young, light-gray bottlenose came barreling around the boulder. When he saw the three divers and the cage with sickly dolphins inside, he stopped abruptly and let out a long ear-piercing screech.

Rodolfo whipped out his dart gun and aimed it at the young dolphin. Before he could pull the trigger, a large adult male came barreling around the boulder and rammed him in the side. Wham! Rodolfo's regulator flew out of his mouth and his body spun 180 degrees.

Flap! The adult male was encased in a net. He thrashed, kicked his flukes and tore at the netting with his teeth.

P.J. watched, frozen. He couldn't focus. He didn't understand. He looked up at Eduardo who was still holding the net gun and was now pointing it toward the young light-gray mammal.

"Help! Help, please!"

P.J. raced over and smacked the gun out of Eduardo's hands then swung around, pulled out his knife and swam toward the net.

The male dolphin was going ballistic. He flailed, thrashed, screeched and squealed, pushed on the net with his snout and attempted to break free. But the net only became tighter around his body and eventually his fins and snout became completely entangled in the web.

The young male looked on in horror.

P.J. desperately tried cutting away at the net. But the netting was made of a material P.J. had never seen before. His knife dulled further with every stroke.

"No!" the young dolphin screeched as he watched the life drain out of his father. The entangled dolphin lay limp.

All of a sudden the net began to move. Eduardo had attached it to a line he'd had strapped to the back of his belt. The young dolphin screeched as the net was dragged through the water at increasing speed—further and further away from him.

Squeals and screeches came from around the corner. An adult female, at full speed, charged toward Eduardo.

P.J. kicked his fins and swam quickly toward Rodolfo. But, it was too late. Rodolfo fired the trigger.

Whop!

A red dart pierced the female above her left pectoral fin. Her body immediately went limp and she spiraled toward the depth of the trench, landing only a few feet away from the net gun.

Rodolfo's air alarm on his BC began beeping. He had to resurface. He pointed to P.J. and then pointed up.

Eduardo swam up behind P.J. and gave him a slight nudge. P.J. glanced at the twelve blackened dolphins trapped within the cage and then toward the young one who surrounded the adult female on the ocean floor. His dorsal fin had distinctly changed color. Like the others behind the cage, it had become black.

A second push from Eduardo made P.J. look away and begin his climb to the surface.

P.J. popped out of the water and tore his regulator out of his mouth, choking. "What the hell just happened down there! What are you people doing?" he screamed. He spun around.

The boat was gone.

Eduardo and Rodolfo were barking at each other in Spanish. The boat appeared within minutes and pulled up alongside the two men. Eduardo hopped in and Rodolfo called over to P.J., who was about ten yards away. He offered to help P.J. into the boat. P.J. smacked his hand away.

P.J. screamed. "Don't touch me! You just killed two innocent dolphins out there!"

*   *   *

"You don't get it, Hans. You just don't get it." He paused. "I am appalled at what your men did to those two dolphins today. What you are doing to all of them is inhumane. It's intolerable!"

"What happened today was extremely unfortunate—tragic, in fact. But you are wrong about the rest, Dr. McMillon. As I suggested on the phone, *Do not judge what you see. Rather, strive for a grander perspective.* These animals are not only helping combat the enemy, they are assisting in the advancement of sonar technologies and intelligence warfare."

"I think you're using these dolphins as some sort of carrier for explosives. I think you are training them to become killers. They're not killers. They'll never be killers. It's not in their nature. You're *killing* them!"

"No. Killing them would not be prudent, Mr. McMillon. We don't kill animals. When they begin to display aggression toward our program, we set them free. Which, by the way, is hardly cost effective. We are teaching them how to track, deliver and eliminate the enemy through placement of self-detonating missiles, yes. The missiles are detonated either upon impact or on a timer when the pack is released, giving the dolphins *plenty* of time to escape unharmed."

P.J. paced the floor. He rubbed his face and eyes. "And you'd call that humane? How long have you been conducting these kinds of exercises?"

Hans didn't answer.

P.J. leaned over the desk and slammed both palms on the metal table. His face was flushed and his eyes filled with disdain. "How long?" he demanded.

Hans' head sprung backward, but he did not take his eyes off P.J. He leaned back in his chair, with a slight smirk. His left eyebrow lifted as he clasped his hands together and remained silent.

"How long?" P.J. growled.

"Six years."

P.J.'s eyes remained fixed on his adversary. "You knew. You knew you were hurting them. Why did you even bother to bring me here."

Hans leaned-in, within inches of P.J.'s left ear and spoke with a soft, firm voice. "Don't think we're the only ones out here, P.J. War is big business and everyone wants in."

Without hesitation P.J. answered, "Well I don't. And, I definitely don't want *any* part of what you are doing here." He pulled back and circled the room, shaking his head.

"Ah, but you are looking at this the wrong way, P.J. This is an opportunity for you. Now you can study these animals that have developed your so called syndrome, find a way to combat the disease and become a hero when you stop it from spreading."

"What would make you think I would *ever* help you?"

"We've had someone at every beaching, and we've read every one of your reports. We expected you to come up with more concrete findings by now, but

—

you haven't. So, we thought we'd offer the missing link and hope you'd join us in combating the illness." Hans continued, "I think if the dolphins understood the greater picture. If they knew why they were being trained, it might alter these negative effects. In fact, in evaluating what happened today, it is greater evidence that if we could tap into their protective mechanism they might be more likely to better assist in carrying out their missions without incident. I think your team might be able to do that."

P.J. knew to whom Hans was referring. There was no way he was ever going to let his daughter near this horrid place. "I am leaving here. Today. My plane will be waiting at the airport in a few hours. And I'll be expected to be on it." P.J. was trembling inside. He had no idea how big a mess he'd gotten himself into. He hoped he'd be allowed to leave.

Han's looked down at P.J.'s bags, pressed a button on his phone and leaned back in his chair again. "So it seems." A moment later a tall, very large man came stomping through the door. Hans pointed his chin toward the bags.

The man bent down and unzipped the backpack.

"Just a formality," Hans said. "I've allowed you to see some highly sensitive situations, Dr. McMillon. You may disagree with them but understand they are all legal. However, highly classified." Hans continued, "When he's done, Jonah will take you where you need to go." He then pointed to the door and looked down at his papers, ignoring P.J.'s departure.

P.J. didn't think he took another breath until he landed safely on the ground at LaGuardia. It was late at night and nobody, except for his pilot, knew he was back in New York. Grabbing a yellow cab, P.J. had the man stop at the nearest bar outside the airport. He asked the man to keep the meter running.

Inside the run-down, cockroach infested hole-in-the-wall, P.J. put a $100 bill on the bar and asked the bartender for a bottle. He poured himself three shots of Canadian Club and walked out the door.

"Okay," he said entering the cab. He gave the driver the address to the penthouse, "Please take me home." He put his head back and closed his eyes. Although he knew he couldn't sleep, the alcohol had caught up to him, and the tension in his body began to wane. He looked down at his knapsack. Opened it, grabbed his journal and began to read. He'd had over four hours on the plane to record all that happened, capture his thoughts and come up with some ideas on how to stop this maniac from continuing this horrid exploitation.

It was after 2:00 a.m. by the time he arrived home. He slept in his study, haunted by the events of the past three days.

> *They were in Hans' office. The room was rapidly filling with water.*
>
> *"How many of them are displaying signs of the disease?" he asked Hans.*
>
> *"All of them," the man answered as his entire office began to sink.*
>
> *P.J. looked around. He was floating underwater in the trench. Alone. He was wearing street clothes with no dive gear or wetsuit. All he could see was the terrified young dolphin circling the adult female's body, which lay upon the sea floor. The young dolphin stared up into P.J.'s eyes, and the animal screamed, "They killed my mother. They killed my father."*

A sharp pain pierced P.J's chest, and he was jolted awake. His body was clammy and his hair drenched with sweat. The grandfather clock, in the corner of the darkened room, struck eight. He jumped up. Light-headed, he made it to his desk, leaned over his trash bin and threw up.

After cleaning himself up in the parlor bathroom, he returned to his desk and picked up the phone. He made several calls including those to his good friends Richard Hughes from the New Jersey Justice Department, John Lindsay (the Mayor of New York), and Governor Nelson Rockefeller. He then spoke with the top brass at NOAA—the National Oceanic & Atmospheric Administration and finally, he called an emergency meeting with the board from the NY Aquarium. By midday, he'd also reached the President of PBS.

He said nothing to Grace. He didn't answer her questions, nor did he share any details of the three-day ordeal. After two weeks of meetings, he called Gracie into his office.

He told her what happened and explained how he'd hired several individuals to do the investigative work on BMD. In order to stop this, they were going to need as much information as possible.

For the next three weeks P.J. gathered information regarding BMD Enterprises' business practices, the history of both The Brewster Group and the MD Corp, and a list of who was involved with them as well as who funded them.

Meanwhile, P.J. struggled with what he'd witnessed. He kept thinking he could have done more. But, he didn't. He froze, shocked under the water. Helpless. And then he left them all behind.

He paced the lab, explaining the latest developments to his daughter. His local political allies had pointed him in the right direction in Washington. There was a bill under development in Congress regarding the protection of marine life. They were extremely interested in his testimony. Having someone as well known as P.J. McMillon would only strengthen the case. His testimony would be vital, and they encouraged him to continue his crusade worldwide.

She reminded him of how much these efforts would help in the long run. "See, you are making a difference," she said. "Ahem, ahem, hem," she stifled a cough. "What you are doing will have far-reaching effects on these and other animals. Ahem, ahem."

She is my strength, even when she is weak, he thought. "Grace, you promised you would rest."

"It's okay. Don't worry about me," she answered. She turned to her little boy, who was looking under the microscope. "Billy, why don't you head to the play room? I'll be there in a few minutes."

The little boy stood and walked over to the door at the far end of the lab. When he left, Grace turned to her dad.

"Daddy, sit down. I have something to tell you." Grace rarely referred to P.J. as daddy, especially at the Mc4.

He studied his daughter's expression. "What is it? What's wrong, Gracie?"

She bit her top lip and turned away from him. Lifting her head, she closed her eyes and took a deep breath, stifling her tears. She opened her eyes, sniffled once and turned back around. "I am sick again, Dad." She said flatly. "I found out while you were away. The doctors think they caught it early and have put me on some medications."

P.J. suddenly felt queasy. He attempted to breathe, but could not find any air. Staring at her, he held onto the counter, reached for a chair and sat down. His hands became clammy, his complexion chalky, and beads of sweat rose from his pores.

Grace came over and gently rubbed his back. "It's going to be okay. I am going to be okay," she declared. "I start treatment in two weeks. Right after Billy gets settled-in with kindergarten."

P.J.'s eyes widened and he sat upright. He knew Gracie wanted to keep Billy with her for another year. He met his daughter's tearful gaze, pursed his lips and shook his head, no.

"It's for the best dad."

He looked down again and wiped his forehead and chin with his left hand. He was scheduled to go to Washington in the next few weeks. Depositions began in thirty days and construction of a proper bill would take all his energy.

"Maybe I can do the depositions from here."

She shook her head. "Billy and I will be okay, Dad. We'll work out a system." She rubbed his back again. "The important thing is for you to stay strong and keep fighting. It's what you're meant to do—protect those animals and find a cure. Promise me you'll do that."

He promised Grace he wouldn't stop until legislation was passed protecting the dolphins. "I'll come home each night. I'll take the train," he offered. P.J. looked up at his daughter. He reached out and touched her face. *How does she stay so strong*, he marveled. "Okay. But please move back to the penthouse."

She closed her eyes and pressed her face against her father's hand. There was a long silence. When she lifted her head, she answered, "Thanks Daddy. But Billy and I need to do this on our own. We'll be okay. And if we're not I'll let you know."

He shook his head, reached for her hands and enveloped them with his. Gazing at the floor, his eyes filled with tears, and his shoulders began to quiver.

"I know, daddy." She leaned-in and hugged him tightly. "I know." She could hear his heart pounding in his chest. "I love you too, Daddy."

Grace stepped back and marched over to her desk. She put a bunch of papers together and picked up her briefcase. She choked back the tears. "I am going to go get my son now and take him for pizza. We have a lot to talk about this evening." She wiped her face, stood tall and said, "His Papa is about to make headlines in a battle with congress for the protection of marine mammals. My dad, the political activist!" Grace laughed, tilted her head and smiled broadly. She then swung around and strolled out the far door, in search of her rambunctious five-and-a-half-year-old.

$$\infty$$

_____

Billy jumped into the back of Lowell's truck. He poked his head through the cab window. "Did you really see them?"

"Been hangin' round here for a few days now. There was a bunch more, but they gone. Be back next year, like always."

The little boy turned back around and leaned on the window. Riding down an unpaved, crater-filled dirt road, Billy's 55 lb. body bounced in the air, uncontrollably. He grabbed hold of the side of the truck and wedged his right foot on a ridge of the bed.

The car came to an abrupt halt along the northern edge of a large salt pond. "Look out there, Billy. See the flamingos. They'll make a racket in the morning worse than any rooster! But, they are pretty."

Billy squinted to find what Mr. Lowell was pointing at. Way off in the distance, near some brush, he could make out some pink dots.

Suddenly he screamed, "I see them, Papa. I see them!"

The trees ruffled and a cluster of small birds flew into the air.

"Okay, Billy. But you don't have to scare them."

"No Papa," Billy yelled. "I see *them*. I can see Phinny and Dolila!"

He was standing jumping around the bed of the truck, pointing the opposite direction of the salt pond's brackish water.

P.J. poked his head out the window, cupped his hand over his eyes and squinted. He could see a smidgen of white sand peaking out between some wild shrubs and a hint of the turquoise water beyond it. He moved his body from side to side and kept searching. He couldn't see anything. Opening the door he stood on the doorstep to take a look from a higher angle. He scanned the horizon, squinted and hunted some more. Out past the darkened patches of reef he thought he saw something jump out of the water. A tiny dark mass soared into the air and back down again.

Then there were two. "Get on in, Doctah," Lowell called out, "let's go get you guys a little closer."

Billy could barely contain himself. He held on, still standing, as Lowell drove toward Cow Wreck Beach. He leaped from the truck and ran down to the water's edge. "Come on, Papa. Come on!"

"You want me to wait for you?" Lowell asked.

"No. I think we can take it from here. It's not too long a walk back. We'll be okay."

"Well, how about I check on you in an hour or so. You don't even have a radio."

Papa grabbed the snorkel gear. "No need to worry my friend. We'll be fine." He thanked Lowell and went running down the beach after his grandson.

Cow Wreck Beach was a pristine, flat stretch of coarse white sand and palm trees. There were no buildings, businesses, homes or people. There was a warm breeze, bright sunshine and moderate chop on the deeper water toward the horizon. About a quarter-mile off shore, the sparkling greenish-blue waters met the darker reef's edge where hundreds of species of fish fed off the rich colorful coral and vast underwater vegetation.

Billy led the way until they arrived at the reef. He stopped swimming, picked his head up and spit out his snorkel. "How do we get through this, Papa?"

Parts of the reef were only two or three feet under water. They would have to be careful not to bump into the jagged edges of coral, abundant spiny sea urchin and less menacing looking, but equally dangerous, fire coral. P.J. instructed his grandson to swim flat, keep his arms to his sides with his palms facing up and limit his movement with his legs. "Let your ankles move your fins. Do not bend your knees. We'll just take it slow, and it will be fine."

Wide-eyed and breathing heavily, Billy's heart raced as he followed closely behind his grandfather. He did exactly as he was told. At first he found the restrictive movement troublesome, but as he got caught up in the beauty of the reef, only feet below his body, he found his rhythm. His breathing slowed and his body stopped shaking. When his right hand hit a flowing purple sea fan, he took a labored breath, but did not panic. His eyes looked all around, but he was afraid to move his head.

He was shocked when he reached the opposite edge. Half his body was in three feet of water and the other half looked down hundreds of feet. The moment his fins passed the reef's edge Billy squirmed around flailing his arms. He spit out his snorkel, lifted his mask and lay on his back, floating. "Wow! That was amazing," he called out.

His grandfather was a few yards away, scanning the surface of the water. "You did great, my boy. You did great!"

Still on his back, Billy tilted his head back and looked up at the clear blue sky. He slowly rotated his arms and kicked his fins. He could hear his grandfather's muffled voice but couldn't understand what he was saying.

"Whistle, whistle, click, click."

The little boy spun around at the familiar sound, threw his mask back on and plunged under the water. He smiled so broadly, he could barely hold tight to his snorkel. About ten yards away, and closing fast, were two bottlenose dolphins.

Phinny came up underneath the boy and scooped him out of the water. Billy laughed, grabbed hold of Phinny's dorsal fin and held on tight as they took off at high speed, blasting past Papa.

P.J. was so relieved. Both dolphins looked healthy and safe. He hadn't been in the water with Phinny and Dolila since the day they saved Angelica. Although he'd watched Billy play on Phinny's back at Georgey Hole, it was very different being in the water with them.

Dolila chirped, cheered and spun around. She did a flip and swam over to P.J. and nudged him with her snout. He clenched onto her dorsal and they took off! Water smacked his unmasked face and his legs lifted up from the speed. He laughed and turned his head slightly to avoid choking on the water. He could feel his mask's strap slowly slipping off his head. "Wait, wait. I'm losing my mask!" but the dolphin wouldn't stop. The mask flew off and slipped under the surface behind him.

Dolila swam harder and faster catching up to her brother and finally passing him before reaching the imaginary finish line. She stopped, wriggled her body until P.J. let go and then took off in the direction they'd just come. When she came back, she swam up to P.J. holding his snorkel and mask between her teeth.

"Thank you, Dolila," P.J. offered.

The young dolphin nodded with her big built-in smile.

"Papa, you guys won. You beat us!"

"I guess we now know who the fastest swimmer is between these two. How are you doing out here, young man? We'll have to conserve some energy for the trip back across the reef you know."

"Phinny said they can take us around to Setting Point. They can go around the reef."

P.J. waved his hands under the water to keep himself upright. "I am not sure about that. It's a pretty lengthy ride in very deep, choppy water. Are you sure you're strong enough to hold on that long."

"Yup. And Phinny knows a shortcut."

P.J. shook his head and rolled his eyes. "Okay. But let's go. I'd feel much safer if you guys played in more protected waters. And, let's go a bit slower this time. No more races, okay."

Phinny looked at Dolila, who had parked herself next to P.J. They both nodded and lay flat so their passengers could grab hold. Phinny led the way through a sometimes narrow, sandy path hidden within the treacherous reef. Billy leaned over with his head in the water. He stared in awe at the razor sharp coral surrounding them. Several frowning grouper chomped on algae growing on the remnants of an ancient cannon from an old shipwreck. When they came around the southwest corner, past a patch of sea grass, Billy's eyes grew wide as he saw a giant turtle.

P.J. held on tight to Dolila and kept a watchful eye on Phinny. He could see what his grandson was concerned about. The blackness now covered most of the dolphin's lower right side. P.J. strained his neck looking to see if it had spread to the dolphin's underbelly. So far, Phinny showed no signs of aggression, and P.J. wondered if it was only a matter of time.

Back at Setting Point, the dolphins dropped off P.J. and Billy on the stern platform of *Amazing Grace*. They didn't hang around very long. Dolila was too nervous about the three other boats nearby. But Phinny couldn't just leave. He wanted to explain himself to his friend and thank him for coming to find him. Their conversation took about fifteen minutes and P.J. remained seated, with his feet dangling in the water next to his grandson the entire time.

He studied Phinny's movements and inspected his upper-body as the dolphin stood vertically out of the water, talking to Billy. The dolphin's eyes were clear and his smile was broad. His bulbous melon, at the top of his head, was a beautiful healthy gray. Phinny's pectoral fins had a solid range of motion and the upper portion of Phinny's contrasting underbelly looked healthy and white.

P.J. leaned over and placed both elbows on his thighs, squinting. He moved his head back and forth slowly, studying the area under Phinny's lower jaw. P.J. had been so pre-occupied with Phinny's dorsal fin and the spread of the darkened discoloration on his back, he'd never noticed the two deep gray, oval shapes connected horizontally at the crease of Phinny's neck. It looked like a rugged figure eight.

"Hmmm," P.J. gently moaned, rubbing his chin with his hand and tapping his finger on his cheek.

By this time both Billy and Phinny had stopped talking and were staring at P.J. Both of Billy's arms were outstretched and his eyes were wide, questioning, "Whaaaat?"

P.J. blinked and jumped back. "I am sorry, I just got lost in thought a moment. Sorry."

A few minutes later the dolphins were gone.

"You have to stop doing that, Papa." Billy looked at his grandfather "It makes us all nervous when you stare it him like that."

"Sorry."

"Can we go back too, Papa?" Billy asked.

"Back where?"

"Phinny and Dolila are going back to Georgey Hole tomorrow." He stopped a moment and studied his grandfather's face. "You still don't understand them,

—

235

do you?" he said in a low tone. "Huh." "Well, Dolila doesn't like it here anymore, and they no longer have to stay." Billy lowered his head and frowned.

"Do you *want* to go back?"

The little boy nodded, but the forlorn expression remained upon his face.

"What's wrong, Billy?"

The boy just shook his head.

"What's wrong? Tell me."

"I am afraid. I am afraid of that storm."

P.J. moved closer to his grandson and put his arm around him. They both sat quietly, looking down into the water.

"Phinny doesn't want that thing to grow anymore. I told him you could help him."

"Do you think Phinny would let me examine him?"

"Yup. Just stop *staring* at him." The little boy grabbed hold of P.J.'s arm. "I want you to fix him Papa, like his friends Char and Ash. Phinny said they got better. They aren't black anymore. He paused a second. "I'll be brave, Papa. I'll be brave. Can we go back to Georgey Hole tomorrow?"

P.J. sat there a moment, lost in thought.

"Please can we go back, Papa?"

P.J. shook his head and rubbed his face. "Of course we can."

That evening they had lobster dinner at Lowell's home and picked up anchor early the next morning. It took less than four hours to sail back to Jost Van Dyke on a gorgeous day with a light breeze. Phinny and Dolila were waiting for them at The Point to welcome them home.

Billy was anxious to get in the water. But first he had to help set the anchor, put away the sails and neaten up the lines.

P.J. stood on the swim platform, pulling out the snorkel gear for his grandson when he finally asked, "Billy, before you go play with your friends, I was wondering if you ever noticed the little spot on the crease of Phinny's neck."

"Oh, don't worry about that Papa." He patted his granddad's arm. "It's just a birthmark. Dolila has one two." In mid-air he shouted, "They got it from their mom."

Splash!

P.J. jumped back. He shook his head and laughed as he wiped his face with his left palm. He watched his grandson swim vigorously over to the small reef along the beach where his friends were waiting.

Mishimo sat on the back deck. Her head rested upon the lower stainless lifeline as she kept a wary eye on her young friend.

P.J. walked past. "Thanks, Mish," before he dashed down below.

At his desk, he opened the cabinet with Grace's books and began scanning the pages he'd read a few evenings before. It took a while, but he found it.

P.J. picked up the radio mic and hailed Danny at The Dive.

Danny came over hours after Billy went to bed. P.J. sat him down and pulled out some rum. "You're gonna need this." He poured his friend a drink and began to tell him everything that happened three years ago with BMD Enterprises as well as all that had happened since they arrived at Georgey Hole.

P.J. grabbed the bottle and took a huge swig "When I came back from Puerto Rico, I made two promises to my daughter; to fight for legislation to protect marine mammals and to find the young dolphin from that day and help him avoid the same fate as the others." He took another swig. "But I was so obsessed with getting proper legislation passed I didn't even realize my daughter was so sick, until it was too late. He shook his head and looked at Danny. "Who would have imagined I'd find him the second day we arrived. I definitely didn't think he'd have a sister and, and, and . . ." He burst into tears. "I need you to do something for me, Danny. I need you to watch Billy for a while. But I need you to do it here, on this boat, in Georgey Hole. Watch him and watch them (the two dolphins). Can you do that for me?"

Danny's head was cocked back and his eyes were bulging from their sockets. "Ummm. I'd do *anything* for you, Doc." His brow was creased and his left eyebrow was askew. "But what are you planning to do? What's goin' on in that head of yours. This whole thing is sounding a bit nuts, ya know?"

"No. No. No. I am not nuts. I am telling you Danny I understood them once too. That day at the trench, I heard Phinny yell for help. It wasn't just a sound. I *heard* him. I understood him. And I think I may be able to make things better. Fix things, at least a little."

P.J. pushed a stack of papers toward his friend along with a pen and some notebooks. "I know all of this is a lot to swallow, but please read the notebooks. They'll help. These are the most pertinent ones, but if you need more information the remainder of the notebooks are in the cupboards surrounding my desk. Both Gracie's and mine are there.

"What about these papers?"

"Wait until you've read the notebooks. Then go over them and sign them if you feel comfortable."

Danny thumbed through the paperwork and eyeballed his friend.

P.J. put his hand on Danny's forearm. "I had them drawn up before I left New York. I trust you Danny. I know you'll do the right thing."

Danny picked up the top notebook and opened it. "I guess I better get reading." Then he looked down at the bottle of Mount Gay. "How much rum ya got?"

—

CONSEQUENCES

Three hundred twenty eight autopsy reports were shipped to Washington along with another sixteen boxes of additional research conducted at the Mc4 regarding the eleven beachings from April 1966-July 1971. P.J.'s deposition lasted six weeks. He would take the train back and forth each day. Most evenings, he would go over to Grace's and help with Billy.

He and his grandson would play in the garden, pruning and weeding, while Grace sat on her bench and watched. Sometimes she was too weak from the day's chemotherapy treatment to sit outside. They'd open the French doors; she'd lie on her son's bed and listen to them chitchat and giggle.

Later in the evening, once Billy was asleep, P.J. would make up the pull out couch, sit on edge of the bed and tell his daughter the latest news from Washington. She'd listen intently, ask questions and lend support when he needed it.

For six weeks P.J. sat in front of a congressional panel and explained how each dolphin's corpse displayed physical evidence of change in body chemistry. Externally their dorsal fins had blackened and the remainder of their epidermis had darkened to varying degrees. The adult dolphins' melons, or top of the heads, all showed signs of discoloration. In all cases, the 83 adolescent males displayed the greatest degree of infection and the 68 adult females the least. There were also 23 calves among the dead.

Internally, the mammals' organs displayed evidence of gross premature aging, even in the calves. Lesions were found on the hearts, lungs, throats, posteriors, melons and inside the mouths.

Over five years of study, in between the beachings, P.J. developed a table of common elements found in the mammals in each group. At the hearings he displayed the results and attempted to explain the intricacies of his findings.

By the fourth week of testimony, those opposing the proposed legislation were ready to attack P.J. They argued that none of his findings supported misconduct on the part of humans regarding mammals in the wild. They unanimously agreed that the ailment was horrific, but did not see the direct correlation with human interference. They wanted evidence.

P.J. had plenty. When he'd arrived back from the shocking ordeal in Culebra, his first phone call was not to his political connections. It was to his *Number One Fan*, James Silver. He spent an hour on the phone with him, giving him details regarding the trench and then asked for his help.

During lunch in Hans' office, P.J. had taken great care in studying his surroundings. He'd noticed a group of filing cabinets behind Hans' desk that seemed out of place for the sleekly designed room. He'd asked Dr. Silver to see what he could find in them.

By the end of the day, Dr. Silver had managed to Xerox enough incriminating evidence to shut the BMD compound down for good. Unfortunately for Hans, fame and memory trumped misguided loyalty.

The proponents of the bill had held back the evidence from Culebra and the trench as a strategic move. They needed verbal sympathy for the horrific ailment before they attacked the source of its manifestation.

The next two weeks P.J. presented evidence regarding BMD's extensive involvement in the mistreatment of bottlenose dolphins and the correlation between that direct mistreatment and Blackened Dolphin Syndrome.

He also described the tragic ordeal he witnessed at the trench, beginning with the twelve dolphins behind the cage. But it was his eyewitness account of the events leading up to the instant discoloration of the young dolphin's dorsal fin that was his most influential testimony.

It took sixteen weeks, but the U.S. military and local Puerto Rican officials were finally given the go ahead to raid the trench. The submarine structure was gone as well as the dolphins. The only thing that remained was the huge metal cage. When the police and military personnel arrived at BMD Enterprises' compound, Hans welcomed them with open arms and let them search the entire grounds. He even took them over to The Toy Box to observe the six healthy dolphins in the pool and showed them the documentation room, which housed all the files regarding the research they'd been conducting on the dolphins at the compound. The entire staff was also questioned.

P.J. never knew the fate of any of the dolphins behind the cage or that of the young one that oversaw the horrible ordeal. But the beachings stopped.

The dolphins were eventually sent to the Mc4 for observation and evaluation. P.J. offered Dr. Silver the opportunity to oversea the dolphins' care until the government hearings were over. But, it seemed James Silver had finally found his calling. He decided he had his own political activism to pursue.

The façade Hans had created at BMD's compound angered the locals. They wanted their island back. James Silver joined the PIP—Puerto Rican Independence Party to help in the crusade to stop the U.S. Military from using the island as a base for target practice. James Silver became a champion for the cause. The military abandoned all operations in Culebra by1975. Silver eventually returned to the University of Puerto Rico where he earned his doctorate in Political Science and decided to call Culebra his home.

P.J. had used every source he could to help in his crusade to stop the gross mistreatment of these mammals. Fourteen months later, on October 21, 1972, the Marine Mammal Protection Act was formally enacted. It was the first legislation of its kind. Among many other things, it prohibited the taking of marine mammals from the wild as well as importing, exporting or selling of any marine mammals within the United States, making the hunting, killing, capture, and/or harassment of any marine mammal or an attempt to do so, illegal.

Twinkle, Twinkle

Breezi stared at the wall in her bedroom. "What if I am not tall enough, Daddy?" she asked. She gripped his arm. "I've *got* to be tall enough."

It was the day before Bill's youngest daughter Breezi's seventh birthday. He planned to take the family to the theme park to celebrate. Breezi had been itching to ride the MONSTER coaster. It was her dream. She had been talking about it all winter long. She hadn't been allowed to ride it the previous year because she didn't meet the height requirement. Instead, she had to watch from the ground as her father and Brooke screamed past her, laughing and giggling. She cried for an hour when they got off.

She studied the marks on the dolphin-shaped height chart. They dated back to when she was barely able to stand. She was nervous. Being tall enough was the most important thing in her young life at that moment. She wanted desperately to ride that ride. Her long legged sister had been riding the same ride since *she* was seven.

"Go ahead, Bree," he urged. "Just believe."

She stepped in front of the leaping dolphin holding its pectoral fin out with the words *How tall am I now?* spread out across the sky and a ruler along the side. She turned around and let her father make the latest mark on the chart.

"Wow. See, I told you to believe."

She spun around. She'd grown almost four inches this year, over an inch more than the height requirement. Jumping up and down, she kissed her dad and ran around the room.

Now, instead of being anxious she was elated. Both were preventing her from sleep. Billy lay down on the floor next to her. He rubbed the back of her hand with his thumb. "Sleep now, Bree. Ride the ride in your dreams. I'll be sitting next to you. Imagine us climbing the steep track together and looking behind us at Mom and Brooke on the ground below. Remember to keep your hands in."

Her breathing began to soften. He waited a few minutes, then slipped his hand out from under hers and walked over to the door. He had one foot in the hallway when Breezi called out in a low voice, "Daddy did you know Grandma Gracie has a star named after her?"

His head snapped back. He turned around and poked his head through Breezi's doorway. "What makes you say that, sweetie?"

"I saw it at the planetarium. They said a man who used to work there named a star, Gracie—after my grandmom, Gracie McMillon. They said it was really far away, and it took the man a very long time to find it. I got to see it today," she said proudly.

"Really?" He asked, "Who at the planetarium told you this?" Bill switched the light back on and sat beside his daughter. She was wrapped in a cloudburst filled, blue comforter. There was a mural of a cloud-covered sky on her wall and a huge sunburst in the corner of the room.

"We watched a show and the speaker made an announcement about the star. He said it was named after the daughter of the founder of great-grandpop's school. My teacher told me the man must have been talking about my grandmom."

"Hmmm." Bill smiled. *I guess he did it, after all.* He shook his head a blinked a few times. "Maybe we can go back, together, and you can show me my mom's star," he said leaning in and kissing his daughter on the forehead. He rubbed the side of Breezi's face and stood to leave, shutting the light off once again.

Breezi lay in her bed with her eyes wide open, looking up at the ceiling of her room. Unlike her sister's room, Breezi's room was windowless. Her father had stuck glow-in-the-dark stickers of stars, moons and planets all along the ceiling so she felt like she could see outside. Breezi wanted them all in precisely the right location. They'd researched it together, looking through several books on constellations.

Now I can add one more star, she thought before gently drifting off to sleep.

The following morning, Bill was putting on his running shoes at the foot of the staircase, when the girls came charging down the steps. They were both dressed.

"Daddy, Daddy. Can we come with you?"

Bill took a stroll through Central Park every Saturday morning. He was leaving a bit earlier today because of their plans to go to the theme park. "Well, good morning girls. Happy Birthday little one," he said and grabbed hold of Breezi, giving her a big squeeze.

It was a little after 7:00 a.m. He knew Ella would be sleeping for at least another hour. He left her a note on the kitchen table before the three of them hopped into the elevator.

It was a beautiful spring day. Bill held both girls by the hand. They crossed the street at 79th and entered Central Park, a few blocks south of the Metropolitan Museum of Art.

"Brooke says she has a birthday present for me, but *you* have to give it to me."

—

"Oh really." He looked at his eldest daughter, "What might that be?"

Ella had been encouraging her husband to share his stories with Breezi. But, he wasn't ready to do that just yet. He'd made a promise to Brooke, not to share them until *she* was ready. For more than two years, it had been something that was solely theirs. Yes, she had shared parts of the stories with her classmates at school, and Bill encouraged it. But, it was up to her when to share them with her sibling.

Recently, Breezi had expressed increased interest in her father's past and a bit of jealousy over her sister's relationship with him. Ella took the matter up with Brooke, who was completely against sharing story-time with her. She told her mom how *she'd* found the box and story-time was something special between her and her dad. She looked forward to it every night, and she didn't want to share it.

One evening, Ella came into Brooke's room and sat with her a while. She expressed her growing concern that Breezi's jealousy might someday turn into resentment. Brooke lay awake for hours that night. She thought about Phinny, Char and Ash. Over the next few days, her attitude began to change.

"I want you to tell Breezi your stories, Daddy. But I have to be there, to make sure you get it right. Sometimes you make mistakes."

"Aha. I see."

They walked along the grass past the joggers and the multitude of early risers walking their dogs. "You can tell her now, if you want. It's her birthday."

He started at the beginning, when Brooke strolled into his office to show him what she'd found. Both girls were mesmerized. Breezi's eyes welled-up at the thought of Grandmom Grace and her whole body stiffened as her father described how the boat heeled from the wind. When he got to the part where he and his grandfather walked out of customs on their way to The Dive, Brooke interrupted him. Again.

—

"You forgot the part about the cows on the beach, Daddy. Remember there were cows on the beach."

They'd managed to cross Central Park and were walking along a path on the Upper West Side. They'd exited at West 85th Street and were halfway up the block before Bill realized where he'd taken them. He interrupted his story and asked the girls if they might like to see where he'd grown up with his mom before she died.

"It's up there, on the right, next to the maple tree." The girls ran toward the steps of the Brownstone. They stopped in front of the tree and both called out to their father.

"Dad. Dad! There's a bird." Brooke waved her arms for him to hurry. Breezi kneeled down in front of it.

"Don't touch it!"

The injured blue jay was hobbling around under the nearby tree. It was dragging one of its brilliant blue and black striped wings across the uneven pavement.

"We have to do something, Daddy." Breezi whined from the ground.

"Yeah, Dad. Can we take it home and try and save it?" Brooke chimed in.

Bill put his arm around Brooke and looked down at the injured bird. He didn't think it stood much of a chance at all, but there was no way it was going to survive very long on a busy Manhattan sidewalk.

A tall, middle-aged man with gray curls stepped out of the Brownstone with a shoebox in his hands. He walked down the steps, handed the box to Breezi and looked up at Bill. "This might help."

"Thanks," Bill muttered with a quizzical glance. He knelt down next to his daughter.

Breezi looked up at her father. "Her name is Blue Belle. She fell out the tree and hurt her wing. But, I don't think it's broken, Dad."

Bill placed some leaves in the box, and gently scooped up the bird.

Its bright white face turned up to look at him. The brilliant crest on its head bristled outward like a crown of feathers as it made a high-pitched screech, "Jayer-jayer."

"It's okay little one," he said softly and placed the lid on top. He turned to thank his neighbor. The man was already gone, but there were several curious onlookers. He meandered past them. "Girls, why don't we go up to the apartment and see if we can save her." He handed the covered box to his youngest daughter and walked up the cocoa-colored step. "Don't run Bree. You'll have to be very gentle with her."

Brooke skipped up the steps. "But wouldn't it be better if we kept her outside, Daddy?"

"We will."

Bill slowly led the way up the three flights of stairs. Brooke stood behind her sister, looking over her shoulder at the box. There was no movement or sound from inside.

When Billy opened the door to the apartment, Brooke slipped passed Breezi and walked inside. She turned left through the door and glanced around the room. She noticed the flowers on the table and how perfect everything looked. "Does someone live here?"

"No. But I come by from to time. There is a service that keeps it clean and tidy. They do a really nice job."

"It's so little."

He smiled and rubbed the brick-faced wall. "It was always enough." Looking down at his two young children, he said, "Come on girls, follow me."

—

When he opened the back door at the other end of the hallway, both his daughters' jaws dropped open. There was a beautiful, lush green garden with huge clay pots and lots of sticks protruding from the soil. A wrought-iron bench sat in the center, and the sun shone brightly along one side.

Breezi took a seat on the ground and placed the box in a shady spot next to her. Brooke stared at her dad. "What is this place?"

He guided his daughter to the bench. They both sat down. "I come here sometimes to think. It's your Grandmom Gracie's garden. It looked pretty sad when I found it, so I thought I'd bring it back to life."

All three of them sat silently, studying their surroundings, lost in their own thoughts.

"Hey. You girls stay out here, I'll be right back. I am going to call your mom and let her know where we are. Breezi, make sure and leave the box covered and stay nice and quiet for a while. Little Blue Belle needs to heal. She'll need it to be nice and serene in case she hurt her head when she fell. Okay?"

Breezi shook her head. Her bottom lip was upturned, and she had a serious look upon her face. Brooke came down off the bench and sat next to her, Indian style. She looked at her dad, nodded and placed her arm around her sister.

Twenty minutes later he returned to find both girls looking into the box. Breezi was whispering, "Hello little Blue Belle. Hello, hello."

He was about to stop her but noticed the crest on top of the bird's head had flattened, and she was chirping, "Chick-a-dee. Chick-a-dee."

Brooke turned around, "I think she's going to be okay, Dad," she whispered. "Breezi's been talking to her."

The blue jay was standing, her wings were perfectly folded and she bobbed her head back and forth. She pecked at the bottom of the box and paced, looking up at the girls from time to time. "Chick-a-dee. Chick-a-dee."

Bill smiled and tiptoed toward the bench. He sat and watched his two girls gently lull the little bird.

"Hello. Hello. Hello Blue Belle," Breezi whispered in a singsong voice.

This continued for almost an hour when, all of a sudden, the bird's wings began to flutter. Breezi and Brooke stood up and stepped away from the box.

Bill walked over to the girls and stood between them. He kissed each one of them on top of their heads and placed his arms on their shoulders.

"We *can't* keep her, Daddy. She has to be free." Brooke explained.

Suddenly, the bird took flight, circling the garden. It sat upon the bench, above Bill's two carvings, and gawked at the three of them.

"Good-bye Blue Belle," Breezi said and waved.

The bird sang, "Hello. Hello. Hello Blue Belle." Then she flew away.

Both girls ran out of the elevator screaming for their mom. Ella appeared at the top of the second floor landing. "What is all the commotion, my angels?" she called down to them.

"We saved a blue jay!" Brooke yelled.

"She talked to us!" Breezi chimed in.

Bill stepped into the foyer with a huge smile, laughing and shaking his head. He walked past the girls and up the stairs with one arm behind his back.

"Good morning, my love," he said and kissed his wife gently on the cheek.

Ella wrinkled her nose and lifted her shoulders playfully. The girls both giggled.

"These are for you, my darling," he whispered, presenting a bunch of fresh spring flowers.

Ella reached out and touched his face. "But it's not *my* birthday." She teased, "It is someone else's, however." Looking down at her little girl, she pointed her finger toward the living room. Breezi's smile grew wide and her eyes sparkled. She turned and bolted down the hallway.

Bill and Ella walked down the steps arm-in-arm as joyous screams resonated through the main floor of the penthouse. Ella stopped a moment to place the flowers in a vase on the table in the entranceway. Meeting up with Bill in the doorway of the living room, she nestled into his arm as they both looked at the scene before them.

A huge easel, with a giant red bow, stood at the epicenter of a newly constructed eight-by-eight foot mini art studio. There were multiple sized blank canvasses, a full-set of acrylic paints, new brushes, and an artist's palette atop a removable, handcrafted washable floor pad that matched the contemporary Italian design of the room.

Breezi was skipping around waving a clean paintbrush in her hand. Brooke was standing in front of the easel, studying all the bits and pieces of the elaborate gift. "Cool."

Bill and Ella looked at each other—laughing. When Breezi settled down a bit, Bill announced, "Isn't it time we all got going? We have a roller coaster to ride!"

Decisions, Decisions

Peter and Grace had been living in the McMillon's guest wing for three months. Peter was finding it increasingly difficult living under the McMillon roof, but their one-bedroom brownstone was not big enough for Peter, Grace, a new baby, a nurse and a nanny. Peter was putting in extra hours at the planetarium attempting to save enough money for a larger apartment. Without Gracie's income at the Mc4, there was no way they could do it anytime soon, and Peter refused to ask his father-in-law for help.

He felt as if the McMillons had taken over their lives.

P.J. had hired a nurse that now lived upstairs in a spare bedroom. He'd also hired a full-time nanny and managed to spend more time upstairs with his daughter than at work or with his own wife. Meanwhile, Nana was busy wielding her networking magic. She was incessantly preoccupied with getting her newborn grandson on the waitlist at the most prestigious schools in Manhattan from pre-K through high school.

Grace had just been discharged from the hospital after her second surgery. Billy was inconsolable, unless he was in Grace's arms and every few hours Grace was being poked, prodded, and probed by the white-capped woman responsible for her recovery.

It seemed anytime Peter went near his wife he was pushed away by a nurse, a nanny, the baby or his father-in-law. He couldn't even get close to her at night. They'd been sleeping in separate beds so she could be more comfortable, and he feared hurting her if he lay next to her in the single hospital bed.

He did manage to have their beds moved closer together so he could at least hold her hand while she slept. Sometimes he'd simply pull a chair over and lay his head on the bed, beside her chest, so he could hear her breathing.

He'd begun using their apartment as a place of refuge. He'd sit in the overgrown garden and dream of how things were back in Hawaii—before Grace was sick, before the baby was born, before they were married.

Grace's mother wanted her to attend Barnard College in New York. Grace had chosen Dartmouth University in the remote hills of New Hampshire. However, on a Senior Class Trip to Hawaii, Grace fell in love with the incredible landscape, the culture and the people.

She came home and informed her parents she had enrolled at the University of Hawaii in Honolulu and would be taking part in some studies being conducted at a newly acquired marine lab on Coconut Island.

Her mother was furious. Her father was proud. He was glad she was pursuing a passion they shared, although it meant she'd be far away for a while.

In mid-August 1962, Grace kissed her mom good-bye and stepped into the penthouse elevator. She was 18-years-old and was finally able to make her own decisions, no longer under her parents' controlling wings.

Peter was a 20-year-old, dark- and curly-haired junior at the university. Majoring in physics with a passion for astronomy, he had spent most of his sophomore year helping with the construction of a new observatory at the summit of Haleakala on Maui.

They met at Freshman Orientation. Peter was immediately smitten and was thrilled when Grace joined the hiking club, of which he was the president.

He spent the next year chasing after her. He'd find any excuse to be in her presence. Grace didn't see it. She was friendly with everyone. She didn't think anything of it, when he'd show up unexpectedly at gatherings or drop by her dorm room several times a week.

When he finally found the nerve to ask her out, she answered, "Great, who else is coming?" clueless to his intentions.

He'd asked her to go on a hike with him, but when she showed up with her roommate Kristine, his head slumped as he packed their gear into his truck. At the very last minute Kristine announced she wasn't feeling well and winked at Peter. He mouthed *thanks Kris* and drove off the moment she shut the door.

It took a little more than two hours for Peter and Grace to hike to the first summit of the Olomana trail. Peter's hands were shaking the whole way. When they got to the top, he had Grace stand at the edge of the lookout to admire the scene below.

She had never seen anything so beautiful. They were thousands of feet above the vast green valley, minute buildings and boundless ocean below. Lost in thought, she had not realized Peter had walked away, leaving her there alone.

When he returned, he stood behind her and gently touched her on the shoulder. Pulling back her long blonde hair, he leaned in and whispered, "Isn't it magical up here?"

Slightly startled, Grace's knees buckled at the feel of his breath upon her neck. She was grateful for his light grip upon her shoulders.

"It's beautiful" she muttered.

He let go of one shoulder to gently clasp her hand. "Almost as beautiful as you."

Gracie became flushed. She turned and looked at him, smiled slightly and turned back away. Butterflies filled her belly, and her heart pounded in her chest.

He turned her around so she could meet his gaze. She was mesmerized. He leaned down to kiss her and then pulled her toward his chest.

Her whole body tingled. It felt the way she'd always dreamed her first kiss should be, and she did not want him to ever let go.

When they finally parted lips, Peter gently touched her cheek and whisked away a piece of blonde hair from her face. He bent down and whispered, "I love you, Gracie McMillon. And I promise to love you forever."

All of a sudden the actions he'd taken in the last year came flooding to the forefront of her mind. She'd been so silly to have not noticed before. She giggled, remembering how she always looked for him when she knew he was in town and how her stomach fluttered each time someone mentioned his name. She thought about how much he made her smile, laugh and how she missed him when he wasn't at a party or a gathering of mutual friends.

At that moment, she could not imagine life without him and whispered, "I love you, too."

"Come with me. I have something to show you." He clasped her hand and led her back toward the trail stopping at the old, indigenous Ohi'a tree. The yellow tentacle-like flowers were in full bloom. He pointed to the bottom of the mangled trunk where he'd just carved their initials bound with a heart

For the next three years, they were inseparable. The only time they weren't together was when Peter had to go to Maui or Grace to Coconut Island. They'd been introduced to each other's parents and had secretly moved in together after Peter graduated in the spring of 1964.

He was accepted into the graduate program and became a student teacher at the university, and Grace was given a paid position at the marine lab while she continued her studies.

They returned to Olomana often and spent many nights up at Mauna Kea where they could gaze upon the stars without the intrusion of the lights more than 9,000 feet below. Peter would point out the constellations and share the stories of how they were named.

Grace would lie in Peter's arms, listen attentively and stroke his chest or shoulder.

"There's an undiscovered star up there that belongs to you," he said. "Someday I am going to find it and name it Gracie's Heart."

*   *   *

When they decided to move to New York to help P.J. open the Mc4, after Gracie found out she was pregnant, she assured Peter he'd still have time to work on his thesis. But with the big wedding production compounded by unforeseen events, including Grace's illness, he never found the time.

Sitting outside the brownstone one bright, cool September morning, Peter excitedly awaited a delivery truck. He decided to set up a small office in the corner of the living room in order to work on his thesis.

Grace was going into the hospital in two days for her third surgery. Peter knew if he didn't have his office ready before then, he'd never do it. So, he disappeared before the baby awoke, took the subway to the design district and picked out a beautiful, handcrafted, classic mahogany desk with rich bronze handles on the drawers. He'd negotiated for the floor model so he could have it delivered the same day. He wanted to make the most of his day away from the penthouse.

He loved Grace, but in helping her live, he felt like he was dying. If he could just have a few hours a day or one full day per week for himself, then maybe this could work out.

Peter had struggled with the concept of being a father. He had sweet mid-western parents who loved one another yet never seemed to have any time for each other because they were always trying to make ends meet. Neither of his parents liked their jobs. Peter's father used to sit with him on the porch late at night, looking up at the stars. He'd tell his son about all the things he wished he'd done when he was young, and they'd both make up stories about what they saw in the sky.

Peter had decided very young he wanted a different kind of life. He wanted to make his mark on the world. He decided the best way to do that was by becoming an astronomer, in honor of his dad.

He'd always planned to have a family. He just thought it would be much later in life. When Grace told him she was pregnant, he was stunned but happy. He knew he loved her. If he was going to be a father at 24, he was glad it was with the woman he adored. When Billy was born, it didn't feel the way he'd anticipated. Maybe it was because he wasn't allowed in the room during the emergency c-section. It could have been because all the baby did was cry unless Grace was holding him, not to mention the fact that his 22-year-old wife was battling an extremely aggressive cancer or that his father-in-law undermined his every move.

Sitting on the bottom step of the apartment that he purchased using the remainder of his college fund (and a little extra help from his dad), Peter stared at the cracks in the pavement. The roots from the small maple tree pushed against its concrete obstruction, but the tree seemed to be winning the battle, breaking free from its barrier.

The sound of grinding gears broke Peter's concentration. He looked up. A small white truck turned down 85th Street and pulled up in front of him. "You Peter?" asked the driver.

It took almost forty minutes, but the two movers managed to get the desk up the stairs and into the apartment. Peter handed them a nice tip and shut the door. It was early fall. He figured if he worked hard enough, he could have the thesis finished by the end of the year. About three hours into to it, he decided to take a break in the garden.

The garden had become a jungle of weeds in the five months they'd been at the penthouse. Grace had always been the gardener. Peter the cook. He suddenly stood up and began vehemently pulling out weeds. The sun beat down with increased intensity and the breeze became still. It didn't take long before Peter's shirt was soaked with sweat and his body reeked from the natural fertilizer.

By the time he stopped, the ground was covered with piles of pulled earth, brown stringy roots and green leaves. The sun had set hours before and the air had grown cold. He cleaned up all the remnants from his work and swept the dirt away.

He ran inside and rummaged through the bedroom bureau. "Aha." It had taken a few minutes, but he found his camera and two unused flashbulbs. When he was done taking the pictures, he opened the metal door to the hallway, turned around and whispered, "I love you, Gracie," and raced out the door to see her.

Tip-toeing out of the bedroom, Peter decided to take the service stairs rather than the front staircase and elevator. It was still pitch-black (or as dark as Manhattan ever gets) when he walked past the doorman and stepped outside.

It seemed the winter had come so quickly. There had been a record-breaking snowfall the day before. It was bitter cold and the wind howled through the streets. Peter lowered his head, lifted the wool flap of his brown bomber jacket, and shoved his hands in the pockets of his blue jeans. Lost in thought, he headed for the park.

Grace's prognosis was looking good. The doctors were hopeful she'd remain in remission and finally her hair had begun to grow back, although slightly darker than it had been before. She'd finally begun to put on some weight, even though she was chasing after an energetic eight-month-old who had every intention of walking soon. She was ready to return to work at the Mc4. P.J. had one of the offices remodeled into a playroom and a nanny available around the clock.

Peter thought about all the discussions they'd been having the past two months. Grace said she understood. It had been a very difficult year for them.

He knew she'd be all right and their son would be cared for. He loved them both very much. But he saw no end to the stronghold the McMillons seemed to have on them. He begged her forgiveness. It was time for him to follow his own dreams.

He'd already been offered a grant and had been accepted to the Institute of Astronomy back in Hawaii. He'd be studying a newly discovered nebulous star system. As it turned out, his position at the planetarium was the pivotal credential in securing a paid internship with the designers of the new Mees Solar Observatory on Kaleala. "Thanks, *Doctah* P.J." he called out in a condescending tone.

Trekking through Central Park, he could barely feel his extremities by the time he made it to the brownstone, almost an hour later.

He walked over to the fireplace, pulled off his wet shoes and socks and laid them on the brick hearth. His feet were red, almost purple.

He sat down at his desk. His thesis lay on the corner of the floor behind him, covered in dust. Pulling out a piece of lined paper, he began to write. When he was done, he folded the paper neatly and placed it in a large manila envelope. Opening the top drawer to the desk, he pulled out a stack of legal documents, placed them inside the envelope and addressed it. He then leaned the envelope against the small lamp in the corner of the desk and pulled out a fresh sheet of paper.

His hands trembled as he wrote. There were no words for what he was feeling. He crumpled the paper and tossed it in the nearby wicker basket.

Standing up, he scanned the room, but could not move. He slammed both hands on the desktop. Eyes shut, chin quivering, his shoulders shook as a stream of tears fell upon the desk. Breathing rapidly, he tried to calm himself, but couldn't.

He told himself he was making the right decision. He had to leave. He had to *live*. He wiped his nose with his sleeve and released the air from his lungs, before drying his eyes with both palms. He inhaled deeply and let it out.

He shook his head up and down, took another deep breath and stood erect. He fiddled with the letter's placement, then turned around and walked toward the fireplace. Putting his shoes back on, he closed his coat but left the two center buttons open. He then walked back over to the desk, bent down and grabbed the pile of papers from the floor. He shoved the unfinished thesis through the opening in his coat and pressed his left arm against his chest.

A minute later, he was out the door and down the stairs, stomping along the sidewalk in the opposite direction of the footprints in the fallen snow.

Correct and Continue

As the plane flew over Jost Van Dyke, P.J. peered out the window and squinted. He could barely make out *Amazing Grace* in the tiny cove. But, it was there. He knew he'd left Billy in capable hands with Danny. And he knew his friend would ultimately understand.

It was almost midnight when P.J. finally arrived at JFK airport without a plan. He didn't tell Nana he was coming. Instead, he went straight to the Mc4 and slept in his office. The following morning he went into Grace's old office, and began rummaging through her files.

The last time he'd been in the room was they day of his daughter's funeral. He remembered shutting all the shades before he locked the door behind him. He'd given one of the student teachers the task of looking after the one dolphin that remained from the BMD tragedy. He swore he'd never step foot into the pool area again. There were just too many memories.

Thinking back, he could not believe he'd missed the connection all this time. Rifling through some paperwork, P.J. quickly became frustrated when he couldn't find what he was looking for. He walked over to the window and pulled on the cord to open the shades. Across the hall was the quarantine pool.

For several minutes, he simply stared. Finally, he reached down and turned the knob to the office door. He walked across the hall and opened the door to the quarantine pool area. Inside there was gentle music playing over the speaker system, but the room was empty, except for the beautiful bottlenose dolphin lying along the pool's floor. A slight smile appeared on P.J.'s face as he remembered Gracie telling him how much the dolphin loved listening to music.

P.J. walked over to the ladder and climbed the steps to the platform. Sitting down, he dangled his feet in the water. "I am here, sweet Dee. I am finally here," he said to the still, gray form at the bottom of the pool. "I am sorry it took so long." His voice cracked. Tapping his right hand on the water he said, "Please, come talk to me."

*   *   *

Danny was going stir-crazy. He'd been sitting at anchor on *Amazing Grace*, taking care of Billy, for three days. P.J. had run off in such a hurry, there had been no time for Danny to make any arrangements. He missed his wife and his bar. He picked up the radio and called The Dive. Marta answered immediately. She missed him, too.

"No," Danny told her, "I haven't heard from him. But just because I promised I'd stay here and watch Billy and the two dolphins doesn't mean I can't have you with me," he paused, "can you come on over and keep me company?"

It was summer so the bar and restaurant were pretty slow. Marta knew her husband didn't like being far away from her for very long, so she decided to ask her two younger brothers if they would take care of things at The Dive for a while. She then loaded up the Whaler with supplies and headed over to Georgey Hole.

For the next three weeks, Marta made lunch and dinner every day. Danny was in charge of breakfast. He'd make coffee in the morning and bring it to

Marta in bed. Then they'd all enjoy a feast before the familiar knock on the hull. Danny would clean up while Marta watched Billy. Once he was done, he'd join her in the cockpit where they enjoyed the opportunity to spend quality time together.

They'd watch Billy swim and play with Phinny and Dolila and listen while Billy shared stories of the day's events over dinner. Then they'd all help clean up before settling in for the night. It was the first time in Danny's adult life that he managed to get to bed before midnight on a consistent basis.

Danny, Marta and Billy were sitting at the saloon table playing cards when Mishimo jumped from a nearby shelf and ran up the stairwell. A few seconds later the hatch opened, and they all turned around to find Papa climbing down the steps.

Billy squealed, "You're back!" And flew out of his seat and into his grandfather's arms.

Marta made eye contact, smiled, and nodded her head. Danny remained silent.

Marta walked over to the young boy, put her hand on his shoulders. "Billy, why don't you and I head off to your cabin?"

"But, I don't want to go," he whispered, "I want to tell Papa about everything he missed."

"There will plenty of time, my young man," Papa interrupted, "You go with Marta and I promise we'll catch up in the morning." P.J. walked over and patted Billy on the head. "It's time for me to talk to Danny for a while."

Marta guided Billy toward his room. "You can read to me," she suggested.

The little boy nodded his head and walked inside his cabin.

Meanwhile, P.J. sat down adjacent to his friend. "I know I just up-and-left, but I have a really, really good reason. It's exciting actually."

He went on to tell Danny how he'd gone to New York to confirm some things he'd read in Grace's journals.

"Does it have to do with Phinny, the trench and the dolphins from the . . . what did you call it?" He made a jester with his hands indicating quotation marks. "The Toy Box."

P.J. looked at him. "Well yeah. How did you know?"

"You gave me a stack of books to read while you were gone. Remember? And you were gone so long, I got to read them more than once." Danny's voice became more agitated as he continued, "In fact, I started taking notes trying to figure out *why* you would abandon your own grandson. I mean really, P.J., three weeks!"

"I know. I know. But I knew he was in good hands. I knew he was safe."

Danny rolled his eyes and swung his head back and forth wildly. He stood up. "Are you kidding me? You are that selfish that not only do you leave your own grandson, but you don't even consider how it might affect Marta and me. Come on, P.J.!"

P.J. rubbed the top of his head with both hands. "But it was for my research, to fix things somehow." He closed his eyes and rubbed his temples. He lowered his head and remained silent for while. When he finally spoke, the only words he could come up with were, "I am sorry."

They talked for a few hours. P.J. explained that things in New York took a lot longer than he expected, but that everyone would understand very soon. He was aloof and evasive when Danny pressed him for more concrete information. "I want it to be a surprise," P.J. said. P.J. explained how he still had some big things he needed to do in order to prepare Billy, Phinny and Dolila for what was to come, and that he was finally going to confess that he was at the trench and witnessed what happened to Phinny and his family.

"I've been incredibly busy trying to get back here," he told Danny, "it's quite exciting actually." P.J. leaned over and patted Danny on the shoulder, "Thanks so much for taking care of Billy for me. I really appreciate it."

By the time P.J. finished talking, Danny wasn't mad anymore. He decided to let it go. "Okay. I guess I can't really complain. Things weren't all that bad." He leaned back in his chair. " I got to lie around on a beautiful boat for three weeks at a gorgeous remote anchorage, hanging out with one of the coolest eight-year-olds on the planet and smooching with my wife, while my friend was on a personal mission to save the darn world or at least the whole marine world!" Danny winked. He looked at P.J. "All I ask is that next time you just let me know approximately how long you'll be needing me to watch over things for you. Okay?"

"Got it," P.J. nodded, "I understand. Thanks Danny."

The following morning P.J. was sitting in his routine spot drinking coffee when his grandson came up top. The little boy was smiling and bobbing his head back and forth as he danced around the cockpit.

"What are you doing, young man?"

Billy hopped onto the settee and looked up at his grandfather. "I am just happy you're back home."

P.J. liked the sound of that. He leaned over and grabbed Billy and pulled him closer to him. "Me, too."

Marta and Danny left shortly after breakfast. A few minutes later there was a familiar knock on the hull. P.J. followed Billy out to the aft deck and onto the swim platform. When Billy went to put on his snorkel gear, Papa stopped him.

"Do you think I could speak with you, Phinny and Dolila this morning?"

Billy turned around, surprised by the formality of the request. "Do you want to examine Phinny?"

"Nope. I just want to talk to you guys. But I realize I may not understand any of their responses. Do you mind translating for me?"

"Translating? Hmmm." He liked the sound of that. "Sure."

A few minutes later, both dolphins were standing erect and clicking away.

P.J. asked all three of them to hear him out before they made any judgment on what P.J. had to say. He warned that there may be parts that might make them really angry or that they may not necessarily understand.

Once they all agreed P.J. began his story. He explained how he left New York with Billy in hopes of finding the young male dolphin he had met at the trench three years ago. He further explained how he thought it might be very difficult at first. But then Billy met Phinny after the race. P.J. immediately suspected Phinny was the dolphin from the trench, but was afraid to get to close to him for fear he'd pre-maturely recognize P.J. and would not allow P.J. to help him.

P.J. interrupted his explanation and looked over at his grandson. "I didn't know how to tell you and then I didn't want to tell you. I was afraid it might affect your growing friendship with Phinny."

It wasn't until they were in Anegada that P.J. could confirm Phinny was, in fact, the dolphin he'd been searching for. He'd noticed Phinny's birthmark at the crease of his neck. It not only confirmed who Phinny was, but also confirmed that Phinny was related to someone else P.J. knew.

"What?" Billy interrupted.

"Let me explain," he said to his grandson and went back to his story.

P.J. had been so pre-occupied with getting legislation passed, he neglected to do the most important things – listen and take care of his severely ill daughter.

P.J. would take the train to and from Washington every day. He raced from the train station to his daughter's apartment where he usually played with Billy a while, made (or ordered) dinner and then sat with Grace. They'd begin their conversations with talk of Billy, school and treatment, but it always tended to veer off quickly into how things were going in Washington. P.J. would babble on until his daughter's eyelids grew heavy. Thinking back on it, they rarely ever talked about what happened at the Mc4 or how the remaining two dolphins were doing.

Grace had been fine *not* talking about her illness. If she was having a bad day, she figured talking about it would only make it worse. And she didn't want to worry her father anymore than he already was. The only two people that actually understood how gravely ill she was were her driver and Billy.

There was no way for Grace to hide her illness from her son. Her skin was pasty white before she applied her morning make-up, and clumps of hair sat atop her pillow each morning. Her garden bench would become covered in long blonde strands as well. The retching sounds emanating from the bathroom at night were also a give-away that her illness was consuming her.

Grace did not want anyone to see how weak she had become. Her driver became her confidant. She'd have him bring the Town Car around so she could sit (or sleep) for a while without being disturbed. She'd have him chaperone her wherever she needed to go. He was on-call 24 hours a day.

"It should have been me taking care of her," Papa said.

P.J. hadn't only been absent for Grace's illness but also for the events at the Mc4. Grace didn't tell him (or quite possibly he wasn't listening when she did) that one of the female dolphins that remained was actually the female from the trench. As it turned out, she'd been shot with a tranquilizer gun. The captain had called for the rescue team to come get the dolphin and safely transport her back to the quarantine at The Toy Box.

All the records from The Toy Box were sent to the Mc4, and Grace was placed in charge of the dolphins' healthy transition back into the wild. All the dolphins were badly traumatized. But four of the six dolphins flourished and were successfully released within a few months. There had been no mass fanfare, but the story was written up in several journals and was on the national news as a *tragedy-to-triumph* piece.

By that time, things in Washington were in full swing. They'd used the news coverage for leverage to help move the new bill being proposed in congress. P.J. was traveling back and forth from Washington daily and Grace was on her second round of chemotherapy.

She'd come to the pool even on her treatment days. Sometimes Grace could only handle an hour at the pool before she had to rest. She did not have much strength by then. Her driver would help her up the ladder to the feeding platform and stay by her side while she coaxed the despondent dolphin to eat and exercise.

By the time the new Marine Mammal Protection Act was passed, Grace had been declared in remission again and was strong enough to come back to work full-time.

P.J. had become somewhat of a celebrity, and Nana decided to use it to the Mc4's advantage. P.J. announced a new division at the Mc4 geared toward high school students. They kept it very small but elite. It focused on students interested in pursuing a career in Marine Biology or Marine Mammal Studies.

For the next year, Grace struggled to keep the forlorn dolphin alive. The dolphin had slipped so far into a depression she would no longer use her innate echolocation abilities to find food. She relied completely on Grace to take care of her. The other dolphin was doing beautifully, and Grace was afraid if she kept her much longer, it would be detrimental to the dolphin's progress in the wild. She made the hard decision to set her free, leaving Dee alone.

Then in the summer of 1973, Gracie got sick again. They were out on the island and she didn't feel well. She decided to lay down for a while and didn't get up for three days. P.J. forced her to see a doctor, and Grace came back telling her father she was diagnosed with a bad case of the flu and would have to take it easy for a while.

She had lied. Her body was riddled with cancer. It had spread to the lungs, bones and liver. Her physician's best-case scenario was a year with treatment and three to six months without. Grace chose the latter but cited doctor confidentiality. She did not want her family to know.

She spent every day at the Mc4 working with Dee. She'd lean on the pool and talk to her. Finally she begged, "I am dying, and I want to be able to help you before I go. Tell me what you need from me. Tell me how to help you live."

But the dolphin never answered back.

Time was running out for Grace. Her body, once again, began to fail her. When she became so weak she didn't think she could come into the Mc4, it was time to tell her father the truth. Over his tears, she made him promise he would search for the dolphin's young one.

P.J. thought it was a virtually impossible task. But his daughter believed otherwise.

They were sitting by the edge of the pool. P.J. had to help Grace into the chair. She was now using a cane to stand and her breathing was always labored. "If she is traumatized, he is too." She paused. "You must find a way. Otherwise he dies because of the blackness and she dies from immense sorrow. She has given up. We need to give her a reason to live." Grace lifted her father's hand in hers and kissed it. "Daddy, she saved *me* and my son once. It's our time to save them. Promise me, daddy. Promise me you will find her young one."

"I promise."

P.J. kept looking at his watch during his explanation. "I am sure you all have plenty of questions, but I know they will all be answered soon," P.J. assured them. He would mumble every once in a while, "4.5 days at 7—10 knots . . ." then he'd drift off in silent thought and fidget with his watch again.

Phinny did not run away. Dolila was in shock and Billy's brain was filled with questions. "I am sorry I was unable to fix this sooner. I hope some day you will forgive me," P.J. said, lowering his head. "Come on girl," he said looking at his watch again.

They all looked up as they heard the clicking sounds coming toward them. Phinny and Dolila spun around in the water, and P.J. and Billy stood up and peered around the boat.

A beautiful, perfectly healthy, shiny gray adult female dolphin came charging toward them and leaped into the air. Phinny and Dolila circled her, nudged her with their snouts and ran their pectoral fins down her back.

Billy and his grandfather both cheered as the three dolphins flew out of the water and did flips in unison. Phinny was in the center. All three of them had the same small birthmark on the crease of their necks.

They danced around the water for almost an hour when Phinny swam up to the swim platform. "I am going to show my mother the cave," he said, looking at Billy. "It will be a good place for her to rest. She has come a long way to get back to us," Phinny announced proudly.

As the three dolphin headed out of the cove, the adult female turned back and called out, "Thank you," before racing her two young ones past the point. They all jumped in the air one last time before diving deep below the underground boulders.

"Wow, Papa! Did you see that?" Billy exclaimed. He tugged at his grandfather's arm. "Did you see that? Did you see that!"

Phinny's blackened back and dorsal fin had suddenly turned soft white.

P.J. nodded slowly, his mouth upturned and he looked to the sky. "I saw it," he whispered.

—

Always Do Your Best

Bang, slap, crash, stomp, stomp, stomp. SLAM!

Bill could hear the commotion from his study at the opposite end of the long hallway. He dropped his pen on the desk, shut off the lamp and looked out his door curiously. Schoolbooks were scattered across the penthouse entryway, along with several bits of paper littered with red ink marks across the top and down sides. A small envelope was stapled to it. Bill picked it up, read the letter and gazed up at the top of the landing.

Upstairs, he knocked gently at Brooke's door. She was lying face down on the bed. Muffled sniffles rose from the pillows.

Brooke was in the 7th grade now and had been taking advanced courses for more than two years. An overachiever like her dad, Brooke didn't like doing poorly at anything, especially something as simple as schoolwork She had just received her first failing grade. "Are you okay, sweetie?"

Startled, Brooke turned around and stared at her dad. She stood up and paced the room, explaining what happened on her science test.

When she was done, he patted the bedspread.

Her tears fell steadily as she nestled her head into his arm.

Releasing her from his embrace, he held both her hands and asked, "Was it your best effort with the tools and knowledge you possessed at that moment?"

She sniffled. "Yes. But, I could have done better. I was absent and didn't . . ." She shook her head. "It wasn't an A."

"Did you get the work from your classmate?"

She nodded.

"Okay then. Did you give it your A?"

She looked at him, confused.

"Have you ever taken a test that you knew you were going to ace, so you didn't worry about studying, went in, took it, got an A and shrugged your shoulders thinking it was no big deal?"

"Yeah."

"So in that situation, do you think it was your *best effort* or did you just get lucky?"

Her eyes looked away as she pondered the question.

"My point is; it's not always about the grade. It's about the effort. You *know* when you've given something an A effort." He held up the folded 3-page test. "If this grade reflects an honest A effort, then so be it."

Brooke shook her arms in the air. "But Katie didn't tell me we were having a test today!"

"Brooke, if it was sincerely your best effort with the information you had at that moment, there is no need for excuses or explanations." He placed his hands on her shoulders. "You are an excellent student. I am tremendously proud of you."

He gently wiped the tears from her face. He could not believe how fast she was growing up. It ached a bit. He wanted her to remain his little girl forever.

She slumped her head on his shoulder. "Daddy, can you tell me a story."

He smiled broadly at the sound of his favorite words in the world.

"You've been listening to my stories for a long time now. You're not bored yet?"

"No way Daddy, I love your stories."

(Chasing) False Echoes

P.J. and Billy spent the following eight months chasing after Phinny, Dolila and Dolly making sure they were healing, healthy and happy.

Dolila had begun spending more time away from her brother and mother. She preferred spending her time at Georgey Hole with Angelica or naively flirting with the adolescent male dolphins that had found where she was hiding. She'd managed to fend them off so far, but an increasing number of them had begun vying for her attention.

Nana had flown down around Thanksgiving 1974 and spent all of her time questioning Billy about whether he really wanted to stay in the BVI for the spring academic year. She'd recognized her husband's handwriting on the homework she'd been sporadically receiving and wanted to ensure her grandson was keeping up with his grade level. She even gave him a formal test provided by the New York State Association of Independent Schools. Upon matching the answer key with Billy's test papers, she could no longer argue he didn't know the work. Billy managed to miss only three questions on the 12-page comprehensive exam.

She still disagreed with the idea that a young boy with such talent and intelligence should be surrounded by so many grownups in an environment that she didn't feel offered enough culture and diversity. Finally, on the last day, she broke down and admitted that she simply missed them both terribly.

Nana and P.J. sat across from one another at the dining table in the saloon.

"I am almost done here," P.J. told her. "Why don't you just stay with us?"

Five days in the sweltering heat onboard a 60-foot sailboat in the middle of a remote cove with only the simplest of amenities was already too long for Nana.

"I know this is important to you, Patrick. But aren't I important to you anymore?"

They'd been together almost 36 years. He'd always traveled extensively. It wasn't until the Mc4 opened that P.J. began settling down. Nana had gotten used to having him home the past eight years. She missed having him close by, even if P.J. was pre-occupied with his research, his daughter and most recently, Billy. She was lonely living in the penthouse alone.

"Ah, you know what the city does to me," he complained.

"Well. I was thinking we could spend more time on the island. You and Billy could play on the farm and I have plenty of things to keep me busy out there. I was thinking of opening a showroom."

Another one of Nana's notable pastimes was attending enumerable Sotheby's auctions each year. She was always searching for additions to her vast art and antique furniture collection. After graduating from Barnard College in 1936, with a degree in Art History, Nana went to work for the distinguished Parke-Bernett auction house.

In the spring of 1942, Nana was asked to represent Parke-Bernett during an exclusive auction in the model room at the renowned New York Yacht Club. She met Patrick James McMillon, otherwise known as P.J., after he successfully bid on an intricately detailed replica of the sailing yacht—*Vigilant*.

They talked for a few hours afterward and he'd asked her to dinner, but apologized for not knowing where to take her. He was in the city on business and the only restaurant he knew was his hotel's room service.

Nana offered to be his tour guide through Manhattan and pulled strings for center seats for the revival of the comedy opera *Pirates of Penzance,* which had recently opened at the St. James theatre.

While sitting at a quiet lounge after the performance, P.J. asked, "Do you believe in love?"

"I think so. I know I believe in commitment."

"I travel a lot you know. My work has always been my life."

She nodded, "I know what you mean. I am pretty independent myself."

Six months later they were married. Grace came along soon after.

*   *   *

P.J. leaned across the table and took his wife's hand. "I promise I'll be finished soon. The purpose for this expedition is almost complete." He changed the subject, "Besides, Billy is thriving here. He loves it."

He explained how their grandson had been learning a lot from Danny's crew. They were looking forward to celebrating the New Year at The Dive and were gearing up for the 1975 spring racing circuit. Billy had been practicing with the boys every weekend and Spidy was training Billy to take his place helping the bowman, Scat. They'd been consistently winning little local regattas and were feeling pretty good about themselves.

Nana was unimpressed.

Three days after their talk, Nana left the BVI. Billy joined her on the lengthy ride up the channel aboard Danny's boat. Luckily, it was a beautiful, clear day and the seas had cooperated. Even Nana seemed to enjoy it. She sat with Billy on the bow as he pointed out *all* the little coves on the north side of the main island of Tortola. As they passed a much smaller island on their left, Billy highlighted the protruding rock formation in the shape of a giant iguana, explaining how Guana Island had been named. Billy then asked Nana to help him point out the shallow areas of coral reef so Danny could make it safely through the cut near Trellis Bay.

"I love you, Nana," Billy said with a cheerful lilt. "I'll be good and do my homework. I promise!"

She kissed him goodbye and stepped onto the rickety dock. Billy waited in the boat with Danny while Papa walked Nana over to the tiny, remote airstrip where a four-seater commuter plane was sitting on the tarmac, refueling.

P.J. fidgeted. "How long is your wait in Puerto Rico?" he asked.

Nana shrugged her shoulders. "Just a few hours."

A local woman came over and told Nana it was time to board. P.J. offered, "I'll wait here to make sure you take off okay." He paused. "Don't worry about Billy. He's going to be fine." P.J. kissed his wife on the cheek. "I am *glad* you finally came." He leaned in and gave her a quick hug. "Good-bye, dear. Have a safe trip home."

Nana nodded, looked down and turned away. She climbed into the plane without looking back.

The next few months Billy studied hard. He'd aok his granddad for help with words he didn't understand. By late March, Billy had read every one of his grandfather's books on sailing. He'd monitored Scat and Spidy's movements closely and always had plenty of questions for them after a race.

Billy was fascinated with hull design and construction and the mechanics of the rigging and sails. But he had a passion for standing behind the helm. So he'd pick Danny's brain with *why this* and *why that*. He'd even asked Phinny to explain how the dolphin used the angle and shape of his body to ride a wave, to steer or pick up speed while swimming through the water.

One day, after Phinny complained about losing another race to his sister, Billy offered to coach him. "I think I know how you can beat her," the young boy said. "I've been watching how your sister swims and it's different than you."

For months Billy put Phinny through drills, rode on his back and gave him advice on how to subtly change his movements in the water. They'd practice secretly in another bay around the corner from Georgey Hole or sometimes they'd go to the cave to dive and talk about strategy.

Eventually, Phinny challenged his sister to a race. She just laughed at him. "Phinny you can't beat me. You know I am faster than you. I am faster. You're bigger. Remember?"

"Not anymore. I *know* I can beat you."

Dolila had been so pre-occupied hanging around the reef with Angelica and discouraging her entourage of new suitors; she hadn't noticed what Phinny was up to with Billy.

"Okay, fine. I'll race you."

"Mom's going to be the judge. Billy and Angelica can be the committee."

"Judge."

"Yeah. So things are fair."

She looked at her brother with a quizzical expression.

"That's how they do it in sailing," Phinny informed her. "There's always a committee to make sure the racers are following the rules."

"Rules?"

"Yeah. To make sure you don't cheat."

"Okay, Phinny. Whatever you say. I am ready when you are."

The two dolphins engaged in three races of varying lengths with multiple obstacles. Whoever won at least two out of three races would be declared the winner. Each dolphin got to choose a race route. Dolly and Angelica designed the components of the third race. But Billy refrained from giving his opinion because he felt it would give Phinny an unfair advantage.

Dolly acted as a marker for the start of each race. Each race began with her sounding three long clicks, before the two dolphins took off! P.J. and Billy were in the dinghy at the end, acting as the finish line.

Beneath the surface, Angelica put together a team to ensure the dolphins followed the designated route. By the time the third race rolled around, there were quite a few spectators, both below and above the water.

Phinny won all three races. Billy was ecstatic. Papa was amused. Dolly was proud. And Dolila was wildly angry. It took several days for Phinny to calm his sister down. Eventually, she listened to his explanation of having been practicing with Billy. She ultimately accepted defeat and refused to ever race her brother again.

Meanwhile, Billy and the rest of the *Silver Bullet* crew were equally elated at their stellar performance in the 1975 racing circuit. They'd managed to beat their biggest competitor, Peter Haycraft, on board *Pipe Dream* in both the Rolex Regatta off St. Thomas in the U.S. Virgin Islands, and down Sir Francis Drake Channel at the BVI Spring Regatta.

For their final race, P.J. and Billy sailed *Amazing Grace* 150 miles to Antigua so the boys could have a comfortable place to sleep during the island's infamous Race Week. By the end of the last day, the crew of *Silver Bullet* was celebrating their third trophy of the circuit. It was their biggest win of the year and they'd managed to achieve an unprecedented clean sweep in their division.

Phinny left his sister and mother behind to join his best friend in Antigua. After *Silver Bullet* crossed the finish line, the dolphin leaped into the air for a

10-minute performance filled with twists, turns and flips, reaching 15-20 feet high.

Big John had taken over as Captain for the race in Antigua because Danny didn't want to be far from Marta's side. She'd gone into labor with their first child the day *Amazing Grace* left. Danny managed to reach P.J. on the single-sideband radio two days later to let him know Marta had given birth, at home, to a beautiful baby girl named Grayata Patricia Waters.

P.J. could hear the panic in Danny's voice during their last radio transmission. He was trying to juggle being with his wife and new baby and manage The Dive. Danny had always relied so heavily on his wife's help, even at nine months pregnant. She was much more organized than Danny and without her The Dive was suffering.

P.J. had offered to stop in Roadtown on the mainland of Tortola on his way into the BVI. After clearing-in with Customs and Immigration, he'd pick up supplies for The Dive and do some larger shopping at the big general store.

The boys had other plans. They were having so much fun they decided to stay a few extra days in Antigua. P.J. couldn't imagine any of them had managed more than a few hours sleep the entire week and he doubted they'd spent any of that time sober.

In order to have enough room for the five of them to sail back aboard *Silver Bullet,* they put all the extra sails and most of their personal gear onto *Amazing Grace*. Scat, Spidy, Bubba and Big John promised they'd head back to Jost Van Dyke in just a few days. Big John shouted, "Tell Danny not to worry. I promise to get his boat *and* the boys back safely!" as he watched *Amazing Grace* pull away from the historic remains of the old 17th century British Royal Navy shipyard known as Nelson's Dockyard.

The first six or seven hours of their journey Billy chattered away, recalling every little detail about the race. "Did you see Spidy and me change out that last sail? We did that in *seconds*! I think it was a world record, Papa. I am telling you, it was *fast*!" He barely took a breath between subjects. "And wasn't it cool to watch Phinny at the end. It was cool. I was listening to everybody screaming and egging him on. I think that's why he kept going. I think he likes the attention." The boy stood up and looked over the starboard lifelines. "I wonder where he is now. He said he was going to go ahead, so he could get back to his mom. But, I thought he might change his mind." Billy walked briskly back to his seat. "Maybe we'll see him tomorrow."

P.J. estimated their trip would take a little more than 24 hours. They had pulled away from the dock at eight a.m. on Friday. He was hoping to be at the cut between Norman and Peter Island somewhere around daybreak the following morning. Nothing was open on Sundays so this would be there best chance to get things from the market or general store.

He had Billy on two watches: four to eight p.m. the first day and four to eight a.m. the following morning. He figured he'd let his grandson maneuver between the two islands and see what it was like to sail with unseasoned traffic on the water. He was looking forward to giving Billy the chance to utilize his skills behind the helm.

P.J. had been looking forward to the peace and tranquility of a beautiful night sky out at sea. Instead, he was listening to his grandson point out star formations and telling stories of astronomy.

"I've been reading your celestial navigation books. It's amazing how you can never get lost if you know where you are in the sky," Billy said.

"Triangulation is not that easy my young man," P.J. chuckled. "It's pretty complex stuff."

"I hope you don't mind, Papa. I played around with your sextant on the trip down to Antigua. I was very careful with it and when I was done, I put it back in its case."

P.J. shook his head, astonished. Most boys Billy's age were thinking about G.I. Joe and army men while his grandson was fiddling around with intricate navigational instruments. "Nope. I don't mind." He smiled. "Are you ever planning to get some sleep, my dear boy? You are on watch in a few hours."

Billy finally headed to bed around 10:30 p.m. Mishimo was already down in their cabin. She hadn't come up all day.

Finally alone, P.J. let out a huge sigh. He'd been racing with the boys on *Silver Bullet* for almost two months and he was tired. They had managed to surpass any of Danny's dreams for a successful racing crew. P.J. was looking forward to handing the final trophy of the season over to his friends in exchange for holding their new baby girl.

P.J. thought about all that had happened since arriving in the islands a little more than 10 months ago. He was amazed at how grown-up his grandson had become and all they'd accomplished since being here. It warmed his heart thinking about Phinny and Dolila's reunion with their mom. His understanding of Blackened Dolphin Syndrome had come full circle and he was so grateful for being able to help Phinny overcome the disease. But, at that moment, P.J. was most amazed at the fact that his diehard, renegade best friend had just become a daddy.

"Hmmm. Grayata Patricia Waters," he said looking up at the twinkling midnight sky. "It's a great name."

P.J. enjoyed the quiet solitude for the next few hours of his watch. Shortly after three a.m., however, he began to feel increasingly fatigued. He could barely keep his eyes open. Even singing his favorite Bing Crosby song wasn't helping. His eyes became heavy and his head started to bob as he began losing his battle with exhaustion. "Wake up, P.J. Wake up," he said, smacking himself in the face. He shook his head rigorously from side to side. "Stay awake old man. Stay awake!"

When the hatch opened up and he saw his grandson's silhouette climbing out of the stairwell, P.J. had a sudden burst of energy. "It's good to see you, Lucky Charm."

Groggily Billy looked up. There was this huge twinkling light in the sky above his grandfather's head. He stood there a moment staring at it through his half-opened eyelids. It was beautiful and stunted all the other stars surrounding it. Billy walked over and sat next to his grandfather. He was about to tell him about the star, but P.J. began to speak.

"It's been very quiet. Very, very quiet. I haven't seen another boat or heard anybody on the radio since you went to sleep. It seems we are out here all alone," he said. He gazed upon the dark horizon to his left then right. "But, that will change soon. We are getting very close now. Almost there."

"Why don't you go down to bed, Papa? I can man the helm alone." Billy stood up. "I can call you when we get closer to the islands."

P.J. considered it for a second. He was worn out and yearned to sleep in his comfortable bed down below, but he'd taken enough chances with his grandson over the past 10 months. He'd be fine on the settee.

Running down to the saloon, P.J. came back up with a crocheted green blanket Marta had given him for Christmas. He laid down next to Billy and covered himself up. P.J. immediately felt his muscles release all their tension. Within minutes his breathing slowed and his mind quieted completely. "I love you, Billy," he murmured before drifting off to sleep.

"I love you too, Papa."

Billy walked over and shut the top hatch. He'd left it open when he came up and the lights from down below were affecting his ability to see out past the bow. He turned around and saw Papa had shifted his body on the settee. The blanket had fallen to the floor. *I wish he'd listened and gone downstairs so he'd be more comfortable*, Billy thought as he picked up the blanket and wrapped it around his papa, tucking him in.

Behind the boat, the night sky sparkled. The same huge, vivid star shone brightly. Billy couldn't believe how intense it was. He remembered a lullaby his mother and he used to sing in the garden. They'd sit out there and pretend they could see past the reflective barrier caused by the city below. They'd imagine how it looked far beyond the Milky Way and then they'd sing.

"Starlight, star bright," Billy robustly chimed. He fixed his eyes on the brilliant luminescence behind the boat, "first star I see tonight. Wish I may, wish I might, have the wish I wish tonight." Billy closed his eyes and held his hands to his chest and whispered, "I wish I could live in the islands forever."

A shooting star streamed across the night sky as the sound of Billy's voice lulled his grandfather back to sleep.

P.J. serenely slipped into a dream.

> *He was at the helm on a beautiful, bright sunny day. The spinnaker was flying. A depiction of three dolphins jumping in opposite directions, one beneath the other, was embroidered in the huge piece of thin white fabric. Both dolphins had beautiful gray backs and brilliant white underbellies, each with a birthmark at the crease of their neck.*
>
> *As the sail flailed, it looked as if the dolphins were in motion.*
>
> *P.J. felt a gentle hand press against his back. "Hello, daddy."*
>
> *He knew who it was before she'd said anything. He turned to look at her, but she was gone. He swung his head in the opposite direction then spun around all together. She wasn't there.*
>
> *"Over here." He heard his daughter call. "On the bow."*

Grace was standing to the right of the huge sail, looking up at the dolphins. "I knew you'd find a way," she said. Her hair was long and blonde once again. She was wearing a beautiful white cotton dress and she looked healthy.

Tears rushed down P.J.'s face. He wanted to go to her but knew he couldn't. They were in shallow water with protruding rocks all around them. If he let go of the helm the boat would surely crash.

Grace walked over to the lifeline on the starboard side. She leaned her legs against the stainless cables, holding on with both her hands. "It's okay." She looked down into the water and inspected all the jagged protrusions and the hidden coral mounds inches beneath the surface.

Shaking her head, Grace turned to face her father. "They're not for you. You're no longer meant to be at the helm."

P.J. shook his head violently. "I can't Gracie. I can't let go."

"It's okay," she called back to him. Grabbing the mainstay for support, Grace lifted her leg and climbed onto the lifeline. Once again, she turned to face her father.

He looked at her, horrified. "Gracie, No!"

"It's beautiful, daddy. Come up and take a look."

"I can't," he whispered. "I can't."

A small voice from behind him drew closer with each word. "I can do it, Papa. I can man the helm."

P.J. jumped back at the sound of his grandson's voice. He looked down to find the young boy at his left side. He was holding Mishimo.

"I can do it, Papa. I can steer through this. I know I can. I promise."

The older gentleman put his hand on his grandson's shoulder. "Do you remember what I told you about making promises."

"A promise is a promise, a contract of the heart. It's bound by truth and therefore bound by me," the young boy recited. "I can do this, Papa. I'll find my way."

P.J.'s hands were trembling. He glanced at his daughter, standing on the lifeline with an arm outstretched toward him. He looked back at his grandson, who had placed his cat upon the settee. Billy looked eager to take the helm.

P.J. worried for the little boy. He was concerned Billy's overzealousness had blinded him from the unforeseen consequences awaiting him, up ahead.

"Are you sure this is what you want?"

The boy nodded. "I know you're tired, Papa."

P.J. took a deep breath. When he let it out he warned, "Don't stop. Don't stop listening, *Billy. It will only make it more difficult for you to have your wish."*

"I won't, Papa. I won't."

P.J. released one hand from the helm and waited for Billy to grab hold. "I love you," he said then he let go with the other and slowly made his way to the bow. Grace reached for her father's hand and kissed it gently.

"I'll go first," she said and jumped into the water.

When P.J. climbed up onto the lifeline he looked down and saw the water had changed. It was now completely black with billions and billions of twinkling lights. Grace was the brightest amongst them and he could hear her voice.

"Come on daddy. Don't be frightened. We'll still be there helping to light his way."

—

Mishimo leaped up and began pacing. She stood in front of Billy a moment, meowing incessantly.

"Shush, Mish. You're going to wake Papa."

Papa Joe was sleeping soundly, not moving at all. Once in a while his deep breathing would cause the blanket to quiver. Billy thought he looked peaceful.

Mishimo finally settled in next to Billy, lying in a big ball behind him. Her head was hidden beneath her paws. Billy relaxed again, glad Mish had calmed down. It always made him nervous to see her upset.

About two hours into his watch, Billy quickly ran down below to grab a snack. Coming up he noticed a slight chill in the air. He decided to cover Papa Joe with another blanket. There was no need for him to shiver and disturb such a serene sleep.

Papa Joe had a slight smile to his face. His tummy moved up and down. His breathing had become quiet, unlabored. Billy was glad to see him finally getting some much needed rest.

The cat began to pace once again. She glanced over at Papa Joe, then back at Billy, then back at Papa again.

She did this for a few minutes before Billy finally asked, "What is it, Mishimo?" He stared at her, uncomfortable with her odd behavior.

Mishimo turned and looked up, out into the distant water. Then she looked back at Billy and slowly made her way to his lap.

The starlit sky began to twinkle. Billy glanced up. The moon was not visible which allowed the stars to shine even brighter still. Staring up, he thought he saw them dull for one brief second. Then they lit up again, even brighter than before.

Billy's entire body shivered. The night suddenly felt strange. He didn't like it.

He looked over at Papa who continued to sleep peacefully. Billy took a deep breath and shook his head. He tried to ignore the oddities of the evening. It would be over soon, he thought. He could see the south side of the islands that made up the BVI.

Mishimo purred as she brushed her head against Billy's left leg. She paced the deck and climbed behind Papa Joe. Then, having never done so before, Mishimo began to meow. The sound struck Billy in an instant. Something was very wrong.

Billy did not want her to wake Papa just yet. "Let him sleep, Mish. Leave him alone."

He walked over, scooped her up and caressed her gently in an attempt to calm her. She wouldn't stop meowing.

He tried stroking her belly and even hugged her to get her to stop. Walking back over to the helm, Billy sat down with Mishimo in his arms. He put his hands under her front legs and stood her up, erect. "Mishimo," he commanded, "What is wrong with you." Then he saw them. Tears.

Billy's chest felt heavy as he quickly pieced the last few hours together. His heart beat against his chest as if it wanted to break free. He jumped up, dropped Mishimo on the settee and ran over to his grandfather.

He shook him, hard. No response.

He called out his name. No response.

The little boy screamed. He screamed again and again and again.

The sky began to lighten as the first signs of a new day drew near.

Billy shook his grandfather once more. "No Papa! No! You have to wake up. You have to!"

No! Billy shouted walking up and down the side decks. No! No, no, no, no!

The islands were quickly approaching. Billy let in the jib and took down the mainsail. His tears never stopped. His face was expressionless. The sun crested over the horizon as he motored through the cut between Norman and Peter Islands, entering into the BVI. There were already quite a few early birds sailing the waters of Sir Francis Drake Channel. Billy turned the corner at West End and continued on to Jost Van Dyke. He sailed alone with his grandfather's lifeless body beside him for almost three hours.

When he was almost to the harbour, he called for Danny on the radio.

Danny was elated to hear the boy's voice, "Young Billy, is that you! I've got a new baby girl I can't wait for you to meet."

Billy couldn't hold it in anymore. He burst into hyperventilating sobs. He pressed the receiver button but could not talk. He could barely breath. Finally he managed, "I need help."

Danny's panicked voice came back over the radio, "Where are you, Billy? Where are you!" he screamed. Danny stepped away from the mic and looked out onto the water. He could see the shiny blue hull headed toward Great Harbour. He ran back to the radio and said, "Stay there, Billy. You're doing great. Stay there. I'll be right there."

Danny ran out of The Dive. He raced down the beach and jumped into his dinghy. Gunning the throttle, he meandered through the spattering of anchored boats. He pulled alongside *Amazing Grace*, tied a line to her and climbed aboard.

Running over to Billy at the helm Danny immediately noticed the adult form wrapped in the crocheted blanket, head covered. There were no signs of an accident. And other than Billy's filthy, snot-ridden, tear-streaked face, he did not look injured.

Mishimo stood on the backboard of the settee, above the body.

"Are you alone?" Danny asked.

Billy didn't answer. He just stood there. His hands were tightly gripped around the helm as he blankly stared ahead. Danny gently peeled Billy's fingers from the wheel. He wrapped an arm around him and whispered, "It will be okay. Everything is going to be okay." He maneuvered the boat to the far corner of the harbour and told Billy, "I have to drop the anchor now. Do you want to stay here?" No response. "Okay, stay here. I'll be right back."

Running back and forth from the cockpit to the bow Danny growled, "Come on damn it!" After several more tries, he finally set the anchor.

Billy never moved.

There would be ample time for questions. Right now, Danny wanted to get Billy cleaned up and off the boat. He planned to wait a while before notifying the authorities. He wanted to go see Val at Immigration first. She'd know how to handle this delicately. She loved P.J.

After helping Billy get cleaned up, Danny grabbed both Billy's and his grandfather's passports, Mishimo's documents, some extra clothes and the wicker basket. He carried Billy down the deck and placed him in the dinghy. "Come on, Mish," he said and scooped up the cat. On shore Danny carried Billy in his arms. The boy rested his head on Danny's shoulder and wept. Up past the General Store, Danny made a right. Marta's family owned the majority of the land from this point on. There were several houses bunched together. Marta and Danny lived in the one in the center.

Marta was nursing the baby in the bedroom when they entered. Danny left Billy in the modestly decorated living room and went in to tell his wife what he knew so far. A few minutes later Marta came out with her head down low. Her eyes were puffy and red. She'd left the baby in her crib.

While Marta sat with Billy, Danny began making arrangements. It would turn out to be the most disturbing day of Danny's long life. By the time the authorities left and the bereaved community finished stopping by to extend their condolences, darkness had descended upon the harbour again.

Danny prepared himself for one last phone call. It would not be easy to do over ship-to-shore radio from The Dive, but he had to do it. He slapped back three consecutive shots of Mount Gay rum and got Virgin Island's Radio on the line.

The following day, Danny waited as long as possible to tell Billy about the arrangements his Nana had made. He sat the boy down on the back patio. There was a plentiful garden and a bundle of banana trees. Beside the house there was also a huge, sweet mango tree. It was Danny's favorite place to spend his leisure time. He loved to dig his hands in the dirt and literally see the fruits of his labor.

Billy held onto his basket and stared blankly at the garden. He still hadn't uttered one syllable.

"I am sorry, Billy, but your Nana wants you to go back to New York. Today." It hurt to *say* the words. Danny winced as they came out.

Billy's head lifted slightly. Otherwise there was no reaction from the boy.

"I am going to go with you. I'll make sure you're okay."

Danny kissed Marta and their new baby good-bye before solemnly departing his home and family.

The commuter flight landed in San Juan a little after 5:30 p.m. When they got to Customs and Immigration Danny asked the official if Billy could sit down while they went through all the paperwork. And there was a lot of it. Danny, Billy, his cat and a coffin it wasn't exactly a quintessential day in paradise.

When they passed through the doors to the main terminal there was a dark-haired Italian man in a suit standing with a sign that read: McMillon.

When Danny approached, the man said, "I'll take it from here, sir," and reached for Billy's hand.

"Like hell you will."

"Oh, but I will," the man said sharply, "This is a *private* aircraft and you are not on the manifest for the flight back to New York." The man sneered at Danny with a menacing sternness. "We've been instructed to pick up the boy, alone." The man attempted to be delicate. "And the rest of the cargo of course," he said.

This was not the place for a scene, Danny thought. It's not going to help Billy and Danny knew he'd lose the argument. He got down on both knees in front of Billy.

"Billy. They're not going to let me fly with you. But I want you to know I'll be right behind you. I am going to grab the first commercial flight out to New York and I will come to the penthouse. Okay?"

He waited for a moment then placed his hands gently around Billy's upper arms and finally made actual eye contact. "Do you understand?" he asked softly.

Billy closed his eyes and put his head down. He clutched the basket to his chest.

Danny stood back up and looked at the dark-haired man with disdain. He motioned for him to step away from the young boy.

"This kid is not even nine years old," Danny sternly imparted, "and he has lost his mother and the only father figure he's ever known. And he didn't just *lose* them. He watched them both die. You take care of him. You treat him like he is your own son. Do you understand me? *Do you?*" He thrust Billy's passport and Mishimo's papers into the man's hand and rushed back to Billy.

On his knees again, he waited for Billy to make eye contact again. "Billy, I am so sorry I am unable to get on that plane with you." Tears rolled down Danny's face. "Remember I am always, always going to be there for you. I will never, *not* be there for you. Okay?"

Billy suddenly dropped the basket and thrust his arms around Danny. He started balling and wouldn't let go. Even the man with the sign was choked-up watching the scene.

When Billy finally exhausted himself he lay limp in Danny's arms. "He just fell asleep and never woke up," he said in a garbled whisper.

Nana had given strict instructions not to let Danny or anyone else join her grandson on the four-hour flight home. Danny stayed with Billy as long as he could. He watched the boy climb the stairs and step into the aircraft.

When the plane taxied down the runway, Billy looked out the window. He could see Danny pressed up against the glass inside the terminal. Billy's stomach churned and his face became flushed. Beads of sweat began to stream down his face. He ran to the bathroom and threw up. When he returned to his seat he scooped Mishimo out of the basket beside him. Squeezing her tight, he began to cry.

Danny scrambled to find a flight. The earliest he could leave was first thing in the morning. He spent the night drinking at a local hotel bar.

Arriving at Kennedy Airport shortly after 9:00 a.m., Danny took a taxi to the penthouse where he was refused entry. He scrambled to find a pay phone and called Nana several dozen times.

He checked into a hotel a few blocks away, on Madison Avenue. A look of horror came over the woman's face as he approached the expansive marble reservations counter. Danny was wearing ratty old shorts and flip-flops. He hadn't noticed the remnants of a late April cold snap that remained in the air outside.

He didn't care to explain himself as he threw his outdated and torn Massachusetts driver's license, his passport, and his American Express Gold Card down on the counter. "Just give me a damn room, lady."

For the next five days, Danny camped out at the Carlyle. He managed to pick up some proper clothing, including a suit for the funeral. He kept tabs on what was happening through the local paper. Nana had made an announcement in the obituaries on the day Danny arrived in the city. Both the wake and service were private, by invitation only.

Danny was turned away at both. He couldn't even get a glimpse of his best friend's grandson. Billy never even knew he tried.

CATHARSIS

It had been more than seven years since Brooke coaxed her father out of his office to open the tattered box she'd found. The abandoned contents lay on their shelves like misplaced relics in the recently renovated room.

Much like Brooke, her room had grown up, too. The pink butterfly bed had been replaced by a luxurious American Cherry sleigh bed and deep burgundy duvet with gold accents. The ceiling-to-floor sheer olive-hued curtains were held open with wrought-iron brackets. Natural wood floors with an intricately designed throw rug had replaced the fluffy-white carpet. The room had a subtle sophistication less the giant, white-faced, smeared red-lipped Heath Ledger poster on the wall and the half-dozen schoolbooks strewn across the floor.

Brooke was on her cell phone when her father peeked into the room. He walked over and sat beside her on the bed. She did not hang up right away. Bill looked around and sighed heavily. They'd managed to grow apart so quickly over the past few months. Brooke had been coming home almost inconsolably. She blamed it on the pressures of school. It was possible. After all, his daughter was taking several AP classes for early college credit, she kept an incredibly busy sports calendar with both volleyball and gymnastics. She was also captain of the debate team this year.

Bill and Ella had always questioned their decision to keep their daughter at Arelbery. Brooke maintained that she liked it there and actually seemed to thrive under the pressure, most of the time.

He sat there, waiting for her to get off the phone, wondering what angle to take on his newest attempt to get his daughter to open up to him.

"Just leave me alone, Dad. Please."

Brooke stood up with a stone-cold expression and walked over to the window.

He waited a moment, silently, then stood up and gingerly walked toward her.

"Honey," he began, "you can tell me anything. Just talk to me."

His daughter spun around and met his gaze. She stepped toward him, teeth clenched. Swinging her shoulder to the right, she breezed past him and burst.

"I don't want to hear any more of your damn stories," she screamed and walked over to the shelves. She resisted the urge to scrape off all the silly stuffed toys and ridiculous pictures from both ledges.

She didn't care about them anymore, but also refused to let her sister have them. Several years ago she'd been dumb enough to start sharing her few moments of personal time with her dad. She wasn't willing to let her sister have the only thing for which she had sole possession. She'd never admit to her dad, but she still slept with Angelica every night.

She lashed out at him. "I don't even believe you anymore. *You* stopped believing once. Why shouldn't *I* stop believing?"

Bill felt like someone had punched him in the gut. He thought he might be sick. He stood up and tried to catch his breath. He spun around and sucked in some air. Leaning his hand against the window frame, he looked down upon Park Avenue. "I don't know what to say," he mumbled. He turned around and stared at his beautiful teenage daughter. She was the spitting image of her Grandmom Gracie.

With a forced smile and pained expression he repeated, "I don't know what to say." And walked out, gently shutting the door.

Ella knocked lightly before opening the door. The office was dark. Bill was sitting behind his desk, staring at a picture frame. His face looked heavy. His eyes and mouth down-turned.

There was an empty space amongst the collage of family photos on the wall. Ella knew exactly which image he was holding in his hand. She had taken it a few years ago. She'd snuck into the room and snapped it before they even knew she was there. Brooke and Breezi were on either side of Bill. They each had an arm around him. Bright smiles lit up their faces as they listened to their dad expressively convey one of his astonishing childhood memories.

She'd printed it in black-and-white and the girls had helped pick out the custom frame. They'd presented it to him on Father's Day along with some drawings the girls made depicting scenes of dolphins jumping in the air, sailboats beneath a cloud-filled sky and children splashing in the water along a sandy beach.

Ella looked over at the wall. Amongst the pictures there were also pieces of Breezi's award winning artwork and the abundant ribbons and trophies from Brooke's gymnastic meets, tennis matches and scholastic achievements.

"Do *you* believe me?" Billy said without looking up.

"Of course I believe in you. You are my husband. I love you."

"No. Do you *believe* me?"

She knew what Bill meant. She walked over to him and sat on the edge of his desk. She offered a warm smile and leaned in to hold his hand.

"I said, do you believe me?" he asked in a sharper tone. "My stories."

Ella tilted her head. She gently blinked her eyes and said, "You've never shared any of them with me."

Bill was shocked. The comment rattled him. He turned away from her with a look of consternation. He rubbed his chin and closed his eyes. *She's right.*

They talked for a few minutes. Mostly, Ella talked. Bill sat. Ella held his hand and told him how she'd overheard their daughter's outburst and suggested she have a talk with Brooke to get to the bottom of her true frustrations. She knew Brooke cherished her relationship with Bill and usually turned to his stories for comfort when she was troubled.

"The important part is that *you* believe them."

Bill spread his massive hand across his face, covering his eyes. His shoulders began to shake and his breathing became labored as he sobbed, sometimes gasping for air.

Ella sat silently. Once Bill's chest began to rise and fall more naturally, she walked behind his chair, leaned over and wrapped her arms around him. She offered one last kiss before stepping toward the door.

"You're coming up, right?"

Bill sat, head still down, eyes still closed.

Ella's whole body began to tremble. She swallowed hard. It took a moment for her to regain her composure. She pressed the palm of her hand to her mouth and made a small puckered sound. Then flattened her palm in front of her and blew. "*Une millione di baci,*" she said with an unsteady voice. *Much love and kisses.*

She gently closed the door behind her. Leaning against the wall a moment, Ella struggled not to cry. Upstairs she lay in bed, praying her husband would soon be there.

Shortly before 7:00 a.m. Brooke tiptoed down the stairs. She hadn't gotten much sleep. She wanted to apologize to her dad. She didn't mean to get so angry. She was just upset.

She'd been made fun of the entire three days after the gymnastic meets in Orlando, Florida. She'd won balance beam and uneven bars, missing the all-around by one tenth of a point. Her coaches and teammates were ecstatic. For the first time in several years they'd beat their rival school and were rated number one for their high school division.

But Brooke didn't feel like celebrating. With the competition over, they were one day away from celebrating at Discovery Cove and her feelings were quickly changing as to whether or not she should go.

At first she'd been excited by the idea. She had used her own money and forged the permission slips, afraid her father would not let her go. Each of the girls was to have the opportunity to swim with the dolphins. Brooke had imagined doing this her entire life. But as she looked around Orlando nothing seemed to fit. She wasn't meant to do this in some manufactured environment. She wanted to do it for real.

Her parents called her a few hours after the meet was over. Bill was surprised at the sound of his daughter's voice. He expected her to be bouncing off the walls. She achieved what she set out to do and had even been approached by a scout from a national coaching team wanting to chat further about her future interest in gymnastics.

The girls could not understand why, at the last minute, Brooke refused to go to Discovery Cove.

"You can't simply not go," her coach told her. "We can't leave you in the hotel by yourself, Brooke. You're a minor and it is against school policy. You must be chaperoned."

"What if I am sick?"

"That's different. You're not sick."

Brooke and Ms. Englebert had a wonderful rapport. Brooke felt safe with her. Ms. Englebert was tough but fair and they'd developed a special bond Brooke didn't have with all the other teachers, or the students.

"Okay. I'll take care of this."

Ms. Englebert offered to stay behind, sighting a recurring injury Brooke experienced in competition earlier in the year. The head coach, Ms. Jones, bought the story. But the girls on the team knew it was a lie.

For the next month Brooke was teased about 'not wanting to hurt her daddy by riding the pretty little dolphins.' Before then, she'd never had any trouble at school. Soon it felt like the whole campus was making fun of her. She hated it. She'd even resigned from the debate team because some of the girls thought this would be a great topic of discussion.

Brooke raced into the kitchen, expecting to find her father drinking coffee and reading *The New York Times*. Instead, she discovered her mother sitting at the kitchen table. Her eyes were bloodshot and swollen.

"He's gone," was all her mom could muster.

There was a note. Brooke picked up the folded yellow, rough-edged lined paper. There were no promises inside. No reassurances. It simply read:

I have to go.
Ti amo,
Bill

Ella had already searched Bill's office. There was nothing in his desk, on his computer or in his briefcase to indicate where he might have gone.

Brooke had an idea. "The apartment, mom." She walked over and rested her hand on her mom's shoulder. "I know that's where he is. Come on, let's go."

They found the spare key in Bill's top desk drawer. Brooke ran upstairs and told her sister they'd be right back. "Mom's just going to go with me up to school a minute."

Breezi was pre-occupied drawing in her sketchbook. "Yeah, whatever." She was used to her parents taking Brooke *somewhere*.

Outside they grabbed a cab. Within 10 minutes they were sitting in front of the brownstone. Ella chose not to go up. She didn't mind that her husband had this private place. He'd told her about it after he'd gone there the first time. But she felt, if he'd never brought her there before, it wasn't her place to go drag him out of it now. She just wanted to know he was safe.

When her daughter didn't come back, Ella sighed and closed her eyes. Brooke and her dad had a lot to talk about. Calmness came over Ella and her natural breathing was restored. Her lips upturned thinking about how her daughter and husband were probably laughing by now.

The door flew open. "Mom. Mom," Brooke cried. "He's not there. He's not there, mom. He wasn't in the garden or anywhere mom," she rattled off. "A neighbor stopped me on the way back down and said he hadn't seen Dad in several days, maybe a week." She jumped back in the car. "We have to find him!" she screamed. "Oh mom. What did I do?"

Back at the house Brooke and Ella sat at the kitchen table. Neither of them knew what to do next. Breezi came down the stairs. She'd heard the elevator come up but then everything went silent again. She entered the kitchen with a furrowed brow. Her eyes darted between her sister and her mother.

"What's going on?" she asked them.

"Nothing, honey. Everything is okay." Ella replied.

At the same time, Brooke blurted, "Dad left."

Breezi winced. She walked over to her mother, sat in her lap and put her arms around her with her head resting on Ella's shoulder. Breezi was 12 years old and resisted the idea of becoming a teenager. She'd ask her mother all the time why she couldn't have just stayed little forever.

Brooke stood up. "Humph." She paced the floor and tapped her fingers on the counter near the sink. "We've got to do something."

Ella took a deep breath in. "What are we supposed to do if we don't even know where to begin? I have no idea what your father was thinking when he wrote that note. He could be anywhere. Jeez, the last time he took off for Hawaii for goodness sake!"

Brooke had no idea what her mother was talking about, but she didn't like the feeling in her stomach. She walked over to the refrigerator and poured a glass of orange juice. She drank half of it and then filled it up again with the last bit of juice in the container. She pressed the foot pedal to the stainless steel garbage bin and went to throw the empty container away.

"Mom. Mom, there are all these crumpled bits of yellow paper in here." Brooked leaned down to get them.

"Don't touch those!" Ella commanded.

Breezi picked her head up and looked at her mother. She slowly peeled herself off her mother's lap.

Brooke stared at her.

"Girls, go inside. Go wait for me in the living room. I'll be there in a few minutes."

"But ..."

"Do as I say, Brooke."

The girls slithered out of the room. Ella sat back down. She eyeballed the garbage bin for a few seconds and took a big gulp before standing up again and walking over to it. She picked each piece of crumpled paper out and placed them on the table.

One by one she read different versions of the same thing. Her husband said he needed answers. He had to know if it was true. If it really happened the way he remembered.

Nowhere in any of them did it say he was coming back or when. Ella scooped them all up and threw them back in the bin. She sat down and slowly shook her head back and forth. She cried, hard. When the tears finally stopped, she walked over to the sink and cleaned her face.

The girls were waiting for Ella in the living room. Breezi was sketching in one of her books and Brooke was pacing.

"Girls. Girls come sit with me," she said with a sigh as she made her way to the long gray couch.

They camped out in the living room for the next three days.

"Mom, do you think . . . do you think dad will ever come back?" Brooke's voice cracked.

Ella had been asking herself the same question. She leaned her head back and closed her eyes a moment, calming her mind. When she opened them again, she turned to her daughters. "Hold on a moment," she said, "I have to go get something."

She climbed the steps, swung open the door to the closet and rummaged through all the forgotten junk until she found what she was searching for.

Downstairs she wedged herself between her girls and put the old book on her lap.

"I want you girls not to worry anymore. Your dad will be back. I don't know when exactly, but he'll be back."

"How do you know that, mom?"

"I know because he loves us." She turned her head back and forth smiling at her two beautiful daughters. They had both grown into such lovely young ladies and she was so proud of them. "Do you guys remember the story of how your father and I first met?" she asked.

The girls nodded.

"Well, your father and I always chose to leave out a part of our journey together." She opened the book. "These pictures in the beginning are of the day we *first* met. We were madly in love. This is true. But then your dad disappeared." Ella sighed deeply. Brooke stared at her, hanging on every word. "We always told you that we were married six months after we *first* met," she hesitated, "but these wedding pictures were actually taken six months after your father came back to me." She looked at each of her daughters, "I think it's time to share a little more of our story."

At MIT, Bill was offered an incredible opportunity to spend the last six months of his college senior year on an overseas internship with Brooke Marine in Lowestof, England. He was assigned to assist the architects for Richard Branson's *Virgin Atlantic Challenger II*, which was commissioned for the sole purpose of breaking the Trans-Atlantic speed record. Bill advocated for the team to make a few unconventional structural changes and he also made some unusual design suggestions. The 72-foot boat went on to break the world record by more than 2 hours.

Bill's internship officially ended the moment the boat crossed the finish line at Bishop Rock off the coast of Great Britain. He was scheduled to fly back to New York three days later. His co-workers finally convinced the reclusive young marine architect to change his flight and join them on a celebratory vacation in Italy. One of the designers had a home in Siena and the annual horse race through the city's piazza was in a few days.

"Come on, Bill," they coaxed, "you've been in Europe for half a year and the only thing you've seen is your desk and some boat plans. Come on, Bill, live a little. Where's your sense of adventure?"

The *Piazza di Campo* was covered in dirt and concrete bleachers lined one side of the massive downward-sloped town square. There were already thousands of spectators scampering around the streets vying for the best view of the 90-second, centuries-old battle between the *contradas*, which are townships of the great city. There were spectators hanging out of windows, standing on rooftops and climbing on the grandstand where the officials were gathered. People screamed out the name of their *contradas* such as *Onda*, *Tartuca*, and *Nicchio* and held up flags with their *contrada's* crest.

Since Bill's co-worker had an apartment that looked onto the piazza, Bill did not have to fight his way through the pushing and shoving of the crowds. He hung out the shutter-lined window of the living room, studying the chaos below. When the horses entered through the grand archway of the inner city, the crowd went wild. The sound bounced off the brick-faced buildings, reverberating as it rose toward the rooftops.

Bill held his ears and looked around. Suddenly everything was muted as his eyes fixed on the stunning, dark-haired woman in the window of the apartment next to him. His hands fell to his sides and his jaw fell open as her deep, chestnut eyes locked onto his.

Three guys pushed on Bill's shoulder to get a closer look as the winning horse threw his jockey off and crossed the finish line alone. "Oh my God, did you see that, McMillon? Holy shit that's gotta hurt!" his friend screamed in Bill's ear.

Bill shook the man off his shoulders and leaned further out the window. The girl was gone. "Damn it," he said under his breath. He punched his buddy in the arm and walked into the kitchen. Grabbing a beer from the fridge, Bill opened it and gulped it down. As he lowered his head, Bill's eyes grew wide and he wrenched his neck forward. The beautiful young woman from the window was standing in the kitchen doorway, staring.

His eyes blinked profusely. "Ummm. Uhhhh."

She stepped toward him. "I am Ella."

"Ummm. Uhhhh." He could not get his mouth to move in sync with his thoughts. He looked away from her for a moment, took a deep breath and blurted, "My name's Bill. Bill McMillon. I am from . . . America. You're not, apparently." He looked up at her, "But, but you speak English so well. Wow."

Ella giggled.

Eventually Bill found his pace and the two of them enjoyed a very natural conversation. Ella shared a brief history of the horse race they both just missed and Bill told Ella about what he was doing in Italy as well as what brought him to Europe in the first place.

"I just saw that on the news. That's impressive, Bill. Are you going to stay in England now?" She asked curiously.

"I wasn't planning on it. Brooke Marine *did* make me an offer though," he thought about it a second, "I bet they'll make me a better one, now." They both laughed.

"I am off for the summer, but I go to school at the Royal Academy of Arts in Piccadily. If you stay, maybe we could have a coffee or something sometime," Ella suggested.

Bill put his head down. His face became flushed and he could feel his nerves re-entering his belly. But he found his courage. "I'd like that. I'd like that a lot."

They continued to talk for hours, never leaving the kitchen. People came in and out and even tried to talk to them, but neither of them paid any attention.

It was almost midnight when Ella suggested they take a walk. Billy hadn't seen the outer circle of the city and Ella offered to take him on a short tour.

Seven days later, Ella and Bill stood in front of his gate at Heathrow airport. Ella had followed Bill back to England after they spent several days exploring the majestic hilltop towns of Tuscany, visiting many of the wineries of Chianti, and even stopping in Montisi at Ella's family home.

They hugged until his final boarding call. Wiping away her tears, Bill re-assured her, "I'll be right back. Don't worry. I'll be right back."

Bill had accepted a full-time position at Brooke Marine. He was headed back to the States to tell his Nana and to pack up his dorm room at MIT. Graduation was in a few days and he didn't want to disappoint Nana. He had to go.

He held Ella's face in his hands, leaned closer and kissed her one last time. "I love you," he said, "and I'll be right back. It's only five days. Just five days."

Nana was thrilled to have Bill back in the States and in the penthouse. Bill decided to wait until after graduation to tell her about the job offer. He struggled to find the right time and the right words.

Their relationship hadn't been the best over the years, but she was still family and he didn't want to hurt her. Finally, two days before he was scheduled to board the plane back to England, he sat Nana down in the living room to talk.

She was completely devastated. And when she heard a girl was involved she was mortified. "How could you choose some girl you do not know over your own family?" she asked.

Bill hadn't had girlfriends growing up. He barely had friends at all. He had isolated himself for so many years and finally felt *alive*. He not only loved Ella, he told Nana, but he was *in love* with her and planned to marry her the moment she said yes. He was elated and he wanted Nana to be happy for him.

"Billy," she began, "you are a very smart young man. You have achieved enormous success and you have barely even finished college." She bit down on her bottom lip. "How do I say this delicately?" She tapped her finger on the arm of the chair. "Remember, you not only have your mom's genes coursing through your veins, you also have your father's. He was a very intelligent young man like you and he claimed to have the same kinds of feelings for your mom that you are describing to me now. But look at what he did." She paused to meet her grandson's gaze. "He left you. He left your sick mother. Don't you think you should be careful not to make rash decisions about love for fear that you may be just like him?"

Bill felt like she'd just hit him in the head with a baseball bat. He was unable to breathe, unable to move. After his initial shock wore off, he stood. "Whew." He shook his head, rubbed his face and walked to the nearby window, staring out at the courtyard.

When he finally turned around, he held his head high, marched over to Nana and with a quiver in his voice declared, "I think you *must* be one of the most vile people I have *ever* known."

He walked out, stepped into the elevator and spent the next several hours walking the streets of Manhattan.

He didn't call. The last time they spoke was after his graduation. He was just about to sit down with Nana. Ella kept telling herself everything was okay. He was safe. Everything was fine.

She sat in the airport until the last flight from New York arrived. She called and left messages at his London apartment. She even made a visit to Brooke Marine. Nobody had heard from him. His rent was paid until the end of the year, Brooke Marine wasn't expecting him for another few days and MIT wouldn't give out any personal information.

Desperate, Ella picked up the phone and dialed the overseas operator. She had them search until they found the number for the McMillon residence in Manhattan. There were three. Ella took them all and began dialing.

The second number picked up on the third ring, "McMillon residence," answered a very formal employee.

Ella's whole body shook. The receiver vibrated against her cheek. In a soft, questioning voice she asked, "Is Bill okay?" She closed her eyes, "Please tell me he's okay."

The woman on the other line said, "Who is this, ma'am?"

"I am a friend," Ella managed. "I was expecting him back in England yesterday."

"I am sorry, ma'am, Mr. McMillon isn't here."

"Is he alright?" she asked, again.

The woman didn't answer.

"May I speak with Ms. McMillon?" Ella gently asked.

There was a small pause. The woman asked Ella for her name and her association with Bill then said, "Let me see if she is here. Please hold."

The phone went blank. Ella gulped down some water. She was sweating profusely and her hands were still trembling.

"This is Ms. McMillon," a stern older voice answered.

"Ms. McMillon, I am . . ."

"I know who you are," Nana interrupted, "My grandson is not here."

"Is he okay?" Ella attempted to halt her tears. "Is he hurt?" But they wouldn't obey.

There was no sympathy on the other end of the phone. "I do not know. Bill doesn't live here anymore." And she hung up.

Bill told himself he had lost his chance—that Ella would never forgive him. But as each day passed, he pined for her. Each day he wondered what he'd done.

He was afraid. He was afraid of possibly losing her one day or worse—maybe Nana was right. He could not bear the thought that he might be like his father and not have the courage to stick around.

Grace had never spoken ill of Bill's father. She always made sure to tell him that his father loved him very much and that leaving was a mutual decision. He never actually thought about it much, until Nana released her venom.

Bill spent the next several weeks at a hotel downtown. He walked the streets like a zombie. He had done everything she asked of him: attend the schools of her choice, make the best grades, double-up on courses, accompany her to every function she asked, always be polite, never ask questions or speak of the past and manage to put himself through one of the most rigorous and competitive programs at MIT in record time.

And now she had tainted the one thing that had brought him joy in over a decade. He needed to know if she was right.

On a whim, Bill jumped on a plane in search of his father. He arrived on Oahu nine hours later, in search of answers. He was sure he knew where to find them. After cleaning himself up, he booked a commuter flight to Maui then rented a car and headed to Haleakala Observatory.

When he got there the woman working behind the desk said, "I am sorry sir, Mr. Annesley hasn't worked here in many years. I believe he's at Mauna Kea now, on the big island of Hawaii." She added, "But you won't find him there. There is no public access to that area."

Bill flew back to Oahu feeling defeated. He had questions. He wanted answers and he wanted help. Early the following morning he packed up his gear and headed up the Pali Highway to the southeast side of the island. He followed the instructions he was given, parked at the country club and walked up the paved road to the hiking trail. He looked up at the massive green pointed peaks and began to climb.

It took him almost three hours to get to the first summit of the Olomana trail. He didn't take notice of the majestic beauty before him. Instead he studied it, wondering where his mother stood the first time she was there and where his parents positioned themselves the day they got married. He walked back to the wooded trail in search of the tree his mother used to talk about. There were no blooms to guide his way but eventually he found it. He bent down and traced the worn initials deeply embedded in one of the lower limbs of the twisted tree.

Bill heard some voices from further down the path.

A group of five hikers approached. As each one passed they acknowledged Bill and shared cordial greetings with him. The last one in the pack was a fit, older woman with short silver hair. "You okay?" she asked, "You up here on your own?"

Billy nodded.

She pulled out a bag of granola. "Want something to eat?"

"Thanks." Bill grabbed a hardy handful, gobbled it up and took the first swig from his water bottle.

A tall, slender curly-haired man walked up and joined them. He looked at Bill curiously. "How's it going?"

"I'm good. Just have a bunch of things on my mind." Bill was surprised by his own answer.

The woman patted Bill on the arm. "If you want some more, I'll be right over there." She walked over to the remainder of their group sitting by the edge of the cliff admiring the vast ocean, plentiful greenery and mass of buildings below.

"Would you like to climb with us, so you're not alone?" the man asked. He had taken a seat next to Bill and didn't seem to have intentions of leaving anytime soon.

Bill shook his head, no.

"Well you are welcome to join us. We'll be heading back down in about 15 minutes."

"May I ask you something?" Bill requested.

The man scrunched his shoulders, "Sure."

The man simply sat and listened as Bill poured out the story of the past few weeks. He told him all about meeting Ella, how incredible she made him feel, how much they laughed and how easy it was to be with her. Bill also told the man what he'd done. That he didn't show up. That he never called.

He explained that he didn't call because he was afraid he'd someday leave her or lose her. He had already lost so much of what he loved. What if he was so damaged that he wouldn't be able to truly love anyone?

When Bill was done, the man did not offer answers quickly. He let Bill take in his surroundings and breathe the fresh, clean air. "Look at that mountain over there," the man said. He pointed to the third summit in the trail, a steep, green peak with jagged rocks. "It's beautiful from afar. It might even seem to be an enticing and exciting challenge to conquer." He paused. "But I guarantee there are some unforeseen treacherous and definitely scary parts of it that would make any new climber wonder if they shouldn't turn back." He paused, "But somewhere, deep inside, you know you are capable to reaching the summit. You're just a little stuck. That's when you look for help. But remember, ultimately you conquer it alone. When you get to the top, it's the best feeling in the world and all of a sudden you forget the difficulties along the way."

The man patted Bill on the back. "If this young lady is as fantastic as you say, then isn't she worth conquering your own fears and taking the journey up the mountain together? Why give up so easily? If she is as wonderful as you've expressed don't you think she probably feels the same way about you? She'll forgive you, if you're honest and explain things to her the way you've explained them to me. Forgiveness is a powerful thing."

Bill leaned over and stared at the man. "How do you know so much about this?"

"Experience." He looked away, "Personal experience." The man stood up, leaned over and shook Billy's hand. "Go after her. The worst thing that could happen is she rejects you. But let me tell you, rejection might be painful, but it's not nearly as excruciating as regret."

One of the guys in the group called out that they were packed up and ready to move on. "I guess it's time to go. Good luck to you, young man."

"What's your name?" Billy asked his friendly stranger.

"My friends call me Astro."

"I am Bill. Bill McMillon. It was nice to meet you."

"Hmmm . . ." The man looked down a moment then back at Bill. "I see. Well, it's nice to meet you too, Billy." He paused. "Why don't you come with us? We can continue to talk."

Bill thought about it a moment. "No." he shook his head slightly. "No thanks. I don't think I am ready." He looked up at the next two summits.

The man smiled. "Okay then. I'll leave you to it. I hope we see each other again someday."

"Hmmm." Billy nodded and glanced up at the man. "Thanks for listening. I really appreciate it."

"It was my pleasure," he replied with the utmost sincerity.

Bill watched the five hikers begin their descent. They were quickly engulfed by the deep, wooded trail. Strolling over to the edge of the rocks, Bill sat and contemplated life *without* Ella. No other climbers passed.

When the sun lowered in the sky behind him, Bill stood up and walked over to the tree. "Mom," he said, "I am going after her."

Bill returned to Siena just in time for the second *Il Palio* of the summer. Five weeks had passed since he and Ella said good-bye at the airport. He walked around the crowded grounds and chose the perfect view. He wanted to make sure he could see what was happening.

When the horses entered the piazza, people's heads began to poke out from the windows above. Bill stared. He watched, waited. Out from the familiar window high above the screaming spectators, Bill saw an older gentleman coaxing a young woman toward the shutter-lined frame. His heart pounded as he squinted to see her face. When she continued to struggle not to look outside, he knew.

He took off running on the dirt-lined pavement. He maneuvered through the dense crowds, up several flights of stairs and stood in front of the door to the apartment where he knew he'd find her.

His brow was dripping with sweat and his shirt was drenched. Bill knocked vigorously. A gray haired, well-dressed gentleman answered the door. He took one look at Bill's disheveled appearance and stepped out into the foyer. He closed the door behind him.

An ear-piercing sound rang through the piazza. Screams, squeals and shouts emanated through the cavernous stone breezeway. The man raised his voice loud enough to be heard above the competing noise. Sternly he shouted, "Are you the American boy?"

Bill's shoulders shrank. His mouth turned down, he fixed his eyes on the floor and nodded.

"What do you think you're doing coming here?" the man demanded. "You have caused enough grief to a girl already filled with so much sorrow. How can you show your face? You should be ashamed. I am ashamed to be talking to you. Leave here now, before I have somebody hurt you."

The verbal assault actually escalated Bill's valor. He stood up tall and faced the man. Strengthening and taking a deep breath, Bill called back, "I love her and I will not leave until I explain. Then, if *she* wants me to, I will get on a plane and never return. But, I will not let you or anyone else stop me from telling her why. She deserves to know why I failed and that I promise to make it up to her for the rest of my life. I love her!"

Bill was shaking. He hadn't noticed the door had opened halfway through his hearty retort. Ella was standing there gawking, dumbfounded.

She went to step into the foyer. "No, Ella," the older gentleman said.

"It's okay, Uncle. It's okay. Go ahead inside."

The man flashed Billy a cold, menacing glance then kissed his niece on the cheek lightly and walked through the door. He closed it slowly, never taking his eyes off Bill.

Bill made a gesture with his hands, "Will you walk with me," he shouted.

He guided her past the mayhem. He got close to her, but was afraid to take her hand. They strolled silently. The crowds were muffled slightly. Bill took a seat halfway up the marble steps of the city's ornately designed, colorful cathedral and patted the space beside him. Billy talked as the hyper crowds came and went and eventually Siena became calm. Ella remained silent, but listened.

In the end, Bill could *not* promise he would never have to go away and think. He needed to offer her the truth and hoped it would be enough. "I love you and I will love you, forever. I may *have to* go away for a while sometimes, but I *promise*, I will never leave you. I *promise* to always come back."

She agreed to see him for a coffee, sometime.

They both moved on. Although he was five weeks late, Bill showed up at Brooke Marine. The boatyard still hired him, but put him on probation. Ella returned to the Academy of Art where she continued to thrive. For three weeks Bill repeatedly called Ella. At first she only offered idle conversation, but the calls soon grew into deeper discussions. Finally, Ella agreed to meet for coffee.

A few months later, Ella graduated. Bill quit the boatyard and followed Ella back to Italy. He worked odd jobs and did some maritime consulting. Ultimately he won Ella over. He asked her to marry him. They had an intimate ceremony in the tiny Tuscan village of Montisi, where they flourished for many years.

—

NATURE'S LITTLE SECRETS

Bill stepped off the nine-seater aircraft and was immediately smacked with a wall of heat causing beads of sweat to soak through his cotton t-shirt almost instantly. He wiped his brow several times with the back of his hand before the last of the six passengers disembarked.

He'd only been to Beef Island airport once, three days after his grandfather died. Somehow even then he knew he'd never return to these majestic islands and although he recognized some scenes from the air, it all felt quite foreign to him.

The plane landed on the tarmac shortly before noon. It was a relatively sunny day in late October with temperatures in the mid-90s. Clouds quickly joined forces and a light rain began to fall. Misty steam crept up from the ground as the cooler water hit the intensely hot asphalt.

The pilot hurriedly guided the six passengers across the tarmac toward the Customs and Immigration office. The airport was no longer a tiny airstrip with a small shack for a terminal. It was a full-size, contemporary structure and the runway was a bustling highway of commuter aircraft, several good-sized commercial planes, and a few parked private jets.

Bill's heart thumped loudly in his chest as he looked around. There was a sign over the entranceway door: Welcome to the BVI—Nature's Little Secrets.

The line for Immigration was long. Three planes had landed in relative succession. Bill waited his turn, patiently, taking in the scene around him. Individuals were toting full dive gear. Some carried multiple surfboards. Families hauling huge pieces of luggage, car seats, and uncomfortable, sweat-drenched babies surrounded him.

He thought of his girls.

"Next," the woman behind the counter called out. "Next," she repeated more sternly, breaking Bill's trance.

He walked up to the Plexiglass-encased booth. Remembering what his grandfather had taught him, Bill approached the woman and offered, "Good afternoon."

The immigration officer looked up. She had dark, black skin and green eyes with her hair pulled back severely. "Good afternoon," she responded.

Bill smiled at the sound of the accent he so fondly remembered.

The woman returned the smile and extended her hand through the small round opening to retrieve Bill's passport. "How long are you planning to stay in the BVI?"

He hadn't thought about it, really. "Just a few days."

"Do you have a return ticket?"

"Oh, yes." He pulled his itinerary from his jacket pocket.

"Let me see it." She glanced down at his paperwork. The woman's face became more serious. Her voice was no longer as friendly as before. "This ticket say you are returning three weeks from now."

"Oh, yes. Yes it does."

She looked at him with an irritated expression. "Where are you staying while you are here in the BVI?"

Good question, he thought. His departure was so sudden—spontaneous. He hadn't made any hotel arrangements. He didn't even know of any hotels on the island. He'd never slept on land during his travels with his granddad. He didn't realize it could be a problem. "Um, I am not quite sure yet."

"What is the purpose of your visit?" she demanded.

"Well," he hesitated. Caught off guard, he rambled, "Well, to find answers I guess. You see, I haven't been here in many, many years and I have been having some trouble with my daughter and I thought coming back here might help me understand some things."

The woman cut him off. "You cannot just come here without purpose or accommodation." She pointed to a door in the corner of the room with several seats on either side. "Take a seat over dere."

Bill was no longer so thrilled with the aggressive tone the woman's accent produced. But he also remembered his grandfather telling him to always be polite with the authorities on the island. He could hear Papa Joe's voice. *Remember, you're in their country, respect their customs.*

The immigration officer stepped away from her booth and walked over to a man in a suit chatting with one of the customs officials and several other men. The group of men looked over at Bill. The man in the suit stood upright and buttoned his jacket before walking over. One of the other men in the group seemed to grow increasingly curious at the situation. He watched intently as the officer marched over to Bill and chatted with him a few minutes.

A crowd had gathered to watch the spectacle. Bill felt increasingly nervous at the unwarranted attention. He explained to the man in the suit how he hadn't meant to do anything wrong and could well afford a hotel of their choosing. He didn't wish to cause any problems. He was just looking to find some personal answers regarding his childhood.

Bill noticed a huge, strapping local man standing in the corner, staring at him.

Suddenly, the stranger walked toward him. The stranger towered over the man in the suit.

Smacking Bill on his right shoulder with his immense jet-black hand, the stranger leaned in and said, "Billy?"

Bill pulled back a moment, startled. He straightened himself up and faced the man head-on. Mustering up as much strength in his voice as he could, Billy answered, "Yes." He looked into the man's big, bright hazel eyes and then he remembered.

Except for some scruff, Billy's childhood friend hadn't changed since they were nine years old. "Oh my goodness, Ritzel. How've you been man? You look great!"

The head of Airport Immigration was confused. "You know this man?" he asked the tall, burly islander.

"Sure do," Ritzel replied, "That's Billy McMillon. He's Doctah P.J.'s grandson." Ritzel pointed to the wall beside them, which displayed pictures from Tortola's past. There was an image of Bill's grandfather standing over a piece of ground with a shovel in his hand. It was the groundbreaking ceremony for the BVI Marine Learning Center on the east end of Tortola. Standing beside P.J. were Chief Minister Willard Wheatley and former Chief Minister Lavitty Stout (for whom the new center was dedicated). In the background were Lowell Wheatley, Foxy, Danny, Marta and Billy. Above the picture there was a quote. *May the research and knowledge gained from this school help preserve Nature's Little Secrets*—P.J. McMillon.

Bill's chest tightened. He sniffled, cleared his throat. His grandfather never saw any additional development of this dream. He passed away weeks after the photo was taken.

"Don't be givin' him no hassles, Red," Ritzel announced with a beaming white smile, "He wit me." Ritzel smacked Bill on the back, "It must be over 30 years since I seen ya face. Boy, you been gone too long!" He grabbed Bill in a bear hug. His voice became lower, softer. "It's so good to see ya, my friend."

Bill smiled.

"My dad is going to be so happy to see ya. He still works over on Jost. Every day he goes over there. He's 59 years old this year, but he still working odd jobs for Danny."

The name made Bill shiver. *Danny is still here.* In a hurried tone he said, "Mr. Red, I apologize for sounding so vague to your immigration officer. I am here to see Danny Waters over on Jost Van Dyke. Maybe you can put The Dive down as my destination."

Red made a scrunched up face and looked at Ritzel.

Ritzel shook the officer's hand and said, "Ah, come with me, Bill. I'll get you all sorted."

They jumped into Ritzel's taxi, a dark green, six-passenger SUV and headed out of the airport. "I see you're traveling light, my friend."

Billy left New York with his wallet and the clothes he was wearing. He didn't have a plan. He just left. All of sudden the severity of that decision came flooding in. He struggled to catch his breath. *Deep breaths*, he told himself, *Calm breaths.* He closed his eyes until his heart rate slowed and the moment passed.

When he opened his eyes, Ritzel asked, "You mind if I show ya a few things before taking you to the ferry?"

"No. No, Ritzel. Of course, I'd love to." He thought he heard a hint of sadness in the man's voice, "Back there . . . well. I just heard Danny's name and I," Billy didn't finish. He didn't really know what he wanted to say. "I am in no hurry, Ritzel and I'd love to hang out with you."

"Great." They drove up a steep hill and then down into an even deeper valley below. Billy held on tight as Ritzel drove up a narrow, winding hill. The roads were curvy and the terrain was rough. Ritzel navigated the road like a New York cabbie—maneuvering and weaving around potholes, swerving and jutting out of the way of other cars.

They stopped in front of a dirt driveway filled with boulders and big craters in the dirt. Ritzel put the car into first gear and slowly crept up the mountainside until they reached the property Ritzel was so proud of. He'd purchased it only a month before and had marked out the land where he would eventually build a house. Meanwhile he already completed his garden with a fully operational cistern irrigation system.

"The water collects in the barrels and the weight turns on the pump," his friend's huge chest puffed with pride as he explained, "In this small part of the world, I am growing tings nobody else is. Fresh herbs like lemongrass, rosemary, basil, chervil, thyme and veggies like okra, bok choy, and bananas. Everybody thought I was crazy. But look how it's all growing now." Ritzel pointed to the tier-stepped garden all along the side of the mountain. "I just had to show you."

Bill was genuinely impressed. He listened as his friend spoke of his dream to have a farm stand at the base of his property. "Wow, Ritzel. You've done a lot here."

They headed back onto the dangerous road. About a half-hour later they'd arrived at the West End ferry dock. "The next ferry leaves in about 10 minutes. You pay on the boat."

Billy shook Ritzel's hand and opened the door to the car. Before he got out Ritzel asked, "So, how life been treating ya anyway?"

Bill thought about it. "Much like these roads, life has led me down a winding path, my friend."

Bill's belly filled with butterflies as the blue, dinged-up, steel ferry pulled away from the dock. His heart beat quickly, pounding in his chest. He stuck his head out into the air and looked around the West End anchorage. He liked all new Caribbean-colored gingerbread buildings and the beautiful homes along the hillside.

The islands themselves were lush and green, even more brilliant than he remembered. They turned the corner and Bill immediately locked-in on the large protruding mass a few miles away. *Jost Van Dyke*, he thought. His eyes welled up, "Wow." He closed his eyes and took a few deep breaths. His lips curved upward slightly.

In 1974 the mountain was an unending mass of green. There was only one road along the hillside, which was obscured by brush and trees. As the ferry grew closer, Bill could see several brown horizontal slash marks embedded in the mountain. Tears poured down his cheeks. The new roads looked like deep, painful scars inflicted upon the place he held so dear.

The obnoxiously loud engine noise and the rattling metal from the ferry drowned out Bill's sobs. But they did not go unnoticed. A little girl asked her mom if the strange man next to them was okay. The woman held her daughter tight and turned away. With his head in his hands, Bill leaned over the unoccupied metal chair in front of him and wept.

Without warning, the engines slowed. The sound of his own hysterics startled Billy. It was an immediate off-switch to the teary faucet and he was grateful he was able to stop.

He picked his head up as the boat entered the mouth of the harbour. Billy froze when he saw her. Her shiny, blue hull glistened in the sunlight. Her sails were safely tucked away beneath the canvas covers. As they got closer, he took a double take to see if he might be dreaming. She swung around on her mooring, just enough for him to see the scripted emblem on her transom: *Amazing Grace*.

How? He thought, *How is it possible that she is here, 33 years later, exactly as I remember her?*.

As the ferry passed, Bill stood up and walked toward the stern. He didn't want to lose sight of *Amazing Grace*. He was afraid she might somehow disappear if he looked away.

The ferry tied up at the new commercial dock on the western edge of the harbour. Bill stood at the companionway, squirming. The moment he was allowed, he jumped from the ferry and ran up the road. Then he realized something was wrong. He spun around looking for a reference.

He saw the church in the center of the beachside village. It was butter-colored now, but very much the same. A little further down the road was the Customs building, now white. But the remainder of the beach remained virtually unchanged. Deep on the other side of the harbour even Foxy's place was still there. It looked like it had grown and had its own small dock in front of it.

Bill looked back at the commercial dock again and realized it was in the very spot where The Dive once stood. His head dropped and his shoulders sank. *How do I find him?* He lifted his head and looked around. Up on the hillside was a newly painted, yellow, concrete-block home with four balconies nestled in the mountainside.

"Hmmm." Bill swung around and bolted up the steep paved road. He crossed the street and stood in front of the yellow house. He caught his breath and stood there studying the structure for several minutes before he got up the nerve to approach the door. He raised his hand and knocked tentatively. A beautiful, slightly graying black woman opened the door. She looked the same as the day Bill had first met her. Behind her was a tall white man with a long white full head of hair, pulled back in a ponytail. He looked beefier and weathered, but otherwise there was nobody quite like Danny Waters.

"Oh my goodness, Lucky Charm!" Danny bellowed. "There ain't no mistaking your momma's big blue eyes." He grabbed his wife around the waist, "Look at him, Marta." Danny slipped passed his wife and held out his arms. "He's all grown." Then he grabbed Bill in a huge bear hug.

"Come in, come in. We have so much to talk about." Danny pushed Billy into the house.

They walked out onto the balcony off the living room. Marta brought them a cool drink as the men sat quietly admiring the view.

Danny explained how he closed the bar several years back after he stopped drinking. It was hurting his liver and he didn't want to end his dreamy life in the islands prematurely. The government bought back the lease and he purchased the land above it with the proceeds.

They had three daughters; Grayata, Dani and Maya and now had six grandchildren. "That's why I had to build such a big friggin' house!" Danny growled in jest. He dropped his head suddenly and quietly asked about Mishimo, "Did she take good care of you?" His eyes instantly became damp.

Mishimo was Bill's final connection to the life he knew with his grandfather. He explained to Danny how he managed to sneak her into his dorm at college. Even his roommate didn't know she was there for several months.

When the dorm master found out, Bill let the guy meet Mish. It only took a few minutes for the fat gray tabby to win him over. Mishimo became a bit of a low-key mascot on Billy's floor.

"She was a gift from Papa on my first birthday, ya know," Bill said with a smile. His grandfather had told Bill that he was in his mother's arms when she helped him open the box. The fluffy gray kitten had looked up at the infant Billy and meowed. He reached out and grabbed her, squeezing her tight and said, "Mishimo." Or at least something that sounded like that.

"Yes. She always took care of me."

She stayed with him until his last semester at MIT. He was lying in bed talking to her about whether or not to take the internship. Somehow knowing it was time for them to both move on. At the age of 20, she died in his arms, purring.

"I didn't leave you, ya know?" Danny blurted, "She wouldn't let me near you."

Bill leaned over and put his elbows on his knees, "I thought you did for a very long time," he paused, "but then I stopped thinking about this place altogether. I pretended I made it up. That nothing ever happened and Papa didn't exist." Bill wiped his face. "I blocked all memories of *everything* that happened after my mom died," he took a sip from his drink, "from then on, it was just Nana and I in that concrete jungle."

Danny grimaced. He had no words to offer. Marta came out with a few snacks. She leaned over and gave her husband a kiss then turned to Bill and caressed his arm gently. When she went to leave, Danny reached out to her. He pulled a chair out for Marta to sit and held her hand while he talked.

"She's been waiting for you." Danny said staring at the beautiful blue hull in the corner of the harbour. "We even had a mooring put in."

Billy was so choked up he didn't know if he could speak. His voice cracked as he said, "Nana said she sold it."

"It was never hers to sell," Danny said, "It's yours my boy." They all looked out at the harbour. "It always has been," Danny explained, "Your nana didn't know everything about your papa. He was a smart man and knew if anything happened to him, she wouldn't understand how important it was that you had that boat. So, he created an offshore company down here," Danny turned to his wife and smiled, "and named Marta the President."

"It was written in his will and in your trust that if you hadn't been told by your eighteenth birthday, we were not to intervene in your life." Danny choked back his emotions, "I tried so hard to be in contact with you," he gritted his teeth, "but Nana wouldn't let me. She blocked all communication with any of us to you. Back in those days we didn't even have electricity on the island, much less a cell phone and the Internet." He shook his head, "Crazy, huh, how quickly things change."

Danny leaned over the table and put his hand on Bill's forearm. "*Amazing Grace* is yours. She's part of your grandfather's legacy." He motioned for Marta to go get something. A few minutes later she came outside and placed two large bundles at Bill's feet.

"These are yours too," Danny pointing to the ground, "I think they might fill in some gaps for you. After all, it's been a pretty long time."

"Have you read them?"

Danny nodded. "Many times. I miss your papa to this day."

They continued to talk for a while. Marta offered the spare bedroom for the night.

"If it's okay, I think I would like to stay aboard the boat."

"Of course," she answered back.

Marta gave him enough provisions for a few days and Danny took him via dinghy.

Amazing Grace was as beautiful as ever. Bill walked along the deck for a long while, touching everything he saw. At times he would close his eyes and envision his days aboard.

He didn't venture below or into the cockpit right away. He preferred to stay on the bow. He lay on his back and looked up at the clear blue sky. White cottony clouds slowly glided past as a warm breeze filled the air. "Puff, Fluff and Snow," he recalled naming them as the clouds made the shape of a smile.

Bill remained up top. The tears fell rapidly as day turned into night. He looked up at the hilltop where Danny's house was. Two lights were on and he could make out a blurry image emanating from a huge television screen. He was struck by the notion that somewhere along the line, Jost Van Dyke had gotten electricity.

Bill finally made his way to the stairwell. He stood in front of the settee where Papa lay their final night together. "I love you, Papa," he whispered in the dark, "And I miss you."

Down below Bill placed both stacks of journals on the dining table next to a massive box filled with Danny's correspondence. Inside the box were cards, letters and gifts Danny had sent to Billy for almost 10 years. They were mailed back to him several years ago by the law firm that settled Nana's estate.

Bill looked over and noticed a leather-bound book on top of Papa's desk. He wondered what it was, but decided to begin his reading with his granddad's journals. It was dawn by the time Bill closed the cover of the final book. Hidden inside were extensive explanations about Papa's sincere love for Nana, his unending commitment to his research, and his fears concerning his increased fatigue and deteriorating health. Papa's last entry was made a few hours before they left Antigua. He wrote about how proud he was of Billy and how much he looked forward to watching him grow into a healthy and happy man.

Bill closed the book and stood up to make some coffee. He poured a cup and went upstairs to sit in the cockpit and admire the sunrise. The water outside the harbour glistened from the morning sun. Closing his eyes, Bill imagined Mishimo scampering along the decks and hissing at Papa because she disagreed with something he'd done. "Hmmm," he gently murmured. He smiled at the thought of being awakened by a familiar knock on the hull. But he pushed the thought aside. He stood up and made his way back down the stairwell, picked at some food and paced the saloon. Hours passed before he finally got up the nerve to loosen the string from the second stack of journals.

Unending tears fell upon the aged pages as Bill heard his mother's voice in every word he read. His mother had always been open with him. The pages, although nostalgic, lent no additional insight for his troubled mind.

It was after 2:00 a.m. when he hauled his exhausted body up the steps to look out at the night sky. It was pitch black. The lights from the island were all extinguished and the clouds barricaded any illumination the moon and the stars typically offered.

Bill was frustrated, confused and immensely overtired. He wasn't sure what he was looking for and he was too afraid to ask Danny his most pressing question. He'd suffered so much loss, so much pain. He wondered if it weren't better simply not to know.

"The past is just that—past," he said aloud.

The skies began to grumble and the wind began to howl. Bill looked up as the deluge descended upon him. He ran down the stairwell and slammed the top hatch closed.

Looking around he quickly grabbed a towel from the back of the desk chair and noticed the leather-bound journal again. He dried himself off and mopped up the stairs then sat at the desk. Bill placed both hands around the bottom edges and pulled the book closer. He rubbed his left hand up and down the handsome, handcrafted, brown leather surface. In the center of the cover was a gold embossed title: *Ohana*.

He looked back at the previous two stacks of books he'd spent the last 36 hours reading. The mysterious journal before him was the only one of its kind. He took a few deep breaths before slowly lifting the cover.

Sometime around 6:00 a.m. Marta jolted from a dream when she heard the incessant knocking at the front door. Danny jumped up and raced to answer it.

There was Bill, soaking wet and smiling.

"What happened? Are you okay? Is the boat okay?" Danny asked. The rain had stopped hours ago.

Bill nodded.

"Well, why are you all wet then?"

"I need to know." Bill pleaded. Danny rubbed his eyes and attempted to focus. Bill continued, "I need to know if *they* are still here." He charged past Danny, skidded across the tile floor and ran out onto the balcony. Grabbing hold of the railing, Billy studied the movements in the still water, searching. He twisted around, "I have some things I need you to do for me. I have a plan Danny."

"Does that plan include scaring the bejesus outta some old people?" He motioned for Bill to stay right where he was and ran to go get a towel.

A moment later he returned. Marta was with him. She walked into the kitchen to make some coffee while Danny handed the towel to Billy. "Here you go, but why are you all wet?"

Bill looked down at himself. He looked back up, shrugged his shoulders, then raised both hands and gave Danny a goofy smile.

"Where is the dinghy?" Danny demanded.

"Dinghy?"

"Yeah, that small vessel used to get ashore from larger boats. The dinghy?"

Billy didn't respond. He just stood there, mouth closed tightly, stifling his laughter.

"You swam here, didn't you?" He didn't wait for an answer. "Aaaah. Hold on a second. I'll get you some clean clothes."

Danny made Bill shower and change before he would listen to him. Then they sat out on the balcony and talked. "I haven't seen the sunrise since I owned the bar. Thanks," he said playfully. "I know what you're asking," Danny said. "Yes. They are still here. They circle the boat from time to time to see if you've come back." Danny lowered his head, "The mom passed away about 6 years ago. But I think she must have been very old by then."

Bill listened with his eyes closed. He remained silent for a few minutes after Danny was finished. He shook his head and opened his eyes. "Danny I have to go. I have to go back. Can you take care of a few things for me?"

"Of course."

"Do you have some paper and a pen?" Billy asked.

Danny chuckled, "Long list, huh?"

Bill looked up and giggled, "Sorry. No, just some instructions. I want to draw you a map."

While the two men talked, Marta found flights for Billy. She booked him on a flight that afternoon. When she was done, she walked into the kitchen and prepared some breakfast. She thought Bill looked gaunt and very tired.

—

"Ya be needin' your strength ya know," she said as she pushed Bill's list away and put the plate down in front of him. "No use writin' if ya don't have the power to be doin." She kissed Bill's forehead and whispered, "I love ya like me own ya know."

At the airport Danny waited with Bill until his flight arrived. They struggled to say good-bye. Bill was about to go through the security gates when he turned back and called out, "Quit crying old man, I'll be back. I promise, I'll be back."

Unlike the small commuter aircraft Bill had arrived on, Marta booked him on a dual engine American Airlines flight, back to Puerto Rico, that held about a hundred passengers. Bill was the last person in line as the passengers of the relatively full flight marched across the tarmac and waited for the ground crew to affix the boarding ladder. Bill looked around, astonished at the amount of growth the country had apparently experienced and wondered if it was actually *Nature's Little Secrets* any longer.

He noticed a familiar symbol on the side of one of the private aircraft that had just parked in front of a large gray hangar. The aircraft's door unfolded and the passengers from the private Leer jet began to disembark.

"I'll be right back," Bill called to the ground crew before he ran over to meet the passengers from the private plane.

"Mr. Branson. Mr. Branson," Bill shouted.

The silver-haired Englishman was halfway down the stairway. His pilot wedged himself between Bill and the steps attempting to stop him from approaching further.

Bill blurted, "I heard about the race. I know how you can win. I can help you break the record!" Bill knew this was his best shot at getting to this guy, "I helped you on *Virgin Challenger II*. I can help you win this too."

—

Richard Branson and his family had recently failed an attempt to break the world record for sailing across the Atlantic in their 90-foot sailboat. They had gotten slammed with some bad weather and had to abort the trip.

"Let him through," Mr. Branson told the pilot. But it wasn't just the pilot who was attempting to stop Bill. One of the ground crew from the American flight and two local police officers were about to pounce on Bill.

"It's okay. It's okay. Let him be," Branson shouted with his arm extended.

"I have to go, but I know *we* can win that record." Bill professed.

Mr. Branson approached Bill and stared at him. "Do I know you?"

"No, we never met. But my design helped you break the record on *VG II*." Bill explained how he'd been an intern and made a few suggestions and changes to the hull design.

"Hmmm. Interesting. Those boys at Brooke Marine said they'd come up with that themselves," Branson commented.

They exchanged a few more words before the ground crew tugged at Bill's arm and demanded, "Sir, if you want to make your flight, you must get on the plane right now!"

Bill reached out and shook Mr. Branson's hand. "I've gotta go," and ran off to catch his flight.

Richard Branson stood there, dumbfounded. He shook his head and looked at his pilot. "All that and the guy didn't even give me his name."

Picking Up the Pieces

Unfortunately Bill's connecting flight out of Puerto Rico didn't leave until the next morning. He booked himself into a nearby hotel and walked up to his room. He thought he would go stir crazy, but the moment he put his head on the pillow he fell fast asleep. There were no dreams that night. When the front desk woke him at 4:30 a.m. Bill popped up, anxious to get back to New York. He'd only have a few hours to pull it all off in one day, but Bill was determined to complete his plan for himself and his family. On the plane he asked the flight attendant for a piece of paper and spent the entire three-hour journey meticulously mapping out his day.

Bill skipped up the stairs of the brownstone around 10:00 a.m. At the top he turned and looked to his right. Leaning over he ran his index finger up and down searching through the nameplate next to each buzzer. He stopped at P. Annesley. Bill nodded and let out a huge sigh. The door swung open and startled him. A middle-aged woman hurried out. *Another nameless neighbor*, he thought. Bill flashed her a quick smile and headed through the doorway.

He sprinted up the three flights of stairs. Struggling with his key, Bill finally managed to open the door. He ran over to the desk and flipped through a bunch of papers. As soon as he found the manila envelope containing the deed to the apartment, he bolted for the door. Holding onto the knob he turned around and studied the room. Taking a deep breath, he looked up and said, "Thank you. Thank you, mom," and dashed down the stairs.

He stopped one flight down, turned left and briefly froze. There wasn't a nameplate, just the number 2A. Bill knocked anyway. When the slender older gentleman with graying curls answered, Bill's eyes welled up. He struggled to keep his composure. There was so much he wanted to say, but simply didn't have the words. *In the car,* he thought. *We can talk in the car.* "Will you come with me?" Bill asked. His voice trembled.

The man nodded, grabbed some personal items and walked out the door.

They spent the next hour sitting in the car talking, crying and explaining a bit about each other's lives.

Peter stared at Bill, the son he left at eight-months-old. He didn't see him again until Bill was a grown man, when Peter accidentally bumped into him on a hilltop in Hawaii. The son he'd been looking out for from afar since Peter moved back to New York after Nana died.

There were times Bill wondered about the man in the building that somehow consistently showed up whenever Bill needed someone, but he never questioned why. It had been his grandfather's journals and his mom's final diary that confirmed his suspicions.

"Will you come with me," Bill asked his father.

With tears rolling down his face, Peter grabbed his son's hand and cried, "Absolutely. I don't ever want to miss another second in your life."

Bill nodded and with a crackle to his voice he said, "Well then, we have an awful lot of work to do, fast."

—

It was just before noon when they pulled up in front of the penthouse. Bill flung open the door and jumped out of the black stretch limousine before the doorman had time to approach.

"Hello Gregory, are the girls upstairs?" Bill asked.

"Yes sir, I believe so."

The doorman leaned into the car to grab Bill's things. "No. No. No need, Gregory. I'll only be a minute."

Gregory nodded his head, shut the car door and turned toward Billy. "Mrs. McMillon and the girls have been home all afternoon, Sir."

"Thanks," Bill called out as he stepped into the elevator.

It seemed like an eternity before the door finally reopened. Bill dashed into the foyer of the penthouse and called out, "Ella, Brooke, Breezi, where are you?"

Each one of them came running from a different part of the house, Breezi almost mowed her mother down as she descended the steps, racing to get to him first.

But it was Brooke who managed to get there, wrapping her arms around her dad, "I am sorry, Daddy. I am so sorry, Daddy," she cried.

"Hey, hey. There is nothing for you to be sorry about." He pulled her away from him, moved her hair from her eyes and said, "It is me who is sorry. I promise not to do that again."

Ella and Breezi wrapped their arms around both Bill and Brooke. All of them held on tight and wept.

Finally, Bill pushed them away slightly so he could talk. Girls, there is so much I have to say to you." He turned to his wife, "Ella, *mi amore.*, I am so sorry for what I've put you through all these years." He kissed her softly on the cheek then addressed his daughters, "Come on, my darlings. Listen carefully. Go grab your most precious things and be back here as soon as you can." The girls stared at him, stunned. "I promise, you will not be disappointed."

"*Tesarina, my treasure*," he touched his wife's face, "I promise no more secrets, no more hiding, no more running." He reached for her hand; "I give you my whole heart now. I am sorry it took so long."

Bill didn't want to let go. He dragged her with him while he ran to his office, grabbed some things out of the safe and some papers from his desk. Back at the elevator he called for the girls, "Come on sweet angels, it is time to go!"

"Bill. Bill," Ella was shaking her head, "Where are we going?" she questioned sharply.

He looked at her and grabbed both her hands in his. "I know I have a lot of explaining to do. I promise I will. I promise." His voice was solid, commanding yet tender. "You'll see, my love. Sometimes you just have to go where the wind takes you. Trust me, please."

"Bill that's just not good enough. We're not leaving until you tell me where we are going."

"In the elevetor, I promise to tell you in the elevator." Bill pressed the button to the elevator. "Girls, we are leaving, now!"

Brooke came running down the stairs with her backpack and Breezi came flying out of the living room with a paintbrush in one hand and artist's case in the other.

When the doors closed Bill quickly explained where he had gone and that he was now taking them back there with him. It was time for his family to see the BVI's.

The girls were enthralled, but Ella was not as excited. When Bill added the part of an older gentleman joining them, Ella was exasperated. She tugged at her husband's arm, gritted her teeth and whispered, "What the hell are you doing?"

"It's okay," he mouthed back.

They stepped out into the foyer as Gregory opened the front door and the chauffer did the same.

One by one the girls climbed in and greeted the mysterious guest.

"Hey aren't you the guy from grandmom's apartment?" Brooke asked.

Breezi sat next to him and said, "You're the man that gave us the box when we saved the blue jay." She held out her hand, "Hi, I am Breezi."

"My name is Peter," the man said, "But my friends call me Astro."

Bill was the last to enter the limousine. Holding his wife around the waist he said, "Peter, this is my beautiful wife, Ella." He looked at his daughters and then back at his wife. He rubbed her arm with his free hand and stared into her eyes, "I'd like you to meet my father, Peter Annesley."

The car went silent. The girls looked at one another and eventually it was Breezi that said, "You both have the same curly hair. Did yours used to be dark too?"

Breezi and Peter continued to talk. Brooke sat in the corner of the limo across from her dad, looking out the window with an agitated expression, while Ella and Bill remained in a quietly heated discussion.

At Kennedy Airport, the driver took them to a remote terminal where a private plane was waiting. The girls jumped out. Brooke looked around soaking in the noises, the activity of the workers inside and outside the hanger and marveled at the bright white jet with its door slung open for them to enter.

Breezi extended her hand to help Peter as he climbed out of the car. They strolled over to the flight crew, followed by Bill and Ella. The driver opened the trunk and took out three large suitcases and two long, black, mesh duffle bags.

"Come on, Brooke," Bill shouted from the base of the steps.

She stayed in front the car and stared at the ground.

Bill looked up and motioned for Ella to go ahead inside. He scampered over to his daughter and put his arm around her. When she finally looked up at him, he wiped away her tears.

"I've waited so long for this. What if it's not what I expected," she sniffled.

He hugged her tightly as they both sobbed.

He released her from his grasp, "It will be exactly what it's meant to be for you. But you'll never know unless you actually go?"

She took a deep breath and nodded, "I love you, Daddy."

"I love you, too, little one."

They both boarded the plane. The door shut and they were soon taxiing down the runway.

Onboard Ella and Bill sat next to each other facing an L-shaped couch at the back of the plane. The girls sat on either side of the couch and strapped themselves in. Peter took a seat toward the front of the plane.

The last time Bill had been on a plane like this was when he left Puerto Rico, alone. There would be no change of flights this time. His was taking his family directly to Beef Island Airport.

Once in the air, the girls stretched out on the couch. Ella and Bill were leaning over their seats talking. Breezi was drawing in one of her sketchbooks while Brooke, who was sitting directly across from her father, studied the aircraft's interior.

Brooke looked down and noticed a leather-bound book at her father's feet and asked him what it was. He didn't answer her right away. He picked it up, placed it in his lap and invited Peter over to sit with the girls.

"It's one of Grandmom Gracie's journals."

The entire plane became quiet. Brooke and Breezi both sat up straight Peter took a seat between them and Breezi held out her hand. Brooke scooted her body to the edge of the couch and leaned in, staring at her dad.

Bill rubbed the front cover. He opened it and took out a piece of paper that was left inside. On it were instructions Grace had written for Papa to give Billy the notebook, when Papa felt Billy was ready.

Bill grabbed his wife's hand and squeezed it tight. He got up and kissed her then handed her the book. When Bill sat back down he asked, "Will you read to us?"

Ella sniffled and wiped away a tear, "I'd be honored."

There was an inscription on the inside cover that read:

My beloved Son,

I love you and I am so incredibly proud of you. Not only for who you are at this moment, but also for whom I know you shall grow into.

I watched you watch me die. Although you were given the hugest burden, you did not allow it to lessen your spirit.

As you continue on your journey, each loss will affect you differently. Remember everyone in your life has a purpose. It's important for you to find yours. Always remember to return to innocence.

There are paths we choose to take. Some are windier and filled with unforeseen obstacles. It will all be a matter of how you handle them, not whether the obstacles are there at all. There is no room for blame, pity, anger or upset. It only causes more pain.

I do not know when this journal will find you. But trust me, you are reading this at the most perfect moment in your life. Whether it is your grandfather or someone else he has entrusted with the task, know you have found this when you were ready. When you need it the most.

In the Hawaiian culture, when one passes on, they continue to fulfill their obligation to those they've left behind.

You'll never be truly whole until you find all the pieces of what make you, You. And only you know which pieces are missing.

This book is meant as a guide to help you find your way.

I can tell you this:

Your father made sure the love within our home remained, by leaving you the apartment when he said goodbye.

Your grandfather, Papa Joe, found a part of him that was missing until you were born. All of his actions have been done out of love.

The same goes for Nana. Whatever role she ends up playing, she only wants the absolute best, safest thing for you. Love her. Forgive her.

In Hawaiian, 'Ohana' means family. But for these beautiful people family means community. I urge you to keep your dearest friends close to you, find them if you've gotten lost. They are the pieces that make you who you are.

By now we've said our good-byes, but I hope you are always able to keep me with you.

Whenever you're in doubt, simply look to the sky. Even if you can't see it, know there is a star with my name on it, looking down on you.

I love you,

Mom

The flight attendant came over to check on them. She had several small packets of Kleenex. Brooke was at her father's knees now and Breezi in her mother's lap.

Bill took the book back from his wife and explained, "Please feel free to read this at any time." He looked up at Peter and asked Brooke, "Can you please hand this to my father?

Peter held the book closed, staring at the cover. "Where should I start," he asked.

"There is an index. But, I believe it's meant to be read from the beginning." Bill suggested.

They both nodded and Peter made his way back toward the front of the plane. He opened the book and became engrossed by the words of the woman he never stopped loving.

As they entered the Caribbean airspace, Brooke and Breezi had their faces glued to the windows asking thousands of questions. Bill tried his best to answer them as quickly as the girls rattled them off. He and Ella were on the couch too, looking out an adjacent window. Ella was as fascinated as her daughters at the incredible spectacle below.

Ritzel was waiting for them on the tarmac. After some sweet introductions and a few silly tales, he helped carry their luggage to Customs and Immigration.

The burly West Indian winked at Bill, "You not travelin' so light this time, me friend. Dis mean you hangin' round a while?"

"I surely hope so," Bill said as he squeezed his wife's hand.

All three of Bill's angels were awestruck with their surroundings. Breezi rode up in the front with Ritzel and asked him questions. Brooke sat with Peter and looked out opposite windows.

They all held on as they turned up the treacherously steep hill. Winding around a turn, Ella grabbed Bill's arm and closed her eyes. The girls were hooting and hollering as Ritzel swerved around some cars.

"We got a quick stop to make, me friends." Ritzel parked the car on the side of the road. "I'll be right back." He walked into a small shack and came out a few minutes later with two brown bags. He got back in the car and handed the bags to Brooke. "She be the oldest," he said to Breezi.

Brooke began distributing the contents. There was a Johnny Cake with cheese for each of them and fizzy grapefruit drink called Ting for the ladies. "The other is for your father and your grandfather," Ritzel told Brooke. She passed the men the two ice-cold glass bottles of famed Caribbean beer, Caribe. "Welcome to the BVI everyone," Ritzel announced.

They arrived at the dock just in time. People were already boarding the final ferry of the day. Peter helped Ritzel with the luggage as Ella and Bill kept the girls focused on getting to the ferry. The sun was setting as they pulled away from the West End dock.

The girls were mesmerized the entire trip across the channel. They had plenty of questions, but the engines were too loud for their father to hear them. They'd have to wait until the ferry slowed down

There was no containing the girls' excitement as they came closer to the harbour. Brooke was the first to see the beautiful blue hull. She screamed, "Oh my God, Dad. Mom, Mom! Do you see it? Do you see it?"

Bill and Ella walked over to their two children who were hanging on the side rails of the ferry, gawking at *Amazing Grace* and the surroundings of

Great Harbour. As the engines slowed Brooke looked at her father and said, "Everything is exactly like you said it would be." She put her head on his chest as he wrapped his arm around her.

At the dock Danny and Marta stood with their entire family to welcome the McMillons to their island. They had set up a big party over at Foxy's. The live band was already playing as the ferryboat gently bumped into the dock.

It was not part of the plan Bill had explained to Danny, but in the end he was grateful. After an overwhelming amount of introductions the entire gang headed down the beach. Breezi immediately made friends with some of Danny's grandchildren, but Brooke stayed close to her dad. Marta chatted with Ella, telling her the story of when she first met Billy at The Dive. And Peter followed close behind, gazing at the twilight sky.

When they reached the end of the beach the music was blaring. Four older gentlemen stood in the sand at the entrance to Foxy's. They hadn't seen Billy in more than three decades. Scat's dreads were curled up into a colorful knitted cap. Bubba and Big John had a little less hair than Bill remembered. And Spidy was as wiry as ever. All four men charged Bill the moment he was close enough for them to see his mother's eyes. "Lucky Charm!" they screamed as they came running. Brooke jumped back and Danny shook his head and laughed. Danny walked over to her and apologized, "Your father's old friends get a little bit excited sometimes."

Brooke looked at him, "I've heard," she said with a smile.

Danny nodded his head and wiped his face, "I am glad. I am so glad." He put his arm around her, "I never used to be such a mush. I think it comes from having kids," he chuckled. "Let's get inside and dance!"

Scat was behind the microphone singing up a storm as the entire restaurant became a dance floor. Everyone was there including Val and the other ladies from Immigration. Even Foxy made an appearance.

A few hours into the party, Bill informed Danny that it was time for him to get his children off to bed. They had all had a very emotional day and Bill wanted them to get a good night's rest.

"You still want to give them their present tonight?" Danny asked. "It was on your list," he chided, "you can't just leave it in a box overnight."

"Oh my goodness you haven't left it in a box have you?"

Danny laughed, "No. It's upstairs in the office here."

Bill chased after his daughters, "Come on, girls, it's time to go." Both of them protested, claiming they were having too much fun. Eventually they followed him. The three of them met up with Peter and Ella chatting near the water's edge.

Danny had one of his son-in-laws bring his Whaler over to collect the group at Foxy's dock. After they boarded the boat, Danny handed the hole-punched box to his friend and waved good-bye.

"What's in the box, Daddy?" Brooke asked. They both smiled broadly at the question. Bill began to laugh and Brooke shook her head and giggled. "Really, what is it?"

The sound from inside answered her question. Brooke and Breezi looked at each and screamed inaudibly. "Hey, hey girls calm down. Let's get to the boat first." Bill passed the box to Ella and tied up the bowline of the Whaler to *Amazing Grace's* swim platform. He jumped off, took the box back and set it down just above his head on the stern. He helped each of them aboard and they all climbed up the steps.

Their luggage had been brought over earlier in the evening and was sitting in a corner of the aft deck. The fridge, freezer and cupboards had also been fully stocked.

Peter had been aboard *Amazing Grace* several times before, but still marveled at her beauty. Ella looked around and sat on the aft deck bench. The girls jumped up and down, not noticing their surroundings. They were pre-occupied by the box at their mother's feet.

"Dad, Dad, come on Dad!" They both begged.

He picked up the box, kissed his wife and turned to his two girls. "Every boat needs a mascot. I hope you two are always protected by ours." With that he sat down on the deck and placed the box on the teak. The girls followed suit, anxiously waiting.

The cries from inside the shoebox became louder as Bill lifted the top off. A nine-week-old, black-and-white patched kitty jumped from the box and hopped between the girls. "Meow, meow, meow," he called out, "meow, meow, meow."

Bill let the girls play with the kitty while he, Ella and Peter got settled in. Bill offered his father the room that he slept in as a child. And placed the girls' bags in the other.

A little while later, Ella ushered the girls down the stairwell. Everyone gathered in the saloon and watched the cat explore. As the girls chased after him, they all threw out ideas for a names. Yachtie, Patches, Cookie, and other names were called out. It was Brooke who said, "I think he should be named P.J. for your Papa," as the little cat scurried up the chair and stood on top of the desk at the navigation station.

They all agreed.

Early the following morning Bill found Brooke on the bow of the boat playing with P.J.

He left her undisturbed. He stood a few minutes looking up at the main mast. His hands trembled as he walked over and uncovered the mainsail.

"Would you like some help, Daddy?"

"Sure sweetheart, I'd love some."

The two of them got the sails ready, did final engine checks and brought up the anchor together. Brooke listened intently at her father's explanations and followed his instructions carefully. They sailed out of the harbour sitting next to each other in cockpit.

Nobody else came up.

When they got to Georgey Hole, Bill asked Brooke to stand on the bow and give him signals he had taught his daughter along the way. Once they were through the reef and had set the anchor, the hatch door opened and Breezi came flying out. "Mom made me stay below and watch P.J." She looked around, "Wow!"

It was a perfect day in the picturesque cove. The sun shone brightly and the water was clear turquoise. Peter and Ella came up as well. They sat in the cockpit and watched the girls run around, while admiring their surroundings.

"Why don't you girls sit on the swim platform," Bill suggested, "I believe there might be some individuals very eager to meet you."

The girls raced down the stairs, sat down and hung their legs over the side.

"Where are they? Where are they Dad?" Breezi questioned. Brooke remained quiet, studying the water.

"They'll be here. Be patient sweetie."

Soon two dolphins came around the edge of the point. Both jumped in the air. One had a distinct whitened dorsal fin and his back was a few shades lighter than his sister's. They swam over to the boat and stood erect, chirping and clicking away.

Breezi immediately began explaining who she was and how they had gotten there. She rambled as they responded and looked back at mom when she came over to sit in the very spot Papa used to write. Bill placed his hand on Ella's shoulders and waved at his old friends.

—

Brooke sat there, staring and watching. She watched as her *sister* carried on a conversation, frustrated that she could not understand. She took her feet out of the water, stood up and climbed the stairs, stomping past her parents as she made her way to the bow.

She began to cry. She couldn't figure why she couldn't understand. These were *her* stories. This was the place *she'd* dreamed of coming to her whole life. And now that she was finally here, everything was completely wrong.

She could tell the dolphins were happy to meet her. She could even decipher some of the basic premise of certain portions of her sister's dialogue with them. But she couldn't make out the words. She couldn't convert the sounds. None of it made sense and eventually she stopped listening altogether. She just sat there, watching.

She wanted to go home, forget this place. She wanted to turn back time and wished she'd never opened that box in the first place.

"Honey, what's wrong?"

She jumped at the sound of her father's voice. "I want to go home," she said in a muffled tone.

"I thought you'd be happy here. I thought this was what you wanted?"

Brooke sat, kept her head down, silent.

"What is it, honey? What's wrong?" Bill asked again.

Tears streamed down her cheeks, her face turned red and her nose began to run.

"Talk to me, sweetie. Talk to me."

She couldn't look at him. The giggles from her sister on the swim platform made her cry even harder. Her shoulders tightened and she squeezed her eyes shut. She wanted the tears to stop.

Bill lay down on the deck. He urged Brooke to do the same. Once they both horizontal Bill simply said, "Talk to me sweetheart. Tell me what's going on."

"Why, dad? Why can't I understand them? It's not fair, Daddy. It's not fair." She was crying heavily now. "I've listened to your stories, I begged you to take me here over all these years and now that you have, I don't understand them. I am supposed to understand them. I *believed* you. I believed for so long!"

Bill took her hand in his. He held it tight and remained silent for a while.

"I know I was wrong not to bring you here years ago," Bill began, "but, we are here now. And, I know you understand them, Brooke. You're just not *listening*." He sqeezed his daughter's hand, "Simply let go and remember. Remember how it felt the first time you heard about me meeting Phinny. Or remember the first time you and I searched for deer in the middle of Central Park. Nobody believed we would, but you and I found one." He continued, "Let go of your mom, your sister, and me. Let go of school, your friends, New York. Let go of the noise and simply begin to listen."

Brooke sniffled and turned her head toward her father.

"Let go of the anger toward those icky girls at school. Stop being mad about Ms. Klein or that horrible girl, what's her name?" he asked.

"Penelope."

"Okay, Penelope." He paused. "Lie here. Lie quietly and don't just remember, but *feel* what it was like the first time you heard me tell you the story of how I met Phinny," he reached over and touched Brooke's face, "You'll *hear* them, babe. You just have to let go of all that other stuff. Get quiet and let go." He took a deep breath and squeezed her hand more tightly before sitting up. "Stay here a while. I'll be right on the back deck when you are ready."

"Can you stay with me, Dad?"

"Of course I can." He lay flat on the deck next to her, "Just close your eyes and let go."

Brooke sobbed. Her body jerked a bit and her breathing became choppy. At times she didn't even know why she was crying. Other times she knew exactly why. She cried for almost 10 minutes before her breathing finally slowed and eventually mirrored her dad's smooth, rhythmic breaths.

They were breathing in unison. After a few more minutes Bill finally asked, "Would you like to meet them again?"

Brooke shook her head, yes.

"Are you ready?"

She didn't answer. Instead she just turned her head, stared at her father and said, "I love you, daddy."

"I love you too, sweetheart."

They stood up together and made their way to the back of the boat.

Ella saw them coming. "Okay, Bree. Let's give your sister a chance, too. Say your good-byes and come on up here with me for a while. You'll have plenty of chances tomorrow."

Breezi turned around, "But mom!"

"Up here, now honey."

Breezi said her good-byes and Ella escorted her into the cockpit. "Peter, do you mind?" Ella asked.

"Of course not," he said with a smile. "So, Breezi, tell me what your new friends had to say."

"Thanks," Ella whispered and tip-toed back to the aft deck.

Brooke and her dad were already on the swim platform watching the dolphins circle the boat. They jumped in the air and passed each other before splashing back down into the water.

Dolila got there first. She stood up and nodded at Brooke.

"Why don't you tell them how you dragged me up to the closet upstairs?" Bill suggested.

Brooke held her father's hand, smiled and began her story.

They sat out there for more than an hour. Brooke told them some of her favorite parts of the stories her father had told her throughout the years. Phinny and Dolila barely had room to interject but Phinny managed a word or two whenever he disagreed with the specifics of Bill's tales.

Ella sat behind them, smiling. She never said a word.

Later that evening, Ella and Bill sat in the cockpit watching the girls on the bow. They were lying on their backs next to their newly found grandfather, who was telling them wondrous stories about galaxies and faraway treasures in the sky.

"I am sorry I kept this from you, especially since I shared it with both the girls," Bill said. He looked at his wife, "You would have believed me, wouldn't you?"

Ella nodded.

"You understand them, don't you?"

Ella hesitated, "Yes."

"But how?"

"Because, unlike you," she said, "I never stopped believing."

Bill enveloped Ella in his arms. Behind them sparkled two huge illuminated forms in the sky. Bill leaned over and whispered in Ella's ear, *"Siete la mia aria. You are my air."*

She looked up at him, smiled and responded, *"Siete la mia stella. You are my star."* Reaching up, Ella touched Bill's face then kissed him gently, "Can *we* live here forever?" she whispered.

Tenderly, he stared into her eyes, "Absolutely."

EPILOGUE

"I think it's them!" Brooke squealed. She thrust the large black binoculars at her sister, "Look for the emblem on the side," Brooke commanded.

Breezi fiddled and fussed with the black, metal contraption until she could see clearly through the magnified glass. With the binoculars plastered to her face, she scanned the harbor. "It's too busy out there. I don't see them," she said.

It had been the girls' first time back to New York since their father whisked them away to the British Virgin Islands several years before.

Brooke looked out past the Statue of Liberty and surveyed the mayhem of boat traffic in the harbor. There were huge ferries, pleasure boats and law enforcement all competing for space. It was definitely the most chaotic environment Brooke had been in since leaving the city. "I think I see them. That has to be them!" she screamed.

Brooke yanked the binoculars out of her sister's hand. Her eyes fixed on the white hull with a red circle on its side. Inside the circle was the letter V. "He's at the helm. He's at the helm!" she screamed, placing the binoculars back down quickly.

Richard Branson's sailboat, *Virgin Crossing*, was under full sail as it approached the New York Yacht Club committee boat. Heeled over and flying at an intense speed it zipped past them.

Hoooooooonk! The committee boat sounded.

"Wahoo!" Brooke and Breezi shouted. The girls screamed, yelled, and jumped. Breezi rushed over to hug her mom, who was looking at her watch.

"They did it," Ella whispered. "*He* did it."

Virgin Crossing's mainsail was dropped and jib furled. The boat immediately slowed and sat upright on the water. Branson smacked Bill on the back. "We did it. No," he paused, "*you* did it."

It had been a tough go. They'd sailed through some nasty weather, had suffered a few mechanical issues and had even torn a sail, but they crossed the finish line in New York Yacht Harbor, having shaved 72 minutes off the World Record for an eastbound transatlantic crossing under sail.

Branson continued his praises, "Damn, that was awesome. I think you've got to be one the greatest helmsman I have ever known," he thought about it, "In fact, at least at this moment," Branson grabbed Bill's shoulder and shook, "I think you're probably the greatest sailor in the world!"

"Thanks," Bill said. He scanned the multitude of boats that had come out to witness their historic arrival, and smiled. He marveled at the familiar shiny blue hull with a young woman at the helm as it motored between numerous boats. It was the proudest moment of Bill's life. His three angels had come to surprise him at the finish line.

Bill held the wheel with one hand and waved as he steered *Virgin Crossing* past *Amazing Grace* on her port side. The girls screamed, "We love you, Daddy." Ella called out, "*Mia stella!*"

Branson grabbed the magnum of champagne and offered it to Bill, "You want to do it?"

"Absolutely!" Bill bellowed. He looked down at the magnum and back at Branson. "Thanks, Richard," he said and handed over the helm.

Bill walked up to the bow. He paused a moment to admire the massive brick, glass and concrete buildings that make up the New York Skyline, and smiled. He ripped the gold wrapper off the top of the champagne, twisted the wire and shook the huge bottle. The cork popped off and a fountain of bubbly burst high into the air. *"This* is for you, Papa Joe!"

ACKNOWLEDGMENTS

If you are reading this it means I actually am published, yeah!

The initial basis for this story began from a mural on the wall. I was cooking for a family aboard their yacht and the mural was in the galley. It had gone unnoticed until one day; I saw a story.

But it was my father's unexpected passing that was the true catalyst for bringing this story to fruition. I was out to sea, working aboard the yacht. My sister and brother struggled to get hold of me, but the boat was not in phone range. Eventually they enlisted the help of the U.S. Coast Guard. I received an emergency radio call from them that informed me of our family's heartbreaking tragedy. In that moment, the resounding message was; the time is now. Three months later, I left the yachting industry to embark on this new journey.

I could not have done this without the unending love and support from my mom. She has had her own huge struggles and immense loss in her life, yet her love and belief in me has remained strong. I am forever grateful for her generosity, patience and for being a true fan. Thanks Mom.

Although the main characters in the book are not based on a specific individual, their names are. Brooke and Breezi—I love you both very much. You are the closest I have to having my own daughters (to date) and I love you with all of my heart. I am so proud of you both and wish the world for you. Bill, take care of them. Remember you are their example. And learn from them. They have so much to give you in return.

My brother-in-law, Mario, the best storyteller on the planet. Thank you for loving my nephews with all of your heart. John, Dominick and Max—I hope you always remain true to your innocence. You are such incredible human beings. Look out world; here you all come! M.J. thanks for being such a supportive big sister.

Thanks, Angela Talentino-Kurkian, for listening to me tell you dozens of tidbits from the book and continually supporting me and this project's growth. I am so grateful for our friendship. Jen Englert-Francis, You Rock! Thanks for the incredible cover design, unending patience with my A.D.D. and for making me laugh all the time!

To the children of the Babe James Community Center in New Smyrna Beach, I love you all. Thank you for bringing such joy into my life, teaching me how to grow as a person and supporting me in my dream. Know that I promise to be there to support you all in yours. Reggie and Dave you do such special work each day. You inspire me to keep growing and remembering that giving back is what life truly is all about.

Special appreciation for Google, Wikipedia and the Internet in general, there is no way I could have done this without them. Wow, what an age we live in.

To my Peak Potentials' Family and especially Marjean Holden, Doug Nelson and T. Harv Eker. I always thought I was strong, talented and had what it takes to succeed. Through your guidance, training and unbelievable motivation, I not only believe it—I *know* it because I've *done* it. A-ho!

Jess Webb, thank you for taking the time out to look over my work, make corrections and suggestions. You were patient, understanding and were able to help me get through some truly sticky moments. Sara & Evan Rivers—Wow! And to Teri Taylor, the most meticulous individual I know. Thank you for all your incredible enthusiasm and immense attention to detail. You Rock! I am so grateful for your friendship and eternally grateful for Evan taking the time to clean up my act. Thank you. And, to my dear friend Sean Adams, our paths have so newly crossed yet I know I've known you forever. Thank you for all the 'handling'. I look forward to our continued journey.

There are people who've inspired me: Matt Damon for never giving up with *Good Will Hunting*, the creator's of *Lost*—6 ½ days!

And those I wish to someday meet: Nelson Mandela you are the person I would choose to be on a desert island with. The conversation would never end and the wisdom gained would be everlasting. Oprah Winfrey for consistently challenging, educating and informing the masses while remaining *true* to yourself.

The influence of art imitating life, imitating art. We gain insight and meaning to our own lives through the incredible imagination of fiction. Whether it's through watching a movie or reading a great book, positive, motivational art has a way of inspiring people, lighting their flame of creativity to do wondrous deeds of service for others. I hope somehow I've been able to evoke emotions within you that help light your way to a return to your own innocence. As with all acknowledgements—there is never enough room to fit them all. If I've somehow neglected to mention your name specifically, know that if I have in any way affected your life than *you* have affected mine. Hello. Hello. And thank you.

Things I Know for Sure

Jost Van Dyke found electricity somewhere around 1989.

Foxy's bar and restaurant remains one of the biggest draws not only to Jost Van Dyke, but also to the BVI themselves. If you are ever planning a visit to this beautiful part of the world this place is surely worth a trip. It's been more than ten years since I had the pleasure of sitting down at his bar and listening to his rough and raspy, fabulous storytelling. But I can still hear it in my heart. Old Year's Night is one of the biggest parties of the year! You can reach Foxy's via radio or take the ferry from West End, Tortola or directly from St. Thomas or St. John.

The island of Anegada is simply magical. Rustic, flat and surrounded by white sand. The pink flamingos are really there and so is one man's dream. Anegada Reef Hotel—Lowell Wheatley's dream really did come true. Sadly Lowell passed away in 2002, but I remember him fondly. And I hear his children continue his legacy of offering warm hospitality. The rum punches are amazing as well as the incredible lobster feast each night. Dine with your feet upon the sand and dance to Caribbean music. You'll be well taken care of and have a great time. It is worth the trip if you are staying anywhere in the BVI's or make a reservation at the Anegada Reef Hotel at: AnegadaReef.com

If you are looking to charter a boat in the BVI's for a holiday, visit CharterPort.com or contact Dick Schoonover at 1-800-386-8185. They are the friendliest, most helpful charter agency in the area and are happy to point you in the right direction for an incredible holiday around *Nature's Little Secrets.*

The BVI Welcome Guide—For Great Information on what's happening, where to stay or what to do in the British Virgin Islands visit: bviwelcome.com. This handy online magazine offers helpful information on all the major islands in the chain as well as places to dine, stay, ferry schedules and more.

Enjoy your journey,

Kathleen

A personal chef for fourteen years, Kathleen Beales has traveled extensively, living in the British Virgin Islands for almost five years. After her father's unexpected death she was compelled to pursue her true passion—writing. She is dedicated to encouraging others to follow their dreams. This is her first novel.

To learn more about Kathleen Beales please visit:

KathleenBeales.com

A Return to Innocence

In the summer of 1974, after losing his mom to cancer, Billy McMillon, an inquisitive eight-year old boy with an innate need to be near nature, goes on a sailing expedition with his eccentric grandfather, a famous scientist who is on a mission to uncover the truth behind a mysterious illness plaguing pods of bottlenose dolphins.

Suddenly tragedy strikes and young Billy's life is turned upside down for a second time. He is back in New York, living with his Nana and shedding the memories of his extraordinary adventure with his grandfather.

Years later, Bill finds himself looking back on his accomplishments. A Marine Architect, he seems to have it all - a great career, a beautiful home in New York, a loving wife and two healthy, well-adjusted daughters. By all accounts, he's a success. Why should it matter he hasn't stepped foot on a boat in over twenty years, he prefers the countryside to the big city, or that he's quite reclusive and distant toward his family?

When his inquisitive eight-year old, Brooke, urges him to explain the contents of a mysterious box she finds, Bill comes face to face with his past and suddenly *everything* matters.

A reflective tale of one man's attempt to build a relationship with his daughter through sharing stories from his own unconventional childhood. Rich with a bounty of unusual characters amidst the beautiful canvas of the British Virgin Islands, A RETURN TO INNOCOCENCE offers a rollercoaster ride of emotion, imagination and adventure.